# The Corner Store

# THE CORNER STORE
## a Novel by Albert Idell

DOUBLEDAY & COMPANY, INC.

Garden City, New York

*The characters, the location, and the incidents in this book are entirely the product of the author's imagination and have no relation to any person, place, or event in real life.*

Library of Congress Catalog Card Number 53-5755

# Dedication

*To Clyde Lisk and Max Abrams, keepers of corner stores,*
*for whom I have respect and affection,*
*and to all of their trade.*

# Part I

## Chapter 1

It was almost midnight and Chester Jones was hungry, but he did not like to close the store while Mary Plotko was seated at one of the tables with a new date. This must be the fellow who had been calling her on the telephone every day for the last week. Often there wasn't anything to do in the store but listen to the girls and boys talking in the phone booths. The grownups, too. How well he knew the affairs of many of his neighbors through those one-sided conversations! Strange that folks didn't realize that the closing of a glass-paneled door did not shut them off from the world—especially when they also listened to others' conversations while they waited for an empty booth.

Mary and the boy were taking a long time to finish their chocolate sundaes, but then, they were busy getting acquainted. I like Mary, Chester thought. All the years that she had been coming to the store —as a dirty-faced child who never had proper care taken of her; as a young girl in her early teens, when sometimes she'd be crying and run upstairs for Kit to console her. Kit had a wonderful way with children. Now Mary was almost grown and having dates. She'd always, since she was little, had the pale, fine hair that she now combed to a smooth sheen, but who would have thought she would become so attractive? She had self-respect, too, and more dignity than most of the younger girls around the neighborhood. Right now he wished she'd go.

He walked to the front of the store, where young George was about to take the reading of the front cash register. "Better lock up first, son, but don't turn off any of the lights. We don't want to rush Mary."

"You're too easygoing, Dad. If you made eleven o'clock closing time and just told people, like they do in the chain stores . . ."

"This isn't a chain store. Sometimes we do our best business after eleven, when the movies are out. But it's more than that." Chester meant to add something else, but he felt pretty tired. Instead he said, "Sometimes slow evenings make me more tired than busy ones."

"You should have had me come down earlier. I didn't mean we had to close at eleven when things are busy, but tonight I told Mother we'd be closing in a few minutes and she's getting supper ready. Gosh, Dad, I'm hungry."

"I'm hungry too, but we're still not going to hurry Mary. Let them sit there until we balance the registers, anyhow. Now go lock up. We'll let them out when they're ready."

He walked back to the soda fountain and noticed that Mary and her date had finished their sundaes but were still sitting there looking at each other, the way young people did.

She jumped up. "Oh, I'm sorry, Mr. Jones. I didn't think. We're keeping you up. This is Bill Sullivan. He works at the A & P on Thirteenth Street."

Chester said, "Take your time" and "Glad to know you, son." The boy was taller than Mary and blond too. They made a nice-looking couple. Not many years ago Mary had been the most un-cared-for kid in the neighborhood, with her hair a tangled snarl tied up with a dirty ribbon. Now she was beautiful. He wasn't being very polite, but then, he was tired.

When they were gone he relocked the door and pushed the switches that threw the store into darkness except for single lights over the registers. He lifted the cash register lid and took down in a little book the amount of the day's sales and then, to please George, the number of transactions. He looked over at George, standing in the area of light cast by the bulb over the other register, and saw the frown of concentration, the intensity with which he was figuring the day's business. George had been born to run a store. Strange how he loved it, when most boys were not supposed to like the business in which they grew up. In that way I'm pretty lucky, Chester thought. George not only likes storekeeping, but I think he'd rather do it than anything else on earth. For me it's been a way to raise a family and still be my own boss.

Chester was so deep in his own thoughts that he didn't answer right away when his son asked and then repeated, "What was your reading, Dad? I bet it was down. Mine's down four dollars and thirty-eight cents."

"Yes, I guess it is down, son, but not much. Mondays are always slow days."

"I'm talking about Mondays, Dad. Of course it's down over yesterday. But it's also down over last Monday and it's down over Monday a year ago."

"Maybe it's the heat. People are just too hot to come out. Besides, I don't see the good of keeping all those figures. How much we did last week is all right, maybe, but a year ago . . ."

"That's how we know where we stand, and it's not down because of the heat, either. It was only ninety-four. Last week it was ninety-seven. People came in last week to buy ice cream and drinks to cool off. All you do is guess. You guess it's too hot, or you guess it isn't hot enough. With this sales record we know when ice cream's up and when it's down, when we sell lots of sundries and what things are moving and what lines we ought to get rid of. Honest, Dad, if you'd only co-operate a little we could make this store into a really paying proposition."

No, you couldn't help liking young George. He was so earnest, and what he was saying was probably right—except what was the use of going to all that extra work when they'd got by all right until now?

"Tell you what I'll do, son. Tomorrow afternoon, when it's slow, you show me all of those figures of yours again. Right now, though, let's get this money counted and have supper. What do you suppose your mother's fixing for us upstairs?"

George didn't bother to answer, and for the next few minutes Chester, balancing the cash in his register, heard with partial awareness sounds which indicated that George was having trouble.

"This is impossible, Dad. I'm short thirteen dollars and ninety-one cents. You know what I think? Mother's been taking money out of the register again without marking it up. Somebody has. We're never short that much, especially when I'm in the store."

"Don't get yourself excited. We'll ask her."

"Thirteen ninety-one. She wouldn't have taken out thirteen ninety-one even, Dad. Or uneven, I guess it is. You know what I bet? I bet that's newspaper money. After I told everybody not to put paper money in the drawer. Helen did that. She was in the store while I was up eating lunch, I bet. You wait and see."

George pushed the counted money into a small white bank bag and charged back. "It seems to me you should lay down the law to Mother. She's always taking money, and Dick and Helen with their ice cream and candy bars. How can you make a profit when your own family is eating up stuff on you? You should say to both of them, 'If you want candy, go out and buy it. Don't eat up the profits here.'"

"You said you were hungry. Let's eat first. If your mother took some money out of the register, she'll probably remember about it. Sure you didn't give change for a twenty instead of a five? That would come out somewhere around fifteen dollars." He shouldn't tease the boy, but somehow George's indignation was amusing. Chester enjoyed it for a moment, then said, "You should know I'm only having a little fun with you. Now go ahead and I'll come right along."

Chester tried the doors a second time. It seemed like a waste of electricity to leave on the lights over the cash registers, which was another of young George's ideas, but the registers hadn't been broken into since they'd started it.

There was Kit calling now, "Chester, aren't you ever coming?" He called back, "Right away," and heard her again, "Hurry up, it's an omelet and it won't wait after it's ready."

While climbing the stairs Chester tried to recall when they had first begun the custom of having supper after the store closed. He could remember years ago, when one or another of the family would run upstairs for a hurried meal earlier in the evening, the way they still did at noon. Probably the midnight suppers were one of Kit's ideas, or more likely still, had just grown from some late snack into the best meal of the day, to which the whole family looked forward almost as much as he did.

Kit came in from the kitchen and gave him a light kiss on the cheek. "It takes dynamite to blast you out of that old store. If the omelet's gone flat, you have nobody to blame but yourself."

"Sorry. Mary Plotko was in with a new date, and I didn't want to hurry her. Afterward George was giving me a lesson on how to run a store. Besides, the cash register was short." He seated himself at the head of the table, with Dick and George at their usual places along the wall.

Kit put her hand to her mouth. "Oh, Chester, I took fourteen dollars from the cash register. Kay wanted a new dress. She's going out tomorrow night and had nothing to wear. I clean forgot to tell you."

Honey brought in the omelet—high, fluffy, and golden-brown—and cut large wedges of it. "Here you are, Mr. Jones. You look like a hungry man."

"I am hungry, and it sure looks good." Chester liked Honey, her coffee complexion, her smile, the easy way she laughed.

There were two empty chairs at the table. "Where are the girls?" Chester asked, after sampling the omelet and approving it.

"Kay's out with Sig," Mrs. Jones explained, and Dick cut in, "The great Sigmund. Honest, what she sees in him I don't know. He's an even worse dope than my older brother."

Young George said, "I'm not even listening, but I think you're unfair. Sig is going to be a great success someday, and Kay will be darned lucky if she can land him."

It was relaxing just to sit there and listen. George and Dick were always bickering, but it didn't mean anything. He was pretty lucky, having a business of his own, even if it wasn't a very big one, and a good wife and nice children. With the possible exception of Helen he had no reason to worry about any of them—which reminded him that her place at the table was still empty.

"Mother, this is pretty late for Helen to be out, don't you think?" From her glance toward young George, Chester could see that she thought so too, but didn't want to discuss the matter before the others. Well, there was nothing like another piece of omelet, made as only Honey could make one: with bits of finely chopped onion green folded in, and a touch of cheese, not enough so you knew just what it was, but enough so you wondered about it if it wasn't there.

Chester was tired, very tired and sleepy, and his feet still hurt, though he'd taken his shoes off first thing. "Mother, you straighten out with George what you owe the cash register. I'm going to bed."

He didn't, though, for Helen came in and took her place at the table as if it were the ordinary thing for her to be out until after midnight. Too bad she hadn't waited five minutes more, so he wouldn't have had to make a decision.

At fifteen it was a little early to tell, but there was every indication that Helen would be prettier than Kay when she grew up. Maybe he'd spoiled Helen by fussing over her so much when she was the baby of the family. He didn't want to be too reproving now, especially with her brothers watching, but he had to say something. "Helen, don't you think you should explain why you're so late?" That wasn't the way he had wanted to say it at all. Helen always confused him; the one member of his family that he could never handle. He didn't like the way she was doing her hair. It was between blond and red in color and looked best when it fell softly over her shoulders, instead of with that big roll, or whatever it was, on top.

"It was nothing, Dad. Vee Maguire and I went to the movies, that was all. There was a double feature at the Avon. You can ask Vee if you don't believe me. It didn't leave out till ten after twelve."

Before Chester could answer, Dick said, "Vee Maguire. The name is Veronica. It's like you telling everybody that your name's Penny, Penny Jones. It makes me sick. If it was Penny Postcard, I'd take you out and mail you—all the way to California."

"To Hollywood, where I'd be a star, no doubt."

Dick pushed back his chair and stood up. "I'm going to bed, Dad. There's nothing bothers me like infantile minds. It's bad enough when I have to cope with them in school."

Where was he—trying to tell Helen not to stay out so late. No, that wasn't it, either. What had she said? If he didn't believe her

. . . Why, that's what he had tried to instill in his children: that he did believe in them and that they should believe in themselves. That was what his own father had failed to do. "Of course I believe you. There was a double feature down at the Avon, and it didn't leave out till ten after twelve, and you came straight home. Where I think you were wrong was not to go to the earlier show. School's out now. You weren't working in the store today."

"I was, too, while George had lunch."

George, who had been busy eating in the slow, stolid way he had, broke in. "Yes, and I bet you put nine cents of newspaper money in the cash register. It's over that much."

Chester was surprised. "I thought we were short. You said the register was short, didn't you?"

"Thirteen dollars and ninety-one cents. Mother took out fourteen dollars, which she shouldn't have, which leaves us nine cents over. Three newspapers, three cents each. You've got to keep the newspaper money separate. Personally, if I had my way, we wouldn't sell newspapers. There's no money in it."

"It's a service, son."

"Yeah, I know. In a minute you'll say it brings people into the store. Out of three hundred papers a day we make a little over a dollar. The wear and tear on the hinges swinging the doors open and closed is more than that."

Chester wondered if he noticed a glance of thanks pass between Helen and George. Had the boy changed the subject just to help Helen avoid a scolding? There were so many of these subtle little things that went on in the family that it was hard to say. "In the future, Helen, if there's a double feature, go to the early show."

"The name is Penny, and you're treating me like a child. After all, it's only a block away. Vee was with me. What harm could there be?"

"You're putting your mother out, for one thing. Besides, Honey could be going home now instead of waiting to wash your dishes."

"I'll wash my own dishes. Honey can go whenever she's ready. Honest, Dad . . ."

Kit came in from the kitchen. "Your father's tired, dear. He's been in the store all day, practically. Stop arguing."

"What about Kay? She's not home yet. When will she eat?"

"She's having dinner with Sig's folks. Now you go along to bed. George, you want some more omelet? I'm having Honey make a fresh one for Helen."

Helen said, "I wish you'd stop calling me Helen. I don't know any name that suits my personality less."

Chester liked the soft, indulgent smile with which his wife accepted the foibles of her family. "Well, Penny, then. Now you go ahead and take your time and then go to bed, but don't sit up reading. Honey, you run along. The dishes you haven't finished will wait for tomorrow." That was how Kit Jones was. Chester slapped her lightly on the back, where she bulged over her girdle.

"Kit, you're a great girl."

He went into their bedroom, the corner room directly over the store, where the light from the street lamp outside cast an almost moonlike glow over the mahogany bedstead that they had bought over twenty years ago, soon after they were married.

He hadn't really reproved Helen the way he'd intended to. Dick and Helen, young George, Kay visiting the Dobrzanski family: these all became natural, commonplace things, largely because of the way Kit handled them. She never got nervous, excited, or worried. A pretty remarkable woman in her way. He undressed without switching on the inside light, then lowered the blinds to shut out the light from the street. There were always things that Kit had to do before the day ended. He knew that he would be fast asleep before she came in beside him.

When Sig's car reached Twelfth Street and she could see the darkened corner where the store was, Kay Jones said, "The ice-cream sign is out. I knew the store would be closed; Monday night is always slow. I do hope Mother isn't waiting up."

"She knows you're out with me." He pulled in to the curb in front of the store and shut off the engine.

She tried to keep her voice firm and not to show the way she was feeling. "We're late, Sig. I should go right in."

"I'll only stay a minute. You've been sort of quiet. You haven't said a word all the way, and there's something I have to know. How did you like my family? Tell me the truth."

Sig wanted to marry her. She knew he did, though he had never said anything about it. Taking her to his home for dinner before he proposed had been his way of letting her know more about him before she might accept—that was how honest he was. She couldn't hurt his feelings now. Before, when he invited her, she had thought he was being silly and that his parents wouldn't matter—that nothing mattered but Sig and whether she loved him or didn't love him.

"Please. I have to know."

"I think they're very nice, Sig."

"You don't sound enthusiastic."

"It's so hard to explain. Did I behave all right? I felt strange. Not being able to talk with your mother was hard, too."

"She doesn't speak English very much. At home she and Pop always talk Polish, but he gets out more. He has to speak English and she doesn't. She's wonderful, though, when you get to know her. She's worked hard all her life—on a farm in Poland before she met Pop and came to America. I bet she worked harder here than in the old country, bringing us up, making it easier for us. That's the difference between her and Pop. He thinks we should have things the way he did and is angry sometimes that we don't. I hope you get to like them both."

While Sig was talking, Kay was thinking that he looked like everybody else. He didn't look Polish the way the Italian fellows in the neighborhood sometimes looked Italian. She hadn't thought of him that way until tonight. "It's hard meeting people you never saw before that are so different. I hope I behaved all right."

"You were very nice to them, trying to make them feel at ease. I liked you even more for it."

She couldn't talk about it to Sig any more now; all she wanted to do was explain to Mother how mixed up she felt. "I must go now. I'm sure Mother is waiting up."

Sig never asked for a good-night kiss the way other boys did. Like everything else about him, it made going out with him more comfortable, somehow, more secure.

He ran around the back of the car to open the door on her side. That was like him, too. Any other fellow would have let her open the door herself—and why shouldn't she? Still, it was nice. She fumbled in her pocketbook for the key. She found it and Sig opened the door because the lock to the front door always stuck, it was used so seldom.

"Good night, Sig. Your mother's an awfully good cook—so many things I never ate before!"

"I'll see you at the office in the morning."

She heard from upstairs, "Kay, is that you?" and answered in a low voice while she ran up the stairs, "I'm coming, Mother."

Her mother asked, "Have a nice time?" and Kay controlled herself no longer. She began to cry. "Oh, it was awful!" They moved together to the kitchen, where the lights were on full, and sat down in opposite chairs across the white enameled table. "I'm being silly, I guess. I tried so hard all evening."

"Sigmund's family?"

"Yes—oh, I don't know. I guess there are lots of fellows who would come here and put their noses up at us, living over a store."

"Well! I like that!"

"People better off than we are, I mean, or who have never had a store."

"Why, Kay, you've never talked like this before."

"I never thought of it before."

Kay saw the worried look on her mother's stout, usually placid features. "I'm sorry, and don't you worry. I'll be over this in the morning. It's only that I'd like to tell you how I think now, and why. I always felt just as good as anyone else, but not better than other people. But I felt as good. Then when I went to Sig's house I felt superior. I didn't want to, Mother, and I tried to keep Sig from noticing. I didn't want to hurt his feelings."

"You're going out with Sig, not his parents. Go to bed now and you'll feel better in the morning."

"No, I'd like to talk it over with you now, while it's all fresh. I do like Sig. He's dependable, for one thing. He's like Dad in lots of ways. You know you can always trust Dad, don't you?"

Mother's way of laughing—soft, easy. Mother pretended to be

stupid about a lot of things, always saying she couldn't count, making mistakes on checks, but Mother knew how to run a family. If she could only be like Mother, who never got upset, instead of being all tense inside, as she had been tonight.

Mother was saying, "Go on with you, Kay. I never trust your father any farther than I can see him."

"Oh, you do. You're just fooling. I want you to be serious. I shouldn't have felt like I did tonight, but their house is on a back street up in Kensington. There was no furniture, much, and what there was was awful—a lot of colored photographs of the family in ugly frames, overstuffed chairs in red velvet—the most awful taste, Mother. And when you talk to Mrs. Dobrzanski she just nods her head and smiles. Sig's father looks like Mr. Plotko down the street, except maybe he doesn't drink. I don't know. He's a foreigner and he looks like a foreigner. Mother, I'm all mixed up. I know I shouldn't feel this way. It's hard to imagine Sig eating food so different from what we have; living so different. He doesn't look different, does he, Mother? He doesn't look Polish? He's real nice-looking—not handsome. I never liked handsome men except in the movies. Even there I think I like the homelier-looking ones best. I like men like Dad, that you can trust; but I said that before."

"You can't say it too often. Do you want me to go down and bring up a plate of ice cream for you?"

"After that Polish dinner? You can't believe the amount of food we had. Sig seemed to think nothing of it. I think he ate even more than Dickie does, but Dick's fat . . . Oh, this is crazy, but I feel better now."

"I wouldn't let Sig's people bother you. I'm sure they're nice, well-meaning folks."

"But, Mother, you've missed the whole point. It isn't that Sig's family bothers me so much. What upset me was feeling better than they were, until I began to think about me and all the people that would think they were better than Kay Jones. I'd never realized how horrible I could be. I knew I was wrong. I know I'm wrong now, believing that I could never marry Sig, if he asked me to, and hating myself for feeling that way."

"You've always known foreigners in the neighborhood, Jewish

and German and Italian. Mrs. Martino hardly spoke English, but you used to be up there all the time."

"The Martinos were wonderful. I was in love with Joe . . ."

"Kay Jones, you never told me!"

"I was, though. He used to sing while the kids played mandolins. They all belonged to the Caruso Marching Club of the Mummers. Remember the New Year's we went just to see them parade and all six Martino boys were in the first line of their group and how everybody applauded them? And Mrs. Martino was wonderful. She cooked the best ravioli. I was heartbroken when they moved to Brooklyn. But that was years ago."

"Almost three." Mother moved over to her, gave her a hug. "Mrs. Martino's food was different from ours and I'm sure her husband looked Italian, when he was alive. Their home was different, too. I'm not saying you should marry Sig . . ."

That was Mother again, planting seeds of thought instead of saying them full-grown. "I feel better. Just telling you things sort of solves them." She yawned. "Guess I'll go to bed now."

Mother hugged her again, differently this time. "Good night, pet. Maybe you can sleep a little late tomorrow. Sig shouldn't mind, seeing that he kept you up till all hours."

Kit thought of how Sig would look tomorrow, as Mr. Dobrzanski, sitting at his manager's desk at the rear of the billing department, and of how disapprovingly he would glance at her if she came in as much as five minutes past eight-thirty. "Oh, Mother, but he would mind. In the office he's very strict—with me especially. He wouldn't show favoritism during working hours for anything. I like him for it, too, in a way."

## Chapter 2

When the delivery from the candy jobber arrived Chester was selling a bottle of iodine to an excited Mrs. McShea, whose Johnny had just cut his finger, and the store was filled with customers. Chester saw Spewack's old Dodge truck stop at the side entrance and thought that he'd have to tell the salesman, on Monday, when he came for the order, not to deliver on Fridays. Before places began to give Saturdays off it hadn't mattered, but now Fridays were busier than any other day in the week except Sundays, when the regular stores were closed.

The youngish peroxided blonde, who was probably the mother of the family that had moved into 1207, asked to look at silk stockings. If she *was* the mother of all those children, she kept herself up pretty well. He showed what he had in stock while she stood leaning against the showcase, a thoughtful frown on her face.

"I wanted something paler—more flesh-color. I don't know . . ."

"We don't have much assortment. Every now and then somebody asks for a pair, which is why I stock a few." Chester waited, anxious for the woman to make up her mind so that he could check off the candy delivery. She was going to be a difficult customer, he could see that. She decided not to take the stockings and wanted a lipstick, but again couldn't find the right color, though Chester thought that he carried just about the best stock of them anywhere near. She bought a *True Story* and a *Life* and asked him to save a

*Bulletin* for her every afternoon, so maybe she would work out all right, even if she was a little hard to please. He wrote her name on a slip of paper for Dick, who kept charge of the people who wanted regular newspapers. Mrs. Canuso! She didn't look Italian; maybe she was married to one.

When she left he apologized to the driver of Spewack's truck for keeping him waiting so long.

"I got to wait longer than that sometimes, Mr. Jones. And we're short two items on your order. Milky Ways are out of stock. They should be in by Monday, though."

He was still checking the delivery when Old Man Meyer came in. It was a warm day, but he had on the black velour hat and the greenish-black overcoat that he always wore, winter or summer. There were pieces of string tied to several of the buttons, and Chester knew, from the long years that Mr. Meyer had lived in the rooming house at 1211, that the strings were reminders, but Mr. Meyer never remembered what the strings were to remind him about.

"Good morning, Mr. Meyer. It's a nice day, isn't it? What can I do for you?"

"What can you do? Oh, yes, what can you get for me? A pack of Melachrinos, please, the plain ones. I used to smoke the cork-tipped, but now I always seem to get the wrong end in my mouth."

His voice carried a very slight accent and he used little gestures as he spoke: shrugs of his shoulders; a way of turning his hands, palms upward. A nice old fellow, but Chester didn't feel that he could put the candy away while he was there, and there were some bills to be checked over.

Mr. Meyer opened the package of Melachrinos and lit one. He didn't hold a cigarette the way most people do, between the middle and index fingers, but with his first two fingers and thumb, very delicately. It gave him an air of elegance, in spite of his faded coat. Yes, undoubtedly Mr. Meyer was going to stay awhile. He seated himself on one of the stools in front of the soda fountain and said, as he always did, "There is nothing like a good Turkish cigarette, Mr.—ah—Jones. It has flavor—bouquet. It is for the *cognoscenti*. You can have your Camels and your Lucky Strikes. They are made for the mass taste. Mass production has spoiled everything—automobiles exactly like each other, all of them noisy and smelly. In the old days, with horses, each team, each carriage reflected the personality of the owner."

One thing, Chester thought, with Mr. Meyer it wasn't necessary to do any talking yourself. Customers came and went—children for penny candy, men for the early afternoon paper, women to use the telephone, mostly to place bets with a bookmaker—but Mr. Meyer talked on. "Those were elegant days, my friend. Everybody knew of Paul Meyer. My name was in the newspapers then, sir. I gave concerts that filled theaters all over Europe, all over the world. There would be encore after encore; there would be no satisfying my audiences, thousands of people who paid their money to hear me. People had taste in those days. They liked me for the special quality in my music, not because I could stand on my head while I played some drivel such as 'Humoresque.'

"Today people have lost discrimination, except for a few of us, out of the past. That is why I smoke Melachrinos. They cost more and my funds are very limited these days, but I would rather smoke fewer cigarettes and indulge my own taste. You understand, Mr.—ah—Jones?"

This was one of the old man's habits, to have to stop and recollect Chester's name. He nodded. "I keep Melachrinos for you and Mr. Gerson. He's from someplace in Europe. You don't know him, I guess."

"Of course I do. You say he smokes Melachrinos? How extraordinary! You surprise me."

"I don't know why. He doesn't speak much English, but I like him. He has a son who hangs around the store a lot. A nice boy—one of the nicest in the neighborhood. He plays the violin, too."

"For the radio I suppose. Atrocious music, on the radio. My wife and I listen only because we no longer have an opportunity to hear anything better. How can people have taste when all they hear is such trash?"

Honey came into the store by the side door. "Morning, Mr. Jones."

Chester said, "Good morning," and looked up at the clock behind the cigar counter, wondering if she was early. No, it was almost noon. Lunch business wasn't much during the summer, but there'd be people in for sandwiches and coffee, as well as ice cream. Honey would bring down the sandwich fillers, but he had clean forgotten about the coffee. "You'll pardon me, Mr. Meyer, while I make coffee? Honey, tell Mrs. Jones to send down a pound." He busied himself at the row of Silexes. Funny how people drank coffee even in the hottest weather. Every now and then, while Mr. Meyer's voice continued, Chester said, "Uh-huh," just to show that he was listening, but when he turned around, finally, the old man had gone. Chester hoped that he hadn't hurt Mr. Meyer's feelings, but anyway he'd have forgotten by tomorrow. He forgot everything that had to do with the present and its hardships, but remembered his past and its glories. Nature was being kind to him.

Dick came in. It didn't require any power of deduction to tell that he had been playing baseball in the school yard, which was kept open during the summer as a playground. The strap was undone on one leg of his knickerbockers and it hung to his ankle. His shirt was out in back. His hair always had the same uncombed look, but his face was unusually flushed and perspiry. "Hi, Dad, want help?"

"Not while you are looking like that. Run upstairs and get washed and your hair combed. Isn't it about time you wore your long trousers for everyday and gave away those?"

"These are better for playing in, especially baseball. How about taking me to see the A's play tomorrow? They're playing the Yankees. George can run the store; it won't be busy anyhow."

"You go if you want to. I'll listen over the radio."

"Know what I think? In a hundred years Americans will be nothing but a big, round bottom to sit on and a pair of ears. Come on, Dad. It will do you good to get out of this old store. We'll sit out in the bleachers and get some sunshine. You've forgotten what that stuff is."

Chester laughed. Dick had something irresistible about him—he always had. And even as a little boy he had talked like an adult. "We'll see tomorrow. I'd sort of like to see that young Di Maggio . . ."

The bell in the first telephone booth began to ring, and Dick grimaced. "Bet it's Mr. Malone. He called up the same time yesterday. Did I tell you? You were upstairs. He came home drunk Wednesday and she threw him out and now he's trying to make up. I sent one of the Green kids, but she wouldn't come to the phone and wouldn't even pay the kid his nickel."

Chester took the call, and as usual Dick was right. "Hello, Malone. Yes, Dick told me. She was in last night, and I don't think it would do any good. Do you mind my giving you a little advice?" Malone was a touchy Irishman, but a good fellow. A better man than she was a woman, the way she spent his money on the races all the time.

"O.K., Jones. You're a good Joe, I know." It was said in a firm voice that showed that Malone was stone sober now.

"Don't try to reach her today. She'll be in here on Monday, placing bets, around this time or a little later. Why don't you try her then? I don't want to snoop, Malone, but in my place I can't help knowing the cause of the trouble between you. If you could break it up and straighten out at the same time, I'd be glad."

Malone had never been a good customer—all their money went to the bookies—but Chester was happy at the way he said, "Thanks, pal," over the phone. When he went into the store again he realized that Dick had been listening. Where did the kid get that strange, knowing grin of his? Why should he say, "Out at Shibe Park it would be sort of hard to play God, I guess"?

"Trying to straighten out the Malones isn't playing God. Perhaps, in fact, it's the opposite; I doubt that God interferes in folks' lives as much as I do. Now run up and wash, like I told you to, and maybe I will take you tomorrow. The A's won't win, I guess, but it would be worth while just to see Lou Gehrig hit a home run."

"Even better than on the radio?"

"Get upstairs and washed, and stop trying to needle your father."

There were always transients dropping in for lunch. Chester liked to wonder about them: what they did for a living, why they happened to be in the neighborhood. One kind I can always spot immediately, he thought when the man came in. It was hard to have a breezy smile on such a hot and humid day, but this man had it. "Hello, friend. I want a cup of the best coffee in the world."

Two in the last week, Chester thought. Part of one of those books on salesmanship. If I could buy from him, I would, but he's wrong thinking that a five-cent cup of coffee entitles him to a sales spiel.

"How come you know about our coffee?" Chester asked, and then was sorry. Underneath the man's assurance was fear. How many had he sold of what he was trying to sell? How many cups of coffee had he ordered this morning, using his flattery in the hope of making a sale? The man dove his hand into the shabby brief case he was carrying and drew out a gaudy folder. Both of them would be losing their time, but there was no stopping the man on the talk that he had probably learned by heart.

"What food does everybody like? What meal is never served without it? Bread, you say? Think again, Mr. Jones. Potatoes. Good old spuds. Who would want to eat a meal without them? Don't you agree? The universal food: taste-rich, taste-full, zest-rich, and zest-full. Spuds, Mr. Jones. We call our product Spudlets. Adults love them. Children cry for them. Install a Spudlet machine in the front of your store . . ."

"I was going to give you an order for a couple of dozen," Chester interrupted, "just to try it out. But what's that about a machine?"

The fear showed in the salesman's eyes, the knowing that he wasn't going to make a sale. Maybe, if it's not too dear, I'll buy one anyhow, Chester thought.

"Spudlets are made fresh, right before the eyes of your customers. When they see the succulent golden-brown color they can't resist. Instead of this empty store, my friend, imagine your place crowded with customers, eagerly buying this new and delicious food treat."

Chester asked, "How much?" and then wished that he hadn't.

"That's the wonderful part about it. There is no cost to you whatever. A Spudlet machine pays for itself."

"Sold! I'll take one under those terms. Deliver it as soon as you can, and I'll agree to turn over every cent it earns until it's paid for."

Another man had entered the store, and Chester said, "Excuse me a minute."

The newcomer said, "Don't let me bother you. I'll wait till you're through."

The first salesman looked annoyed while he explained that Chester's proposition was exactly what his company wanted, except that Chester would understand the need for some small down payment, say $150, and then a regular amount monthly. Chester wished George would come down; he could say no. Sometimes too abruptly. And yet, that way, he saved the time of both himself and the salesman.

"Seems to me that's a long way from your first proposition." They were both acutely aware of the other man, and Chester, who had been through such scenes hundreds of times, wondered why they still annoyed him. He was saved by the beginning of the luncheon trade. The three painters who were giving 903, across Camac Street, a needed coat over the old paint covering the bricks were followed by a couple of strange girls, who ordered ice-cream sundaes. Eddie Bryant, whose daytime beat this was every third week, sat down at the small table in the corner behind the telephone booths. There was no need for him to sit there. The law, as well as his blue uniform, entitled him to sit where he wanted, regardless of the color of his skin. If Eddie preferred his place, that was up to him.

The salesmen still waited, and Chester said, "I'll be busy for a couple of hours. Come back later." After they had gone he remembered that the one had not paid for his coffee. Well, that was all right, just so he didn't come back.

Business stayed brisk all afternoon, which wasn't surprising, the way the day had warmed up after last night's rain. He pressed the buzzer button for help, and Kit came down. He didn't like his wife to work in the store; she had done more than her share of that in the early days. He knew that George was uptown and Helen—Penny—out with Vee Maguire, but what had happened to Dick? He must have sneaked out by the private entrance on McClellan Street, which was like him if he had some project of his own in mind and didn't want to tend store.

The rush kept up, mostly youngsters with dishes, wanting two or three dips of ice cream to take home, and Chester forgot about Dick. He dipped ice cream while Kit served the tables. She could still get around quickly, in spite of her increasing weight. He recalled when they were first married, when she was in the store all day while he worked at Strawbridge's. She'd always been short and plump—Dickie took after her that way—but she could serve three people to his one, then and now. The trouble was that he liked to talk to customers, which wasted time.

Chester was so busy dipping ice cream that he didn't notice when Mary Plotko came in. There she stood, at the end of the fountain. His wrist was hurting from digging with the ball-shaped dipper into the too hard cream. Only the pineapple was of the right consistency, but hardly anyone ordered pineapple. The vanilla was like a brick; the chocolate and strawberry weren't much better, though the lids had been off all the cans ever since the rush began. His thumb was numb from pressing the lever that pushed the balled ice cream out of the dipper.

Mary stepped behind the fountain and began to help. He had never known her to do this before, though she had often run errands or earned nickels by taking telephone messages, but she made four fountain Cokes and a double chocolate soda the way Kit used to do. There was a swing to working behind a fountain, and Mary had it. When a troop of children gathered in front of the candy case she pushed him out of the way. George wanted to get rid of penny candies, and he was probably right, but there was nothing more fun than watching kids spending pennies, except when the store was busy. Mary had first come to them that way, but all the memories of her as the cutest and dirtiest kid in the neighborhood made it impossible to remember any single time as the first.

When the decisions had been made between licorice shoestrings and gumdrops, chewy caramel and sour balls, nonpareils and chocolate nigger babies, Chester hurried back to the fountain, but Mary had already caught up with business. Beads of perspiration stood out on her forehead and her cheeks were flushed. "Oh, Mr. Jones, isn't it fun working at the soda fountain? I've wanted to, often."

"You could have, any time."

All the people at the fountain had gone; there remained only a stranger at one of the tables and two neighborhood women in the phone booths, placing late bets. Kit gave him a glance that included Mary, and when he nodded she went upstairs.

"It *was* wonderful, Mr. Jones. I can't tell you. I've—I've dreamed about it, even."

"You and George are a pair. You should run it together and let us retire." As soon as he finished saying the words Chester knew that he had made a mistake. Mary's chin and mouth began to quiver. She threw her head around so that her long, almost straight hair made a kind of golden veil to hide her face and its show of emotion. She said, "I'm sorry, I've been through so much today," and ran for the stair door. What the hell had he said to make her behave like that? One good thing, Kit would be waiting for her upstairs, to straighten things out. Kit was wonderful at that.

After George relieved him, Chester joined the two women in the kitchen upstairs. "Better send Honey down to wash dishes. By the way, what happened to Dick?"

"Now Chester, darling, don't be angry. Somebody offered him a puppy. I said he could have it, and he's going for it. You know he's been miserable ever since Buddy was run over."

"I hadn't noticed it. And I'm not angry, except that a store is no place for a dog. There's no room inside, and he's not safe outside."

"When your cats get killed I always notice you get new ones."

"Cats are different. They keep down mice, for one thing. And they're never in the way. Let's hope this pup doesn't grow to Buddy's size."

Kit laughed. "We never knew that Buddy's father was a great Dane until Buddy was full-grown. This one's parents are both fox terriers, more or less."

"I'll believe that a year from now. Feeling better, Mary?"

"I'm sorry. I'm all right now."

No wonder boys were always calling up to date her. Her appearance of grave reserve came out of her childhood—the pain of having the worst clothes of any child in the neighborhood, the pain of being taunted because her father drank, the pain of a negligent mother. Even Kay, three years older, didn't possess her air of maturity, an inner beauty. The truth is, Chester thought, I love Mary as much as my own girls. She needed love, and it was nice to think that both Kit and himself had done all they could for her over the years.

"I guess I shouldn't butt in, but why don't you get a job? You could work for us. Just to have you in the store would increase our business. Guess I'm getting to think like George. Let's see, there are one hundred and nine single men in this neighborhood under the age of sixty. Add ten per cent for others looking in and seeing you . . ."

"Stop teasing, Mr. Jones. Mrs. Jones thinks I ought to leave home, too. You have to understand; it's not Mom keeps me home. It's Pop. You see him at his worst, but he's O.K. He works every night, and he works hard. He makes good pay, too, because it's over at the Atlantic Refinery. They have all kinds of safety rules, but it's still dangerous. You know Mom never used to take care of me. That used to make him mad. Now she plays the numbers and the horses. Pop can take just so much. He gets mad and fusses, then when it doesn't do any good he gets drunk enough to beat her up. But he loves me, Pop does. If I left home, he'd go to pieces."

Kit said, "Maybe he should leave too."

"He won't. I've told him he should. You know, when you see him on the street Pop don't look like so much, but he tries and goes on trying. He loves Mom, too, in spite of her losing his money. It's hard to explain. If Pop sticks, I have to stick, but sometimes I can't stand being home. That's why I keep coming to your place. That's why I date more fellows . . ."

Kit and her wonderful, gurgly laughter. "Now you're boasting. Date along, but make sure who you want, like I did."

"I already know."

Chester looked at Kit and she looked back, surprised at Mary's bitterness.

It wasn't the words, but the way she said them. Chester felt better when Kit's soft, warm, vague attitude took over. "You're like Helen. Isn't she a scream? A month ago she wanted to be called Dawn, and now she's Penny. Not that you're like her that way. But you've set your sights on some movie star or other, when you should be setting them nearer home."

"Oh, but I have, Mrs. Jones. Let's not talk about it. It's so good just to have you here."

Children, even the neighbors', were too much of a worry. Chester was glad when Dickie came in, displaying his usual excitement. "Look, Mother. Dad, you're not going to fuss?"

You might think, from the way he talks, that I was the worst father in the world, Chester thought. Then he saw the puppy cringing in the kid's arms, as though knowing it wasn't wanted.

It was too short in the legs for a fox terrier, but looked more like one than anything else he could think of. Its face was white, save for a black spot around one eye.

"Isn't he a beauty, Dad?"

If the kid wanted a dog that much, Chester felt that he had been wrong in fussing about it. "What are you going to call it?"

"Floyd, Dad. Isn't it perfect?"

"Floyd? Doesn't seem right for a dog."

"Floyd Gibbons, that's why. The fellow on the radio who has a patch over one eye. Boy, can he talk fast!"

"The truth, Dick?"

"How would I know? It's what we're supposed to listen to. Besides, Floyd won't care. I'm naming him for his looks, not for what he believes in. Floyd. Hello, Floyd. See, he knows!"

The pup did turn his head sidewise, with a very knowing eye in the center of the black patch.

Mary said, "He's cute, Dick. And he does know his name. Here, Floyd. Here, Floyd." She frowned. "It's a good name, and he knows it already, but somehow it doesn't sound like a dog's name."

"It'll stay Floyd," Dick said, and knowing him Chester thought it doubtful that there would be any change.

There went the buzzer, just as Mary was saying, "I'll have to be going home to fix supper." That meant the first finals of the *Evening Bulletin* had come in, which always made Chester wonder, "How final is Final?" To the anxious women who had placed bets in the phone booths earlier in the afternoon the results of the early races were pretty final, particularly if they lost, as they usually did.

The news wasn't final at all, though, when the Phils were ahead in the fifth inning—they'd end up by losing.

He said, "Come in any time" to Mary, trying to sound casual, while she opened the side door and looked back gratefully from the sidewalk. Friday was a big magazine day, too, so George was too busy to take care of the fountain—the Coke drinkers, the chocolate-soda kids, the men and women who still needed Bromos at this time of the afternoon. What new headaches had they acquired? Chester handled them without George's desire to make further sales, or Dick's ease, or Kay's and Helen's quick dashings. The long days were telling on him, and when the early rush was over he was glad to escape upstairs again.

Unusual for all the children to be home; Kay usually dated Sig week-end evenings, and Helen was always with Vee. He remembered Veronica Maguire as a little girl, when she had been one of the worst kids in the neighborhood. Maybe he was prejudiced now because she had been such a bad child. No time to think of that; it was evident from all their faces that something was up. But there couldn't be, not on a Friday.

Kit said, "Chester, dear, know what today is?"

"Sure. Friday. Say, with you three kids home, as well as young George, you're going to have to work something out among you to give me a lift. I'm tired already."

He could see Kay and Helen look at each other and then at Dick, who said, "The articulate member of the family wants to remind you that twenty-three years ago today you married Katie Schweitzer, a daughter of the butcher in your neighborhood."

The little devil—that came of all the reading he did. "A daughter of the butcher in your neighborhood," and him standing there, waiting to see what I'll say. How in hell did Kit and I get such a child?

"All right, so I did. But that doesn't make this any silver anniversary." Kay like Kit, and George like me—but each with a bit of the both of us. Helen and Dick so different, and with none of either Kit or me. Funny how children worked out.

Dick took him up fast, "No, Dad, not silver—pasteboard. Two tickets for *Romeo and Juliet*—a present from the four of us, though

Kay gave the most, as Penny and I are practically broke, and you know how tight George is."

Kay interrupted, "Dick, you promised not to, and then you go right ahead being mean. It's from all of us to two wonderful parents."

"Well, now, that's wonderful. We haven't seen a real live show in years."

"Dad! Don't be a dope. It's Norma Shearer and Leslie Howard, at the Aldine. He's wonderful. You can just close your eyes and imagine he's holding you in his arms."

Hard to remember to think of Helen as Penny, and he wished she wasn't so full of ideas like that, but now, while she looked at him with flushed, eager face, he felt a paternal pride that none of the other children inspired quite so strongly. Gosh, she was beautiful! As beautiful as—well, as that girl they were using on the Coca-Cola ads. They both had the same color of reddish-blond hair and dark violet eyes.

"Dad would rather think of holding Norma Shearer," Dick said.

All this movie stuff wasn't good for kids. Chester thought that he'd rather sit quietly upstairs and listen to the radio, but Kit was dying to go, he could see that, and the tickets were already bought. There was nothing to do but make the best of it. "I'll settle for Kitty Schweitzer."

"As she was twenty-three years ago?"

"Fishing for compliments, Kit? I had one all ready, but you won't get it now."

"Well, if we're going, who's to help George?"

Dick again, "We planned all that a week ago. We're all going to help."

"We won't be that busy, even for Friday night."

"It's so that we'll all take part." Kay looked at Dick and added, "Equally. Now you and Mother get ready. We've ordered a Yellow cab for eight."

After the theater, Chester wanted to take one of the Yellows that were parked in a line in front of the Aldine, but Kit said, "Oh, Chester, let's walk. I really mean it; the night's so beautiful. And a cab will spoil all the feeling of the show."

"Won't the kids be disappointed? After all, it's their deal."

"I want to walk anyway. And wasn't it thoughtful of the children? They didn't tell me until just before you came upstairs from the store. Who do you suppose had the idea first?"

They turned down Nineteenth Street and had almost reached Rittenhouse Square before Chester answered, and she wondered why he took so long when the answer was so evident.

"Kay, I'd say."

"I think it was Dickie. Chester, he scares me sometimes. He's so much smarter than we are. Ever since he was little I've always felt that when I said no to him, he knew more about things than I did. Goodness knows, I'm at my wit's end with Helen a good part of the time, but with her it's different. I worry over her. I do, Chester, and I don't over Dick. He engineered this whole evening, even to Kay and little George paying for most of it, and then taunting them."

"George wasn't even there, sweetheart. Besides, what does it matter? The kids arranged it, all of them. How did you like the show, anyway? Did Leslie Howard affect you the way Helen says he does her?"

"Yes, a little. Not the way he looks, but the sound of his voice. I didn't even listen to the words, the sound was so beautiful." Kit tried to remember when she had heard anything that was quite the same. She loved Chester and they had four children, but he had never aroused the particular kind of feeling that Leslie Howard —or William Shakespeare—had. Was it the actor or the author?

While they walked along, she thought of Chester Jones as a stranger and not as her own husband. He wasn't a very imposing man; he was only five feet six. His hair was still thick, but its neutral brown was graying rapidly. Although she couldn't tell by the street lights, she knew that he had a perpetual pallor from spending so much of his time in the store, and he always had a tired walk that came from the same reason. They shouldn't be walking home; Chester was on his feet so much during the day. But he was smiling, looking at her with that amused expression that had first interested her in him.

"Stacking me up against Leslie Howard, and I don't come out so good?"

She nodded her head. "Uh-huh. I made a mistake. I should have waited."

This was by far the worst lie, and she snuggled up to him, to let him know, thinking to herself that his question was surprisingly like one that Dickie might ask. They turned onto Broad Street, its midnight emptiness and quiet broken only at South Street, where the colored people seemed to be as wide awake as ever. When they were past, she said, "I'm happy, Chester. The way people like us should be happy—no wild excitement, but no real tragedy either. A quiet happiness, which is the best after all. Even the worst times we can look back on and find some satisfaction in them . . . Chester! You don't feel that way?"

"How? That I'm no Romeo?"

"I know when you're teasing. That isn't what I mean at all."

Here was McClellan Street, and they turned eastward, toward the store.

"I'm not teasing. It's that way, sort of. Men can make a Juliet of almost any woman, as I did of you and still do. To me, you're perfect. Aw, hell, Kit, it's too beautiful a night to try to philosophize. How did you like Norma Shearer, by the way? All our talk seems to have been about Romeo."

Chester opened the store door—he never liked to use the front one—and she answered, "I didn't like her at all. She's pretty, I guess, but I hated her all through the picture."

"For Pete's sake, why?"

"She looks like Vee Maguire, that's why. The same butter-won't-melt-in-her-mouth look, and I'm worried about Helen. Veronica is just the kind of girl who . . ."

She couldn't finish, because Chester had begun to kiss her, right there in the store where anyone could see, if they looked hard, because of the lights over the cash registers. Why, he hadn't kissed her in the store since shortly after their marriage, when he used to steal a kiss sometimes behind the old telephone booth, the one they'd had before the store was enlarged and a row of booths put in the rear window. It felt good, awfully good. Maybe Leslie Howard had been married two or three times, or wasn't living with his wife. Chester was good and wonderful and dependable.

## Chapter 3

George had worked late the night before and was still sleeping. Dick tiptoed out of their third-floor back bedroom and continued dressing on the way downstairs. By the time he reached the store he felt presentable, except for his tie, which hung over one shoulder, and his hair, which he combed with his fingers at the sink behind the soda fountain. There, that was good enough. He scooped a dipper of vanilla ice cream from the electric cabinet into a parfait glass, poured on chocolate sauce, and played a thin jet of soda water over the mixture. When he'd finished eating it, he helped himself to a second. Smoky, the cat, rubbed against his leg, and he put down a dipper of ice cream for her.

Five minutes to six; Mr. Oberholtzer, who lived at 1236, would be along in a minute. Dick took a pack of Camels from the rack behind the cigar counter, unlocked the front door, and removed an *Inquirer* from the thick bundle that had been thrown on the front sidewalk.

The streetcar was over a block away and Mr. Oberholtzer only about thirty yards—which was darn good timing. He handed over newspaper and cigarettes as Mr. Oberholtzer raced by. He'd pay in the evening, when he picked up his Final *Bulletin*.

Inside, Dick rang up fifteen cents in the front register, which took care of tobacco, candy, and sundry sales, wrote on a slip of paper, "Mr. O. 17¢," and took out two cents, which he dropped in the cigar box labeled "Paper Money."

34

George gets the craziest ideas, he thought. He put on a short apron with a change pocket in front, broke the paper wrappings on two dollars' worth of pennies, and stood by the front door. He handed out papers and made change automatically for the line of impatient customers that began to move past. Why didn't people allow themselves a few minutes' more time to go to work? This was the mill and factory trade; shortly there would be a lull before the office workers came.

From sounds behind him in the store he knew that Kay was making coffee in the row of Silexes on the back bar of the fountain. She'd drink a cup herself and leave enough brewed coffee and boiling water for early customers.

When she hurried past him, a package of peanut-butter sandwiches in her hand, he called, "Robbing the store again?"

Usually Kay only laughed when he ribbed her, but she had been touchy the past week or two. She turned and walked back. "I'll pay for them when I get home if you feel that way."

"Why should I feel that way? Eat all you want, I say. It's George's rule, not mine—and here comes your car."

She made a face at him and ran; the first paper rush was over, but there'd soon be breakfast trade. Dick went back to the soda fountain, helped himself to another black-and-white soda, placed eggs and bacon by the electric grill, and turned it on. Another of George's ideas, and it was a pain in the neck. Every time George had an idea it meant more work. The bread box under the small door that was cut into the large one on Camac Street needed to be checked off from the delivery slip. Six sandwich loaves, three dozen doughnuts, and a dozen coffee cakes. He carried them behind the fountain and arranged the cakes and doughnuts on plates along the marble fountain.

Usually Mr. and Mrs. Rivkin were first in, then Saul Gerson, when he was working, but this morning Mary was first.

"Hello, Dickie. How's about coffee and a doughnut?"

"O.K."

"I forgot. You don't like to be called Dickie. I'm sorry."

"Who told you that? I don't care at all. You just have to pronounce an extra syllable. Now me, I'm labor-saving, that's all. Say

Dickie four times and you've wasted the energy to say a sentence, if it's not too long. Here's your coffee. I didn't make it—Kay did."

Dick liked to make Mary laugh. Maybe it was because she had pretty teeth. Anyway, she was four years too old. "Saw your new date."

"How'd you like him?"

"Why you waste your time! You and Kay. Her Sigmund—ugh! And Polish." He put a doughnut on a plate and placed it beside the coffee. "I'm sorry. Forgot you were Polish too."

"I'm as American as you are, Dickie Jones. My father's Ukrainian. I bet you don't even know where the Ukraine is."

"You should bet with George. It's in the southwest part of Russia. So you're a Communist."

"Here's my dime."

"Cut it, Mary. Why should you pay when the rest of the family doesn't? Besides, didn't you help out the other night?"

"I've no time to argue with children."

Why didn't Mary wise up? Or maybe she had, and it bothered her. Anyway, she had stuck in the harpoon where it hurt the worst. "O.K., we're even."

The Rivkins and Saul. Mary nodded to them. Saul was a funny fellow. Quiet and smart, but he couldn't keep a job, ever. Maybe he was too intelligent.

"Hi, Saul, the usual?"

Before Saul could answer, Mrs. Rivkin cut in. "Be a good kid, Dickie, and draw us two coffees quick. Ben and me are late now. Butter a coffee cake and cut it in half."

"You get no bread with one meat ball." Dick poured the two coffees while Mrs. Rivkin said, "Meaning what?"

"Meaning we can't butter a coffee cake unless it's a nickel extra."

"So who is kicking?"

"You. Every day. Saul, how's the new job?"

"O.K., so far. Funny thing, Dick. I try hard, every job I get. I organize my work, anticipate what the boss wants. You know—all the things that are supposed to get you ahead in the world. All it gets me is fired."

"I've been giving you some thought. My conclusion is that you're

36

too intelligent. I'm the same way; I'd be fired by any boss I worked for within a week."

The Rivkins downed their coffee, wolfed their cake, and rushed out. Dick said, "Take your choice. They have their own business. I don't know what it is, but they're always broke. Everything goes into the business. They owe Dad from way back. She always has stomach trouble. *They* should be working for someone else. With half the work and worry they'd be a lot happier."

The store filled, until all the seats along the soda fountain were occupied. If he pressed the button of the upstairs buzzer for help, Mother would probably come down. She'd be letting George and Helen sleep late, when it was she who needed the rest most of all.

Four Bromo-Seltzers in a row. Eggs fried, sunny side up and over, scrambled and poached. Eggs one minute, two minutes, and three. Why did people need to eat their eggs in so many different ways? If Dad wanted to do something really worth while, he'd buy a bigger grill instead of listening to George's ideas. The buyers of the late morning papers. Bill Thomas, who lived right across on Camac Street, still looking for a job, peering through want ads while he drank two cups of coffee. "Hello, Dickie," or "So long, Dick," over and over. The first users of the public telephones.

A call in, to be answered. "No, Mr. Malone. There's no one here I could send. Why don't you take Dad's advice?" Malone was drinking again; it was in his voice. "Look, Mr. Malone. We only keep a store. No, this is Dick."

"Little Dickie. Nice kid. Known you since you was a li'l fat squirt . . ."

Dick hung up. This could go on forever. Besides, there was Breyer's truck outside, with the ice cream delivery. He was still so busy when Dad came downstairs that he didn't hear him until Dad said, "Good morning, son. Keeping you stepping?"

"Not much. I could handle it. You should have slept awhile longer. Now you're here, though, I'll run upstairs for a minute and see how Floyd Gibbons is doing. He was sleeping in George's bed when I came down. Not very faithful, when you consider he's my dog. And Dad, add Luckies to the tobacco order—we're fresh out."

One thing about Dickie—he never presented any problems. That was all young George did. Just to see him come in the front door from wherever he'd been, Chester knew that he was popping with problems. There was no one in the store, and Chester sat at a table listening to the ball game and idly wondering why anybody paid admission to watch either the A's or the Phillies. Which reminded him that weeks ago he had half promised to take Dick to a game. Which should they see? As both teams were in last place in their respective leagues, it couldn't matter much.

"Dad, I want you to come across the street with me."

What had got into George? He sounded as though it was a matter of life and death. Chester turned down the radio and followed George outside. There was almost no traffic on McClellan Street, and they crossed the car tracks with what seemed unnecessary haste. When they stopped on the brick pavement in front of Joe Spinelli's shoe-repair shop, George faced him. He waved his arms toward their own store and commanded, "Look, Dad. I want you to tell me what's wrong with that picture."

It was years since Chester had looked at the store this way; not since he replaced the brick pavement with concrete. What was wrong? There it was: the four-story yellow-brick building at the end of a solid row of buildings exactly like it, except for the store front. The two top floors did not run all the way back on the Camac Street side, but stopped where the two-story addition had been built after Helen's birth. There was a curious-looking arrangement of wire fencing up there that Chester had not seen before. Then he remembered. "Now, George, that's nothing to get so excited about. I told Dickie he could fix a place up there for that new pup of his. It's rather unsightly, I admit. I'll get him to move it back."

"That! It looks terrible, but I didn't mean that. Just look at the store."

The store looked just like it always did: the narrow private door to the upstairs living quarters, the large plate-glass window, the front door set at an angle. The builder who made the alteration had sold him on that, to make it easier for people to come in from either street. Maybe he had been right, but it had cost a good deal more, and besides, everyone from Camac Street used the side door, between the two long windows on that street. "Looks pretty good to me, son. You should have seen it when we moved here. Two little show windows on McClellan, with the door between and ordinary window sash on the side. The kitchen and dining room were in back of the store, and behind that was a board fence. There was a little yard, too, where nothing would grow, hard as your mother tried."

"Oh, I remember all that. You still don't see!"

"The private entrance, maybe? Your mother's idea, on account of the girls, when we did the place over. It cuts off from the store, but she thought when they entertained . . ."

"No, Dad!" George's exasperation would have been funny if the kid weren't so darn serious about it. "I heard all the talk between you and Mother when the front was remodeled. What I want you to see is something else. You've lost your sense of perspective, Dad. That's why I brought you over here. Whose store is that, anyway? To look at the signs, you'd think it belonged to the Coca-Cola company, or to Breyer's. Look at all the signs. 'All-ways Delicious'! 'The pause that refreshes'! 'Nearly everybody reads the *Bulletin*'! 'Phillies, handmade'!

"Where's your name? You can hardly see it. 'Chester Jones, Confectionary and Sundries.' What are sundries? Besides, those glass letters on the windows are old-fashioned. They were old-fashioned when you had them put on, even. We're behind the times. I admit I'm almost as bad as you are. It just happened that Mother sent me down to Little Italy. Honey's husband works in a spaghetti joint and taught her how to make it, so we're having it tonight, but we didn't have the spices.

"That's beside the point, except that usually I come from uptown. I tell you, when I saw our place from over here I was shocked, really shocked. It looks a mess, Dad. A mess."

"We're doing all right."

"That's what you always say. But we're standing still. If we don't go ahead, we'll go back; all the merchandising magazines say so. We should take all those signs off and put up a big one, around the top, with nothing but our name on. Do you see the Rexall stores advertising anything but Rexall? Or Schulte's? I bet they sell

Phillie cigars too, but they'll have special brands to push—their own."

"Five or six years ago, when things were tough and we still owed two or three notes on getting the new part built, the Phillie people gave us credit. When we bought this place it sold Crane's ice cream. It was good ice cream, but Breyer's gave me a big, new cabinet and a lot of signs. They advertised a lot—that 'All-ways Delicious' slogan that you don't like. I don't know just what it means myself, but our business doubled. When electric cabinets came in we got one of the first. They paid for it; they still own it. Know what their investment in cabinets must be, George? I'm real proud to be selling their ice cream, and I don't see any sense in not letting people know we sell it. The same with Coca-Cola. Sure, we could get cheaper sirup, or cut theirs, like some places do . . .

"Anyhow, there goes Mrs. Malone to place bets with her bookie. That's one thing I don't like. Seems to me if the phone company and the police really wanted to, they could stop it."

"Mrs. Plotko is as bad. She doesn't come in our place any more, but Mary says she hasn't stopped. She plays the numbers, too."

All afternoon the bettors would be trooping in to the phone booths. The horses and the numbers caused more trouble among the married folks around than drinking or anything else. The women betting the men's money. People spoke of playing the ponies as the rich man's weakness, but it was also the poor woman's. Both men and women played the numbers, but this was a racket that didn't seem to affect people's lives much. Neither did the baseball pools, or those on football, which only the men played. It was betting on the horses that caused trouble.

Would it do any good talking to Mrs. Malone? Back in the store he looked at her through the frame of the telephone-booth door. Not over twenty-five, black Irish, and pretty as the picture she made. Raised to bingo and chances on almost anything, could she really be blamed for graduating to the ponies? Right now, as she placed her bets, the tenseness, the hope of winning gave her face a peculiar, alive attractiveness. No wonder Malone got drunk from worrying about her. How much had he tried to stop her failing, instead of taking the easier way for himself?

George was talking behind him, complicating life further. "There's something else, Dad. I don't want to go back to school this fall."

"I don't like to hear you say that."

"It's how I feel. What's the use? I'd learn more working for a chain—Woolworth's, maybe—and learning how they operate. I'd watch everything."

"If you went with Woolworth you'd have to take some pretty unimportant kind of job."

"That wouldn't matter. Even working in a stock room would teach me more than intermediate algebra. What good will it do? Learning to do logarithms is sort of silly these days, when people can't even add and divide any more. Take in the store here. Every time any of us makes a sale of more than two or three items it's apt to be added up wrong—with Helen and Mother especially. Dickie has his failings, but he figures pretty good."

"Better than any of us, you might add. But what are you proposing now?"

"I'm not proposing anything. I just got the idea. Maybe we should have little adding machines at every counter. I bet we'd save what they cost in a couple of years."

"We don't run an A & P, George, just a little corner store. You're changing the subject, which is school. I think that when you start something you should finish it. Suppose you should change your mind about storekeeping?"

"There's nothing I'll ever want to do but have a store. Someday there will be dozens of Jones Brothers stores in this town."

"Dickie isn't as interested as you are."

"He'll be the silent partner. Dickie's smarter than you think, in spite of the way he goes around half dressed."

"Well, I'll be damned."

"He is, Dad, really."

"You don't tell. I understand him better than I do you, sometimes."

"How can you? Dick changes his mind every week about what

41

he intends to be. The only reason I'd cut him in is that Jones Brothers has a better sound to it than just George Jones.

"I just wonder what color store front we ought to have. Red is best, of course, but Woolworth and A & P and a lot of others have done it to death. I'm not for green or yellow either. What I've thought of is purple."

Chester watched him screw up his face and knew that the kid was actually visualizing with his mind's eye a purple-fronted store filled with every merchandising gadget there was.

"You've only another term, George. Finish it out."

"I'm two years older than the rest of the class."

"Not your fault. You were pretty sick, and you licked it."

"I couldn't do any of the things the other fellows did."

"You can now."

"Not like Dickie. You should go see him play baseball up at the playground. He's the best there. I can't even run much."

"You don't limp, George. Those were worrisome days for your mother and me. We did what we could, but it was your courage that won."

"I have to be best at something . . ."

"Maybe I haven't always understood you, son. I think I do now. I'll make a deal. Graduate, and from then on anything you want to do, I'll go along the best I know how."

Chester knew he would never forget that summer of the first big infantile paralysis epidemic. People had said it came from the war, like Spanish flu. It had been in their neighborhood. The two children of Abe Isaacs, who had the drugstore at Thirteenth and McClellan, which was now Weisberg's. Then the boy who worked at the corner American Store, before the Acme Supermarket was built. The tailor's little girl. What had been his name? Anyway, the little girl had died, and so had the son of Ed Burke, who still owned the oyster saloon across the street.

Chester glanced over at the closed store, with its shades pulled down. Almost a month until September, the first r month, when they'd be having a couple dozen of Burke's special fries for midnight supper.

Yes, Sonny Burke had died and the epidemic seemed to be limited to the families of storekeepers in the neighborhood, so they all talked of closing—but how could they, when the stores were their livelihood?

Suddenly every family on Fawn Street—completely shanty Irish then—seemed to have a stricken child. Fawn Street, with outside toilets and only one cold-water spigot for some eighty people. A living cesspool that no one cared or thought about, because you had to turn down McClellan and go up Camac and turn again on Cristobal to reach it. The people on Fawn Street came into the stores, though.

The first time he had thought of getting into politics was then. Bill Lewis, who was division leader, took them to the mayor, who promised a cleanup.

Not soon enough! Little George with a slight fever, which they wouldn't have worried about ordinarily. The overworked doctor, who came long after midnight. Kit sitting with him beside the tossing youngster.

Gosh, it seemed like yesterday. Fawn Street had gone colored since then, but the WPA had put in sewers and repaved it. As if because he was thinking of them, two of the Green boys, who lived at 922 Fawn, skated by the door on the smooth macadam paving of Camac Street. It was beautiful to watch them. Somehow the white boys skating by never seemed to have the grace and rhythm of the colored kids. They jumped the curb, crossed the sidewalk, pushed open the screen door, and sailed across the store floor. George sold them the edition of the *Daily News* that they had come for. Horace Green couldn't be over eight, but he turned the paper to the stock-market share clearings, on which the winning numbers were based, with the same eager anticipation that the women in the phone booths had, awaiting calls from their bookmakers.

The sudden flatness of feature and expressionless mask that didn't belong on a child showed that the Greens had not won today. They cluttered out, Horace ahead, clutching the pink sheet, to bear the bad news home, without paying any attention to Chester calling after them that they shouldn't come into the store on skates.

And it wasn't the Green kids, but George, that he had been

thinking about. The doctor saying, "Polio." Kit, those months after, never giving up hope. Their fears for Dickie and the baby. Strange, come to think of it, they'd never worried about Kay being stricken, that he could remember. How could they have got along without her? So little older than the others, but like a second Kit, the way she had taken responsibility.

George walked outside and cranked up the awning over the front window, now that the sun had gone, then put on the short apron with change pockets that Dick usually wore in the mornings, ready for the evening paper rush. Yes, Chester thought, no sign of a limp. He'd do everything in his power, everything he could, when the right time came, to heal the deeper hurt.

# Chapter 4

The Saturday morning before Labor Day, George stood in the front doorway of the store and watched the solid line of one-way traffic. On McClellan Street it was westbound, which meant that all these cars were headed toward the country. On the eastbound streets they would all be going shoreward.

"Go west, young man!" One of Dad's favorite jokes, because that was the only way you could go by automobile or trolley if you lived on McClellan Street. What would happen if you drove the other way? Right now, if he walked up to the Sley Garage, where Dad kept the Lafayette, and drove down Camac and made an east turn on McClellan, what would happen? Today, an accident, right off. But other days, when it wasn't crowded? He'd get a ticket from the first cop who saw him, that was what. You had to do everything according to the way it was marked out for you. You followed signs and arrows, you stopped at red lights and waited impatiently while they turned to amber, you stepped on the gas when they became green. Everybody talked of having freedom and liberty, but where was there either, in this? It was like having to go back to school next week just because a high-school diploma was a mark on the road that fellows were supposed to take. Sheep had the same liberty —to follow each other.

Look at all those people going to the country. All the way out, and Monday night all the way back, they'd have to stay in line, stopping and starting, following the signs, obeying the lights. Dad was right in saying that he'd rather stay at home for his vacation instead of closing the store and wearing themselves out on the road to the shore. George remembered how busy they used to be, Labor Day week ends; now, in an hour or so, the city would be practically deserted. They went away knowing the trip would be unpleasant, that when they got wherever they were going it would be over-crowded, knowing that it was dangerous and there'd be accidents and people injured and killed . . .

He wondered what put such ideas into his head. He was afraid of them. They showed an unwillingness to accept things as they were, and that was wrong, besides not getting you anywhere. He was glad when Mr. Rivkin came in and asked for a bottle of aspirin.

Actually Mr. Rivkin wasn't much taller than George, but he gave the impression of being so because he was extremely thin—not only thin, but narrow. He had narrow, sloping shoulders, a long neck, and a long, narrow head dominated by a huge nose that was always slightly red.

While George wrapped up the aspirin, he asked, "Not going away for the week end, Mr. Rivkin?"

"Who, us? No indeed! My wife is down at the office right now, getting work ready for Tuesday." There was bitterness in his voice. "It's easy enough for the people that work for you. They come in at all hours, leave on the dot, get holidays off, and expect to be paid just the same. Are there holidays for the bosses? I should say not.

"And what do we get out of it? We'd be better off working for someone else. *Then* we could take a nice vacation—down at Wild-wood maybe. We was there on our honeymoon and haven't had a vacation since."

George said, "Anything else?" but Mr. Rivkin went right on talking. "I should be down helping Stella, but I've been getting a cold for three days now. I think I'll take some aspirin and go to bed. One never has any effect on me—I need two. Maybe if I took three it would be better yet. What do you think?"

"On the bottle it says two."

"I know it does. I've been a two-aspirin man for a long time, but lately I notice they don't do me as much good as they used to. I'm going to try three."

"A lot of our customers take a Bromo or Alka-Seltzer for colds. They say that either of them helps."

"That's an idea. Maybe you better give me a bottle of Bromo. A small one, to try. I'll take it first and the aspirins after. What do you think of that? Or should I try the other way around?"

Funny, the questions people asked. George tried to think what to say. "It's not on the bottle of either one. I don't think I'd mix them, though."

"With me, colds are very persistent. It's like Mrs. Rivkin with her stomach, but in her case I think it's just nerves, and I tell her so. Her stomach actually jumps. You should see it. She's always taking medicine of one kind or another, but like I tell her it's a waste of money, especially in our case, with everything going in the business.

"I know what I'll do: I'll take the Bromo first, like you suggest. I get worse colds than anybody I ever met. I don't think even three aspirins would help, but with the Bromo to start things . . ."

Another man had come into the store, a stranger, and George was anxious to wait on him, because he might be somebody just moved to the neighborhood, but it was hard to interrupt Mr. Rivkin. He told all over again how his wife's stomach jumped, and George tried to imagine how it must look, but that turned out to be pretty difficult. He said, "Uh-huh," a couple of times, then turned to the stranger anyway and asked, "Can I serve you?" the way the clerks in the chain stores were taught to do.

Maybe Mr. Rivkin took the hint, for he left, and then George almost wished that he hadn't—not that Mr. Rivkin would be much good in a pinch, but he didn't like the stranger on closer inspection. He was dressed nice enough, in a gray pin-stripe suit and felt hat to match, but there was a look about his face . . .

The store hadn't had a holdup in more than a year, and besides, anyone would know there'd be little money in the registers so early in the day.

"You earn your money the hard way, listening to guys like that.

Why don't you put in a couple of machines? You'd get a good play here, and we pay fifty-fifty. Your old man around?"

"No, he's not. But if you mean gambling machines, I don't think he'd want them."

The man laughed. He's not much older than me, George thought, but I hope I never make a sound like that when I'm supposed to be laughing.

"If we want to put in machines, it won't make much difference what your old man wants. Right now I'm just looking around, that's all."

What was this—more green lights, more red lights? I won't say anything to Dad, anyway, George thought. He'd only be mad and upset. That was the trouble with having only one store. Suppose he had ten? Or twenty? Or a thousand, like maybe Walgreen's had? Would any little gangster, or a big one, try to muscle in with slot machines then?

The man said, "We'll be seeing you," and George tried to be unafraid—maybe he was only a bluff and not the way he sounded—and answered, "So long." He watched while the man walked slowly toward the door and turned around only when he'd gone, to find Saul and Mary sitting on the stools at the soda fountain. "When did you two come in?"

"Just now," Saul said. "Who's your boy friend? Grandma, what big teeth he had!"

"Slot machines. All these rackets make me sick—and Dad, too. It's bad enough having to listen to customers losing their money over the telephone . . ." George remembered that Mary's mother was bookie bait and let his voice trail off.

"Where's everybody?" Mary asked.

"Sig Dobrzanski and Kay took Dad and Mother to the shore. Dickie is in the exhibition game at the playground this afternoon and is practicing, I guess. Helen is where you might suppose—with the Maguires, on a picnic or something. I stayed home to rest, which Dad wanted to do but couldn't, and that accounts for the whole Jones family. What gives with you?"

"Mary and I are orphans for the week end. My folks went to New York to visit my brother."

Saul had lived in the neighborhood almost as long as Mary. Everybody knew that Mr. Gerson was a freethinker, though he looked like a rabbi, with whiskers and a little black cap that he always wore. Saul looked Jewish too, which was sort of a shame, for he was otherwise the best-looking fellow in the neighborhood, and the nicest and most intelligent. The trouble with Saul was that all he cared about was playing the violin, when he should be trying to get somewhere in the world.

"Pop has to work, holidays or no holidays," Mary said, sticking her chin out to show that she wasn't ashamed about her parents. "Mom went out."

There were times when Mary looked real pretty, like now, when she seemed to be half daring him to say something. George said, "I know! Let's have a picnic right here in the store. There won't be any business to amount to anything." George wondered why he'd made the suggestion; he hadn't even thought of it a moment before, but it was a good idea just the same. "We have Bologna and hot dogs, pickles and pop—most everything we'd have on a picnic, except ants. What say?"

Mary said, "It sounds wonderful, but I'll be the only girl. George, why don't you invite your girl, the one you brought to the store last month? I thought she was pretty. Saul, she had the most gorgeous black hair, with reddish lights in it."

"Are you kidding?" What had got into Mary, anyway? His girl? Why, he had only been out with her twice—well, not over a dozen times altogether, if you included the time when he met her and the last evening, when he brought her back to the store and she was high-hat because that was where he lived. "Honest, Mary, I'd hardly remember her name, even, except that it's the same as Helen's. I don't think she's so pretty, either."

"You don't need to be so angry about it. It was only a suggestion, that's all. It seemed a nice idea to bring your girl, this Helen, or whoever she is."

"I don't have a girl. Is that final?" Honest, if he hadn't known Mary for so long, he'd have thought she was trying to pick an argument. To make matters worse, Saul began to laugh.

"Good grief," muttered George, "all I suggested was a little picnic at the store."

"Whereupon Mary tries to explore the present status of your love life. She's partially right, though—there should be another girl, just to make things even. Too bad Kay didn't stay home."

The way he said it made George wonder. All the time Saul and Kay were kids they had been inseparable. In the old days they had dated, until Kay had gone to work and met Sig. At first she hadn't been too crazy about Sig either. At least that was what she always said, but you couldn't tell with girls. Anyway, for the last year she hadn't dated Saul once, that George could remember.

"Suppose I run around to Fawn Street and get Gertie Cameron. She's most sure to be home," Saul went on. "Besides, her father is usually away."

"He's a Communist," George objected. Why should Saul want to ask Gert Cameron, anyway? "Besides, she's drippy."

"Wrong on both counts. He's a labor organizer and she was the brightest girl in our class at South Phillie." As Saul ran out the door, George called after him:

"It still makes me right. O.K., see if she wants to come while I fix up some stuff, but she'll be your girl; Mary will be mine."

"You shouldn't say something like that." Mary wasn't just fooling; George had never known her to be so touchy. "Especially when I know you don't mean it."

"For our picnic, I mean. Didn't you start the idea of having another girl? You don't think I want to have Gert Cameron? She'd start trying to unionize our store, and we'd have to strike against Dad. I can see Dickie and me carrying signs out front while you'd be scabbing behind the soda fountain."

Suddenly Mary was smiling at him. "George! I never knew you had such a good sense of humor. O.K., I'll be your girl—for the picnic—and I'd scab for your dad. I think he's wonderful. Now let me help get things ready. What are you going to have?"

Gertrude Cameron came up outside and spoke through the screen door. "Hi, George. Hi, Mary. If I seem to smell of turpentine, I do. I've been painting the floors in our place. I can only stay a little while with you guys, because I want to get finished before my old man gets home, beginning of the week."

That was like Gert, always trying to talk tough. She was wearing blue denims with the legs rolled up to different lengths and a paint-splotched white shirt. When she came to the store, which wasn't very often, she usually had on some kind of funny outfit. George didn't like the way she wore her hair, either—straight, and bobbed so that she looked Japanese, or Chinese, whichever cut their hair that way. She might be pretty if she dressed up and wore her hair different, he thought.

Saul came in after her. "Gert played hard-to-get. I hope you're going to have pickles, George. It was the promise of pickles that broke her resolution."

"Sure," Gert said. "When the old man's away I live on canned beans and wienies. Wienies taste the same, picnic or no picnic. I want pickles."

Mary was doing all right at fixing things, so George let her go ahead. She had pushed two of the tables together and thrown over them a colored kitchen tablecloth that she had brought down from upstairs. "It looks more like a picnic table," she explained. "Shall I open a bottle of pickles, George?"

"There's an open gallon jar of Jewish pickles under the soda fountain. We'll have those—no use opening others." He sat down at the newly made long table and watched while Mary hurried around. She put wienies on the grill and began to toast some rolls. She speared pickles from the jar and cut them in quarters length-wise. She sliced all the tomatoes left over from yesterday's lunch and arranged them on a plate with lettuce and sliced sandwich meat. She put mustard and ketchup, pepper and salt on the table. Gert didn't help her, but sat talking to Saul about the war in Spain and the fascists winning. George thought that she would only have been in Mary's way, anyway.

She was asking him now, "George, can I take a package of paper plates out of the front showcase? They'll be more like a picnic and save washing besides."

George said, "O.K.," but what Mary didn't think about was that the plates came out of stock, while washing a few dishes didn't cost anything. When she asked, "Shall we have bottle Cokes or fountain Cokes?" he said, "Fountain Cokes," quickly, before anyone else could say differently, but he was still glad he had thought of the picnic, even though Gert Cameron was such a pain in the neck and Saul proving to be not much better, under her influence. Who cared about Hitler and Mussolini sending armies to help Franco? He turned on the radio to drown them out. A dance band began to blare out a tune he didn't recognize, and Mary said:

"Isn't that wonderful, George? It's from *Swing Time.* Gert, did you see it? I just love Ginger Rogers—she's my favorite star."

Gert looked at Saul in a way that George resented. What was wrong with what Mary had said? Instead of answering Mary directly, Gert went on talking to Saul, only changing the subject. "I hardly ever see a movie. I don't have the time, with all the important books there are to read. Did you read *Steps Going Down,* by John McIntyre? It's laid right here in Philadelphia—over around Franklin Square. The old theatrical section."

No, Saul was a good skate. He understood that Gert was pretending most of the time. Pretending to be tough, with her "guys" and "old man" stuff. Pretending to be high-brow. Saul was grinning at her, and George heard him say, "Sorry, I guess my tastes are just too low for you. Right now my favorite author is John Marquand. You know, the fellow writes for the *Saturday Evening Post,* about that Jap detective. Hey, George, did you read 'Think Fast, Mr. Moto,' in last week's *Post?*"

George hadn't, but he knew Dad had. Dad followed all those stories about different characters that ran in the *Post*—Tugboat Annie and Florian Slappey and Mr. Moto. Why should Gert look so snooty when he said so? He was glad when Mary put the first round of wienies on the table. She sure knew how to cook wienies so they were an even golden brown all over. Mary said, "Try these, Gert, and you'll see that wienies aren't all the same. Mr. Jones pays more for his and gets them six to the pound, instead of eight or ten like some places. Isn't that so, George?"

Yes, it was, but there was no need for Mary to go on about it. He remembered that he had wanted Dad to buy cheaper wienies, to make a better profit. Maybe Dad had been right.

They ate wienies and quarters of Jewish pickles and drank Cokes from the fountain, and the radio played "I've Got a Feelin' You're Foolin'." Mary toasted some more rolls and grilled another batch of wienies, and Saul imitated Baby Snooks. Saul could really be a scream when he wanted to. George wished he could be like him that way, but he could never think of anything funny to say or do and he couldn't sing or play. Even Gert broke down and stopped posing. George noticed that she ate more than anybody else, too. She needed to, skinny as she was.

All this time no customers had come in to interrupt, but now the screen door banged. It was Mr. Meyer, in his long black coat with all the strings hanging from the buttons to remind him of things he'd forget anyhow. He looked surprised, and George almost resented having to get up—but a customer was a customer. He went to the tobacco case and took out a package of Melachrinos even before Mr. Meyer asked for them. The old man hesitated, as though he was about to say something, then started for the door.

"George, ask him to stay and have a wienie. Please do. He looks awful lonely." He hadn't heard Mary come up behind him, but it was O.K. if she wanted him to.

"We're having a picnic, Mr. Meyer. Won't you join us? Everybody has gone to the country on picnics, so we thought we'd have ours right here."

"A picnic? Oh, yes, a picnic." He looked confused, but Mary led him over to the end of the table and took off his coat.

"Sit down here, Mr. Meyer. Do you like mustard or ketchup on your wienie? This is Gertrude Cameron, who lives around on Fawn Street. You must know Saul Gerson. He plays the violin too. You should hear him."

Maybe Mary shouldn't have said anything about Saul's playing. Mr. Meyer looked at him very strangely. "Jazz, I suppose—like this awful noise. I remember you, young lady, from your beautiful hair, even when you were a child. When Mrs. Meyer could still sit at the window she used to say that the sight of you lit up her life . . . But can't we shut off that thing?"

George turned off the radio, and Mary brought out a newly grilled wienie on a toasted roll.

"What was I saying? What did you ask me? Oh, yes, a 'wienie.' Now I understand. A wienerwurst. And 'picnic' is a day in the country. Would any of you know of the Prater? But how could you

53

know of such beauty, brought up in an American slum? You, who play the fiddle, could you possibly play 'Tales from the Vienna Woods' without standing on your head?"

George hoped Saul wouldn't be angry with the old man, but Saul just laughed. "Sure. I'll run down the street and get my fiddle."

He was back in a minute, in time to hear Mary coaxing Mr. Meyer to try a Coke. "No, no. I loathe them."

"Have you ever tried one? Honest, now."

"They look like medicine."

"Just take a sip."

George watched the old man's expression and Mary's. Then Saul began to play, and Mr. Meyer picked up the glass and kept time with it. He must have forgotten all about how he thought the Coke would taste, for he drank it all, and when Mary offered him another he nodded.

Gert Cameron was the first to leave, to get back to painting floors, but every time Saul stopped playing Mr. Meyer begged him to go on. "I, Paul Meyer, can no longer play, because of the arthritis, but I can still teach, and you shall be my successor," he promised before he finally left, taking Saul with him.

Mary washed the dishes—there weren't many, because of the paper plates and cups—while George began to do some figuring on an unused paper napkin. "How many wienies did you cook?"

"Gee, George, I don't know. I didn't count. Why?"

"I have to charge myself for them, that's why. It was my picnic."

"It's your store. Dickie and Penny take stuff all the time—I've seen them. Even your dad. I bet he doesn't charge himself for cigarettes when he helps himself."

"And I get after them all the time. 'How can you know how much you make when the whole family is living out of the store?' is what I'm always asking. Now let's see. We must have had four wienies each, which is sixteen, and Mr. Meyer had two. How many Cokes did everyone have?"

"You should have told me you wanted me to keep count. I'm sorry, George, really I am."

"Never mind. I'll figure it out approximately. Oh, darn. I was going to ring it up on the register, to help out the day's sales, but that wouldn't be good either, because that would throw out my comparative sales figures for next year."

Mary looked so puzzled as to what he should do that George said, "It's O.K. I said I'd figure it out."

She cleaned off the tables and the top of the soda fountain, then said, "I guess I'll go now. It was a wonderful picnic, George. I enjoyed it a lot."

George decided to ring up what the picnic had cost anyhow and remembered also that he hadn't rung up for Mr. Meyer's Melachrinos on the front register. He said, "Uh-huh," and wondered why Mary didn't go, as she'd said she was going to. Say eighteen wiener sandwiches at a dime each and three Cokes apiece at a nickel . . .

"Something else—I liked being your girl, for the picnic. So long."

"So long." He rang up $2.75, which didn't include the Jewish pickles, which were a kind of garnish and had been moving slowly anyway.

# Chapter 5

This afternoon the pinochle game was at Max Herbster's, and Chester thought back to when he had first bought the store—when Max had dropped in just like any customer and had bought a couple of cigars, then drawn Chester into conversation. Cautious old Max, making very sure of the kind of chap who had bought the store before he finally came to the point.

"Phil Glickman, who you bought from, used to play pinochle with us. With him leaving the city we'll need a fourth. Want to come next Thursday to my place?"

Gosh, that had been a long time ago. There were two Maxes then, but Max Klein had sold out to Ed Shaughnessy, who still played with them, and Ralph Verna had sold out to his cousin Tony, so Max was the only original member left. Well, it was a nice friendship, four men with their own little businesses, who worked hard for long hours. Fortunately for him, he had the children to help out. Max didn't have children, so there was only his wife to take turns with him. Max was getting older, too. He'd be selling his store one of these days. Talked about it all the time.

The taxi turned sharply at Sixteenth Street and shot northward. I've picked a real cowboy this time, Chester thought, watching for Max's place. They went for blocks through an all-colored neighborhood. Max said that colored money was as good as white, but it would make his place harder to sell just the same.

The taxi stopped with a jolt. He shouldn't have been sitting forward in his seat. Damn near ran his head through the glass. When he'd paid the driver and the Yellow shot off, Chester thought the store looked pretty run-down. Max had never expanded much, the way he had done. He pushed open the screen door, startled as he always was by the little gong that announced his entrance. The kitchen and living room were still back of the store, where they had been in his own place when he had bought it.

Max called to him, "Late as always. Don't tell me it's because you've got so much business down at that dump of yours."

The men had been playing three-handed while they waited for him, but now they threw down their cards and Ed Shaughnessy dealt.

"We already cut for deal to save time," Max explained, as if they didn't do that every week when one or another was late.

Ed and Chester were partners, and after they won the first game in three straight hands Max said, "I think it's time to have a drink for luck." He pushed back his chair and got up heavily, went to the sideboard and returned with a bottle. The gong at the front door sounded, and Saidie Herbster came through from the kitchen. She didn't approve of drinking, or of the pinochle club for that matter, and walked past to wait on the customer, but Max called after her, "Saidie, bring us back a couple of bottles of soda, will you? Cold ones."

"There go the profits," Tony said, and they laughed at the old joke.

During the next hand, while Chester was having trouble making a three hundred spade bid, Ed Shaughnessy asked, "Say, have any of you fellows had a visitor drop into your store recently—a special visitor?"

Max nodded. "You mean those one-arm-bandit fellows—a lot of gangsters they are. Yeah, they were in my place."

"What did you tell 'em?"

"At first I said no, but when they said they'd make trouble I said O.K. I'm getting too old for trouble."

Yes, Max was old. He was looking real old. A big man, Max, but soft. He had a belly that seemed to sag down deeper into his trousers every year.

Chester asked, "What is this, Ed? Who's coming around making trouble?"

"You'll find out. There's a new slot-machine racket with protection, heavy protection. A judge is supposed to be in on it and some other fellows from City Hall. They're putting machines in stores all over town."

Chester shook his head. "Not for me. I'm running a store, not a poor man's Monte Carlo. I've seen places you can't hardly get in between pinball machines and one-arm bandits. They draw a bad crowd, too." He lost the last trick and protested, "Why did you start that business about one-arm bandits? Which side are you playing on?"

Ed said, "Just happened to think of it. They came into my store yesterday. It's a fifty-fifty proposition, which is O.K., and me, I've nothing against gambling. Half the women in my neighborhood come in to phone bets, anyway, same as they do everywhere. I've got the space, too. You know my store. A crowd of fellows could play down at the end, beyond the fountain, and wouldn't disturb anybody. I'd have said O.K., let's try it, but the way these fellows operate made me sore." While Ed talked he shuffled and dealt. "Three of 'em came in: a tall, well-dressed young guy and two hoodlums. At first I thought it was a holdup."

"They came here the same way," Max said. "If I was younger I'd have said no and be damned to them."

"I'm a sucker for three hundred," Chester said, "but I'm going to bid it again, take it or leave it."

They left it, and while he melded, Ed went on, "This tall fellow says, 'This is the setup. We're putting in a slot and two pinball machines. The slot machine we'll put behind your phone booth.' He said this all real soft-like, but without asking me whether I wanted them or not. It made me mad."

"I'd have popped him," Tony said, but Ed shook his head.

"Not with those two other fellows standing there. They were real goons, like you read about in the paper. I said something about I'd like to think it over and to come back and see me again sometime, and this fellow says, 'You'll have to think it over fast. We're putting those machines in Monday'—still soft-like. 'And if I don't let you?' I asked. 'You'll let us, all right,' this fellow says. 'In fact, you'll be begging us to before we're done if you give us any trouble.'"

"With me the same," Max broke in. "Exactly. Where will they put them in my store, crowded the way it is? I don't know, but I said O.K. anyhow, just to save trouble."

Chester tried to decide what he would do in a similar situation. Operators had wanted to put in machines before, but he'd never agreed, and for some reason they had not insisted. It looked as if this time, though, they might.

Tony said, "Come on, Chester. This is a pinochle game, not a debating society. To hell with those fellows! Let them come to my place. Racketeers get caught up on. Like a few years ago—those bums coming around wanting protection money, protection from themselves."

The game went on. They finished the bottle and Max was going to bring out another out of hospitality, in spite of their unspoken rule to limit themselves to one. Nice fellows all, Chester thought. Young, tough Tony, who had grown up in the slums of South Philadelphia but had married the right girl, so instead of becoming a hoodlum he had a store of his own and was raising a family. Then wiry Ed, with his shock of graying red hair. About his own age Ed was, the scholar of the group and the only bachelor among them.

"Come on, Chester, deal the cards. Put some pep into it."

Yes, Chester thought, that was his trouble. He lived too inwardly, always a little apart from what was going on, even from the pinochle game.

During the last round of hands Ed brought up the matter of the pinball machines again. "Have you thought yet what you're going to do, Chester, when those bums come to your place?"

He made up his mind on the spur of the moment. "I'm going to say no and stick to it. I'm glad you told me, Ed. These rackets make me sick. It was bad enough during prohibition, but it's getting worse."

"They may get ugly."

"I'll do the best I can. If we give in, they'll be running us. The reason I keep store is because I want to be independent. All of us. We work twice as long hours as most people just to be independent, and we won't be if we let those fellows tell us what to do."

"I thought you'd say that. My advice is, change your mind."

Ed was the practical man among them, but he could be poetic or could involve you in some little-known phase of history, and when you looked it up in the *Book of Knowledge* that Chester had bought for George while he was in grammar school, Ed would be right.

"O.K., you're going to be stubborn. I can tell from your expression." Ed's grin was sly as he laid down a hand that covered every trick. "I don't see why you fellows let me play with you. You should beware of the Irish; we're an evil race."

Verna said, "It's luck, that's all. The luck of the Irish."

"No, Tony. You fellows don't have a chance with me. God is on my side."

"Get away, you never go to church. Even I go more than you do."

Max suggested one more hand, and Chester thought how good it was to get away from the store; he wouldn't miss these Thursday afternoons for anything. Ed went on talking.

"My friends, beware of irreligious Irishmen, like me, as much as those of us who are too religious. When we're religious it's to excuse our dishonesty. We slough off our sins in church. An Irishman at Mass is salving his soul, and those who don't go are in revolt against society."

"You don't win by luck or by cheating," Tony interrupted. "You talk us unconscious."

Ed went right on, as he always did. "Look at all the Irish who are Communists. What made them that way?"

Somehow, Chester forgot Ed's explanation by the time he got back to the store and told Kit about the afternoon. Honey was downstairs, helping George by cleaning the tables and the fountain, and he and Kit had the kitchen to themselves, which didn't happen very often. "What I like about Ed Shaughnessy is the way he says things that make you think. I always thought it was only Jews who were Communists; now I remember there are a lot of Irish names among them. Like the time he said that God made man in his own image, but that the Irish had made the Old Gentleman over into *their* image."

"The idea!"

"I know—almost sacrilegious, I guess, but interesting just the same. Today the talk started over some fellows who have been to his place and Max's to put in slot machines. I'm a bit worried about them. He said something else—I wonder if I can remember just the way he said it—about we fellows who have small stores having a responsibility the chains don't have. He said, 'The merchandise on their shelves may be a bit cheaper sometimes, but it's unsweetened by personal interest and unsoftened by the milk of human kindness.' I tell you, Kit, I enjoy getting together with Ed and Max and Tony —fellows who all have the same problems we have."

Kit looked wonderfully sweet. She said, "I know, Chester. I'm glad for you to get away from the store. You don't do it nearly often enough." She hesitated. "Funny I should feel this way about it after all these years, but you're going to have a problem that neither Max nor Ed Shaughnessy has to think about."

"That Ed doesn't have to think about?" What was making Kit behave so oddly? By gosh, it couldn't be! He jumped up and ran around the kitchen table. "Kitty, darling, you really mean it?"

"Chester, what will we tell the children?"

He kissed her on the ear. "Romeo and Juliet! That's what Leslie Howard is responsible for!"

"It wasn't from thinking of him at all, as you very well know. *You* thought you were holding Norma Shearer. You'd never been like that."

"I should have known I'd get found out. I hope the child looks like . . ."

"Like Veronica Maguire? Well, it won't. Oh, Chester, stop fooling. What will we do? The thought of telling Kay, at her age, and especially right now—I'll feel downright ashamed."

"Why, for Pete's sake? Kay's a grown woman. Three years older than you were when we married. Say, I'll never forget the way Dickie presented those tickets. Remember? Katie Schweitzer, the butcher's daughter. Your father will be glad to hear this. We'll drive up real soon."

"We should drive out to see Pop—we don't go nearly enough. But not to tell him about this. It seems silly, Chester. There's a time when it seems decent to bear children, when you're young and just married. Then suddenly it seems like two old fools carrying on, like we did that night. It began with you kissing me down in the store—what it would have looked like if there had been anyone around! Remember?"

"Sure I remember, but it began with you going off the deep end for that movie actor. I had to show you that Chester Jones had something too."

"And look at the trouble it's got us into. I hope I stop feeling this way about it, but right now I'd die before I could tell Kay or Helen. After me warning them all the time!"

Chester poured cups of coffee for them both, then patted his wife on the shoulder. "Our worry is getting you through this all right, not about our girls. They know more than you give them credit for. Why every girl in the neighborhood, including ours, read *Married Love* when it was in our lending library, especially after that priest down at the Little Flower spoke against it. The library company must have made a mint off that book. Which reminds me, George was after me about that new book, *Gone with the Wind*. There's been a lot of call for it and the driver for the library dropped off a copy yesterday, but it's disappeared. Are you reading it?"

"A real thick book, with a brownish jacket on it?"

"Could be. You better get it back, or your son will be on you like a ton of bricks."

"Chester, isn't young George funny? He almost kills me sometimes, he's so serious. Every time I take a can of talcum powder from the store, or a hair net, I feel downright dishonest. The last time he caught me helping myself to one of those Whitman's Samplers I almost died."

"Between getting killed and dying so often, I'm surprised how you hold up. And we're getting away from that book. You better read it later."

"Oh, I don't have it, but maybe Helen does. She was deep in something last night that looked awful thick for her to be reading.

You know, she generally sticks to Ethel Dell and Faith Baldwin, or Kathleen Norris. My heavens, if we had to pay for all the books she reads out of that library in the store . . ."

"From what I've heard, this is no book for her to be reading anyway."

"You thought she should read that *Married Love.*"

"I let her sneak it out of the bookcase because I don't think facts do any harm, and that Dr. Marie Stopes—or Stokes—put everything pretty well. What I don't like are the books that give wrong ideas about what life is really like. You tell her to put that book back. It's not fair for us to read the popular books before our customers do unless we pay rental—that's where the library's income comes from. Even then, maybe it's not fair. The books that everyone wants to read help carry the others."

"Land alive, Chester, you sound like young George."

"Anyway, tell Helen to put that book back in the library. From what I've heard about it, listening to women in the store, what ideas she may get about us won't be anything besides what Scarlett O'Hara might give her. No wonder she goes around calling herself Penny, when they give names like that to characters in books and in the movies. Ginger Rogers! Any day now I expect Helen to announce that she's Lavender Jones."

"Oh, Chester, you go on about nothing. I remember at home the time I had trying to stop Pop from calling me Kate and you saying Katie, when nobody did it any more. I wanted to be Kittie, and you just wouldn't. Then with Kay. You started calling her Katherine. No wonder her childhood was so unhappy. She thought of Kay herself, when Kay Francis became popular. You don't know how important those things are to children."

"I hear you talking about me." Kay came in by the stairway from the store. She kissed Chester on the cheek and gave her mother a hug. "What a day!" She sank into one of the straight-backed kitchen chairs. "Mr. Shapiro, the New York sales manager, wanted a lot of figures, and Sig and I worked overtime digging them out. And I mean digging. Honest, the mere mention of suitcases and overnight bags . . ."

"Why, I thought you and Sig had a date tonight."

"We have, Mother. And you can't guess what. Roller skating. Last week it was bowling, because Sig thinks exercise is good for us. Honest, the things I do for that man! He has a friend with a rink down in South Phillie somewhere. Thank goodness he doesn't know Connie Mack, or I'd be pitching for the A's someday."

Chester laughed. "Couldn't do much worse than his men are. But why don't you go skating out on Camac Street? Your mother and I used to skate on South Broad Street after we first met."

"You couldn't now, with all the traffic. But if you and Mother will skate on Camac Street with us, Sig will have to—I'll make him."

Kit said, "Oh, go along. The neighbors would think we were crazy, and what would George say?"

Undoubtedly there was quite a bit of her mother in Kay. It made her a nicer girl. "Now you go out with Sig and forget this foolishness. At the rink there'll be music and other young folks. You used to skate pretty good out on Camac Street. I can remember when you and Saul used to skate together, on an evening like this, under the trees, with the moon showing through. You were just about tops, I thought."

"Dad! Why bring up ancient history? I haven't even seen Saul in years. But let's skip it. Dad is always going off some way. Why you can't be understanding!"

"I thought I was. But I'll skip it. What about you and Sig having supper with us after—after the store closes?"

"That's what I was going to ask about. What are you going to have?"

"You know Honey—since her precious Shelley started working down on Eleventh Street."

"Spaghetti?"

"And she makes it really good, only . . ."

"Sig is crazy about it, anyway. We'll be in, if I'm still alive. Right now all I want to do is run and take a nap. Tell Dickie not to be nasty when Sig comes in the store. That is, if he's there. I know Dickie's smarter than any of us, but there are times he makes me madder than George does."

Kit all over again, Chester thought, and how he loved the both of them! "Sure, bring Sig up." He started to tell what was uppermost in his mind, but Kit was shaking her head, and he knew what she meant.

The buzzer sounded, which was odd for this time on Thursday, after the newspaper rush. Chester hurried downstairs feeling pretty good, thinking of an addition to the family, chuckling at the way Kit felt about what had happened. George was waiting in the doorway. He whispered excitedly, "Thought I better ring for you, Dad. Some fellows in the store want to talk to you. They were in this afternoon, one the other week. Take it easy with them."

George was usually excited about something or other, but this time he had reason to be. Chester remembered Ed's warning and tried to put on as impressive an appearance as he could; he didn't want to look like just another little storekeeper. George kept whispering as they walked toward the front of the store, where the three men waited. "It's machines, gambling machines. They . . ."

"Ed Shaughnessy told me about them while we were playing pinochle. They're covering the city I guess."

There they stood by the cigar case, just as Max had described them. What gave the youngest of the three, evidently the leader, the same odd quality of apparent viciousness that some of the kids from around the neighborhood of the store acquired when they took up with the wrong company?

Chester said, "You want to see me?" and the boy—he couldn't be much older than George—smiled. If it wasn't for the cold impassiveness of those two others, would this kid look so mean? Chester wondered.

"I'm from the Ace Amusement Company. You have a nice location here, a nice, clean store. We'd like to put in some machines—you know, nickel, dime, quarter . . ."

"Gambling machines. My customers gamble too much already."

"No gambling, mister. These machines are legal, perfectly legal. It's all on the up-and-up. You give away candies if some guy wins—like Life-savers, only they ain't. You'll be surprised at the play you'll get. We split fifty-fifty."

"There's some catch."

"We don't want you to play for candy. Be a wise guy. Figure your customers. Keep it legal for anyone you don't trust. That's where you can make the real dough. It'll bring young fellows into your place, too. They stand around, play the machines, buy smokes, drinks. You can't go wrong, I'm telling you."

Words that tried to make one thing into another, just by giving the thing a different name. "We have a family trade. I don't like a gang hanging around here, and we've discouraged it. Count me out."

"Dig your own grave if you want to. I've been trying to be friendly, but we got to place our machines. That's a nice soda fountain you have there. Cost a lot? Bet you ain't finished paying for it. What a couple of cracks of a sledge hammer would do to that marble! Not that we need to, understand? There are other ways."

"I don't believe in gambling and I don't want machines in my store. Now you better go." The protection racket all over again, Chester thought. Or the time when the newspapers cut the profit of the dealers and they had all refused to sell papers, until they had been intimidated by chaps like these. Well, he had survived then and he would now.

The young fellow didn't argue any more. He said, "You'll be sorry," as though it were some kind of joke he was taking part in. His companions followed him out to the street, their silence more disturbing than further threats would have been.

George said, "Gee, Dad, what will we do if they come again?"

"Maybe they won't. Anyway, I'm going to fight them. Now we have to get settled about help in the store, with all three of you back in school next week. This is as good a time as any to talk about it."

"I thought it was all figured out that Honey would come in early and stay to wash up after lunch, like she did last winter. Dickie can handle the papers mornings, like always, and I'll close up. If we get stuck, there's Mother to help out."

"Now we're getting to the point. I want your mother to take it easy. We'll get another girl to take Honey's place for the housework, and Helen . . ."

"She's too flighty, Dad. I'd almost rather not have her in the store at all. And she steals cosmetics. I caught her taking nail polish yesterday—that awful reddish-purple stuff."

66

"Don't say 'steal,' son. Helen's going through a stage."

"I bet Kay never went through it the same way."

"Anyway, we've all lived out of the store. There were times we used more stock than we sold—before they put people on relief so they had some money to spend—so you can't expect us to change our habits too soon."

"You could write it down . . ."

"Let's get back to help in the store. We'll need someone. Would you object to Mary Plotko?"

"Gosh, no. But you asked her before."

"Maybe she'll be willing now."

"Fellows are crazy about her; it ought to help sales."

"Sometimes I wish you weren't so commercially minded, but skip it. I'll see what I can do."

Mrs. Canuso for her *Bulletin,* and Mrs. Malone all excited. "Mr. Jones, George, you'll never guess. I won the daily double at Aqueduct! Something told me to play those two horses. The good Lord, I think."

"Maybe He'll tell you to stop playing now."

"When I'm winning at last? Mr. Jones!"

The phone rang in the first booth, and Chester answered. "Malone? Yes, she's in the store right this minute." He beckoned through the glass, and when she had taken his place and closed the door he could hear her telling Malone the news. Then the phone in the next booth rang, and it was for Gertrude Cameron. "I'll send over for her."

He told Henry Green, who was waiting outside. The Green brood must pick up a lot of nickels, acting as messengers for all the stores in the neighborhood. They seemed to have worked out a plan of their own: little Horace had hung around all last evening, and Billy the day before. Chester watched through the screen door while Henry darted off. Too bad their father couldn't get work. Maybe if he had less time on his hands, the Greens' production of children would slow down. Anyway, between relief and the children running errands, none of them went hungry.

Henry came back, skating at full speed over the macadam paving of Camac Street. When he came even with the side door he put one skate sideways, as a brake, swung around, and came to a stop in front of Chester. "Gert's coming right away, Mr. Jones."

"She pay you?"

"Ten cents." He held up the dime, and Chester said, "Mrs. Malone owes one of you boys a nickel from last week. You better hit her for it when she leaves the store. She just won a daily double."

Gertrude Cameron came in. She was all dressed up; he had never seen her in an evening gown before, and she looked prettier than he would have thought possible, with a dark, slender aliveness. He could see George give her a second look, too, before she went into the booth. Chester chuckled. George was always so particular about girls, and he had always said he couldn't stand Gertie Cameron. He sure looked interested in her now.

Mike Cameron came in behind her, four books from the lending library under his arm. When Gertrude's father was in town he was one of the library's best customers, especially as he used to forget to return books after reading them. He went directly to the book racks, and George figured out the amount of rental from his card. Another of George's ideas, keeping the library money separate.

Cameron was a strange fellow. He had a huge head, which looked even larger because of a great shock of silvery hair. His eyebrows were as bushy as those of John L. Lewis, but gray. He had a long nose and face, with a mouth that seemed to carry a perpetual half-sneer. He was handsome, though. Distinguished was a better word. Chester had never seen an English lord, but he always thought that Cameron looked like one. Too bad the fellow was so short—not much over five feet, most of which seemed to consist of that leonine head.

He had a sonorous voice, and even in talking to George about books he wanted from the library truck next time it came around he sounded like an orator. "One of the most significant authors of our time," he was saying, but Chester missed who he was talking about. Why did Mike Cameron (where had he heard that he only adopted the name of Mike when he became a labor organizer?) live on an otherwise all-colored alley like Fawn Street? With the whole city filled with vacant houses—there were a dozen on their block of Camac Street alone—it could hardly have been from economy. It

68

must be hard on Gert, too. Probably her usual pose of being unconventional came out of that. While he waited on other customers he could hear her telling someone to pick her up at the store. He saw her hang up the receiver, but she continued to sit in the booth. Probably she didn't want to hang around in such formal clothes.

Dickie came rushing in, with Floyd on a lead. The puppy seemed to be all feet, and from its panting and Dickie's flushed face it looked as though the evening walk had been a run. "Get that dog upstairs." Silly thing to have said; that's where Dickie was taking him anyway.

A horn began to toot outside, and there was a big roadster with the top down. It looked like a Marmon or a Pierce-Arrow, and a young fellow at the wheel was keeping his hand on the horn button. Couldn't he see that Gertie was getting out to him as fast as she could?

It had been an exciting day: first the pinochle game and then what Kit had to tell him. Not to mention his visitors. Damn it, he had almost forgotten about them. They'd be back; he was sure of that. Tomorrow he'd talk over what to do with Eddie Bryant, the policeman on the beat who was on day duty this week. Well, it would work itself out.

The real thrill had been Kit's news. Five Joneses instead of four. Wouldn't that be something!

# Chapter 6

Roller skating was more fun than Kay Jones had expected. She hadn't skated for ever so long—not since the time Dad had reminded her about, when she and Saul Gerson used to go up and down Camac Street under the double row of trees, where there was always a breeze. On the street they used to race each other, or couples would race other couples, and she and Saul usually won. But they had been kids then.

Here at the rink no racing was allowed, which was a good thing. It was respectably run, too. There were attendants in uniform who skated around the floor in the opposite direction from the crowd, ready to caution anyone who got rough or fellows who held their girls too closely.

Sig was a good skater, too, which surprised her. They glided around and around the smooth maple floor to the music from the loud-speakers. In each corner of the rink there were lights that changed color, so that they seemed to skate through a dream world that was now rosy and then green or yellow or purple, when all the women appeared ghastly and Kay worried about how terrible Sig must think she looked. Thank goodness she didn't have to live in purple light all the time. Then the white lights were cut off completely, and there were only the colored ones—moving around, making blots of color on the walls—and the sound of skates swishing and the music.

It changed to a waltz, and some of the couples left the floor. Others tried a few turns and then left too, but Sig waltzed very well, and it was much more exciting on skates than just dancing.

Afterward they went to the soda fountain, and Sig had a Coke while she had ice cream. It seemed funny, sort of, to order ice cream at twenty-five cents, when she could have it at home for nothing and customers paid only fifteen cents for dips the same size. Wouldn't George love a place where you could charge a quarter for a plate of ice cream!

Sig's friend, the owner, came over to them and asked how everything was. Sig had told her that he was Polish too, but he had a long, thin face and was very dark.

Sig said, "Kay Jones, Gus Koval. Gus and I used to live on the same street in Kensington. You've got a nice place here, Gus."

"I don't allow any roughstuff. We keep it high-class. I expect to put in a live orchestra instead of canned music, soon as I get the mortgage paid off a little more."

Kay hadn't thought of it as canned music, and what difference did it make, as it would come out of loud-speakers anyway, alive or canned?

After Gus had gone the music shifted to the "Beer Barrel Polka." Sig said, "Come on, Kay. Let's try a polka on skates. I never have, but when we dance at our house it's usually the polka."

She remembered the large, bare rooms in Sig's home, with the wood floors scrubbed white, and visualized him and all his family and Polish neighbors cavorting around to the polka and drinking beer, the way he had told her about, and suddenly she didn't want to skate any more.

"We have swell times at home—usually Saturday nights. What's the matter, Kay? Let's try it."

"It's awful—awful strenuous. I don't think I can."

"Oh, come on. It'll be fun here, with so much room."

She had never fallen on skates that she could remember, but she objected, "I'm afraid I'll fall."

"No you won't. I'll see to that." Sig skated out on the floor, dodging the swirling couples, pulling her along. It turned out to be wonderful after all. More exciting than the waltz, even, because they went around so fast. Sig sang against her ear, "Roll out the barrel, we'll have a barrel of fun . . ."

The words weren't romantic, but they were having a barrel of fun all right. When the record ended Kay was breathless and could feel how flushed her face was. Sig was panting. A lock of his straight yellow hair hung over his eyes, instead of being combed flat back as it usually was, and he streamed perspiration, but she liked him better than she ever had before.

He looked at his wrist watch. "Golly, it's after eleven. We'll have to go if we're eating with your folks. Personally, I'll be ready for spaghetti. This is more exercise than bowling, even."

"I like it better too."

Sig gave her what she thought of as his bleak, blue-eyed look. "But last week you told me you liked bowling."

"Oh, I did, but this is *real* fun. Let's come here again sometime."

Sig took off her skates and then his. "We'll get regular shoes with the skates fastened on."

A lot of the girls on the floor had high white skating shoes, but Kay didn't think she would want a pair like them. "These are fine, for all we'll use them. Besides, the others would cost a lot."

As they drove home Sig said, "Maybe Gus is right and I'm wrong. I've always had the idea of being in a big company, because there's more chance of getting ahead. I started in the luggage-manufacturing business because it was the only job I could get. In five years I've become office manager. Fifty dollars a week is a darn good salary for these days—almost enough to get married on. Our firm is just about the largest in the business, but the whole industry is small compared with—well, paints and varnishes. Do you know how many million dollars' worth of paint is sold a year?"

"No, I don't, Sig."

"Well, a whole lot more than there is of luggage. I mention paint because I had an offer from a paint company, but it wasn't good enough. Sometimes, though, like when we were talking to Gus Koval tonight, I get to thinking. He's got a business of his own. I know he's mortgaged to his ears, but he's paying it off, some every month. His folks are helping. Soon he'll be independent, while I'll still be working for someone else. Like having to dig up all those old sales records. I knew they didn't mean a thing."

"I was glad to help."

"What do you think? Is it better to work toward being a really big shot or toward having something of your own—like your dad, say?"

"Why, Sig, I don't know. Lots of small businesses go into bankruptcy every day—look at the columns of sheriff's sales in the newspapers. You have to decide for yourself what you'll do with your own life. I wouldn't know what to say."

"It's your life too, Kay. It's on account of both of us."

"You don't say."

"Well, it's understood we'll get married, soon as we make enough to live on and put a little away besides. We could right now, except that we couldn't count on your working for much more than a year."

"Sigmund Dobrzanski, if you don't take the cake! When did I ever say I'd marry you? For one thing, you've never asked me."

"I've always taken it for granted. It never occurred to me you'd want to go through all that business of being proposed to."

"Taken it for granted! I like that! And this not working for much more than a year—it doesn't take a map to figure that out. I'm surprised at you, and disappointed. If you had proposed, I don't know what I would have said, but it wouldn't have been yes, I'm sure. It wouldn't have been no, either, maybe, but I don't know yet."

They were practically at the store by this time. Sig drove along in his careful way, just as though she weren't furious with him. He put out his hand and made a right turn, then waited at Thirteenth for the light to turn completely green and not just amber.

"Do you have a piece of chewing gum in your pocket, Sig? I'm so mad at you I could spit, but my mouth's too dry."

Kay could hear Dick saying, "Hot damn. That was sure a break for us when Shelley started working in that spaghetti joint," and her mother reproving him, "You shouldn't use expressions like that —and your third plate! Dickie, you shouldn't eat so much."

Dickie was an awful pig. Kay hoped that her mother wouldn't notice from anything in her expression that she had been quarreling with Sig. She tried to put on a carefree look and said, "Hello, everybody. Sorry we're late."

Dad jumped up. "Sit over here, Sig, next to—ah—Penny. You're not late; we closed early. Thursday is always slow."

"Its volume is coming up, according to my sales records." You'd know that would be George.

"I didn't know roller skating at a rink could be such fun. I was afraid it would be rough, but it wasn't at all." Kay wished that Sig would play up a little, too. He had moved into the extra seat at the table with hardly a word, and he sat glumly while Honey filled his plate.

Mother said, "Have some meat balls, Sig, and help yourself to sauce. I'm glad you had a good time."

"It was all right." Honest, she wished she could reach him under the table and kick his ankle. No use letting the whole family know of their private affairs, especially Dick, who'd rib her for months.

Dick came to her help without realizing it. "I still think you followed the wrong tactics," he said to Dad, who explained:

"We had some visitors this afternoon, Sig. A rough-looking crew. They want to put gambling machines in the store, and I won't have it."

"They said they'd smash the soda fountain," George added.

"What they said was that they could smash it, but there were other ways to make you come around. Isn't that right, Dad? Now where you were wrong was in not saying, 'O.K., boys, I guess you win,' and letting them put in their old machines. Fight force with guile, I say."

"I don't see . . ." George began, and Dickie interrupted, "You wouldn't, dear brother, so I'll draw you a map." He paused to take a last, huge mouthful of spaghetti, and Kay thought, I wish he wouldn't take such mouthfuls.

"Ever hear of hostages?" Dickie continued. "Those machines are worth a lot of money. Take them into the store, but don't use them. Hide them away in the basement. Or put out-of-order signs on them. Suppose you only play for Life-savers, and keep them strictly legal? I bet I can find ways of putting them out of commission. Gosh, there are so many ways of handling this sensibly. If they don't make money, that gang will be glad to take them out before long. Anyway, so long as they're there, nobody will bust up the soda fountain or throw a rock through a plate-glass window."

Dad said, "It makes me mad. This tie-up between gangsters and public officials that has been going on the last four years . . ."

"Remember the bootleggers?" Dick asked.

"You didn't have to buy their liquor if you didn't want to. You never *had* to sell someone's newspaper. You never *had* to put slot machines or jukeboxes in your store. But there's no use just sitting here and being mad about it. You know what I'm going to do? I'm going into politics."

Thank goodness, Sig was coming out of his sulk. "How would you begin, Mr. Jones? Committeeman?"

"Councilman. Our customers know me. I think they'd vote for me."

Dick was saying, "On the Republican ticket? With half the people around here on relief? Dad, you know better."

"We've had four years, almost, of things going worse and worse. They made fun of Hoover saying that prosperity was just around the corner, and it's still there—after spending billions. Do you know how many columns of sheriff's-sale notices there were in the paper yesterday?"

"I'll bite," Dick said.

"Thirty-two. I counted them. That means hundreds of homes of poor people being sold for their mortgages."

Mother interrupted, "Now, Chester, Sig has to drive all the way to Kensington. When you get started on the evils of Mr. Roosevelt . . ."

"Damn it, Kit, you're always saying I hate Roosevelt. I don't. I'm disappointed that he has accepted support regardless of where it comes from. During all the years of the Vare machine, which I used to think was pretty bad, there was no visible partnership between politicians and gangsters against ordinary people, such as we're up against now. When there's dishonesty at the top it goes right on down. Take this airplane deal with Russia that the President's son was trying to put over . . ."

Sig cut in, "But there's no use going into politics unless you can be on the winning side, and the Democrats have all the money to spend. This man the Republicans have put up for president—what's his name, Landon?—he doesn't have a chance. I think he's the kind of man I'd like, personally—a businessman who made his money himself, who would run the country like a business—but there's no use voting for him. Besides, he doesn't have a good voice over the radio, which attracts the old people, who sit and listen to it. And there are an awful lot of old folks in the country, Mr. Jones. Look at the influence that man Townsend is having with his pension plan."

It was rare for Sig to talk so much, and Kay felt sort of proud of how sensibly he spoke, in spite of the fact that she was still angry with him.

He said, "I do have to go, Mrs. Jones, like you said. And Honey, tell Shelley he ought to change his name to Giuseppe."

Helen said, "It's so nice of you to come, Sig." Imagine Helen saying that, and the look she was giving him! Honest, Mother ought to give Helen a talking to. Now she was saying, "I'm reading the most marvelous book. There's a man in it who's simply the most adorable . . ."

Well, Sig had sense, anyway. He said, "Thanks, Penny. I think these midnight suppers are a wonderful institution. Good night, everybody. Good night, Kay. See you at the office in the morning."

She said, "O.K.," and then remembered how he had talked about taking her for granted, but she didn't think it showed in her expression.

Mother saw those things, though. Sig's car hadn't pulled away before she said, "I'm afraid you and Sig had a quarrel."

"He asked me to marry him, if you must know. Rather, he said that he had always taken it for granted that I would."

"I think that's rather nice."

"To be taken for granted? Mother!" She was glad when George started in on Penny.

"Say, this book. This adorable man. So it was you who sneaked upstairs with the library copy of *Gone with the Wind* that I have six reservations for right now. You produce that book this minute."

"Oh, George, I can't. I'm right in the middle of it. I must know what happens next." There was no denying that Helen was pretty —Penny; Mother encouraged her in that silly business—but Dad was giving in to her all the time, and the awful way she had carried on in front of Sig!

Dad was giving in to her again. "Your mother told me this afternoon that she thought Penny had your book, and I clean forgot to tell you. The store's closed; let her finish it tonight."

"Dad, I can't. It's thousands of pages—but every one exciting. Please, Dad, let me keep it over Sunday."

"While six women want to read it from the store? Make her put it back."

George could be a pest too, but this time Kay thought he was right.

Penny said, "I'll pay. Isn't my money any good?"

Mother straightened everything out. Imagine her knowing there had been an argument with Sig, but then ignoring her explanation, which hadn't been altogether fair to Sig (and she realized it). Mother said, "You turn that book in first thing in the morning, Penny. George is right, it's not fair to the library company. But we can buy it at the Central News, which sends us the magazines. They have a book department, don't they? And we can get it wholesale, can't we? Mrs. Tomolillo—Tony the barber's wife, across the street—was telling me about it while we were shopping in the supermarket on Eleventh Street. I bet you never even knew Tony was married, but he is, and she's a real nice girl. They're fixing up an apartment over the barbershop. Now let's all go to bed. George, not another word. When we've all read the book . . ."

Dick said, "I read a review about it when it first came out. That Scarlett O'Hara is what all women would like to be, but haven't the nerve or the looks, but they think they have. I bet I could make money writing, but it's too hard work, like the store business. I say there must still be some business somewhere where people will work for you, instead of you working for them."

Mother went on as though Dick hadn't interrupted, ". . . we'll give it to the library company, to make up for any advantage we've taken."

During the night Dick kept waking up. Floyd Gibbons, who slept at his feet, was restless too and seemed to be chasing imaginary cats. If that was so, it was symbolic of something or other, for there was Smoky, Dad's pride of all the cats they had ever owned, sleeping right next to the puppy.

Across the room, in the other bed, George was dreaming too. Dick tried to hear what he was saying, so he could rib him about it afterward, but all George did was thresh about and mutter. I bet a hat the midnight suppers of the Jones family aren't any aid to sleeping, Dick thought. He was wide awake now and looked at the clock by his bed. Ten after two.

A streetcar ground westward on McClellan Street. A half hour until there would be another; he'd try to be asleep before then. One advantage he and George shared was having the back bedroom; let Kay and Penny have the front one. It was bigger, but you were right over the noises of all the traffic. Besides, the back room opened directly on the second-floor roof, where he'd fixed up a pen for Floyd out of chicken wire.

The noise of Bill Thomas' player piano, of people talking too loudly. A man's voice saying good-by to someone, over and over. There ought to be a law against saying good-by; people ought to just get up and go when they are ready. A woman's voice joined in the good-by. That would be Mrs. Thomas. Their relief check must have come in; they always gave a relief party on check nights.

There was the soft, distant sound of a radio, too. Some car parked under the trees along Camac Street. Some fellow and his girl, listening to the soft music while they necked a bit before he took her home. Maybe it was Gert Cameron and the fellow who'd called for her at the store. No wonder Gert was ashamed to have fellows go to Fawn Street.

The rumble of heavy trucks—the first of those from the wholesale produce district. There'd be a steady stream of them soon; they always came out McClellan Street. All the night noises there were; the sleepless city. Floyd began to make curious muted barking sounds again; *he* hadn't eaten any midnight spaghetti.

The Burkes were back. He could see a light in Mr. Burke's window across the street. George would be glad, because of the increased lending-library business and the Cokes that Mr. Burke was always dropping in for. He always said that he read detective stories to put him to sleep, but didn't they, in fact, keep him awake?

I'm glad the Burkes are back, too, Dick thought. Maybe we'll have fried oysters tomorrow night. He looked into the darkness of the room until he could see, in every detail, one of the folded pasteboard cartons with "Burke's Oyster Saloon" printed on it. His eyes lifted the flap onto the row of twelve oysters, covered with bread crumbs and fried to a golden brown, and the handful of mealy French fried potatoes that filled the rest of the box. The Burkes never put in enough potatoes, but who else in the world could cook them like he did? The little paper cups of ketchup. Mrs. Burke saying, as she did every time she came into the store, "If the day ever comes that I can't make our own ketchup, we'll close up. The boughten is never as good." Then a long rigmarole about Mr. Burke driving around South Jersey every week end during the season, buying up tomatoes, which she put up in the kitchen of the candy store they ran during the summer in Wildwood. The way she always said, "Candy is an all-right business for the summer months, but our hearts are in oysters."

And well they might be. Dick laughed to himself, then, in imagination, took one of those wonderful hot *chefs-d'oeuvre* of Mr. Burke's and slowly bit through the flaky browned bread crumbs, through the thinnest of batter and cracker crumbs, into the most delicately cooked of Burke's extra-large-size fryers. My God, the ecstasy of it! Dick thrashed about in bed while he recaptured the taste and the smell. The next oyster and the next—he wouldn't add ketchup until the second half dozen; otherwise his appetite might begin to slacken. At the halfway mark he'd eat some of the potatoes. If he only had some now—just one single strip about five inches long and a half inch square, fried to a lighter color than the oysters, but no less beautifully golden, with sticking to it tiny crystals of salt that were still as dry as when Mr. Burke had sprinkled them there, minutes before.

Dick felt intolerably hungry and wondered if Mr. Burke would fry just a half dozen for him if he sneaked over. But he'd have to put the gas on and heat the fat and make fresh batter, most likely.

Then the light went out in the window on which his gaze was fixed, and Dick sat up in bed. He just had to eat something to relieve the gnawing pain in his stomach. He told Floyd to keep quiet, patted him, and sneaked out of the room. What he'd like to do would be to go down to the store and have a dipper or two of ice cream with chocolate sauce, but if he happened to be seen by the policeman on the beat or one of the prowl cars that came through once in a while, they might mistake him for a burglar.

He switched on the kitchen light and searched the icebox. There was nothing that appealed to him but the sandwich meats for the store tomorrow, and if he helped himself to them, and George found out, he'd raise Cain. No, there was some leftover spaghetti in a bowl, and sauce and meat balls in another. He poured them into one bowl and finished it off. He felt better, but he shouldn't start thinking of oysters again. He'd switched off the light and was groping for the door when his shin banged against something with enough clatter to wake the whole family.

It was that darn washing machine. He put on the light again and surveyed the damage to his shin. Only a scratch, but it hurt like heck. The drain stuck out a bit beyond the white enameled tub and he'd hit against that. Of all the darn fool machines. It sat around unused for six days out of the seven and was in the way most of the time, but Mother and Honey both loved it. There ought to be some kind of collapsible machine that could be stuck away someplace. Or better yet . . .

That was a problem he ought to try to solve. He went to sleep thinking about it.

# Chapter 7

The *Druggist's World* was a lot more interesting than the stuff they taught in senior English. There were lots of swell ideas: how to display merchandise, how to increase sales. Anybody who had a corner store could learn a lot. George forgot entirely that he was in Professor Lowry's "lit" class, he was so absorbed in an article entitled "How to Increase Turnover on Sidelines." Things he had told Dad. Not to be taken in by a gross price that sounded cheap, but what was cheap about it when you were stuck with eleven dozen?

"Jones, can you give us any additional information about this fictional character who was so unfortunate as to possess the same surname as yourself?"

This is the worst year I've had to put in, George thought. I wish I'd flunk, just to show Dad how wrong he was. Lowry, for instance, the whole English "lit" course, but Lowry especially, with that dry, cynical voice of his. He stuck the *Druggist's World* under the desk. This was Lowry's way, talking in long riddles that didn't make sense, but there was no use trying to kid him. "I guess I wasn't listening."

"And where was your mind, this beautiful September day? On the football field, I suppose."

"I was thinking about opening a store—one of my own."

"Indeed! A laudable, if commercial, aim, but man lives not by bread alone, Jones. We are discussing a novel by a certain Mr. Fielding. Does that mean anything to you?"

It was easy to see that the other pupils were enjoying the way Lowry was making fun of him—all those kids who had never made a cent for themselves and wondered why he was in their class anyway. They didn't show it by smiles, for fear of being called on next, but that was how they felt. A certain Mr. Fielding—Fielding? A book he should have read. "I'm afraid I don't remember."

"It was about a young man named Jones. Does that refresh your mind?"

They all began to laugh at him, but Myra Lang tittered first and that saved him.

"Miss Lang, perhaps you can enlighten Mr. Jones and the rest of the class?"

George listened while Myra gave an outline of *Tom Jones*. She was a new girl who had transferred from somewhere out west, near Pittsburgh, and she had a funny way of pronouncing some words, especially words with an *a* in them, like water and wash. She was pretty, though, and smart—the smartest girl in the class, George guessed. He tried to picture a store with all the latest-style fixtures, with electric adding machines and cash registers, and a stainless-steel lunch bar with a formica top, like the one the salesman had been trying to sell Dad last week. Behind the lunch bar, like in pictures in the *Druggist's World,* a girl would be standing, but instead of some paid model who'd be no use in a store whatever, it would be Myra.

He guessed you'd call her hair chestnut-color—a rich brown with nice lights in it. Funny how he usually got interested in brunettes. He'd invite her to the movies. He wondered if she would accept or turn him down.

Soupy Campbell recited when Myra sat down. It's easy to see he's trying to bluff his way, but Lowry never picks on him the way he does on me, George thought.

Now that Mr. Lowry's attention was diverted from him, he sneaked out the trade magazine again. The page opened to some vending-machine ads. Cigarette machines and salted peanuts. Chewing-gum balls that came in colors, with the sly suggestion of ways to profit by giving premiums for certain colors. All kinds of pinball machines that lit up and rang bells—all of them legal, but so easily made illegal.

Why was most of the appeal directed to "operators"? Wouldn't it be better for stores to own their own machines and make all the profits? "Operators" made him think of those fellows who were trying to put machines in the store. Of course they wanted to put in jackpot machines too, which everybody knew wouldn't be played for candy, but maybe Dad was being stubborn in not letting them put in the pinballs, which loads of fellows would play just for the fun of making a big score. Anyway, a week had passed and they hadn't come back. Maybe they were just talking big.

He was glad when the bell rang to mark the end of the period. Myra was right in front of him as they left the room, but suddenly he felt unable to ask her for a date. She was too smart and stand-offish. Thank goodness it was the last class of the day; he had promised to pick up some patent medicines from the drug-jobbing house on Arch Street and Dad would want his help in the store, soon as he could get there. Dickie going to Southern High and him going to Franklin made it bad in one way. There were so many times they needed things between regular orders, but all their jobbers were in the center of town, miles from Southern. But mostly I'm glad, he thought. It's bad enough being the oldest fellow in my class without having Dickie, who's just a kid, only a year behind me in the same school.

Mrs. Waldman, from 915, was asking if he had saved a *Bulletin* for her. Chester shook his head. "No, I didn't. I saved it for three days and you never came in."

"I couldn't, but it doesn't make any difference. Always save me a newspaper. I'll pay for it anyway."

"The next final will be here in a half hour. I'll send one down." He watched the nervous way she bit her lower lip, the quick, tense way her hands moved. He rarely read a newspaper from one week to the next, except the front-page headlines, when they came in; why should people get so upset at missing a single edition of all that came out during a day? Things didn't happen that fast, and if there was anything really unusual, it would be on the radio.

"No, I'd rather have the one-star."

"I'll save it for you from now on. It's only that I get just so many papers in my allotment and I don't want it cut by too many returns."

Mrs. Waldman had been a difficult customer ever since she had moved to the neighborhood, but he had won over her type before by a little extra courtesy, a bit more patience. He smiled, but he felt tired. He should not have carried papers again, after the news dealers' strike that they had lost. George always said they weren't worth the trouble.

Why did women who had dark eyes and swarthy complexions bleach their hair? It looked bad enough when natural blondes peroxided. Chester hoped she couldn't read in his eyes what was going on in his mind. Could her unhappiness be over nothing more than his failure to save the *Bulletin*? What else troubled Mrs. Waldman, of 915? She had lived there too short a time for him to know, but it wasn't much of a place, the third-floor apartment of a done-over row dwelling. Suddenly he felt sorry for her. "I just made some fresh coffee. Sit down and have a cup with me. You'll feel more relaxed."

Maybe she wasn't used to people being friendly. "No, I can't. Really I can't." She fidgeted a moment, then smiled, a genuine, appealing smile despite the rigid, lipsticked lines of her mouth. "I'm edgy this afternoon, but don't pay any mind. I'm that way often. It's not the *Bulletin*, it's everything."

She put a dollar on the counter. "Two packs of Luckies, please." She walked over and picked a copy of *Life* from the high pile of them in front of the magazine rack. "And this. The pictures in it are so depressing sometimes that I enjoy it. Crazy, ain't it?"

"I see a lot of life that isn't in pictures and I say that the good equals the bad—maybe a little more than equals it. *Life* is like the newspapers: it picks out the unusual things to publish. Life isn't near as bad as *Life* makes out."

Her laugh was natural. "I'll have to remember that one." She hesitated. "You have a real nice place. Nice and cheery-looking and as much light as an Automat. I'm sorry I bawled you out about the paper."

"You should hear when I really get bawled out."

"I know, the public. I put up with them all day. Thank God I ain't one."

"Down here we're neighbors. Any time we can be of help let us know."

"Would you call me to the phone if I gave the number to a friend?"

"We have four booths, but often they're all filled, especially in the evening. We'll call you, though. There are always kids around to run and let you know. They expect a nickel."

"That's how it generally is. My calls are awful important."

"We'll treat them that way. All calls are important to the people they're intended for."

He kept wondering about her after she'd gone, until Dick scooted through the store, schoolbooks under his arm, toward the doorway to upstairs. "Hey, how about taking over for a while? I'd like a rest."

The kid turned and gave that smile of his. "Okey-doke, Dad. Be right down, but I have to take Floyd for a walk first." He almost bumped into Honey, coming down to clean up around the soda fountain, and suddenly he was no longer in a hurry. "Honey, I've been wanting to ask you something. How long does it take you to do the wash on Mondays?"

"We don't do it on Mondays if it looks like rain. There's no room. 'Specially since you put that dog out on the roof where we hang up."

"That's what comes of working for our family. You're getting to live on a perpetual tangent. How long does it take to do the wash in that washing machine upstairs, any day you do it?"

"Well, now, Dickie, this family has a lot of wash, especially with all the dishcloths and towels down here at the fountain. Now what piece of monkey business are you up to?"

"Can't I just ask you a simple question?"

"You can, but I can be suspicious, too, knowing you since you was little, and all you get up to."

Chester, listening, was thinking the same thing. Who could know what was going on in Dickie's brain?

"There's a washing machine sitting up there in the kitchen. How many hours a week do you use it? Now, Honey, it can't get you into trouble, answering a simple question like that."

"Two or three, for the wash. It's the ironing takes long. And I'm not one for using those mangles, if that's what's on your mind."

What was Dickie up to? He said, "Thanks, Honey. That's all I wanted to know," and all you could hear was the sound of his feet clumping up the stairs.

Honey was a nice woman, Chester thought. She had been with them for a long time now and had two children of her own to take care of between times. They were both going to parochial school, to St. Peter's. Why didn't she send them to public school, where there would be white children in the same classroom? It cost a good bit to keep them where they were.

If Dickie had clumped upstairs, the noise he made coming down couldn't be described in one word. Floyd was behind him and then in front. A cute pup and not growing too much. He watched through the screen door while they ran down Camac Street and Floyd did his business at the second tree. Did his business? Where had he got that phrase? Mrs. Koehler, who lived at the other end of the block? He couldn't remember.

She had a flock of dogs. The neighbors were always complaining because she picked up strays; but if she didn't, who would? A strange woman. Like Old Man Meyer, she bought cigarettes as an excuse to talk—about her dogs and the way the neighbors behaved.

Whatever he had been thinking about was forgotten with George coming in, laden with packages. "There's a car-bender been arrested down at Thirteenth Street. He sure smashed up a Buick. Hurry down and look. I'll take over."

Car-bending. What would some future historian think of that? Yes, he had been reading about it in headlines; maybe he should see an actual case. He hurried out the front door, waving backward, up McClellan. There was the Buick, smashed sideways against a fireplug. Four prowl cars in bright red and at least a dozen policemen and the two sullen prisoners. Neither of them looked over sixteen, and he was glad that they were not from the neighborhood.

Patrolman Yaeger, who had been on the beat ever since Chester had moved into the store, came over and began to talk. "Afternoon, Jones. Shame to see a nice car like that all smashed up."

"The boys don't look hurt, either."

"They're not. The game is to get the car set right for the fireplug or telegraph pole and then jump. This is the most beautiful job of bending I've seen yet. Car-benders themselves say that their heroes are the two young wops who bent a big Caddie limousine around one of the light standards on South Broad Street. They must of had that car going fifty when they dropped off. They say that big cast-iron standard was broken off at the ground, but the Caddie was so completely bent around it you wouldn't have known."

A patrol wagon pulled around the corner, and Yaeger explained, "It's not my pinch. One of the red cars made it. I'm just as glad. You lose all that time in court, and if they got any pull they'll be out doing it again in a few months."

"Why do they do it, Yaeger? I can understand joy riding, but deliberately wrecking property . . ."

"They've nothing to do but hang around gas stations and garages, mostly. They don't work and couldn't get jobs if they wanted to. It's that age before they can go to CCC camps we have the most trouble with."

"You'd think the fear of punishment . . ."

Patrolman Yaeger spat. "A few months in the jug is just more excitement for them. Those two are from Gray's Ferry, so they're Irish, no doubt, and some Democratic committeeman will be in there pitching for them. I tell you, the way things are going it's pretty bad. I ain't saying they were always good, but the way they'll do anything to get votes is sometimes more than I can stomach."

A nice chap, Yaeger, though Chester never thought of him as a particularly good policeman. He was short and stout and he was always taking his hat off to mop his forehead and bald head, clear to a gray fringe of hair at his neck. But he was honest and didn't belong to the present political crew that was taking over.

Yaeger was just the one to ask for advice. "Feel like walking back to the store and having a drink at the fountain? I'd like to talk to you about something."

"I could stand a Coca-Cola. It's sure keeping hot for after Labor Day."

When they turned toward the store, Chester asked, "Hear anything about a new slot-machine racket?"

"They been after you, too?"

"Uh-huh. What happens if you don't put them in?"

"Most of the stores on this beat are going along. They pay well. You can make your rent out of a couple one-arm bandits. What I can't see is why people want to play something where they know they're licked before they begin. And there's another thing; this is a strictly Democratic racket. If the Republicans should win—and the election isn't much more than a month off . . ."

Both George and Dick were in the store, Dick behind the soda fountain. "Dickie, give Mr. Yaeger a Coke."

"If you don't mind, I like it best in bottles. Maybe it's the way they fit in your hand."

"You should learn what a problem it is to keep stacks of cases until the bottler comes around. But here you are. How I feel is that slot machines are illegal and I don't want them."

"Things have changed a lot since I went on the force. There was always people you couldn't touch—especially during prohibition— but they've really come into their own now. If they give you any trouble, like they're threatening to, talk to Eddie Bryant or me, but not to the cop on the third shift. He's one of the new crowd, and you know how they stick together. By next year I'll have my twenty years in, and I'll be glad of it. The last four have been about all I could take."

Funny how coincidences worked. Patrolman Yaeger had no more than left the store, and Dick disappeared someplace, than a man in a gray suit came in. George was waiting on Mr. Rivkin, but the man cut in. "I'm from the Department of Public Health. We've had complaints about your soda fountain not being clean."

Chester could hear him, back where he was standing, and was glad there was nobody else in the store, but he wished it wasn't either of the Rivkins. He admired the combative look on George's face, the almost peaked expression he had when he was angry or believed that he was very right. "We think we keep our whole store cleaner than most." Good for him!

"We have a lot of complaints."

The man was polite enough, but underneath there was something as though he were going through an act—maybe an act that he didn't like too much, but couldn't help doing.

Mr. Rivkin left, and Chester knew that within an hour everyone in the neighborhood would hear that there had been complaints about the cleanliness of their store. It wasn't that Rivkin really disliked them, but he did like to talk, and this would be an unusual piece of news. Who could have said such a thing, and why?

The man strode by where Chester was standing and began to inspect the dishes and glasses with an expression that became increasingly disapproving.

"You are Mr. Chester Jones?"

"That's right."

"I find this soda fountain to be in a filthy condition. You'll appear in City Hall to answer charges to that effect two weeks from today, at ten o'clock. Here's the room number."

"You show me any filth around this soda fountain, any filth anywhere in the store. You won't find a cleaner store in Philadelphia." Chester felt angrier than he had ever been before in his whole life.

"I don't have to show you anything. I made an inspection. I've taken swabs of dishes and glasses, according to law. They are supposed to be sterile, with some tolerance, but that's only for the record . . ."

"I didn't see you take any swabs."

What in the devil was a swab? And how did you take one? The man was lifting a little rack of glass tubes. "Here they are, and here's your summons."

Chester held the piece of paper without reading the senseless words. Helen, running upstairs and saying, "Hello, sweety-pie," as she came by. George saying, "Honestly, Dad," over and over. Dick opened the door from upstairs and said, "I caught the last half. So they're really putting the bee on you?" Why should he grin that way, as though it was funny? A summons! The first time in his life that he'd ever been given a summons for anything.

Kay, home from work. How she looked like Kit, when he married her! "What's the matter, Dad?" but not really asking, just because he didn't give her a kiss as he usually did. She passed Dick in the doorway and disappeared, while he kept on grinning.

"You better start running for Council pretty quick. Elections are only a month away."

"Stop it, Dick. I'm mad—really mad. If that fellow thinks I'll wait two weeks to be summoned, he's crazy. I'm going to City Hall tomorrow and pull it apart."

"With your own two hands? You better talk it over with Yaeger and Eddie Bryant. Bryant's got a lot of pull with the colored voters, I know, and this election will be a struggle for them. Wait a few days to cool off."

George was saying, "Shut up, Dickie, you don't know what you're talking about. If you'd been here when that guy came in and seen the cheek he had! I tell you, I'm as mad as Dad is."

"No, son, Dickie's right. We need to cool down and think this over."

Dick said, "First of all, I think you're presuming that this has something to do with the slot-machine outfit."

"Of course it has," George said.

"Maybe it's some political dodge. Suppose you go to Al Henderson and show him the summons and he says, 'Chester, think nothing of it. I'll take care of the whole thing.' Then you'll feel you have to vote for good old Al, because he takes care of you when you're in trouble. But it's silly talking. George, give me a couple of dollars in nickels, to be charged to store expense."

"Yeah? And what are you going to do with them?"

"Beginning right now I'm going to every newsstand, cigar store, drugstore, and small restaurant around here. I'll spend a nickel, maybe a dime, and get talking to the storekeeper. I'll find out whether there is any tie-up between the Department of Public Health and those machines."

George looked at him questioningly, and Chester nodded his head. "It's not a bad idea."

"Come on, big brother, fork out. You better make it three dollars. And don't forget, if we fight those fellows, we'll need all the friends we can get. Maybe I'll find some of those, too."

Supper was half over, and still no Dickie. However undependable he was at other times, it was rare that he was late for a meal.

Chester tried to remember. It couldn't have been much after five when he left—the early newspaper rush was just starting—and that was over six hours ago. Could anything have happened to him?

Penny was going on about the new King of England. "Wouldn't it be wonderful to be a queen? Why should he want to marry any Princess Frederica just because she's the granddaughter of the Kaiser? The Kaiser was all washed up years ago—before I was born, even."

Kit said, "Maybe he wants to marry her because she's beautiful, and she just happens to be a relation of the Kaiser."

"Have you seen her pictures? Ugh! Or that other princess, the Danish one? How royal women can be so ugly when the men are so divine . . . I can just see myself sitting across from Edward at the breakfast table. 'A little more marmalade, Eddie, darling,' I'd say, and he'd look at me with those swooning eyes . . ."

"Penny, behave yourself," from Kit.

Where could Dickie be?

"A fine queen you'd make, especially with a name like Penny," George said. "Besides, did you see tonight's paper? He's on a cruise with some American woman."

Penny when she was excited. Eyes like stars. How many people had used that comparison? It applied to her, anyway. Her face was flushed and her mouth half open.

George went on remorselessly, "A married woman, from Baltimore. Honest, Penny, how a fifteen-year-old kid can get such crazy ideas . . . King Edward is an old man. He must be forty, anyway."

"Queen something of somewhere was only fifteen when she got married. It's in the history books."

Kit interrupted to say, "Where can Dickie be?" when there were his feet on the stairs.

He burst in with even greater excitement than Penny had shown over the King. "Sorry I'm late, everybody. I've been to eighty-two stores. I ran out of money and had to use my own, but that will wait until tomorrow. I've made a list of fifty-one stores that have had machines put in, with the ones marked where they took them only because they were afraid of trouble. There are eleven who wouldn't put them in and will fight along with us if they have to, and seven who are ready to give in, I think, after the visit from Public Health.

There's no doubt of the racket tie-up: every one of those eighteen had refused to put in machines and every one has had a summons."

He paused for breath, and Kit asked, "What is this anyway? I've been worrying myself sick over Dickie . . ."

"Something that happened today. We didn't tell you right off, Kit, not wanting to worry you."

"I like that. I want to know everything that's important to my family right away, and I'll settle with you later, Chester Jones. But sit down, Dickie dear, and eat. I'm saving your supper in the oven."

"Couldn't eat a thing. I've had, let's see . . ." He pulled out a list and smirked toward George. "Just in case you wanted a record of how I spent the store money. I've had two dishes of chocolate ice cream and one walnut sundae, two banana splits and seven Cokes—I figured I'd have more time to get acquainted, drinking something, where they had a fountain, or eating. Let's see—eleven, twelve, thirteen nickel chocolate bars, and . . ."

Kit interrupted him again. "Now this has to stop. I've saved your supper for you and I want you to eat it."

Dick looked around at the empty plates. "Honest, Mother, I'm not hungry. In the interests of the Jones family I have martyred myself all evening. I've eaten more stuff in the last six hours than anybody but me could possibly get away with."

"Dickie, I can't believe it." Kit was really distressed. "There's a whole dozen of Mr. Burke's fries waiting for you. Honey, bring them in, please."

"Oysters?" Dickie began to look funny. "Mother, you can't do this to me, the way I like them. Honey, I can't even look at them," he screamed toward the kitchen, but she came in anyway, holding the hot plate on a cloth, the oysters looking as beautiful as they had when Burke had lifted them out of his deep fryer.

Dickie's flushed color turned whitish and then green. "Mother—Honey—you don't know what you're doing to me." He made a dash toward the bathroom while the family looked around at each other in amazement.

Meanwhile, if Dickie didn't want them, there was no use in letting good oysters go to waste.

# Chapter 8

Ed Shaughnessy picked up his cards and said, "I think you're nuts. They've moved machines in here. The pinballs are doing pretty good, considering that I get nothing out of that space anyway. The nickel Bell machine is reaping a harvest. Call it a one-arm bandit or whatever you want to. I'm getting a fair play out of the dime machine, but the school kids are really going for the other. Chester, why not make money instead of scaring it away?"

"Out of kids gambling? Look, I bid thirty-five."

"They gamble anyway."

"In your schools maybe."

"Not my schools, and I'm against chances and all that stuff, but not for moral reasons, understand. Or because some kids get hurt trying to sell chance tickets to automobile drivers going by. I'm some kind of Catholic, which Verna is too . . ."

"Don't get me into this. You know, Chester, I think your kid is right . . ."

Ed, with that funny look of his, "Only or but?"

"Only or but what? You get the craziest ideas."

"I'm bidding forty, and if you won't go along with Chester, I will. When you say, 'I think your kid is right,' I know the next word is going to be only or but."

"Imagine him. A mind reader. I'll bid forty-one, and I'll go with you to the Mayor's office, for all the good it will do."

Verna got the hand, which he hadn't wanted, and as he was partner to Chester, he didn't want either. Consolation for declaring themselves came when Max said, "It's settled, then. Ed and Tony and me will all go when you're ready, Chester. Just give us the day."

Tony said, "O.K.," not altogether meaning it, and Ed said, "O.K.," meaning it but not altogether sure that it was the smart thing to do. "We'll bring all the customers we can, which will be few enough. You know how even people you do favors for all your life hate to get involved with anything at City Hall."

Max dealt the next hand, and while he was riffling the cards he said, "Funny thing, after the way they acted when they wanted to put those machines in, when the truck came around even the kid with them could see there wasn't room. Besides, I don't have that kind of a neighborhood. The folks around here want a run for their money. They don't play the ponies, like the women do in a location like Chester's. Or bingo, or chances on automobiles, like they do in a neighborhood like Ed's here. You don't mind my speaking like this?"

Ed said, "Why should I? Why try so hard to protect my feelings? Now that St. Bingo has joined the category or calendar, or whatever it is . . ."

Max again, "They want action, like the numbers give them. Go to sleep broke and wake up with a couple of bucks in your pockets, without having to pull any lever, which is nothing but work, when you come down to it. That's how my people think.

"Anyway, they only put in one pinball machine and none of those one-arm bandits you talk about. They didn't even try, seeing the neighborhood, and that advance fellow, the real icy one, who could have killed sooner than look at you . . ."

"This is a pinochle game, not a movie, Max." Ed, covering up after his promise, so as not to appear sentimental. He turned to Chester. "That Dickie of yours is a pretty smart boy, and the idea of going directly to the Mayor as a group of storekeepers is practically genius, especially right now with an election coming up. The Mayor is an independent that both regular parties hate and he got where he is by doing spectacular things. He's not afraid of any gun mob, either. I wouldn't be surprised to see him ending up in my store, here, having his picture taken with an ax in his hand, breaking up that nickel machine that could practically finance me a trip to Florida."

"And you'd get your name in the papers, like Chester did."

"When I saw that on the front page . . ."

" 'With summonses already issued against eighteen storekeepers for having filthy premises, the Health Department has begun a crusade . . .' I learned it by heart. That's the reason I'm for what you intend doing. Meanwhile I have thirty meld on a thirty-five bid. Do you concede?" Ed looked at them with that strange, cynical expression he always had when he was winning.

Tony threw down his hand and stood up. "When a pinochle game turns into an old woman's *Kaffeeklatsch* it's time to go home. I'll see you fellows at City Hall or in jail."

As the storekeepers came into the large audience room one of the Mayor's secretaries showed them where to sit. Dick checked them with his list. Most of them were nervous and embarrassed and balanced on the edge of their chairs, but they were all there. It was sure a test of his constitution, rounding them up, Dick thought. The second day he had been more careful, but he had still consumed a quantity of ice cream and candy that surprised even himself; the third day, though he hadn't wanted to look at an Oh Henry, he had finished his canvass.

This was the pay-off; now it was only a question of the way the Mayor would receive them. Gosh, he had made a lot of friends anyway. Everyone he passed was saying, "Hello, Dick," and how many people had he introduced to his father? Dad was a swell guy, but no good at this kind of thing. This needed the thinking out of every detail in advance.

Which reminded him: What had happened to Ed Shaughnessy? He hurried over to where Dad was standing.

"Son, I simply can't figure out how you got them all here."

"Organization, Dad. You know something? I was enjoying thinking about George back in the store and missing all this until I got to thinking of how green with envy he'd be if he saw it. But where's Mr. Shaughnessy? I'm counting on him to do the talking."

Dad shook his head. "Oh Ed? He doesn't care much one way or another. He promised to come, but he may change his mind."

"No he won't. I'll tell you why. He's someone who doesn't like to be pushed around. Mr. Shaughnessy is a very logical man, like me. Remember, when I first heard of this business I said that you and George were handling it wrong. I'm not sold that it's not right for people to gamble if they want to. Mr. Shaughnessy and I see the real issue, which isn't gambling, but whether we'll stay free to make——" There he was now; he'd recognize that thick, untidy mass of pinkish-gray hair anywhere. "Never mind. Here he comes. Don't mind if I leave you, Dad? I have to prepare him—not for what he's to say, because he'll know that better than I would, but for the news that he's the one to say it."

The Mayor entered, made a slight bow, and seated himself behind the desk at the end of the room. He looked like his pictures, Dick thought, but older. A fighting man, in spite of his stout, slightly pudgy figure. Most of the years that he could remember, the picture and name of S. Davis Wilson had been in the papers, and always as the champion of some improvement in government or against some misuse of public money or authority. It was something Officer Yaeger had said that had given him the idea of this meeting. All the old-time police were admirers of the Mayor because he had fought for their welfare. Now could Ed Shaughnessy get him to fight still another battle?

Being a mayor must be hard work. He looked tired and drawn; he talked with his secretary, then lifted his head and surveyed the roomful of people expectantly. I didn't guess wrong on Mr. Shaughnessy, Dick thought, as Ed walked up to the desk holding the lists that Dick had made out for him.

"Your Honor, I'm a storekeeper, and all these people here are either storekeepers or their families and customers, who will vouch for them. The storekeeper's lot is one of long hours, hard work, and service to the community. A lot not unlike your own, if I may say so."

Mr. Shaughnessy was even better than Dick had expected. Everybody clapped, as though it were some kind of political meeting, and Mayor Wilson smiled and nodded his head.

"Some time ago a man called on all these storekeepers and many others and represented himself as a salesman of an organization called the Ace Amusement Company. He offered an arrangement whereby his company would put in machines of the type called pinball, where little metal balls are shot so they set up electrical contact with pins . . ."

The Mayor made an impatient gesture. "I know what they are. In fact, I enjoy playing on them."

This sounded bad, but Mr. Shaughnessy didn't look fazed. "I have two in my store, which this company put in. The baseball one is a lulu, and I challenge you to a game." Everybody laughed, but he went right on, "You must understand that I do not object to these games personally—many of us here do not. This salesman also wanted to put in what are commonly called 'one-arm bandits'——"

"With which I am also familiar."

"Perhaps I should explain that his manner was that of a moving-picture gangster. Two sinister characters accompanied him."

"They are also familiar, especially recently."

No, the Mayor was sticking to the ball, his eyes on it all the way.

"Any storekeepers that didn't accept the deal were told that the company had legal and political protection."

"There is nothing here for me to go on."

"We think there is something to go on, and the reason we are here is that everyone who did not accept the proposition was summoned to this building by the Department of Public Health, in what the newspapers called a crusade. A crusade against filthy stores.

"Here is a list of every storekeeper, from South to Snyder, from river to river, who put in machines of both types. I would be on there except my place is farther uptown. And here is another list, of those who refused. No one on the first list received a Department of Health visit or summons. Everyone on the second list is in this room, with a summons in his pocket."

Ed Shaughnessy had reached that climax in just the right way. Dick wanted to clap when the Mayor jumped to his feet, his face turning red with anger. He was mad all right. Anyone could see that.

"I've heard all I want to or need to. The Department of Public

Health comes under me. I believe in you people and I'm ashamed that this has happened in my administration. I hope you realize that it was not my fault. The last four years of Democratic rule in this state have witnessed an unholy marriage between gangsters and politicians, which I am bound to break up if I can. Tear up those summonses, every one of them, here and now, and go back to your places of business assured that I shall handle this in my own way immediately. There is political strength behind the threats that were made to you. I recognize the methods and have a pretty good idea of who was responsible, but I assure you that the whole power of this city and its police force will be mobilized to protect you. If any one of you is threatened in any way, call me here, where my secretaries will see that I am put on the phone immediately, as soon as you say that you are a storekeeper. If it's Sunday, call my home. The number's in the phone book. From what your spokesman has said I gather that many of you, under the force of threats, put in these machines that prey upon the poor and have been declared illegal by the courts time after time. I propose to take them out of your stores within the next two hours. Ordinarily you would be served with warrants, but there's no time for that."

Gosh, this was wonderful! Dick was so excited that he could hardly sit still. All that he had hoped for and more. Wait till George learned about it, after the way he'd tried to put a wet blanket over the whole idea.

"There's no time for warrants," the Mayor repeated, "because before they could be issued there would be court injunctions to prevent their use. We shall act, and act fast. Good-by now, and thanks to all of you."

As everyone started to file out Mayor Wilson motioned to Dick. "My secretary tells me that you started this thing, got all these people together."

"That's right."

"And the man who spoke for you?"

"Ed Shaughnessy, a friend of my father."

"He worked with you right along?"

"He was sort of against all this, but I figured . . ."

"You figured pretty well. Call him, will you, and we'll get going. We don't have much time."

Before the rest had filed out the Mayor was giving orders. "If there is any leakage on this, I'll find out who was responsible and see to it myself that he's fired, so help me. Miss Fine, get the captains, lieutenants, and sergeants of every police district on the phone. We're going to raid the places on this list, and I'm going to give the orders personally."

Dick said, "You have the wrong list, Mr. Wilson. They're the ones that *didn't* put in machines. This is the machine list." Then he wondered if he should have interrupted.

This was why Mr. Wilson was mayor of Philadelphia, against the wishes of both political parties. When he believed in something he acted, as he was doing now. Miss Fine ran along beside him, taking orders in her notebook, as he pushed Mr. Shaughnessy and Dick into his own office and through a private door.

"If something backfires in this, I don't want either of you two to suffer any reprisals from gangsters—or politicians. But I think both of you should be in on this."

The telephones on his desk began to ring, and Dick, who had learned to know the various sections of South Philadelphia as he had never known them before, felt increasing respect for the Mayor. When Dad had said he'd go into politics Dick had been inclined to make fun of the idea, but maybe Dad was right. Here was a man who had been nothing but a clerk in the tax office, but he believed in himself; he had fought always as he was fighting now, and look at what he had accomplished.

"Lieutenant, I want your patrol wagon with six men to be at the corner of Fifth and Snyder Avenue in ten minutes. That order takes precedence over everything but a four-alarm fire. . . . Captain, I want your patrol wagon to be at the corner of Ninth and Reed . . ." The man had the whole campaign already mapped out. "I want your patrol wagon here. I want every prowl car on duty here."

Then suddenly Dick and Mr. Shaughnessy were being shoved along again. "Out this way. Miss Fine, is my official car downstairs?" Then, almost as though he was ashamed to give the order, "Wait ten minutes, then call the papers. I don't want any leaks there either. Tell them to meet me at Ninth and Reed and I'll have a story for them. Oh, that reminds me, Miss Fine. What happened to that fireman's ax that was around the office? You know—the one I carried in the parade two or three months ago."

Mr. Shaughnessy looked at Dick and winked.

This was more fun than a barrel of monkeys. Surrounded by a motorcycle escort with sirens screaming, the limousine raced down Broad Street, through red lights, past traffic policemen frantically halting the flow of cars on the cross streets and then saluting as the Mayor's car sped past. Dick was so excited he could hardly pay attention to what the Mayor was saying. He was sitting back, not looking excited at all, as though this were an everyday occurrence, which Dick guessed it was. Mr. Shaughnessy was excited, though. He tried to appear calm, but it was easy to see that he was excited inside.

The Mayor was saying, "Now, son, I'm going to count on you to keep track of those stores on your list. Only those that have one-arm bandits. We won't touch the pinball machines, as I'm on shaky ground there. We have to work as fast as possible. If there were no leaks in my office, we have an hour before all hell will be popping. Then maybe another hour before they catch up with us. By then I expect to be back in my office. Here's a memo pad and pencil. There are ten police districts alerted. Divide your list roughly into that many sections. It won't hurt if they overlap."

For a moment Dick found it impossible to think. The speed of the car, the scream of the sirens, the importance of what was being asked of him made it impossible to concentrate. The list of addresses was nothing but a blur of spots on paper. Then suddenly they came clear and his mind began to function with an exhilarating smoothness. Why there was nothing to it; he had prepared the list in sections, as he had visited them. The motion of the car was so smooth that he had no trouble writing, until a tire-squealing turn onto Snyder Avenue almost threw him on the Mayor's lap.

"Here's the first group." He tore off the page and went to work again, visualizing each of the stores as he did so.

"Good boy." The Mayor thought of everything; his mind was racing too, the way Dick's was. "Another problem. If I have those machines stored all in one place, they'll have them out in twenty-four hours and a lot of our work will be for nothing. I'll try sending them to various station houses out in the sticks somewhere."

Parked ahead was a familiar red patrol car, and watching curiously as their own cortege drew up was a detail of police. They saluted as the Mayor spoke through the rolled-down window. "Captain, I have information that a lot of illegal coin-operated gambling machines are in stores in your district."

The officer looked uncomfortable. "There may be a few. We've had no orders about them, sir."

"Why should you need special orders? When you see somebody disobeying the law don't you arrest him?"

"Word got around that they were to be let alone, sir."

"You mean you were ordered . . ."

"No orders; just sort of an understanding."

"I'm giving you orders. You are to go to these stores and remove all spindle machines—know what I mean? Don't touch the pin-balls."

"Yes, sir. The warrants?"

"I'll take the responsibility. And if you do a good job, I'll remember. Maybe you don't know it, but it was my recommendation that promoted you and put you here. You were lieutenant in the Fourteenth District. Maybe I was wrong in your appointment . . ."

"No, Your Honor."

"Show me, then. I want no arrests. If any storekeeper objects, pay no attention. Don't tamper with the money boxes, but treat the machines as roughly as you want. Now I'm wasting time. Get going. I expect every machine to be lifted and your men on the way to the Bustleton Station within fifteen minutes. Throw them in an empty cell there and tell the turnkey to lock it and throw the key away."

That was how to give orders. A curious group of onlookers had appeared; doorways and windows filled while the motorcycle policemen gunned their machines. The Mayor waved, the sirens started again, and they were on their way.

Mr. Shaughnessy said, "You sure gave it to him straight, Your Honor."

"Here's the next list, Mr. Wilson," said Dick, who continued writing. "I'm sorry, I guess I should say 'Your Honor' too, but you're the first mayor I ever met and I think you're wonderful. The cop on our beat said you were. He said all the old-timers were for you."

The Mayor interrupted, " 'Mr. Wilson' is fine, son. Save 'Your Honor' for formal occasions. And when you get your lists finished give me a memo of the name and number of that cop, also your own address and that of your friend here. I don't expect you'll have any personal trouble, but I'm going to put on details of plain-clothes men around your places for the next few days."

At the third stop three other cars stood behind the patrol. "The reporters got here, I see. You two stick to the car. If anyone tries to take your pictures, duck down." Then, to the chauffeur, who also wore a policeman's badge, "Mike, keep our friends out of trouble."

He called through the window, "I'll talk to you boys in a few minutes. Follow me. You too, Lieutenant. Step on it, Mike. Now, son, which store on this list will be best for a spectacular personal raid—something that will dramatize what we're doing? Think fast."

There was no need for Mayor Wilson to say that. Dick's mind was spinning around like the reels in the one-arm bandits. "This would be it. It's a big, new place right across from a junior high school, and they have three of each kind of machine."

"You listening, Mike?"

"Yes, sir."

One of the escorts pulled alongside and grinned through the window. "Where away, Your Honor?"

"Follow us. Now, Dick Jones, I've a new idea that will put you in the act without getting you in a jam. Got some change on you?"

"Yes, sir."

"Good. Mike, pull around the corner by that school and we'll let Dick out. Then we'll step on it and go around the block again. By the time I get back, with the reporters, you are to be in that store playing one of those machines as though your life depended on it. High-school kids gambling, get it? You *are* in high school?"

"South Phillie."

"Beat it now."

Dick slipped out of the car and waited until what had become a whole parade disappeared around the next corner. I don't want to look in a hurry, he thought. He sauntered into the store and bought a candy bar—all this excitement was making him hungry. He put the nickel change in one of the machines and pulled. There was a sudden sound of falling coins, a rain of nickels. Gosh, he thought, I've hit the jackpot!

Here they came. Before he could scoop up the nickels policemen, reporters, and photographers were milling around inside. The store-keeper, who a moment before had been doing nothing more exciting than making a five-cent candy sale, found himself in a bedlam of excited people who kept pushing him aside while he tried to under-stand what was happening.

In came the Mayor, carrying the ax over his shoulder like a musket, a stern, implacable expression on his face. He walked over to Dickie, whose hands felt uncomfortably full of nickels. "What's your name, son?"

"Dick Jones." Darn all those nickels. One slipped through his fingers and rolled across the floor; flashlight bulbs half blinded him.

"You go to school, Dick?"

All the reporters were busy writing. Some of them began to call questions but Dick answered only Mayor Wilson. "Yes, sir. High school."

"And you were spending all those five-cent pieces in this ma-chine?"

"No, Your Honor. I just won the jackpot."

The pictures didn't appear in the early edition of the *Bulletin,* but there they were, right on the front page of the first final. There was the Mayor, talking to Dickie. The photographer had taken the shot so that the nickels in Dickie's hands were clearly visible, as were those still in the machine. The expression on his face was funniest of all. Chester almost doubled over laughing. "Call your mother down, George. No, send a copy of the paper up to her. Son, that's the most realistic picture I've ever seen. You look exactly as though you'd been caught stealing jam or something."

"I felt like it, but Mr. Wilson said that made a prima-facie case that those were gambling machines, and not to sell candy, the way the judge ruled who's been protecting them. What you don't see is all the reporters rushing to play the other machines when they realized I'd won a jackpot."

"Did the Mayor really smash any machines with his ax?"

"The one here, with the money running out of it. He's a great man. You should have seen how nice he was at the meeting, George. Wasn't he, Dad?"

"Wonderful."

"And to me and Mr. Shaughnessy, while we chased around with all those sirens going."

"Where's Ed now? He did a good job at the meeting, I thought."

"I knew he would."

"Sometimes, son, you take me by surprise. I was expecting to explain how we storekeepers felt and had just about thought out what I was going to say."

"I know. But I couldn't tell you ahead of time that I wanted Mr. Shaughnessy, because if he hadn't come you were the only one I could fall back on. You would have been terrible, compared to him."

"Don't know as I like that. I had some very powerful words lined up. Nothing in my life has made me as mad as this business. I'd like to see the expression on that icy-faced fellow right now."

"He wouldn't have any. Expression, I mean. It's only a job to him, Dad. Maybe he's feeling glad to see his bosses get the worst of it."

"Where did you say Ed Shaughnessy is now?"

"Back at his store, I guess. The Mayor whispered to me to go on home, but Mr. Shaughnessy was having a real good time riding around in that big Caddie and everybody wondering who he was."

The store began to fill with people. Nearly everybody bought the *Bulletin,* and those who played the numbers bought the *News* also, where there were other pictures; but because the *News* pictures were on pink paper they didn't stand out like the ones in the *Bulletin.*

Saul Gerson said, "Well, Dick, so you made the headlines!" and Mary Plotko, "Dickie, with the Mayor?"

"You are one person from whom I do not take being called Dickie."

"I'm sorry. Mrs. Rivkin came by with the paper . . ."

"And there I was. Save it. I'm hungry. *Mrs. Burke!* You've come just in time. The events of today have been too much for me. How many extra-large-size fryers can I buy for five dollars in nickels?"

"Well, Dickie, I don't really know. Why would five dollars in nickels . . . ? And your picture in the paper! I see—you won a jackpot on one of those nickel machines. I wonder why your father never put them in."

"Mrs. Burke. This is no time to stand on ceremony. If I'm over in your place in five minutes can I be greeted with heaped-up piles of Burke's fried oysters?"

"Why of course you can, Dickie. My goodness, your picture on the front page of the *Bulletin,* along with Mayor Wilson. Why it's the first time we've ever had a customer who's a—a celebrity!"

# Part II

Chapter 9

When the children had finished decorating the store Chester called upstairs, "Come on down, Kit. Everything's ready."

Honey came down too, as she did every year after the tree was set up and the colored lights finally made to work, but now she kept saying, "Take it real easy, Mrs. Jones. These stairs are tricky."

Surely, by this time the children must know, especially with Honey being so solicitous. It was silly of Kit to be sensitive. Strange, the way women behaved. And what if something went wrong? How would he ever get along without her?

He remembered the first time they had a Christmas tree in the store, the second year they owned it. It was Kit's idea. He had gone outside and bought a tree from Abe Green, who had sold trees out front every Christmas even while Phil Glickman owned the store, which was a lifetime away. Abe was outside now, showing a prospective customer what he always called a "dandy double balm." Five of his boys were watching the transaction, hopeful of carrying home the purchase and making a dime extra.

When that first tree was all decorated Kit had said, "Chester, dear, it seems selfish to have it in the dining room, where our customers can't enjoy it too. So many of them can't have trees of their own, living in one or two rooms the way they do. Would it be an awful lot of work to move it into the store? I know just the place." He had objected a bit, but as usual he'd done what she wanted, and their customers had enjoyed it—then and every year since.

While Kit was exclaiming over the new lights and how thick and bushy the tree was, Chester saw that Abe had made the sale; there behind the customer trotted Billy and Henry, carrying the tree. It was cold outside, the coldest night so far, and Abe was trying to keep warm by flailing his thick body with his arms. A good, well-meaning man, a kind of bull among men. How many years now had he been out of work? Surely he made use of every opportunity to earn money for that constantly growing family, from dealing in Christmas trees and shoveling snow in winter to selling ice on a rented pushcart in summer. Chester usually financed him in these little enterprises and aided in the deception of the government that gave him relief checks.

Strange, how peaked his rugged, almost black features looked. The cold gave him a gray, dull appearance. Chester tapped on the window to get his attention and then motioned for him to come inside.

"Good evening, Mrs. Jones. Your Christmas tree is the prettiest you ever had, I think. I saved it for you right off, the minute I took it out of the bundle." Abe Green was from northern New York and spoke with a precise Yankee accent.

"It is beautiful, Abe," Kit said.

"A dandy double balm." He had been saying that for years, but Chester wondered if he or anybody else knew what it meant.

"Why don't you stay inside by the window? There won't be much business tonight, it's too cold."

"You'd think that, but around Christmastime folks like cold weather. I've done real well today. I need to, too. Mrs. Green is expecting, which means another mouth to feed."

"Abe Green, you've said that almost every Christmas since we've known you," Kit said. "Remember when you wanted to put trees down Camac Street too, before Henry came?"

"I've been very fortunate in the sex of my children, Mrs. Jones. Eleven boys. No, it will be eleven with this one."

With Kay and Penny standing there, looking for empty places to put odd ornaments, Chester couldn't help saying, "I've been less lucky that way, but I guess I can't complain. Suppose I had all girls, like Eddie Cantor? Fifty-fifty isn't a bad average."

Kay said, "Father!" which she never did, and Penny, "I think Eddie Cantor was luckiest."

It was Dickie who upset the applecart, unless the others were only pretending that they didn't know. "Mother is expecting too, Mr. Green. Maybe she should rub your head for luck."

Kit blushed like a young girl, but what could you do with Dickie, especially after his successful engineering of the campaign against the slot-machine racket? He just stood there grinning at them. "Now don't tell me, Dad, that she hasn't told you?"

Penny, screaming, "Mother, you told Dickie and not us? I think that's unfair. After all, we women should stick together."

"Don't be silly. She didn't tell me, so she didn't tell him." Kay hugged her mother. "I don't know why I didn't guess; you've been behaving sort of funny lately. You haven't, so much as Dad and Honey. Imagine Dickie . . . Oh, George, isn't it wonderful? Why don't you say something?"

"I don't see anything wonderful about it. It'll be fifteen years until he or she will be able to help out in the store. We'll all be old by then."

· There went Anthony Plotko to work. As he walked by the side windows of the store it was hard to imagine that he could be the father of anyone as beautiful, as sweet and unassuming as Mary. She was always talking about how wonderful he was. No doubt he had the qualities she described, but as he passed he looked like just another of those little men who crept out of houses here and there in the neighborhood to begin their day after most people ended theirs. That had been the cruel part about Mary's growing up—perhaps the cause of her mother's behavior, though so long as he could remember Mary had been neglected. What was Mr. Plotko's job at the Atlantic Refinery, where he had worked these twenty years? He was short, broad, and hunched over, but during his bouts of drinking he had the whole of Camac Street in a turmoil. That was the wonderful thing about Mary, her sense of loyalty to him. What a wife she would make for anyone!

She came in radiant. "Pop's just gone to work. Oh, Mr. Jones, the tree looks beautiful. And I just heard that Mrs. Jones is going to have a baby. Isn't it wonderful?"

"News travels fast in this neighborhood. As it's only ten minutes since Dickie decided to tell the world . . ."

"I thought it was about time that someone did. Who would want their own mother talked about?"

"Anyway, I'm curious to know how you found out."

"Horace Green. He knocked at the door to tell me. 'Mrs. Jones going to have a baby,' he said, and pelted off."

"A kind of public announcer—an old Philadelphia custom. Anyway, that's why I wanted you to help out in the store."

"If I'd known . . . I said when you asked that any time you needed me specially just to let me know. It's the afternoons, when Pop is up, that I like to be home with him. I could help at lunch and in the evenings . . ." Her face took on that turning inward expression that it so often had. "There's another reason that makes it hard for me, which I can't explain about, but that doesn't matter. You can count on me evenings from now on. Where's George?"

Before Chester could answer, Dick said, "Date. With a girl in his class, name of Myra. They're going to see that new French actress with the redundant name in something."

"Oh. Simone Simon. What did you say her name was?"

"I didn't, you did."

"Dick, you're trying to tease me. I mean George's new girl."

"Myra."

"Oh."

That confounded way that Dickie had of looking *through* people. "Why should you be upset? It's only Mary spelled backward, except for the *m*. But then, George never could spell."

"I'm not upset. Why should you think I'm upset?" Mary looked angry and on the verge of tears at the same time, so Chester said:

"Why do you pay any attention to Dick? You should know him by this time."

"What I came in for was to see Mrs. Jones. Can I go up-stairs?"

She didn't wait for an answer, but ran for the stairway and almost bumped into Honey. Honey said, "It would sure save me a lot of steps if you folks would listen. I've been hollering myself hoarse for five minutes. Mrs. Jones, she say that she clean forgot about supper tonight and would Dickie please take two dollars out of the cash register and go over to the store and buy four pounds of loin lamb chops and that the coffee is running short and get two pounds of the twenty-cent and not the seventeen-cent. She say they close in fifteen minutes and Dickie better do it right away."

Penny tried the effect of the new lipstick she had sneaked out of the store. There, that was pretty good. She wanted to make her lips thicker, so that she would look like a woman of the world, but then Mother would get after her. She powdered her nose again and watched her face emerge from the little cloud she had raised. I am beautiful, she thought, a lot prettier than Vee, but fellows aren't interested in mere good looks. She tried two or three expressions and then thought of the picture she had cut out of the paper. She hunted through her schoolbooks until she found it, folded in half, in her English history.

Elaine. Why hadn't she thought of Elaine as a name before she picked Penny? Penny was schoolgirlish and frivolous, while Elaine —well, it sounded sophisticated, the way Elaine Barrie looked. John Barrymore would never have married anyone named Helen—or Penny. Penny Barrymore. Elaine Barrymore. Imagine, a girl not many years older than herself winning a man who'd been married so often, had known so many great beauties. He looked older than he had the last time she had seen him in the movies, but his profile was as handsome as ever.

She picked up the lipstick again and made over her mouth to look like Elaine's, slipped into her coat, and put on a scarf so that it would partially hide her face. Thank goodness Mother wasn't there. Honey looked at her sort of funny, but she didn't say anything, though she wasn't above being nasty when she wanted to.

Of course Vee had to be early and was talking to Dad, who kept calling her Veronica. Honest, Dad could be drippy sometimes. After practically slaying Vee he turned on her. "What have you done to your face? Your mouth looks like a hunk of raw meat."

You couldn't explain about Elaine Barrymore to Dad, and it was mortifying for him to treat her like a child before Vee. There was nothing to do but be as casual as possible. "I was in a hurry; I knew Vee would be waiting." She controlled her seething feelings while with cool detachment she examined her face in the mirror behind the soda fountain. She pretended to rub off a little of the lipstick; Dad in the meantime went on making himself obnoxious.

"Come back early. You'll have to help in the store."

"Dad, do I have to? Now that you have Mary I don't see why you need me. I hate the store anyway, it's so—so . . ."

"You know we always have a big rush the last few days before Christmas. I want you home by five."

There was little use objecting further when Dad was in one of his stubborn moods, but she had to show Vee that he couldn't walk over her. While she continued to try out expressions in the mirror she said, "There's some last-minute shopping I just have to get done, and you know how the traffic is. I don't see how we can possibly go all the way to Market Street and be back by five."

"Five-thirty is the limit, and I mean that. I don't want your mother in the store, and it's not fair for Kay to work all day and then have to help out."

Anyway, he hadn't said anything more about the lipstick. On the way over to Thirteenth Street, Penny said, "Aren't families poisonous?"

"Mine are pretty good. They let me do what I please."

That was true; Vee could get away with anything. "I guess it's having the store. If ever a girl had a grim childhood! Here comes a streetcar—let's run for it."

Market Street was exciting, with all the tree vendors and the decorations on City Hall and men selling tinsel and Christmas-tree balls and the Santa Clauses ringing their bells and the Salvation Army women standing by their little pots and the way the store windows were decorated, but especially it was the crowds of people pushing along the sidewalks, eager and happy.

She had told a white lie about wanting to shop: all her presents to the others were already wrapped and hidden away in the bottom drawer of her bureau. Besides, it was silly to go out and buy presents when there were so many things from the store she could give. They walked down as far as Gimbel's, and back on the other side. It was cold, and her face tingled. It felt good, and she forgot all about being made up like Elaine Barrie until Vee whispered, "Don't look around now, but there are two of the best-looking men following us."

"Really! How do you know?"

"I've been watching for the last block. Every time I look back at the taller one he looks at me. Let's stop and pretend to be window-shopping."

This was thrilling. Penny could see the reflection of the people passing, and then Vee, who had hold of her arm, pressed it. There they were, grown men who must have been as old as Sig. They walked by very slowly; Penny wanted to give them a provocative look, but she didn't know whether she could. She tried to look interested in the windowful of men's suits, and Vee began to talk excitedly about all kinds of things.

There, the men had gone on, and she breathed a little freer, but no, there they were, standing in the lobby of the Earle Theater. Vee whispered, "Let's go in. Maybe they'll come sit beside us. We can get acquainted in the dark."

"Vee, we can't. I wouldn't dare."

"Oh, come on. Be a sport. It's a good picture, too. I simply adore Johnny Weissmuller and Maureen O'Sullivan. We'll buy tickets and go in. I bet they follow."

"I've seen every Tarzan picture . . ." Penny hesitated, then walked up to the box office and bought the tickets; both of them pretended not to notice the men standing there. They walked down the aisle of the darkened theater, and Penny had begun to feel that she would never reach a seat when Vee said, "Here they come—one down each aisle, so that they can sit on both sides of us."

"Maybe we better not. Let's pick out seats with people on each side."

But the usher was showing them into a row of empty seats. Penny had no more than taken off her hat before the man was sitting by her, and beyond Vee she could see the other man. What should she do? What was Vee going to do?

Vee began to whisper to her, under the sounds of Tarzan saving Maureen O'Sullivan from the Leopard Men, about all the wonderful fellows there were in her class at Hallahan High and paid no attention to the men at all. In here, in the dark, it was hard to realize that outside it was practically Christmas, with people shoving you this way and that in their hurry to buy things. In here it was so quiet, except for the roar of the animals and Tarzan challenging them. Not only was it quiet; now that her eyes had adjusted themselves she could see that the theater was almost empty.

But all she could really think about was the man next to her. The man on Vee's side had put his arm around her so that his hand was right next to Penny's shoulder. She wouldn't have minded so much if the man on her side had done the same, but his hand was on his knee, so that the back of it touched her knee, and for a while it gave her a funny feeling, but gradually, when he didn't move or seem to care about her the way the other fellow did about Vee, she began to follow the story. Just when she had almost become accustomed to his sitting there, as though he were George or Dickie, his hand against her knee was no longer the back, but the palm. She wanted to scream, but couldn't.

Vee and the other man were kissing. They had been holding a long, whispered conversation, Penny remembered, but she herself had not said a word to the man next to her. She *had* to get away. "Please, I have to go to the ladies' room. I'll be right back."

Vee and the other man paid no attention, but a deep voice, somehow different from what she had expected, said, "O.K., baby."

She slipped by him, hat in hand, and practically ran out of the theater. She didn't care what Vee Maguire might say later. She didn't care about anything but getting home. She was waiting for the streetcar when she saw a clock in a store window. Quarter past four. She'd be home in fifteen minutes at the latest. Wouldn't Dad be surprised when she came in before the time he had said?

When the streetcar came along it was colder inside than out, a damp cold. Whether it was that, or remembering again what had happened, she began to shiver. She wanted only to see Mother, to see Dad. She'd tell him she had started thinking about how selfish she was, and came home early on purpose, so he could have a little more rest. But no, he'd probably think that funny and wonder what had happened.

When she arrived at the store she was glad to see that only Dickie and George were there. It had been so easy to tell Dad a white lie earlier in the afternoon, but if he were to question her now, she knew she would blurt out the whole story of what had happened and it would only make him feel bad and not do any good.

It would have been the same with Mother, so she was glad when George ordered her, in a manner she usually would have resented, "Penny, you go to Spewack's right away and get all the one- and two-pound gift packages of candy that he can give you. I've just called, and they've nobody to send down. You can take a taxi back."

Dickie said, "Now, big brother, don't be so stingy. She'll do better taking a Yellow from here. I'll call them."

Instead of answering directly, George said, "I don't see why people wait until the last minute to buy presents. We've carried more gift boxes this year than we ever have and we're practically out of them already. It's a good thing I ordered as many as I did."

"Wrong twice. It's the customers who *do* wait that buy from us. And you deserve no credit for ordering what you did. You'd have been stuck with them if Mary Plotko wasn't jerking sodas for us. You know how many fellows come in just to look at her, and most of them buy candy for an excuse. Meanwhile, do I call a Yellow or does Penny take the streetcar?"

This was wonderful. It was like old times, a hundred years ago, before this afternoon had happened. "It's awful crowded uptown, and I think Dickie's right, George darling." She realized that she was laying it on too thick. "I mean I won't possibly be able to pick up a taxi around Spewack's. And Dickie, do explain to Dad. I promised him faithfully . . ."

Honest, he was worse than Dad or Mother. She practically lost track of what she meant to say, the way he looked at her.

# Chapter 10

Chester's feet hurt; he'd be glad when June came and George graduated. How many miles had he walked since he took over from Dickie, at eight-thirty? Business hadn't been too brisk, and Mary had come in to help with lunch while her father slept, but every sale had seemed to take him the full length of the store. That was the trouble having a place so long and narrow. When they had enlarged the house it would have been better to leave the store the way it used to be and make a storeroom in back. They could have made the store ten feet shorter, with the fountain coming opposite the next-to-the-last phone booth, on one side, and in front of the door to the upstairs. They would have had a place to keep stock where they could see it, instead of under the cases or in the cellar, and it would have been more private going upstairs. There was no drawback, so far as he could see, except that there would have to be a narrow passage to get to the last phone booth and there would be no room for the table beyond, which no one used but Eddie Bryant, the colored policeman, when he ate lunch there during the week he was on day duty. That might be a good thing, too; Eddie shouldn't feel that he had to sit back there.

The store looked more imposing, though, the way it was. George would kick like a steer if he suggested reducing its length, but twice ten feet—all the times he had walked from the soda fountain to the cigar case or the magazine rack—could add up to a lot of extra steps during the day.

Where had he read: "Flat-footedness is the occupational disease of barbers, dentists, and storekeepers"? Or was it one of those things that Dick had said? Toothache wasn't as bad as footache, or was it feetache? He would be glad when Saul Gerson went out and he could take a rest. What had got into Saul, wanting to go to Spain to fight the fascists?

Chester hoped he had given the boy the right advice. "What does it matter to you what Hitler and Mussolini and Franco do? Besides, you're a violinist, not a soldier," he had said. "Mr. Meyer says you're a genius and that he's proud to be your teacher."

Saul admitted that the old man had helped him, and teaching Saul, having some purpose in life, had been good for Mr. Meyer, too. He hardly ever had strings hanging from his coat any more, as reminders for things he forgot anyway.

Saul began a long argument about Jews being killed, about communism and fascism. "Why not let those two fight it out between themselves?" Chester had suggested. He didn't understand Saul and was worried about him; he hoped he'd change his mind. Young fellows were usually itching to get into a fight, but Saul wasn't that type. Likely he had been running around too much with Gert Cameron. She was always full of talk like that and so was her father, always putting in requests for books they didn't have in the library.

Chester turned on the radio. It was almost time for the sports broadcast. He'd forgotten all about the Joe Louis fight the night before until he'd seen the headlines in the papers; maybe there'd be a rebroadcast.

When the announcer's voice came in, it was the general news that went before the sports events. So the sitdown strike was still on out at the Fisher Body Company. Half the country without jobs and the other half sitting down on them. The worst of it was that Governor Murphy was giving in to threats to set the plants on fire.

Packing the Supreme Court. What had happened to the country, anyway? Too bad the President had been re-elected. If ever an election had been bought with the people's own money, that one had. But it was useless to get mad about it, now it was over.

More about Edward's abdication. So the royal family will support him! Nice of them. None of Chester's affair, he supposed, but he resented the idea that a man couldn't marry whoever he wanted, even if he was a king.

His attention wandered until the announcer said something about Amelia Earhart. Imagine a girl planning an airplane flight around the world, following the line of the equator. The world is sure getting to be a small place, he thought.

Of course it had to come—the Spanish Civil War. Mussolini sending ten thousand more men to help the fleeing rebels. Hell, he'd just been through enough of that with Saul. He switched off the radio, intending to turn it on again after the world news was over, but Mrs. Waldman came in.

"Could you send that cute little colored boy over to my place— you know, 915—with a half dozen cold Cokes? Tell him to ring twice, short-like, so I know who it is."

"He'll be back in a minute. Right now he's calling one of your neighbors to the phone. You know Mrs. Koehler, who has all the dogs?"

"The little, thin woman up at the corner?"

"With a heart too big for her body. She's about the only woman around here, except Mrs. Jones, who never played the numbers."

"I don't play them either, Mr. Jones," Mrs. Waldman interrupted. "They're illegal, and I hate anything illegal."

Mrs. Waldman had always interested him; she always looked worried and tense, and he wondered why. Now, as she talked, with more emotion than the situation seemed to warrant, he thought he knew what she suffered from. It was fear. She was afraid, terribly afraid of something. "You know why I hate things like numbers so much?" she went on. "You get started doing something little, that hardly seems illegal at all, and then suddenly you wake up and find yourself a criminal."

"Well, Pierce, the old colored man who lives alone on Fawn Street, started on the numbers, and Mrs. Koehler played a whole dollar, just to help him out, and she hit. When the news got out, everybody she knew called up and tried to borrow money."

"I just wouldn't want that kind of money. And I'm glad the

Mayor is raiding places where they play the numbers, like he cleaned out the slot machines. He's a wonderful man, Mr. Wilson. Well, good-by, and don't forget to send the Cokes."

"They'll be there almost as soon as you are. Here comes Henry now." Standing there, talking to Mrs. Waldman, he'd forgotten how much his feet were hurting, but now he could hardly take a step.

When Mrs. Koehler came in he congratulated her on her luck.

"Imagine me winning all that money! Four hundred and forty dollars! I couldn't believe it when Pierce told me. And I haven't had so many telephone calls since my dear, sweet Goldyeyes climbed the telephone pole and got his picture in the paper when the firemen rescued him."

Chester remembered that and smiled in spite of the way his feet felt. He'd just have to go to a foot doctor, maybe get some special shoes made, with arch supports. Thank goodness, there was George, cutting across McClellan Street. He came in, explosive with indignation about something or other, as he usually was. "Guess what? The chain stores are selling all the leading brands of cigarettes at two for twenty-five. Chesterfields, Camels, Luckies, everything. That's practically what we pay. Now you know the companies must be giving special discounts . . . . Dad, what's the matter?"

"Don't look so worried, son. My feet are hurting—worse than usual."

George caught hold of his arm. Chester felt ashamed to lean on him, but he had to. He heard the door open again, letting in a cold blast of air, and George said, "Penny, stay in the store, will you, while I help Dad upstairs. Something has happened to his feet."

"It's nothing but that I've been on them too much."

He wished they wouldn't make such a fuss over him. The wind had brought out the color in Penny's cheeks and she looked wonderfully pretty. Her kisses had a fresh coolness that was nice, too. He was glad that she had stopped using lipstick. "Dad! What can I do?"

"Mind the store." George's tone was his usual one, which rarely promoted family harmony, but Penny was remarkably docile.

He had to explain it all over again with Kit. Couldn't a man's feet hurt without everybody treating it like a catastrophe? When

George went downstairs Penny came up and, while Kit put Epsom salts in a basin of hot water, helped him off with his shoes. The pain seemed to be between his third and fourth toes, and came and went. Gradually the Epsom salts eased it.

Only two months, or a little more, for Kit, but you would never have known it as she fussed around. The first time he had ever done anything like this, having to be helped upstairs. He said, "Penny, maybe you ought to go downstairs and help George. I feel a lot better."

"Dad, Mother—I've done a good bit of soul searching and I've come to the conclusion that Penny doesn't suit my type nearly as much as Helen does. If you'll kindly refrain . . ."

"Refrain? I'm even going to begin calling your mother Katie again, which is what I've always liked best."

"You will not. I admit that Kit sounds pretty terrible, but it's an improvement over Katie. We'll call Helen whatever she wants to be called, and the same applies to me. I guess that fashions in names change."

"Can't I just be Helen Jones?"

The buzzer from downstairs meant that George was busy. Helen ran out and Chester said, "You know, that kid stumps me."

"You know what she said to me a week or so ago? 'I want to be a nun,' she said, 'but how do I go about it?' I'd have thought it was the influence of Vee's family, except that she's hardly seen Vee since Christmas. Now what could have made Helen say that?"

"Give me time, and I'll come up with some answer. Meanwhile, my feet are feeling a lot better, but I think I should go to a pediatrician."

Kit laughing, the way she did, deep down in her throat. "Honestly, where could I have found a husband like you? It isn't a pediatrician you need. It's a chiropodist."

"Guess I should have done something sooner. It's pretty silly compared to what you're going through."

"Chester, you've never seemed very excited about another Jones."

"What am I supposed to do, hand out cigars before the blessed event?"

"Now, Chester. Are you really happy about it?"

"Happier than I ought to be, considering how my feet were hurting, up to a couple of minutes ago." This was like the *Bulletin*, and how final was Final? Could there be one-star and two-star and three-star happiness? He felt in no mood to go into that, and fortunately Kit changed the subject. "Dear, to go back to the change in Helen—she hasn't been painting herself up, the way she was."

"Besides that, look at the way she helps in the store without fussing."

"And now she wants to be called Helen again."

"Sensible girl. What I want to know is where is Dickie? He should have been home before either of the others."

"Why, didn't he come up through the store?"

"Not unless I was unconscious."

"But he came home before George."

"He didn't come through the store. Maybe by the front door. No wonder we can't keep track of the children. You'll remember that was your idea?"

"Certainly it was. What I went through! Do you remember when you were calling on me, and had to pass all those horrid pork chops in Pop's store?"

"No I don't. You were all that mattered."

"Well, it used to embarrass me. That was the one thing I wanted when we remodeled, so the girls could bring home friends without going through the store."

"So Dickie can sneak upstairs when he doesn't want to help me and George."

Kit giggled like—like she used to before they were married. "Chester, darling, do you know what I think? Have you noticed the way he's dressing up—and combing his hair, even? Other winters he was always going ice-skating. His skates are hanging in his closet right now and he hasn't taken them out once this winter. I think Dickie has a girl! Imagine! Our little Dickie with a girl."

"Could be. And like him to keep it secret, too. Do you think it's a girl from the neighborhood? There's usually a gang of them in when he's in the store, especially recently."

"How would I know? I've hardly been in the store in months.

Every time I go up or down the stairs you or Honey are after me. I admit they're a little steep."

Gingerly, Chester tried putting his weight on first one foot and then the other. Epsom salts were wonderful. The pain was practically gone. What was Kit saying? Oh, yes, about Dickie having a girl. "If she's from around here, everybody else knows who she is already and we will too, before long." Just the same, when Dickie comes back I'm going to get after him, he thought, girl or no girl. Then he began to chuckle. "You know, Kit, we're a very lucky couple, seeing our children grow up and then getting a new life started. I'm all for it."

"A child in the house without having to wait for grandchildren. I'm glad you're glad. But what has happened in the neighborhood? Nobody tells me anything."

"Saul Gerson wants to go to fight the Italians and Germans in Spain."

"Why, for goodness' sake?"

"Because he's Jewish, I guess, and because of what they say Hitler has been doing to the Jews. He says if the fascists win Spain, they'll try to conquer the rest of the world. I tried to talk him out of it, of course. Oh, and Mrs. Koehler, of all people, played a dollar on the numbers and won."

"Did she box it?"

"I don't know. What's that, anyway?"

"You know that the winner has to have the last three numbers of the stock-exchange clearings, like they're printed every day in the *News*, which is why they sell so many. If the last numbers are 7-0-5, say, they win, but you can also play all the combinations of those three numbers."

How in hell did Kit know so much about playing the numbers? Chester was conscious that his mouth must be falling open while she went on, "So you box them by playing 5-0-7 and 0-5-7 and 7-5-0. You can make more boxes than that . . ."

This was getting too much. Chester interrupted, "Mrs. Waldman was in. You know, the bleached blonde who has an apartment at 915. I said something about Mrs. Koehler winning, when she'd never played before, and Mrs. Waldman said that she never played, which makes the two of you about the only grown folks on the street who don't."

"Why, Chester Jones, I always play the numbers. I've played them for years, through Honey. Ten cents a week. Sometimes I win, and besides, it's only a few cents. I can't see what's so awful . . ."

Now Chester knew that his chin had really dropped. Would he ever really know Kit? All he could think of to say was "Well, I'll be eternally God-damned!"

Dick consulted his list. With luck, this would be his last stop. He pushed open the door and entered between rows of whitely gleaming electric stoves and refrigerators, heaters and washing machines. He began to examine these.

"Well, young man, can I be of service?"

He looked up, pretending he hadn't heard the salesman come over. "I'm looking for a washing machine to give my mother on her birthday. What's the difference between the $99.50 and the $129.50 ones?"

"This is our de luxe model. It has an eight-sheet capacity and that only has six. It's a handsomer machine, too."

"I don't have much money. How about the motor on the $99.50 one?"

"Exactly the same. The motor and the drive are identical. The wringers, too, except for a little more chrome."

"You think it would be a good, sturdy machine for a small family? Something that wouldn't get out of whack quickly?" Dick had been going through his little act so often that he felt he was getting letter-perfect in it. It wasn't good to let himself be sold too easily. "What's better about your machine than the Whirlpool, let's say?"

"Well, son, I could give you a long sales talk, but honestly there's not much difference between any of the leading makes, except in little things. The companies have all been making washing machines for a long time. They all buy their motors and their wringers. I don't think I'd get any but a propeller-type machine. They're simpler, for one thing. The vacuum cups are going out and the ones that whirl clothes dry aren't perfected enough, I believe. I honestly think our machine is a little better value—which means something these days. We'll be glad to put one in your home on a two-week trial. Your father or mother would have to sign, of course."

This was the difficult moment, but in all this time he'd had only two turndowns. "I don't need to have it on trial. My name is Dick Jones and my dad has a store at Camac and McClellan, but I'd want the machine sent to where we live, in West Philadelphia." When you were telling a lie it helped to look straight into the other person's eyes and will him to believe in you. "The trouble is, I want to surprise both Dad and Mother and I don't have enough money to pay cash." He began to take dollar bills out of both pockets and then quarters and half dollars. This was the part that convinced them. "I see you'll sell this for ten dollars down and a year to pay. Here's twenty-five, and I'll pay the rest at five dollars a week, which is only fifteen weeks. That's how much I get for helping in the store nights. But they're not to know I'm buying it on time. It wouldn't seem like—like a present."

Earnestness and looking straight at the man did it. He rubbed his chin. "O.K. A contract with a minor isn't enforceable, but you look honest."

"Yes, sir. If I don't pay, you can take the machine back anyway. But you needn't worry. Here's where it goes to. It's an apartment house. It's important the driver leaves it with the janitor—on account of wanting to surprise my folks."

That was that. Dick wondered whether he should buy himself a chocolate sundae now, or at least a Coke, or whether he could wait until he got home, where he could have all he wanted free. He decided to wait, but then got to thinking about the bawling out that Dad would probably give him for sneaking out and staying away all afternoon, and stopped in a store and had a Coke anyway. The storekeeper said, "Dickie Jones! Remember me? I was one of the crowd you got to go to City Hall and see the Mayor. Sol Spiegel, remember?"

"Sure I do, now. But you weren't here, you were at Seventh and Catherine."

"Around the corner from there, but the neighborhood was going down and I had a chance to get this place. I've been going to go down to your store and tell your father what a bright boy he's got, but I'm pretty tied down."

"He already knows it anyway. Right now he's probably mad because I've been gone so long. Here's for the Coke."

"Forget it, boy. I'll always remember the Mayor smashing them machines of those dirty racketeers."

"Thanks, Mr. Spiegel, and if you do get down our way, you'll have a Coke on us."

The pause that refreshes, which the Coca-Cola people advertised about. It had more to it than most advertising phrases, at that. The real money probably lay in inventing something that was even better than Coke, if that was possible. Anyway, he felt ready for Dad.

George and Helen were in the store, and upstairs Dad was sitting in the kitchen with his shoes and socks off. Dick put on his best, most straightforward-looking smile. "Hello, Dad. What's the matter, feet hurt?"

Mother came in. "Your father could hardly get upstairs. Something went wrong with his arches."

"They feel fine now."

"Sorry I'm late. I had an errand to do."

Dad didn't bawl him out or anything, which he was entitled to do, especially when his feet were giving him trouble. Instead, Mother and he got the silliest grins on their faces when Dad said, "You look sort of slicked up, just to be out on an errand, son."

Now what fool idea did they have in their minds?

# Chapter 11

"I sent a letter to my love, I lost it, I dropped it, will somebody look behind them . . ."

Sure sign that spring was here again was the ring of little girls playing the old game on the side street. You could hear the clear, high, flutelike tones of little Shirley Stratford, from Fawn Street, above all the other voices. Who had told him that the new little girl in their house had been named Bellevue, after the hotel? The Stratford family was on relief, but if Shirley's voice continued to improve, they wouldn't need relief much longer.

Did any other neighborhood in the whole city produce as many children as this? The latest Green boy was over a month old, and Bellevue Stratford almost a week. It wasn't only the colored people. Mrs. Malone had twins, which would give her something to do for a while, besides playing the horses. Mrs. Tomolillo, wife of the barber across the street, looked pretty far gone. The women in the neighborhood were like sheep, lambing with the springtime. They had all come through it all right and he guessed Kit would, but she was older and it was fifteen years since her last. She didn't seem afraid, though, unless she was afraid inside.

When he'd talked with her last night while she lay beside him in bed, the light from the corner street lamp filling the room with a reflected radiance that was almost as beautiful as moonlight, he had told her how concerned he was and she had said, "Nonsense.

I'm perfectly healthy and I never had any trouble with the others. Now don't you worry."

He remembered how quietly she lay there for a while, close against him, and then the way she said, "Chester, which would you rather have, a boy or a girl?"

"You sound like Mary, asking if someone wants vanilla or chocolate."

"Don't be silly. I want to know."

"A girl, I guess. Maybe that's funny for a man, but girls are more fun to raise. Remember when Kay was little, buying her dolls and things?"

"I think I want a girl too," Kit had said. "But Dick was a wonderful baby. I can't remember him ever crying, the way George did."

"I always think of George when he was five or six—right after we got him glasses. He looked like a human owl."

"He always had trouble in school, but there was never a boy studied harder."

"Dickie never studied at all and breezed through."

"It's not fair to compare George and Dickie. Kay had to study hard and so does Helen, except Kay wanted to and Helen doesn't. But about the baby . . ."

"Whatever it is, I'll love it."

"Chester, my dear man, I know that, but I like to hear you say it," she answered, before he watched her go to sleep.

"Red Rover, Red Rover, I want Henry Green to come over."

Joe and Bert Cummings had joined the girls, and Henry Green, which meant that he was on duty for telephone calls instead of one of the others. Teresa Maguire, Veronica's youngest sister, was "it" and stood in the middle of the street, chanting her invitation, while the children stood on the curb and Henry prepared to dash to the other side without being caught.

When he'd been a boy, up in Tioga, they had played the same game, Chester remembered, but usually at night, under the gas lamps. It was a summer evening game, really, but with the spring-like weather so unexpected it must have caught the kids off balance. Why, it was only a week since the slush from the last snow was off the street. He'd have to look at their stock of marbles, jacks, tops, and hockey sticks and see if he needed to order any more. Probably George had already attended to it. And kites. The kite season would be on them in no time and it was remarkably good business, between the string, the made-up kites, and all the different kinds of sets for boys to make their own. Too bad it was so seasonal and not like the model-airplane sets, which went on selling all around the year.

Smoky jumped down, with a small plop, from wherever she had been sitting and began to weave between his feet. That meant that she was ready for her afternoon spoon of vanilla ice cream. He was about to give it to her when Patrolman Yaeger came in, which meant that he was on the four-to-twelve shift.

"Mind if I take a smoke?"

"Of course not. A White Owl?"

"Thanks. Ever since I read the ads that said they spit on other kinds to seal them, I've preferred White Owls."

Chester took out the White Owl box and picked out one that he thought was well colored. "Here you are," and when Yaeger went to pay for it, "Not this time. This is on me."

How many years, every third week, when Yaeger was on that shift, had they gone through much this same conversation? Yaeger would now tell about the apples.

"Saw a movie once, with a cop in it. He used to go past a place where some poor wop had a fruit stand and always helped himself to the biggest apple. Sometimes the wop hardly sold anything, but he had to count on losing two–three apples every day. No, Mr. Jones, I enjoy coming in for a few words and a cigar, but I like to pay for it."

When he had his cigar well started, Patrolman Yaeger said, "Hear what the kids are playing? Red Rover. We played that when I was a boy around Sixth and Girard, which used to be a German section. Still is, I guess. Next they'll be playing 'Run, sheep, run.' You know, there's nothing finer than walking down the street, swinging your club, looking out for all the things going on nowadays, and come on some youngsters playing a nice, innocent game like that and enjoying themselves, too."

He puffed away, while the phone booths filled and Chester waited on a few customers. After the store had emptied again, Yaeger said, "Say, there've been some plain-clothes dicks from City Hall hanging around this whole neighborhood the last few weeks. I spotted them because they're the same chaps the Mayor detailed down here after Dickie started the slot-machine raids. Know any reason?"

"Detectives? No I don't."

"There's one now—the fellow just came out of Burke's place. Having himself some fries, I guess. This is the last month for oysters. There's his partner, looking in Spinelli's. Want to bet he goes in for a shine?"

He'd no more than said it than in the man went and took a seat in the high chair beside the polishing machine, where it was easy to see right down Camac Street. Chester never would have realized that the two men were police. They looked like anyone else, he thought, with their blue pin-stripe suits and gray felt hats.

"There's not much I miss," Yaeger said, standing up; he carefully put out the cigar and placed the butt in the sweatband of his cap. "There's another pair of them at the other end of Camac Street. Know anybody down the street might be in a jam?"

Chester shook his head, and Yaeger said, "I better be getting along."

Just then they heard Teresa Maguire say, "I'm tired of this game. Let's play 'Run, sheep, run.' "

Yaeger tipped his cap back on his head and mopped his forehead with his handkerchief. "What did I tell you?"

After he left Chester remembered Smoky, who was sitting on the chair closest to the ice-cream cabinet and looking at him with reproachful eyes. Suddenly customers began to come in through both doors, but Smoky had waited long enough. Chester put a small scoop of ice cream on a paper plate and set it down behind the fountain. He heard her purr of satisfaction as she began to eat, and he walked toward the front of the store wondering why the sound gave him so much pleasure.

The family had made careful plans for the time when Kit would have to go to the Philadelphia Lying-in. "A hell of a name, but a damned good hospital, from all I hear," Chester kept saying to customers who asked. He had wanted her to go a day or two before, instead of waiting until the last minute, but everybody seemed to be having babies, and the hospital needed the space. Patrolman Yaeger, in for his afternoon cigar, inquired, "How's the missus?" He sat down heavily at one of the tables in the back of the store, where he couldn't be seen easily from outside.

"She's going tomorrow. It's all arranged. I sure wish it was over."

George was in a dither about leftover Easter eggs. "Everybody buys them before Easter and you can't hardly give 'em away after. There they are, the best line of eggs we've ever had—everybody said so. Now you can't hardly give them away. The pound-and-a-half ones that we sold for a dollar, which was darn cheap anyway, I've marked down to thirty-five cents—less than cost—and we haven't sold one since Easter."

"Right now I don't care a damn about Easter eggs. We did a good business in them, and right now your mother is lying upstairs waiting to go to the hospital tomorrow. I can't think about anything else. Do whatever you want."

Patrolman Yaeger contemplated his cigar. "My old man had a confectionery—learned to make candy in the old country. What he used to do with leftover Easter eggs was to put them away in tins right after Easter. Everybody eats so many they don't want to look at them for a while, much less buy them. Also it established quite a reputation for my old man's eggs, being as he always appeared to sell out. Then, along in June, when chocolate-coated candies begin turning gray, he'd melt down Easter eggs and make chocolate coconut fudge out of them. The coconut cream would be good and mellow, better than at Easter, and people looked forward to that fudge, never knowing it was left over from Easter."

"That was easy for him, knowing how and having the place," George said.

"Nothing to it. I'll show you how and you can do it on the gas range, ten or fifteen pounds at a time. You're right, you can't give those eggs away right now. Put them away for a while, and when you're ready to make fudge let me know."

There was the distant sound of sirens, and Chester said, "Must be a fire somewhere."

Patrolman Yaeger said, "No, that's a police car—there are two of them, and there's another. Something's up." Almost before he was out of the store, the corner was a maelstrom of red cars and motorcycles, all with their sirens screaming.

Chester remembered Dickie's descriptions of the raid on the slot machines and wondered whether the Mayor's raid on numbers was under way, with his store as a mistaken object of it, but no, cars and motorcycles turned up Camac Street, while police ran up the alley that separated the rear of the McClellan Street houses from those on Camac. Chester and George both ran out to watch; windows opened and heads were stuck out all along the block. Far up at the other end of the street there was similar confusion and noise.

Patrolman Yaeger said, "I better find out what's behind all this," and then saw the detective he had pointed out a few days earlier. "You're from the Hall; I've seen you around and wondered what was up. Can you tell me now?"

"Sure. We got Eddie Waldo cornered up the street—915. His girl lives there."

"The bait in a trap that's all set to spring."

"That's right, flatfoot. You better get busy and tell these people to get off the street. There's going to be a lot of shooting." The detective walked on, with a quietly insolent manner.

"I hate those City Hall dicks. It's a pleasure when one goes back to pounding beats."

"Who's Eddie Waldo?" Chester asked.

"Public Enemy Four or Five. Friend of that Willie Sutton they caught trying to escape from the Eastern Pen a short time back. Eddie grew up on this beat, a few blocks from here. A nice boy then. We were good friends. I bet he'd still remember me. Too bad he went wrong."

Sirens were still screaming, and Chester wondered what the poor man was thinking, trapped in 915. Nine-fifteen? Mrs. Waldman lived there! Waldman—Waldo. Of course. But what about the Piel kids, who lived downstairs? Mrs. Piel always said how worried she was, all day while she worked, leaving the baby and the little boy with Gracie, who couldn't be over seven or eight.

"Yaeger, do you think he'd come down if he heard a friendly voice? All this noise is enough to drive a man desperate."

"I was thinking the same thing, but I wouldn't dare stick my neck out, going up to the inspector there and suggesting it. He's trigger happy, itching for blood, and so are the rest of them. I'd be broke, and I'd hate to take the chance of losing my pension."

"The woman, Mrs. Waldman, came in the store a lot and was real friendly."

Chester suddenly realized what he had to do. Mrs. Waldman was in danger and so were the Piel kids.

"If you won't, I will. Come with me." He could hear Yaeger follow as he ran over.

"You are in charge here?"

"Look, I've no time to talk. We've a dangerous criminal cornered, and he'll fight like a rat. You, patrolman, should know better than to let this man through. Get him away."

"He'll have to carry me then." Chester could hardly believe it was himself talking. "I'm almost certain there's a baby, a two-year-old boy, and a seven-year-old girl alone on the second floor of that house. If one of them's hurt, or anybody else on the street, I'll go right to the top. I know the Mayor personally" (which was stretching it, he thought) "and I'll tell him you made no attempt to get that man out peaceably."

"He's a rat, a cornered rat, loaded down with guns. Say, who are you anyway?"

"Chester Jones. I have the store down at the corner. The woman this man came to see is a regular customer. Is she up there too?"

"So my men say."

"They must be hiding up there, watching from under the shades —I see they're lowered. Let me go out and shout up to them, tell them they'll only get killed. God Almighty, I'd turn into a killer myself if I had to listen to all this noise."

"Get out of here, I tell you. You'd be shot down as soon as you stepped within his range."

"I'll take the chance. Somebody's got to get those kids out."

The inspector turned to Patrolman Yaeger. "What are you doing here? Get those people off the street."

Chester could see that Yaeger was tongue-tied and spoke for

him. "Yaeger happened to tell me he knew this Eddie Waldo as a boy. He'll take the chance, too, to try and make Waldo see reason."

Yaeger nodded his agreement. "He was a nice boy, growing up. I don't think he'd hurt me."

"If one of those kids got hurt it could cause trouble . . ."

"I'd see to that." Chester thought, maybe Dick takes a little after me, after all.

"O.K. Commit suicide if you want to. Go out and plead with those two and see what it gets you."

"You'll have to cut off all those sirens."

There were orders, and gradually a stillness more ominous than all the sirens prevailed.

Chester only now realized that the police were drawn up in semi-circles on either side of 915, but well out of range of anyone inside the third-floor windows. He tried to walk along the pavement opposite just the way he would in the store. Then he thought of Kit. How could he have forgotten her for a moment? She'd be all upset about the sirens and the noise. Then it occurred to him that she'd want him to do what he was doing.

He kept on walking his store walk until he came opposite those two shaded windows of 915. Poor people, what they must be going through! The fear in her eyes, as he remembered it. That was it: she had been hearing the sirens shrieking, day and night, all the time she had been living there.

There was a little stoop on 918, directly opposite. The house had not been lived in for years, and most of the windowpanes were broken. He thought, if I were in command here, I'd have put men inside, from the back. He mounted the stoop's three steps and looked up at the blinded windows.

"Mrs. Waldman. You know me. I've been arguing with the police, who have ringed the whole street. They said you or your husband would shoot if I came out like I'm doing. I didn't believe it, just from talking to you. Besides, if there's any shooting, the Piel kids might be hurt. You were always nice and friendly down at our store, and I'm asking you to give up and come down."

The shade went up and down, an inch or two. What did that

mean? Only that they heard, or that they agreed? He waited long enough for them to come downstairs, and when they didn't appear he tried again. "You haven't a chance. You'll get killed, and what good will it do if you kill some other people before they do you?"

Until now he hadn't realized that Yaeger was standing by him. Yaeger whispered, "Let me try."

He called, "Hey there, Skinny Waldo. You remember Dutch Yaeger, who was cop on the beat where you lived? Sure you do. Remember me giving you some advice on how to stay out of jams? You wouldn't be in this one if you had taken it. Mr. Jones here and me are both friends of yours. I don't want to see a guy I knew as a kid on my own beat shot up. They got you pinned down, fellow."

What was happening to Yaeger? Suddenly he almost screamed, "Come on down, kid, and bring her with you. Jesus Christ Almighty, there are times that I hate cops too, but there's no use killing yourselves over them."

By the time Chester ran back to the store and upstairs he was out of breath, but he managed to cry out, when Kit was not in the kitchen, "Dear, where are you? Are you all right?" Without waiting for an answer, he dashed toward their bedroom. "Kit, are you all right?"

She looked up at him sleepily. "Of course I'm all right. Chester, what are you in such a stew about?"

"I've been worried to death about you. The sirens, and all that noise, and me running up the street at a time when you might have needed me. Didn't you hear all the racket?"

"Of course I heard a racket. There's always one, isn't there, down here? The trucks passing and the streetcars and fire-engine sirens. Was it any different from all the time?"

Chester began to explain about Mrs. Waldman, who was really the wife of Eddie Waldo, and how the newspapers called him a public enemy, and about the police blocking off Camac Street, preparing to shoot it out with him. Then he told how he had remembered the Piel kids, who lived in the apartment underneath. "You would hardly know Mrs. Piel, because she isn't in often, working all the time. Honest, all I could think about was those youngsters and her not home yet—not home for hours maybe. We do have some kind of responsibility toward the folks around here."

"Of course we do."

"I sort of lost my head, I guess. I didn't even think about how you might be feeling. That's what bothers me now. Or what you would do if something happened to me just at this time. I just barged in. Part of it was something that Mr. Yaeger said, but that's no excuse. The officer in charge of the police said I'd be shot, but I guess all that I could think about was the children and how nice Mrs. Waldman always was. Yaeger and I were frightened, I tell you."

"Chester, you weren't! I've never seen you frightened."

"Yes you have. The day I proposed, in the parlor over the butcher shop."

"I don't believe it! Anyway, I'd never have thought it. You were so cool and collected."

"Now that I know you're all right and weren't worried, I'm glad I did it. Nobody got hurt, and whatever happens to the Waldos, or Waldmans, they're better off than they would have been otherwise."

Kit said, "Chester, do you hear what the children are singing outside? They must be jumping rope."

The lower sash of the side window was open only a couple of inches. He pulled it up all the way and looked out. A colored girl from Fawn Street and a white youngster he didn't recognize, with dirty face and stringy blond hair, so that she reminded him vaguely of Mary Plotko as she had looked years ago, stood on each curb; the rope, knotted in several places, turned lazily between them. A dozen other girls stepped into the rope's arc and began to sing while they skipped:

> "My mother and your mother
> Live across the way.
> Every night they have a fight
> And this is what they say . . ."

The rope began to turn faster and faster, and they kept time to it with the crazy chorus:

> "Aca-baca soda cracker,
> Aca-baca-boo!
> Aca-baca soda cracker—
> Out goes you!"

"Why, we used to sing that years ago, when we jumped rope. Don't they look graceful?"

Chester felt a wonderful quality of peace, sitting there by Kit, while both of them looked out on the street, with its trees still in bud and the feel of spring vibrant in the air. Kit went on talking:

"I hope they do 'Mabel, Mabel, set the table, with your sugar, salt, mustard, pepper.'" She gave a rueful look at herself. "I don't imagine that I'll ever be able to do that again, but I used to be able to pepper longer than any other girl in our street."

He put his arm around her as the colored girl who had been turning rope gave her end of the rope to another and began to skip alone, while the others sang. She had the wonderful grace of most of the colored children and she followed the demands of the song with breath-taking ease.

> "Teddy bear, Teddy bear,
> Turn around, around, around.
> Teddy bear, Teddy bear,
> Touch the ground, ground, ground.
> Teddy bear, Teddy bear,
> Show your shoe, shoe, shoe . . ."

For "Teddy bear, Teddy bear, Skiddoo, skiddoo, skiddoo," she ran beyond the turning rope, first to one side and then to the other. "Go upstairs, upstairs, upstairs" was done with higher and higher jumps, and "Say your prayers, prayers, prayers" with a touch of her knees to the macadam pavement.

Chester said, "It's hard to realize that a little over an hour ago this street was about to become a battlefield—that I thought I was going to be killed."

"I know. I've been thinking the same thing, and for the first time what might have happened frightens me. Chester, it's awful, after what you've just been through, but I think you should get me to the hospital just as fast as you can."

Outside, Teddy bear was turning out the light, light, light, but Chester hardly heard. Why hadn't they put in a telephone upstairs, for emergencies like this? He tripped and almost fell on the stairs. He was too excited, almost, to tell George, but he understood anyway. Chester could hear him calling for one of the new cab ambulances that Yellow had put on, and what seemed an endless time went by before he said, "It's coming, the girl says. Better get Mother down." Somehow George's voice seemed to lack excitement completely, as though he had been calling the Yellow for expectant mothers all his life—which he had, practically.

Chester dashed upstairs again. Why couldn't it have happened a little later, when Kay would have been home? But Kit had an overnight case all ready. He was conscious of being more frightened than he had been earlier in the day, until Kit said, "Please, dear, do try to control yourself. You're making me nervous."

God, if only Honey would come back, but that would be another hour. He tried to carry the overnight case and support Kit as well. Then, to add to his confusion, George shouted upstairs, "Dad, the Cabulance is waiting. Do hurry."

Kit said, "I'll take it easy. All of us don't want to fall."

They got downstairs somehow, but it had been a near thing, Chester thought. The Cabulance driver and Chester both tried to help Kit into the vehicle, until she pushed them aside and got in by herself; Chester climbed in after, to sit by her. As the Cabulance jolted away he mopped his forehead and decided that he was getting too old for this kind of thing. He almost voiced his determination aloud, and decided not to, as Kit mightn't understand, but even her sensibilities couldn't keep him from thinking: This is the last child I'm going to have. He was pleased that he had made up his mind about that, and he waved to George and the neighbors who had gathered on the sidewalk.

## Chapter 12

"Kit, my feet are killing me."

"All she wants is to be walked . . ."

"Why at three o'clock in the morning? I've been looking forward to the pleasure of having a baby around the house again, but I guess I forgot the nights we were up with George and Helen. We're too old for this kind of thing; I propose we send her back."

"She's quieting now. Wait, I'll put the light on."

"Don't. That'll start her off again. I can see well enough with the street light." Chester moved toward the bed, holding the now quiet Alice against his pajama top. It seemed the same course that he had covered a dozen times in the last quarter hour, but he veered enough to walk into some large, unfamiliar object and stubbed his toe. He held the baby tighter, involuntarily, and she began to cry again. "What kind of an infernal machine was that? It feels as though it was made of cast iron."

"Oh, Chester, I'm sorry. It's my portable sewing machine. I was doing some sewing this afternoon."

"The most unportable darn thing I ever saw. Now my feet are tied up in the extension cord. You better put the light on, after all."

"You said you could see." Kit switched the light on, and Chester said:

"I think that's a murderous contraption. If I'd hit it any harder, it would have fallen from this confounded bench it's on and wrecked me completely."

"I should have put it away, but I wasn't finished. Here, give me the baby. Did it really hurt you?"

"What do you think? It didn't feel good, anyway. One thing I know—if I'm going to be up every night we'll have to get another clerk in the store. Mary is fine, but she brings in so much extra business it sort of balances out."

He got into bed and switched off the light. Thank goodness the baby had stopped crying.

"Who do you think you'll get?"

"Don't know yet. I'd rather have some woman who could take over from Dickie in the mornings."

"Let's think who there is in the neighborhood."

"Good grief, Kit. Not now. All I want to do is sleep and not have to wake up for a week."

"Chester, you still like the baby, even if she is a little trouble?"

He heard her distantly and faintly, the words penetrating to him through sleep, but he couldn't answer.

"Sometimes I wish we didn't have so much marble business. It took those boys ten minutes to pick out two agates and a bull's eye," George said.

"I noticed you were being a little impatient with them," Chester answered. "That's not a good way to build up customers. We make a hundred per cent on marbles and things like that. Those boys will be coming in again later for hockey sticks. Who are they, do you know?"

"Never saw them before, but there was a drive-yourself moving truck parked in front of 915, and they were taking furniture in. It looked like a large family. Six or seven strange youngsters were standing around or helping . . ."

"Mrs. Waldman's apartment? Has she moved out?"

"Not that I know of, though she hasn't been in and we haven't been saving the *Bulletin*. They were putting things in through the first-floor-front windows, so they must have taken the place under the Piels. It's been empty for a long time."

"That's the trouble around here. There are too many houses anyway, and then every time they make a big old house into apartments, like they did at 915 and around where Mr. Meyer lives, it means more empty places to be sold at sheriff's sales."

"It isn't that there are too many houses, George. There's too little money to rent them. Like as not this new family has moved into an apartment because they can't afford a house any longer."

"You can rent any of those empty houses on Camac Street for twenty or twenty-five dollars a month. The banks that have taken them over would be glad to rent them for that to responsible parties."

"A family with seven children that rents a three-room apartment isn't a responsible party the way banks think."

"Dad, there's something I want to ask you, now there's nobody here."

"Shoot. Bet I can guess—you want to buy new store fixtures. I've been watching you look at that old cigar case for some time now."

"No. What I want is the lend of your tuxedo. There's a dance Saturday night. The senior class, and it's formal. I've already arranged with Dick about working for me. Trouble is, I don't have a tux. The cheapest are $14.75, and a real good one is $18.50, which seems an awful lot of money to put into something I'll hardly ever wear."

"Do you think you could get into mine? You're taller."

"Just an inch, and you're a lot heavier."

"No use arguing. Try it on when you get upstairs. I haven't worn it since I was Worshipful Master at the lodge, four or five years ago. My recollection is that it was getting a bit tight on me, and the girl you're taking will get an awful scent of moth balls."

"Mother can air it out."

"O.K. As soon as Mary comes we'll see." A woman had come in by the side door, so quietly that Chester hadn't heard her. Maybe Max Herbster was right in having that old-fashioned bell at his door entrance. It did announce customers.

The woman walked over to the magazine rack, where he was standing, and said, "Hello, Mr. Jones."

Her face looked familiar, but there was something about her that was different, that made her hard to place. She said, "It's my hair. I'm having it come in natural and doing it the way I always used to.

If there was one thing I hated, it was that bleached blond hair."

"Mrs. Waldman! Of course."

"I won't bother you, Mr. Jones. I just had to come in and thank you for what you did for Eddie and me. You and that policeman. You don't mind talking to me? After all the commotion we caused and everything?"

"Of course not. I've been worrying about you quite a bit, Mrs. Waldman."

"The name is really Waldo, but Eddie and I decided it might be better to stay Waldman until he gets out, which will be in six or seven years if he gets any breaks. All that stuff in the papers ain't true, about me being a gun moll. We were married long before Eddie first got into trouble. I'd meet him places through ads in the *Bulletin*. That's why I always wanted you to save it for me. He'd been out for months, and then I guess we got careless. We both thought it would be all right for him to come to my place."

"There were plain-clothes detectives on duty day and night for weeks. Patrolman Yaeger pointed them out to me. We didn't know they were watching you, of course. When we found out, we didn't want to see you hurt."

"You might of been killed. Not that Eddie has ever killed anyone, but we were crazy from those sirens. We made up our minds they'd never take us alive. It's hard to know what you might do in a case like that. When the noise stopped all of a sudden, we thought: This is it—and then you came walking out, all alone, the way you look in the store. Only thing was, Eddie didn't know you. 'He's a good guy,' I whispered, but he thought maybe you were just being a stooge for the cops and they'd let us have it when we came out. Then that old cop came running out, and Eddie knew him right away. That did it. It wasn't the kids downstairs so much. I hardly knew them, staying by myself the way I had to, but that cop showing he was on your side, that we weren't all alone . . ."

She fiddled with her hands, the way she used to, out of nervousness, but she no longer had the expression of fear in her eyes. "One thing more. What do you think the folks in the neighborhood will say if I go back to my apartment? I've got no place else to live, really, but all the excitement . . ."

"It's your apartment, and all that will be forgotten in a few weeks." Chester had another idea. "Excuse me for asking, but do you have a job?"

"I did, as a waitress, but they fired me when our pictures were in the papers. Never mind, I'll find something. I always have."

Now that her hair was a natural, soft brown she was nice-looking, if not pretty. She'd be trustworthy, too, he knew she would.

"You know we have a new addition to our family—a little girl— and we really need more help in the store. How would you like to work here? You wouldn't make much in tips, but we'd pay you as well as we can and you'd be living close by." He could see George's face storming up, from out of the corner of his eye, but he'd win him over. "Besides, it might help a little for people in the neighborhood to know we're in back of you."

Instead of looking pleased she seemed about to collapse. He helped her over to a chair at one of the little tables. "I'm sorry. You sort of took me by surprise. I stood outside awhile trying to decide whether, if I came in, you'd even talk to me. Do you really mean it?"

"Of course I do. Do you have some kind of uniform to save your clothes? It gets messy around the fountain."

"Sure I have."

"Tomorrow morning, then, at eight-thirty. I'll work with you till you learn to know the stock. Meanwhile I know you'll want to get back to your place. Do you have any food in?"

"I guess so. I don't know. I got in a few extra things I knew Eddie liked, to give him a home-cooked meal—anyway, as good as I could on a gas hot plate. We were just eating when we heard— when we heard them. He knew it was for him, right away."

"Try to forget. Take a rest now."

As Mrs. Waldman went out the side door Dick came in the front. Before Chester could say anything George exploded. "Dick, what do you think Father has just done? He's hired that Mrs. Waldman, whom the police arrested with that escaped jailbird!"

Whatever the cause, a change had certainly come over Dickie. He even had a collar on, with the tie tied up in a knot instead of hanging down four or five inches. As usual you could not tell from his expression what he was really thinking. "So?"

"To work in the store! Imagine!"

"I am imagining. It seems like a good idea to me—better than a lot of Dad's. I bet she'll never take a dime from the registers. What are your objections, O good and noble elder brother?"

George stood in the middle of the room and turned around slowly, catching reflections of himself from various angles in the long mirror of Mother's dressing table. "What do you think?"

"It fits better than I expected," Dad said. "I was afraid that, you being taller, the pants would be too short, but they look fine."

Mother said, "Stand still for a minute. It's so seldom that I ever see anyone in evening clothes, I'd hardly know, but it doesn't look right somehow. Maybe I just imagine it."

"It feels all right, and the sleeves are just right."

"You know what I think?" Dad said. "I think that in order to tell what it looks like you need to put on the things that go with it. Any tuxedo would look funny with those brown shoes and that sport shirt. Kit, where are the fixings that go with this?"

"The shirt and black tie are in your top bureau drawer, and I guess your black slippers——"

"George better wear his own black shoes. Go on, now, and do the job right. Don't worry about the store—Mary came in a while ago."

All this fuss about trying on a suit. But the dance was to be at the Walton and he was taking Myra Lang, who was pretty particular, so he did want to be sure that he wouldn't look funny in Dad's suit. He took the tie and shirt upstairs, and when he came down again he was completely dressed except for the bow. "Mother, can you tie this? I can't get both ends to come out the same."

Dad was right, it did look better now, but it still didn't look quite right, even though Mother said, "George, you look positively stunning. A tuxedo certainly gives you a distinguished air."

Helen poked her head in the door. "Aren't you dressed up! Formal! Turn around and let's see."

Mary's voice. What the dickens was this, a public exhibition? But Mary was pretty smart. She could tell better than Dad or Mother if it didn't look well. "Mary, tell me what you think," he called.

Mary sure was an odd girl. He'd never want to fall in love with a girl like her, of course, or marry her, but he could understand why other fellows might. Maybe it was because he had known her when she was little, and her family. She stood there blank-eyed, the way she always did, without answering.

"It's Dad's suit, and I want to wear it to a dance if it's not too old-fashioned. It fits fine, but somehow it doesn't look right to me."

Surprising how everyone waited quietly to hear what she would say. "I know what it is, George. The trousers are the main trouble. They're making them a little fuller now."

"I hate to buy a tux just to wear once. You don't think they'll do?"

"If you want me to try, I think I could make them do. It all depends how much material there is in the seams that I could let out." She dropped down on the floor beside him and began to turn up the trouser leg. It felt funny as heck having Mary do that, but she didn't seem to think anything about it and neither did the family.

"There's over an inch on the inner seam. I can fix them, all right."

She stood up, and he tried to compare her with Myra, but you couldn't. Myra's folks were pretty well off and she had what the fellows called "class." She was good-looking and awful smart, too, and what a fellow needed who was going to be a very successful businessman was a wife behind him who was worthy of him.

Mary was saying something else. "The coat is fine, but you know, George, you're not quite as broad as Mr. Jones. Besides, they're putting more padding in the shoulders than they did when this was made. I think I could fix that easy with shoulder pads out of one of my dresses. I couldn't do much of a job, because I wouldn't want to change the way the sleeves are set in, but nobody would see the inside, and I think it would make a great improvement."

She was right about the shoulders, that was sure. George remembered that was what he liked about his last suit—the broad shoulders it gave him.

She turned to Mother and asked, "You don't mind if I do it on your portable tomorrow? I couldn't do nearly such a good job on my foot machine."

"Of course not, Mary, dear. We'll all be grateful to you."

Then Dad said, "Yes indeed, son, we want to see you done up proud. You're always talking about this wonderful Myra Lang that you're going out with. Why don't you bring her down here sometime, so we can look her over?"

Mary seemed to get away in an awful hurry. "I better get downstairs and help Dickie," she said, and left.

"This is one time I'd like to drive our own car. We hardly use it enough to keep it from getting rusty."

"That's just it, son. It's so much easier to take a cab, I think, and cheaper in the long run. I don't know why I ever bought it anyway, except everybody else had one." Dad half laughed. "The real answer, George, and one that every storekeeper should keep in his mind when he buys something he doesn't need or shouldn't have, is that I was sold into it. We didn't need the Lafayette, and besides—if I was buying a car—it would have been better to get a kind that everyone knew. Any time you want an example of your dad's bad judgment you have it there."

"But I can drive it?"

"Of course you can. I thought taking the taxi would be more convenient, that's all, and that you were worrying about how much the taxi would cost."

"No, I want to go for her in our own car. They're pretty well off. Her father was one of the top assistants in liquidating those banks that closed."

"I see your point."

"He was transferred here from Pittsburgh. You know, Dad, sometimes I think the only sensible thing for a fellow to do is to try and get a government job. Then you don't have to worry like we do, whether we buy too many seasonal items that won't keep. Except that in the government there's always some boss higher than you are. I don't like that."

"I don't like it either."

"That's one of the reasons I like keeping store, until I get to thinking about fellows like Myra's dad, making a darn good living their whole lifetime out of closing a lot of banks."

"Maybe he's not making such a good living."

"They live out in Overbrook, in a big house. You should see it, Dad. There's lawn all the way around and flower beds. I'm almost ashamed to bring her down here, to see how we live."

"I thought we kept a pretty nice home."

George didn't want to hurt Dad's feelings by telling him the differences. For one thing, out where Myra lived there were no colored and no Italians. And the Jews were all high-class, not like Saul Gerson's father, going around in a funny hat and a long beard all the time.

"Sure we do," he said, "but it's all over the store. It's more dignified, or something, when you can live separate from where you make your money. Mainly it's that they're not hemmed in by other houses like we are. There must be—oh, I don't know—fifty feet between them and the folks next door. Imagine!"

"I sort of thought it was good to be near other folks, instead of keeping them at a distance. It's real nice for me to know that everybody around here is close."

"Sure it is, Dad." And it was, only at the same time it wasn't, but how could you explain? Especially if you had any ambition? Anybody knew that when you really had ambition you never did things the way Dad did them. Things like hiring that Mrs. Waldman.

The way Mary had altered the tuxedo was a miracle, especially the way she had fixed the coat. He looked at himself in the mirror behind the soda fountain. Gosh, I'm almost good-looking, he thought. Anyway, for me.

Dad gave him the keys for the car, and when Mary finally finished waiting on Mr. Rivkin—who was more of a pest than ever, since Mary began working in the store—she came back to where he was standing. "Let me see, George." She put her head first on one side and then on the other. Sometimes she was darn pretty, even when she looked so serious. She felt where she had put in the shoulder pads. "Maybe I could have the pads out a little bit more, but the way the coat is cut I wasn't sure. They help anyway."

"It's like a new suit. I never knew you could do things like that."

"There's a lot you don't know. And your tie's crooked. Let me fix it for you."

She took an awful long time. Gosh, he didn't want to be late and he still had to get the car, which was usually on the top floor of the garage and had to be brought down on the elevator, and that took forever. "I hope you have a nice time, George," she said very low and with something in her expression as though maybe she didn't mean it.

Helen and Kay came downstairs and told him how fine he looked.

Mary said, "Just a second more, George. There's some lint on the back of your coat," and began to pick it off, but he said, "Let it go. So long, Dad. Thanks again, Mary," and hurried for the side door before anything else happened to delay him.

Dancing was a lot harder than walking. The reluctant muscles that he'd forced back into use, so that he didn't have to think of them any more when he walked, were being stubborn now. George had managed before at dances by half-timing, but Myra was a peppy dancer. She kept saying, "The music is too drippy, George. Let's double-time," and he couldn't tell her about his leg.

She was wearing a new dress of bright yellow chiffon and looked beautiful in it. The color seemed to reflect in her skin and eyes, giving them greater warmth. She was nice to hold, just close enough so that he could feel the least softness against his tux, but just the same he was glad whenever one of the fellows in the class cut in.

Lew Langer did now, and George went to the men's room. Reinhold and Quinn were in there, both with pints of whisky that they were offering around, pretending to be half drunk. Quinn said, "Have a drink, Jonesy, old sobersides. Brighten you up a little."

Quinn was almost as old as himself, but there was some excuse for George's still being in high school whereas Quinn was just stupid. This was the third time he'd been in a graduating class, but he probably wouldn't graduate even this time.

George said, "No, thanks," and then, so his refusal wouldn't sound unmanly, "I just had a drink at the bar."

"A fellow who would pay fifty cents up there for just one drink, when you can get a whole pint for a dollar, is nothing but a sucker. Come on, Jones, you better catch up with us."

George retreated into a pay toilet. When he came out Quinn had gone and Reinhold was being sick into one of the washbasins. A silly way to waste your money, just showing off.

He returned to the ballroom as the dance ended, and Lew brought Myra back to him. "She's sharp, really sharp," Lew said, inferring in a way that George wasn't. He led Myra toward the chairs along the wall, opposite where the orchestra was, and she said, "Lew Langer had the most wonderful idea, George. The floor show's on upstairs in the roof garden in fifteen minutes. He's going up with his date. What say we join them?"

The roof garden! That would be expensive. But what could he say? Besides, he wouldn't have to dance for a while. "Sure, I think it's a good idea." He thought of cover charges and minimums. Fortunately Dad had given him twenty dollars out of the front cash register before he left, for emergencies. He hadn't wanted to take it, and had only thought of using it for a flat tire or something like that. Maybe Dad knew what could happen when you went on a date in a tux.

It might be expensive, but he couldn't be angry with Myra, the way she was standing there looking at him, smiling so that most of her even white teeth showed. There was a new expression in her eyes. They were squinted a little in the corners from smiling, but it was something else—maybe the way she turned her head a little and didn't look straight at him. "Tell Lew that we'll share the same table. I'm awfully tired of these kids and this will be a good time to break away from them."

Myra couldn't be nearly as old as himself, and neither Lew Langer nor his date was over nineteen. What were they all but kids? Myra was trying to show off, the way the two fellows had in the men's room. Fellows showed off by drinking, or telling how strong they were, but girls did it by trying to appear older and more sophisticated than they were.

George went over to where Lew was sitting with his girl. "Myra said you were going up to the roof garden to see the floor show and that you'd sit with us."

"Yeah? Why, that's swell of you, Jonesy. Sure we will, won't we?"

His girl was funny-looking, with popping blue eyes like the kind on the dolls they had bought for the store three Christmases ago and still hadn't sold out.

What's swell about it, George wondered.

"By the way, Miss Smith, meet Mr. Jones. Smith, Jones—sort of a joke, huh? But that's how it is. Old Jonesy is in my class."

George was hating Lew more every minute, but he said, "Pleased to meet you. Yes, we're in the same class. Where will we meet you . . ."

"In the lobby," Lew said, and Miss Smith, her eyes rolling as though the elastic behind them had become undone, said:

"I'd like to go to the powder room first." She made signs toward Myra, who nodded. "We'll meet you in the lobby."

Why do they call this place a roof *garden*, George wondered. It was on the roof, all right. It wasn't often that he had to ride on elevators, and the sudden upward swoop of the special elevator had made him dizzy. But there weren't any flowers or plants, and there were no windows to look out of so that you could tell you were so high up. Shaded lights on tables crowded close together furnished the only illumination, but as he followed a waiter and the others trailed behind him he could feel that they were walking over thick carpeting. There was hardly room to walk between the tables. They were finally crowded in at a table facing a stage, where an orchestra was playing.

It was the first time George had been to such a place and he envied Lew, who acted as though he had been going to night clubs all his life. The first waiter left, but almost immediately another one appeared and stood beside them expectantly. Lew said, "Lola, what will you have?"

"Creme de menthe frappé."

Myra said, "I'll have the same. White mint."

"Whisky sour," Lew said.

"Of course you are all over twenty-one?" the waiter asked, very softly and inoffensively, George thought, but Lew was angry right away.

"Lola, listen to that, will you?"

Myra said, "Of all the nerve!"

"It's been a long time since anybody asked me that," Lew said, going on being indignant.

148

"I'm sorry, sir," the waiter said. "Two frappés and a whisky sour. What will you have?"

George had been trying to decide. Should he try a whisky sour just because that was what Lew had ordered? No. Lew was a fake, showing off, and the waiter knew it. "I'll have a Coke, please."

"Yes, sir. Rum and Coke."

"No, just a Coke. I'm not twenty-one yet."

Myra was looking daggers at him, but he didn't care. She had got him to come up to this place, which was for grownups, not for kids, and right now he felt they were all being very kiddish.

The waiter said, "Very good, sir," and walked away. Just as the stage was suddenly spotlighted, George saw the little card on the table. It said: "Minimum check, $2.00 each."

Gosh, that would be four dollars for the two of them. He hadn't thought it would be that expensive, but he guessed there wasn't much he could do about it now. One thing, he'd see they didn't spend any more than that.

Myra seemed to have forgotten she was angry with him and was keeping time to the music by moving her head from side to side. Then the chorus danced in—eight of the tallest girls George had ever seen.

"Jack Lynch's six-foot chorus," Lew said.

George felt almost ashamed to look at them, they had so little on, except for high headdresses of colored plumes that made them look even taller than they were. When the acts changed, Lew beckoned to the waiter and ordered another round of drinks.

A man came out who turned out to be the master of ceremonies. He told some stories and then began to do imitations. He did an imitation of Father Coughlin and one of Huey Long. It was easy to see he didn't like either of them. Then he did an imitation of the way Walter Winchell talked on the radio for Jergens Lotion. Advertising was wonderful—you always thought of Winchell and "an ocean of lotion." Which reminded George that he'd sold their last bottle and hadn't put it on the list to order.

Afterward he sang "Pennies from Heaven" the way Morton Downey would sing it in his light Irish tenor, and then the way Jimmy Durante would sing it, and finally in Bing Crosby's style. As it was Bing's song anyway, and you could hardly tell it wasn't him on the radio, the master of ceremonies got a big hand.

Then there was a magician, dressed in long Eastern robes, who ended his act by bringing out baby chicks from all kinds of improbable places. When the chorus of tall girls came out again, the magician went among the customers and found chicks under table-cloths and in teacups. He came over to their table just as the show ended and the spotlight was turned off.

While he kept saying, "Gilly, gilly," he drew a chick right out of the front of Myra's dress and another out of Lola Smith's hair, but the payoff came when he asked George to look in his own pocket and George himself drew out four, five, then six chicks before his pocket was empty.

George thought it was the best part of the whole show until Lew said, "Jonesy, when a fellow does an act at your table, for you personally, you should give him something. I suggest a couple of bucks."

Come to think of it, he remembered that the gilly-gilly man had been handed something at other tables. A dollar was enough. He handed it to the man, who seemed entirely satisfied.

There were fresh drinks on the table. Lew must have ordered them while I was taking chicks out of my pocket, George thought. Fortunately I'm only drinking Cokes, which can't cost much. He wondered if, when they divided the cost of the check, they should do it equally or on the cost of the drinks each had had. If Lew was fair, he'd want to pay more.

Apparently the floor show was over. Lew said, "I'll be right back. There's a fellow over there I want to talk to," and walked away.

The waiter said, "Will there be anything else?" and Myra gave a squeal.

"George, it's almost one! You shouldn't keep me out this late."

The bill came. Three, six, nine—holy smoke, seventy-five cents each for the Cokes! Lew hadn't come back yet, so George paid with the twenty-dollar bill that Dad had given him. Twelve thirty-seven for just sitting there a little over an hour. Lew returned with the waiter. "Had to see a man about a dog. Ready to go, everybody?"

The waiter held out the change, and George had begun to put

it in his pocket when Lew whispered, "The tip, Jonesy. Better leave a couple of bucks."

George remembered something about ten per cent and left a dollar and the coins. With what he'd given the magician, Lew owed him seven-fifty. The best thing to do would be to step aside somewhere when they got downstairs and settle up. He started to suggest that in the elevator, but before he could Lew said, "Thank you for a swell party, Jonesy. We'll have another sometime, when it'll be on me."

Lola Smith kept saying, "It certainly was." George waited for Myra to explain that there was some misunderstanding, but she didn't.

When they got to the sidewalk Lew said, "If you're taking Myra home in your car, Jonesy, you can drop us off at Sixty-third, which is practically where she lives."

He had been looking forward to driving Myra home, but suddenly he didn't care. "O.K.," he said, "sit in the back."

## Chapter 13

There was a smear on the side window. Honey should have noticed it, or Mrs. Waldman. One thing I do like is clean store windows, Chester thought. He examined the front window and the back, where the telephone booths were built. They were clean, which only made the smear more noticeable. He'd have to tell Mary when she came in.

This was the nicest time of the day, when the newspaper rush was over and most of his customers were having dinner. In another half hour people would be coming in to buy containers of ice cream for dessert, but now the store was empty. It was almost seven o'clock, but out on the street it was still broad daylight. Summer was almost here again; they'd had daylight saving for a week. Why hadn't they named it "daylight spending"? That's what it was, using the daylight rather than saving it. Watching the boys playing hockey on roller skates he forgot the smear. The puck was a short length of broomstick. What if it hit one of the windows? He could hardly chase the kids away—they had all bought their hockey sticks from him. Besides, what difference did it make? All the glass was insured.

He went over to the side doorway, where he could see them better. A colored boy was running the puck, his stick guiding it from side to side, his body swaying toward whichever way he wished to turn. Another colored boy, much shorter and darker, intercepted him and sent the puck down the street in a low arc.

It was the same in all the sports on the street. The colored boys were usually a little quicker than the white ones. That's why they were always divided when sides were chosen. A good thing, too. It would be bad to have all the colored boys on one side.

He wondered who these two were. Several Negro families had moved into houses on Camac Street.

Ernie Murray took the puck from the Thomas boy. Ernie was tall, slender, and handsome, with the complexion of a bar of Hershey's milk chocolate. Which reminded him, he'd have to put Hershey bars on Spewack's order; there weren't any left, unless Helen or Dick had put a box of them in the wrong place, as happened sometimes.

Ernie's father worked in the post office and they owned their own house, up on the next block of Camac. Ernie had the puck again and raced up the street with it, the others in full chase. Wonderful how exciting a street game could be, even just watching it.

Saul Gerson stopped outside. "Hello, Mr. Jones."

"Hello, Saul. Say, tell me something. Why do they call it 'daylight saving' instead of 'daylight spending'? Seems to me these kids are spending it—in the best way possible. I wish I could join them."

"Why is 'saving' something we should do and 'hoarding,' which is the same thing, something we shouldn't do?"

"A question on a par with mine."

"Or when you watch a murderer killing off your own people? When is it good to be neutral and bad to intervene? Can't you see what's going to happen, Mr. Jones? Unless fascism is stopped—stopped cold—there'll be a war. What better time to stop it? Spain is the place and Franco is the enemy. Anyway, he's the front man for the enemy. I'm leaving tomorrow to join the Abraham Lincoln Brigade, and I wanted to say good-by. Is Kay home?"

"I'm sorry to hear you say that. If you were fighting for the U.S., now . . ."

"I will be, just as much as if I were wearing its uniform. You'll see."

"We'll always be thinking about you. And Kay is upstairs, I'm pretty sure. She came home from work an hour ago."

153

Saul didn't seem to be gone more than a minute before he was back again. "I want to go away, Mr. Jones, without any long good-bys. I had to see Kay, though. You don't know how much I've always liked her, except I learned to know, a long time ago, that I wouldn't be right for her. Kay is someone to whom security is more important than anything else, and I would never have been able to give it to her."

"Well, now, I don't know . . ."

"I've never been able to keep a job, and what security does a violinist have? Look at Mr. Meyer. No, Mr. Jones, I try to figure out things as realistically as I can. But I have to hurry around to Fawn Street. I do want to see Gert Cameron. Actually, I guess that she and her father are the only people in the whole world who understand what I'm doing and why. Even my father doesn't. Doesn't that tie you, when you think that he considers himself about as great a dissenter as Justice Holmes?"

"Don't know as I've seen either of the Camerons this week. I've the impression her father is out in Detroit. It usually seems that wherever he is there are strikes going on. If you want me to, I'll tell Gert you were around, next time she comes in."

Well, that was that. I did all I could, Chester thought. Boys going to war again, only twenty years after the last time. Could Saul be right? Was there such a thing as a common enemy to a world that was otherwise peace-loving? After all, Saul was the most intelligent boy in the neighborhood, with the possible exception of Dickie, who would never get himself involved the way Saul was.

Dick came in, as if Chester's thoughts had brought him. "Hi, Dad. Just heard a funny story about old Mr. Meyer. He's in an orchestra—a WPA project that's giving concerts out in the park, in front of the art museum. Seems he forgot to wear suspenders or to button them or something. Anyway, he was right in the front row, and at the end of the piece, when they all stood up, his trousers fell down."

"Now, Dickie, I don't believe that. Mr. Meyer is always complaining about his arthritis. How could he play?"

"You don't have to be able to play in a WPA orchestra. No, it's so; everybody from around here went up to hear the concert, on account of Mr. Meyer being in it. Say, look at George in the Lafayette." They watched him back it into a space across the street. "My all-powerful and benign elder brother isn't so hot at parking."

"I've been going to tell you before, son, that you overwork this elder-brother business toward George. I admit he's a little bossy at times, but you rile him too much."

"Sorry, Dad. All I try to do is cut him down to his own size. I tried for years, but nothing worked until I hit on this. By the way, before he comes in, I want a driver's license, but you have to sign. I have the forms upstairs. How about it?"

"Aren't you a little young?"

"I'll make a bet with you that I pass the test the first time, instead of being turned down twice, like elder brother was."

"There goes that elder-brother business again."

"You will sign?"

"Yes. But I don't want you using the car without telling me."

"Thank you, O wise and noble father."

"Cutting me down to size too?"

It was impossible to dislike Dickie or be angry with him. Who else had a smile like his, or his way of looking at you? "No, Dad. In your case it was a heartfelt expression."

"Get upstairs with you. And tell your mother I'll be up too, as soon as Mary comes in. O young and annoying upstart." Two could play at this game.

"Dad, have you ever closed your eyes and imagined exactly the kind of store you wanted to have, with just the right location and the best-looking fixtures, with everything planned just right, and then, like a miracle, you saw it, just the way you imagined?"

"I sure have. Right here. I imagined this store for a long time before we could do it over the way I wanted, with windows along the side and the telephone booths in the window farther back. There are a few things I might change, but it came out just about the way I imagined."

"Oh, this place!"

"What's wrong with it, George? It has raised a family in some pretty bad years."

"But you've never seen *this* store. Dad, it has everything. You never saw such a fountain. And everything behind it of stainless steel. The breakfast business alone that you could do there! A refrigerated candy case. It doesn't matter whether it's June or January. Honest, you can't imagine how perfect it is. We'll never get a chance to get anything like it again. Not that there aren't a lot of things that we could do, knowing the business, that this man hasn't done. Like a library. Imagine this beautiful store without one! Not that they bring in a whole lot, but the folks who rent books are the best customers we have, aren't they? You've always said so."

"Right now I'm having a little trouble following you. Am I supposed to be interested because this place doesn't have a lending library, which would be profitable for it to have, or the other way around?"

"Dad, you have to realize. This store is in a neighborhood that isn't like ours, but strictly first-class."

"I've always felt this is a pretty nice neighborhood."

"Yeah, sure. The people are all right."

"You don't sound as though they are."

"Sure they are. But they're mostly foreigners of one sort or another. This place I'm telling about has all big houses around—no rows of small houses. There aren't many twin houses, even. The store is right on the corner. There'd be no competition either; there's not another store in blocks and no place to put one. I tell you, it's perfect."

Chester scratched his head. "What do you propose?"

"I want you to drive out to Overbrook with me and look at it."

"Oh, it's around where that Myra lives. You were going to bring her down here sometime."

"This has nothing to do with her. In fact I haven't seen her for weeks. This place was advertised in yesterday's *Record,* under 'Business Opportunities.' It's the chance of a lifetime, Dad."

"I still don't see what you want to do. Sell this place and buy that? If it's all you say, we probably don't have that kind of money."

"What I've been trying to tell you is that we don't need much money. All we need to do is to take over the notes on the fixtures

156

and buy the stock at cost. There's not over three or four thousand dollars' worth of stock—the owner has been buying light, because of wanting to sell. You must let me show it to you."

"It'll do no harm looking, I guess." He'd promised that he'd help George all he could and he didn't want to destroy his enthusiasm, but another store would mean more work, not less. Then, the possibility of leaving the neighborhood. Damn it, this is *my* neighborhood, he thought. "When Mary comes in call me and I'll go with you. Meanwhile I'm going upstairs and play with the baby awhile. As her father, I ought to be entitled to do something besides carry her around at three o'clock in the morning."

All the way out in the car George raved about the fixtures and the location, but when they parked out in front of the place Chester said, "It's a drugstore. You never told me that."

"Because I know that you're prejudiced. That's where the real money is, Dad, in prescriptions."

"I'm not prejudiced against drugstores for druggists."

"You can always hire them. The man who owns this place isn't a druggist either."

"Maybe that's why he wants to sell."

"He had a heart attack."

"When he saw how much he was losing. But I'm not being fair. Come on, son, let's go inside. Before we do, though, I want to explain how I feel about drugstores. I don't like the idea of having someone working for me who has some specialized knowledge I lack and whose decision I'd have to take."

"Walgreen's, Sunray—all the big chains employ pharmacists."

"I like the word druggist better. And I bet the man at Walgreen's or Sunray who hires the druggists is one too. Besides, we're not one of those chain outfits, but Chester Jones and George Jones, and that's how we should think. If a druggist made a mistake on a prescription while working for us, it would be our responsibility."

Inside, the store was everything that George had said it was—an almost impossible dream that somehow had come true. "Look at the cigar case, Dad. A built-in humidifier, so you never need worry about stock drying out on you. This is the refrigerated candy case;

isn't it the last word? That's all double glass, so it doesn't steam up. But what I really want you to see is the lunch counter. He's got away from the old soda-fountain idea of having the customers sit up on high stools. This table-height counter is a lot more modern. The linen-looking finish on top is formica, a kind of plastic that won't chip or crack the way marble will."

Chester found himself getting excited in spite of all his caution. There was a whole battery of electric milk-shake mixers. The tiny deep-fat fryer, the grill, a special sandwich grill that toasted on both sides at once, and the bread toaster were all automatic. "It sure is pretty to look at," he said.

The several customers in the store gradually left, and the man who had been waiting on them came over. "Hello, Mr. Jones. I guess this is your father."

"This is Mr. Pope, Dad."

"Sam Pope. I've been in the store business all my life. Used to have a stand on Christian Street, not far from where you folks are, but I moved uptown. Maybe you knew my place, at Eighteenth and Columbia. Sam Popoff's. I changed the name when I came out here. More dignified, it seemed like, but me, inside, I'm still Sam Popoff. Frankly, my place on Columbia Avenue became nothing more than a dump, the way that neighborhood went down. I made a good living there, but I lost plenty when the banks crashed. I'd made out pretty well from buying houses in the neighborhood, too. I lost all that, but that never bothered me like the twelve–fifteen thousand of store money that I dropped. Money that I worked for."

Sam Pope reminded Chester a little of Phil Glickman, whom he'd bought from. Phil Glickman as he'd look today, going bald and with thick glasses that made his eyes look like distant electric-blue pin points. An excitable kind of chap and a fast talker, so that you could hardly get a word of your own in edgewise.

"If that bank hadn't failed—at Columbia and the Ridge, it was— I'd never have had to buy the fixtures for this place on down payments and notes, I tell you. Anyway, all the years I was in that dump on Columbia Avenue, getting worse all the time with the low class of people coming in, I kept thinking, Sam, before you die you're going to have a store you can be proud of, and this is it. There ain't anything a store should have that I ain't got, except customers maybe.

"I'm being fair to you, Jones, and if you call me Sam I'll be obliged. Business hasn't been what I hoped for, not enough to pay my notes as I went along. Part of it is that this is a new neighborhood, which ain't developed yet. Part of it's me. 'Sam,' I tells myself, 'you should never of left Columbia Avenue. You've mixed with a bad element most of your life and now you try to go society.' Not that this is society the way the Main Line is, but it's society as compared with Columbia Avenue.

"Then comes this heart attack. Right here in the store, over there by the guess-your-weight scales. I thought I was a goner, I tell you. I would of been, too, but my registered pharmacist comes back from lunch and he knows as much as some doctors—more than one I could name right around here."

Chester thought it was time to explain that he had come out to look, just because George insisted, but that they couldn't possibly buy the store. Before he could even begin, though, Sam Pope took his arm. "Wait until I show you our pharmacy department. This refrigerator is for biologicals. Imagine me, Sam Popoff, whose biggest drug business was aspirins, selling biologicals. Mostly, though, it's still like the old place—Alka-Seltzers at night, Bromos in the morning, and aspirins all the time. I've been tempted to take an aspirin once or twice myself and then I think, go easy, Sam, go easy, so I don't, but when I think of the loss I'm willing to take here, I could eat aspirins by the bottle.

"The thing is, I know I got to take it easy. I've got two sons in Miami Beach. They have stores—good locations—one sundries, the other men's wear. They've been saying, 'Pop, why don't you come down here?'

"It's been a wonderful feeling having this store. You folks, being storekeepers yourselves, understand what it means to have a really perfect place. O.K. I've had my fun and I'm willing to pay for it. I've told your son my terms. Everything strictly aboveboard . . ."

Supper was scrapple. "I could eat it summer and winter," Chester said. "Especially the way Honey does it. A good thing we got Mrs.

Waldman, so Honey could go back to cooking supper for us."

"Fried scrapple is like fried oysters," Dick said. "Both too good to have only part of the year."

"You better eat your fill, Dickie, because your mother says this is the last time we're goin' to have scrapple until November, and we're having it now only because you all like it so."

Dick screwed up his face. " 'Eat your fill.' A nice phrase, Honey. Could I ever?" You could see him begin to remember back. "Yes, but that wasn't scrapple."

"It's the way I do it, Dickie. Mostly scrapple is just hog meat cooked in with corn meal and it ain't from the backside of the hog, if you'll excuse the expression."

"Of course, so far as I'm concerned."

Chester thought, Dick and Honey have some kind of double talk that I don't follow, but her scrapple is sure good in any kind of language.

"There's folks just slice scrapple and put it in the skillet, but not me. I put it in beat-up egg and then sift corn meal over it—not the yellow, but the white. When that sets I put it in beat-up egg again, but this time with a little dry mustard."

Dick almost screamed, "I can't stand it, Honey! That first batch was just a teaser."

Kit said, "Dickie, stop talking so loud—you'll wake the baby."

"Don't you think it's about time for her to join our midnight suppers?" Chester asked. "Especially tonight. There's something I want to discuss with the whole family and get your opinions. The baby is entitled to hers, as it will probably affect her the most."

Kay yawned. "Oh, Dad, do I have to, too? I'm sleepy."

"I won't take long. George and I were looking at another store."

He knew how Kit would take it at first. "Move from here? Chester, you wouldn't!"

"Right now we wouldn't, but maybe eventually. There's a wonderful place for sale at a big sacrifice out in Overbrook."

Helen made a face. "George wants to be nearer that stuck-up Myra."

"She has nothing to do with it. I haven't seen her since the senior dance."

"If everybody keeps interrupting, we may be up all night at that. Now give me the floor for five minutes. George is practically twenty-one. He feels that this store here doesn't hold much future for him. The new place is larger, with greater possibilities. It's a big bargain, there's no question about that, but it's a business that will have to be built up. We have money enough to buy the stock; all we have to do is pay monthly on the unpaid notes for the equipment, which amount to about what this store makes. Some of the notes still have a year to run, others longer, but a year would see us out of the woods.

"George and I figure that the other store will just about pay expenses for a time. The man who wants to sell has been very frank in saying that he hasn't made any money, but George has a lot of ideas for improving the business that only need a little time to carry out. The rent is reasonable and there's a long lease. If everything goes well, and I don't see why it shouldn't, at the end of the year we'd have two stores. We might sell this one and move out to Overbrook, or George might gradually buy that one and this could eventually be Dickie's."

"God forbid!"

"Your comments when I ask for them. This will mean some small privations. Especially it will probably mean more time in the store for all of us, as George would be out at the new place all the time, for a while. Frankly I don't like that, as I'm tired most of the time, but I've got new shoes that I think will help.

"Oh yes, one thing more. If this works out, it will be for the equal benefit of each of you children, including the little newcomer in the front room; George realizes that. Now, Mother, what do you think?"

"This is my home and where I want to live. If we can get a store going for George, that's fine. Tell me something, Chester. I'm so stupid about some things. When you say we would be taking over notes, you mean we'd be going into debt. Could the people who hold the notes take this store if we couldn't pay? Or only the new one?"

"We'd be responsible, but that wouldn't mean losing the store. It's seen us through everything and it will go on doing so. If we can't pay off the notes as quickly as we should, I can always borrow from a bank. Maybe that's the way we should do it anyway. Anyway, you approve?"

"Dear, you've always handled business things; do what you think best."

"Kay, any ideas?"

"I'll help all I can, of course, but it won't mean as much to me as to the others . . ."

"As it's always been taken for granted that she'll marry Sig."

"That's not what I was going to say at all."

"It's what you were thinking."

"Dickie, will you shut up?" Chester thought the kid was going entirely too far. It was easy to see, too, that he was opposed to the idea of the new store. "Your turn is coming. I'm taking you in rotation around the table. Go ahead, Helen."

"I'll work hard as I can, Dad. Every night if you need me." This new attitude of Helen's had been going on for months now, ever since Christmas. He'd almost liked her better before she had got so darn co-operative. There was something about it that he still didn't understand.

"All right, Dickie."

"You don't want my opinion, honestly, Dad."

"Every time I want to do something, Dick's against it," George said.

"I value your opinion a great deal, son. I want you to be sure it's not dictated by feeling against your brother."

"It's dictated by common sense. If George wants to start a store of his own, let him save his money until he can get a small one down here someplace. I know two or three he could buy cheap—good stands, too. You talk about this new neighborhood—about all the big houses with grounds around them, and no row houses. If I wanted to buy a store, I'd pick a location where people live six in a room.

"The people out there have money, George will say, I guess, but will they spend it with you? How many boxes of Whitman's Samplers will that air-conditioned candy case sell? If you need a humidifier to keep cigars from getting dry, you shouldn't have a stand where it takes that long before you sell them.

"There's another thing, and it's personal. For very good reasons of my own I've been planning to spend less time in the store, not more."

"I think that's plain selfish," George began, and Chester interrupted:

"Dickie is entitled to be heard. Everything he's said is pretty sensible, except that I don't like this business about not wanting to do his share in the store."

"I didn't say 'wanting' but 'planning.' I'd thought of hiring someone to take my place a couple of days a week."

"Dickie," said Kit. "We always say how old you are for your years, but you're still pretty young. I've been watching you sneaking off every day and not playing baseball or anything. If you've got a girl, don't you think you ought to tell me about her? Bring her around, and I'll be just as nice and motherly as I can be."

"Which is plenty," Chester said.

Dick had just taken a mouthful of the very last piece of scrapple that Honey had brought in for him. He let out a roar and then began choking.

Kit said, "Dickie, not so much noise!" Then, "You shouldn't open your mouth while you're eating—and there, you've wakened the baby."

Chester couldn't hear the baby, but he guessed that Kit was right, from the way she jumped from the table and ran toward their room. He said, "We'll sleep on it tonight. If you have any new ideas tomorrow, give them to me," and followed Kit.

When he got to their room she was holding Alice in her arms, and they made just about the most beautiful Madonna and Child picture he'd ever seen—prettier, even, than those printed on the cards they used to give out in Sunday school when he was a kid.

"Dear, do you really think this is a good idea?"

"George is the only one of our children who is handicapped."

"Why, Chester Jones, how can you say that? He walks perfectly."

"By an effort of will. I guess I should say that he feels handicapped. Dickie has a lot to do with it. He's always been best around here at baseball and football. Remember how he used to roller-skate? Better than the colored youngsters, even. I'm hoping this store will make George into a well man. If it turns out successfully, it will. If it doesn't, I don't believe we'd lose much unless the depression got really bad again."

He sat down heavily on the side of the bed. "Funny, I know Dickie is right from a business point of view, but a store like this, in a poor neighborhood, even if it was his own, would leave George as tied up inside as he is now."

"I don't think this is such a poor neighborhood, dear. We both grew up in ones like it."

"But not with relief checks, WPA, and CCC. The whole damn alphabet brands it as poor. After five years I don't see any improvement. Worries me sometimes." He yawned. "When I came in and saw you holding the baby it was like the old days. Meant to tell you how good it made me feel, but we got started on this store business."

"Really, Chester? And it will work out, I know it will. Imagine you realizing things about George that I never thought of! I can see that you're right. It's not healthy for a boy to be so serious, and it does have something to do with his being sick . . ."

She placed the baby in the new crib and covered her, then got in bed beside him. "Dear, did you notice the look on Kay's face when Dickie said that about her and Sig? I'm sure they've come to an understanding."

# Chapter 14

M̲r. Yaeger! We thought you were sick, it's been so long since you've been around."

"I've been feeling pretty bad, George. On sick leave two weeks. My prostrate gland has been acting up, which you wouldn't know about at your age. Last week I was about as prostrate as I've ever been in my life. Then I got to thinking about your leftover Easter eggs and me promising to show you how to make fudge out of them. This being my regular eight-to-four week, I reported at roll call so I could show you. You kept them eggs the way I told you?"

"They're all in hard-candy tins, but I haven't looked at them since you suggested putting them away."

"Nice and ripe they'd be. Coconut fondant, if it's made right, gets creamier and creamier. If you've the time right now, I can show you. I don't have to make a pull for pretty near an hour."

Mrs. Waldman was down at the soda fountain, making up simple sirup to add to the soda flavorings and to canned fruits for sundaes. She was good, too. It seemed simple to put sugar and water together and boil them, but the right proportions and the proper amount of cooking meant a lot. George said, "I'm going upstairs for a few minutes. If you get busy, press the buzzer."

Instead of just saying O.K. or something like that, Mrs. Waldman dried her hands on the apron she wore to save her uniform. "Mr. Yaeger, I just have to say how much I appreciate what you did for me and Eddie."

George, who could see that Yaeger didn't recognize her, started to explain, but then the policeman said, "Sure, Skinny Waldo's wife. You lived on my beat too, but I never recognized you when you were living here on Camac Street, with all that bleached hair."

"I'm still living in the same place, thanks to you and Mr. Jones."

"Thanks to him. In all the years I been a cop I was never so scared."

"Eddie wouldn't have hurt you, I'm sure."

"Hell, no. I wasn't scared of him, but of losing my pension. Your pop was George Something-or-other—had a Greek hash joint. I used to stop there a lot on the midnight-to-morning shift, because it was the only place open. It got me in the habit, and I began stopping in the eight-to-four, when you'd be there."

"I remember you!"

"Skinny was a nice kid, and so were you. I was glad when you two took up. I never really understood what happened afterward."

"You know the political crowd that moved in. My God, it seems years ago, but it's only five. Eddie got a job at City Hall through a man who got all sorts of government contracts to build places. This man shook hands with the President, even. There were pictures in the papers of him doing it. He was tied in with the numbers racket and gradually he drew Eddie in. When there was a crackdown Eddie was made the goat. 'The Numbers King,' the newspapers called him. I wanted him to make a clean breast of things—tell on everybody—but he was afraid. It would have been better if he had. But I don't want to bother you with my troubles. The Joneses have been wonderful to me."

One trouble with Mrs. Waldman was that she liked to talk too much, like Dad. "Come on, Mr. Yaeger," George said and led the way upstairs.

Mr. Yaeger sure looked funny with his uniform coat off and one of Honey's aprons around him. He stood in front of the gas range and broke Easter eggs into the largest double boiler George could find in the kitchen.

"You see how creamy these are. My old man used to say that eggs should be made in December to be right for Easter—especially starch-molded eggs, like these. It doesn't matter so much with hand-rolled ones, because in them the fondant isn't reheated. That's what we have to watch now, not to reheat any more than necessary. That's why I'm breaking 'em into small pieces. This two-pounder is a dandy. A work of art really, ain't it? But all these roses and sugar decorations have to come off—they'd just make hard lumps. You stir so the chocolate goes all through the cream, real even. Any lumps that don't soften right, mash with your spoon. Now you see that the water in the boiler is warm, but not hot really. We'll shut off the gas and stir a minute or two more, real brisk. Set those pans you buttered down here."

George did, and Mr. Yaeger began to pour the thick, creamy fudge into them. When he had scraped the last bit of candy out of the pan with a kitchen knife, he mopped his forehead. "First time I've done that in forty years, and to tell you the truth I was afraid it wouldn't come off, but it looks perfect. Wait till it's almost cold, then score it with a knife—not too even, but so it looks homemade. There's about fourteen pounds there, and how long did it take?"

"About ten minutes."

"You put a sign up tomorrow, 'Special Homemade Chocolate Coconut Fudge, Forty-nine Cents a Pound,' and see how it sells. Maybe I'll come in and buy a pound of it myself. Mrs. Yaeger is very fond of fudge."

"I'll fix up a big box of it for you, for showing me."

Mr. Yaeger told his story about the Italian and the apples, then asked, "How's your father? Is he around?"

"He's O.K. We're buying another place, out in Overbrook. Right now he's at the lawyer's. There sure is a lot of red tape to buying out a business. Advertising for creditors, taking inventory of the stock and making sure none of it's on consignment . . ."

"You're moving from this place?"

"I hope so, eventually. This neighborhood is getting worse all the time."

"George, my boy, I can remember when everybody around here, except on the back streets like Fawn, owned their own homes—when there wasn't a rooming house or a made-over apartment. In the depression after the World War a lot of folks lost their homes, and a lot more after the banks crashed, when prosperity was just around the corner, where it has been ever since. I'll be leaving— I've my pull to make. Give my regards to your dad. And your mother?"

"She's got the baby out for a walk."

"Wonderful to have another kid in the family, after not expecting any more. I guess your folks are real happy about it."

"I wouldn't know. I didn't approve." Mr. Yaeger shared the failing of Dad and Mrs. Waldman of talking too much. It was nice of him to help make fudge out of the Easter eggs, but downstairs there was a lot to be done.

Mr. Yaeger put on his coat and hat. "No, I guess you wouldn't." He said good-by and went downstairs, with George behind him. "Good luck on the new store. Good-by, Mrs. Waldo."

After he had gone Mrs. Waldman said, "You know, George, isn't it wonderful to meet a cop who can be a good guy at the same time? It sort of renews your belief in human beings."

He said, "Uh-huh," and went on checking the lending-library books that had not been returned, as tomorrow was the day for the library to be serviced.


Why did Kit cross the street at Camac instead of Twelfth or Thirteenth, where there were traffic lights? He'd told her before how dangerous it was, especially with all the heavy truck traffic there was on McClellan. Chester wanted to run outside and call to her to go back to Thirteenth. At the speed the trucks went, it was dangerous for anybody—let alone a short, stoutish woman pushing a folding baby carriage. They had lost four dogs and two cats under McClellan Street traffic; if cats couldn't make it, how could humans?

But if he called to her now, it would only make her nervous. He waited until she entered the corner door. "Kit, why do you take such chances? I've been watching you cross the street with my heart in my mouth."

"Oh, Chester, you're being silly. I can see, can't I?"

"You can see, but I don't think you can move very fast, especially with Alice in that baby buggy." A tractor trailer thundered past, as though to give weight to his words. "That just came around Twelfth Street on the green light. If you had been starting across when it turned, do you think you could have made it?"

"Oh shush, Chester. You're much too concerned."

"Better to be concerned now than after something happens."

"I love you for it." Kit looked about to say something more, when the *Record* truck pulled up in front. The driver threw a pile of newspapers on the sidewalk, gunned the motor, and was gone.

"Now why the dickens did he leave papers at this time of day? And so many of them? Wait a moment, Kit, till I see what happened that could have caused a special edition." Chester hurried outside and saw the headlines on the top paper. The zeppelin *Hindenburg* destroyed by fire at Lakehurst. What a horrible thing! There were whole pages of photographs, scenes of terror and hysteria. What a scoop for the *Record!* Why, it had only happened a couple of hours ago. He took in the papers and gave one to Kit to take upstairs with her.

"All those poor people burned to death!" she exclaimed. "I don't see why people aren't satisfied with staying on the earth."

"There's a long account of how the *Record* got there first and took the pictures while rescue work was still going on."

Chester was just about to pick up the baby carriage, when Mrs. Rivkin came in. She noticed the headlines right away. "The *Hindenburg*. Germans! They deserve it. I don't feel a bit sorry."

"Now, Mrs. Rivkin, you don't mean that. They're people, like ourselves."

"With what they're doing to us?"

"Some of them perhaps, but the way I see it, you can't convict a nation on account of individuals."

Mrs. Rivkin's eyes left the headlines and pictures. "The baby! Oh, please let me see it; I haven't yet." She looked into the carriage with that peculiar expression that childless women get. "Isn't she beautiful! We've always been wanting to have children, but in getting our business on its feet we have to put first things first."

Chester got the things she asked for and waited, pointedly, for her to pay for them. His interest in the Rivkin enterprise was already large enough—too large—though he couldn't help admiring their courage in a cause that must have been lost before it ever began.

She rooted through her bag. "Ain't that one? I thought sure I had a five. I'll drop in first thing in the morning."

The times she had said that. How she must hate the words! How often, Chester thought, the woman goes out and tries to get credit because the man would lose too much self-respect. It wasn't less difficult for her, but she had greater courage.

George would be wild tomorrow, but Chester said, "It's all right, Mrs. Rivkin, tomorrow is time enough."

Kit had been standing there all the time, listening, waiting for him to carry the baby upstairs. After Mrs. Rivkin left she said, "You softie, you," but not with any bitterness.

There was George, the second from the right in the third row. She hadn't been able to see him at first, among all the students in the various sections of the graduating class. Kit nudged Chester. "There he is."

"Darned if I can pick him out. When I went to school we never had such big classes. Looks like a regiment. Oh, I see him now."

Kit said to Mary Plotko, sitting on her left, "Do you see him, Mary?" Funny, she thought, Mary wanting so much to see George graduate. She never paid him much attention when they worked in the store together.

"I saw him come in," Mary whispered back. "He looks nice, doesn't he? Just like Mr. Jones must have looked when he was George's age."

Pop was sitting next to Mary, and Helen, Kay, and Sig beyond. It was a shame Dickie couldn't come, but it would have been too much for Mrs. Waldman to take care of the store alone. Honey wanted to come too, but somebody had to stay with the baby. Kit was glad Pop could come, to see his first grandson graduate.

Not that George had distinguished himself. Kit examined the program. There his name was, halfway down the list of the group taking the commercial course. That Myra Lang, whom he used to talk about, was class historian. How could she be, when she'd only been in the class a year? George had seemed so crazy about her; what had happened?

Music by the school orchestra, and speeches. The principal and one of the school board. Students who obviously had learned their talks by heart. Kit became restless and glanced around the auditorium. It was filled with parents and friends as restless as herself. There, two rows back, a couple her own age beamed and nodded their heads. She bet they were the parents of the boy who was talking about good citizenship. Well, they had a right to be proud. He was real good-looking and he must be smart, to be asked to make the address. She clapped hard for him when he sat down.

She waited for the moment when the diplomas would be given and George would step up to receive his, but when the time came she was disappointed. All the principal did was pass out a diploma, which was handed from one student to another. She could see that it would take a long time to call the names of all the class and give out diplomas separately, the way she had expected, but it would have been wonderful if they could all have clapped when George came forward for his.

She wondered how many of his classmates were going on to college, how many of them would have jobs to go to. Very few probably. George had said that a lot of the fellows were going directly into CCC camps or into the Army or Navy. He was pretty lucky that way, opening the new store next week. The poor boy had worked hard all month. Sometimes she worried that he'd overdo it, but he looked fine and never complained of being tired the way poor Chester did.

When the exercises were all over George came down to where they were—he'd seen them among all those people, from up on the platform. After they had congratulated him, there came the problem of going home. There were seven of them—excluding Sig, who wasn't going their way—and it was a hard squeeze to get six into the Lafayette.

"I'll go home the way I came, in the subway," Pop said.

"You can't. We want to take you down to the store. You've only seen your youngest granddaughter once since she was born."

"Nice of you to name her for your mother. I appreciate that."

Mary said, "I'll go home in the streetcar. Good-by, everybody."

She was starting away when Chester called her back. "No indeed. We'll go together. I'll drive. Kit, you and Kay sit beside me. Helen, sit back there and Grandpop on this side, with George in the middle. As a special reward for graduating, Mary will sit on your lap."

Honestly, the way Chester behaved sometimes! He shouldn't have done that to Mary. Her face had turned red as a beet. But you couldn't accuse her of being a poor sport. She climbed in after Pop, saying, "If George can stand my hundred and twelve pounds on his lap all the way back to the store, I guess I've got nothing to complain about."

Everything seemed to come together—buying the store for George and then his graduation; expecting to open the new place on the first of July and having the block party on Camac Street in between.

How many years had it been held? It always took place right after school closed, by the Eighth Presbyterian Church, out on Broad Street. Chester had forgotten about it until Mrs. Crozier, the pastor's wife, called on him for a donation. "You can always count on us, Mrs. Crozier," he said, and she answered:

"We do, Mr. Jones. And I hope we shall see you in church again soon."

Any other time she would have brought up the matter of the store being open on Sundays, because she was chairman of the blue-laws committee that was against stores being open then. But as he always donated well to the block party, she wouldn't say anything now. He'd tried to explain to her any number of times that, except for July and August, they might almost as well shut up shop without the Sunday business, when the chain stores were closed, but it had never done any good.

Kit was a Lutheran and he was a Baptist. The only reason they'd ever gone to the Eighth Presbyterian was because it was handy. Maybe that made the kids Presbyterians, though he'd never insisted upon their going if they didn't want to. He answered Mrs. Crozier, "Perhaps you've heard we have a new daughter. She keeps Mrs. Jones pretty well tied down." He wondered if he should say anything about baptizing Alice, but he thought the Presbyterians had some funny ideas on the subject, though he didn't remember just what they were. Kit was talking about taking the baby up to her old church, where her father still went, but to Chester a few drops of water on the head didn't seem an adequate baptism. His folks had believed in total immersion.

"You'll order the ice cream for us?" Mrs. Crozier had come back to the block party.

"Sure will."

"And the soft drinks and frankfurters?"

"The same quantities as last year, I suppose. You sold out almost everything but the candy, remember?"

"Oh, and Mr. Jones, do you happen to know where we can hire a team of horses and an open wagon for the hay ride? Every year they're more difficult to find. I wouldn't be surprised if someday we'll have to give up the hay ride or change to trucks."

"I think I know of one. Handsomest pair of horses you ever saw."

"You don't mean it!"

"The only disadvantage I can see is that they belong to a brewery, but you could put drapes over the side of the wagon and nobody would know."

"God would know, Mr. Jones. No indeed. The brewer's big horses won't run over me!"

"Sorry. Guess I misunderstood. You'd be sitting inside the wagon—not standing in front."

"Oh no, Mr. Jones. The Eighth Presbyterian Church will never stoop to employing a brewer's team, not even if we have to use a truck, which won't do as good as horses for a hay ride, I know."

"Maybe it would, Mrs. Crozier. The young folks don't go because of the horses. They go because they want to lie close to each other in the hay."

"I think you are very much mistaken. I often went on hay rides as a girl. We'd sing Gospel songs together, while the horses jogged along. I'm sure it was because of the horses."

Chester chuckled. There was something he wanted to say, but he guessed he'd got himself into enough hot water already. Time to change the subject. "How about rolls for the hot dogs?"

"Of course. Imagine, I almost forgot them. That would have been disastrous. I must rush now, I've so much to do."

"I'll take care of my part; you needn't worry. I hope you have good weather. Remember three years ago when it rained and you had to postpone it?"

"I do indeed. I've been praying to the Lord all week for a nice, clear day, and I'm sure He'll hear me."

The block party meant a lot of extra work in the store, but everybody seemed to enjoy it. Mary Plotko knew that she did. The whole street was lighted up, with booths along the sidewalks and banners stretched across from the telephone poles and lamp standards. Up at the other end of the street one of the Mummers' Parade marching clubs was playing accordions. She could hear them all that distance, even over the music of the organ-grinder right outside the window. The organ-grinder's little monkey kept looking in and grinning at her. He had a cute way of tipping his little red pillbox of a hat every time someone gave him a penny.

Mr. Jones didn't get fussed at all, keeping track of all the cases of Coca-Cola and orange drink and ginger ale. Right now he was helping some of the church people take off the heavy canvas bags that kept the cans of ice cream cold. Breyer's had delivered the ice cream with the regular order that morning, but it was still good and hard.

She wondered what it would be like to belong to a church group that was nice and friendly, the way these people seemed to be. The times Pop had taken her up to St. Vladimir's, on Berks Street, it had been nice of him, but she had felt strange and everybody had been foreign-looking. That was one thing about the Protestant churches, like the Eighth Presbyterian. They didn't call themselves Ukrainian Orthodox or Roman Catholic, or Greek Catholic like they did down where Mrs. Waldman went. Imagine, she'd never thought of Mrs. Waldman as being Greek, until Mrs. Waldman asked her to go to church that time. It was a lot like St. Vladimir's, and this was the United States, where the heads of religions should be Americans and not live in some other country. When she was a child she had first heard her Pop called a hunky. She had been set apart then and she wouldn't be surprised if she still was, except by the Joneses. Sometimes she thought that she loved Mr. Jones more than she did Pop. Pop was on her hands, but she couldn't go to him with problems, like she could with Mr. and Mrs. Jones.

She continued to think about them while she waited on people in the front of the store. Naturally, with the block party outside, there was practically no ice-cream or fountain business—or candy— but they were selling more of everything else. She knew from George that there was almost no profit in cigarettes, even at fifteen cents instead of two for a quarter, like the chains were charging, but there was in cigars and pipe tobacco. Magazines were doing awfully well too, especially *True Confessions*. Maybe the Presbyterians didn't like to buy them over in their own neighborhood, two blocks away.

There were a lot of people wanted to rent books from the library, too, but George had warned her about renting to people out of the neighborhood unless they put up a deposit, which scared most of them away. Still she had rented all of Jack Woodford's and Tiffany Thayer's, besides *Steps Going Down,* which was all about Philadelphia, over around Franklin Square, and what it was really like.

It was so crowded in the 900 block that the hay-ride truck was in the 1000 block, but it went out full every time. Every few minutes some fellow invited her to take a ride with him, but she turned each one down, hoping that George would ask her. Why did she like him so much? Was it just because he was so like his father?

Well, George didn't ask her, though she hinted several times. Maybe he hadn't liked having her on his lap, coming back from his graduation, which was all Mr. Jones's fault.

Of course George was busy, too. Maybe when the store quieted down a bit he'd ask her to go for a ride. But Gert Cameron came in dressed in pink organdy, which made her look real pretty. Usually she went around in blue denims, but recently she'd been dressing up more.

"Hi, Gertie, want to go for a hay ride?" George asked, which surprised Mary, as he'd always said he didn't like Gert.

When she nodded her head George said, "There's not much of a rush now. Think you can handle it, Mary?"

"Sure. Have a good time." She felt disappointed, though why had she expected anything different? George never paid any attention to her.

They'd no sooner gone than Mr. Jones hurried in. "They've sold out of wienies. Run upstairs and get all there are in the icebox. All the rolls too."

"There aren't any more. I gave them all we had a while ago."

"Sliced sandwich bread, then. It'll have to do."

There were only two five-pound boxes of wienies in the refrigerator and two long loaves of bread. She ran down with them just in time to see the hay-ride truck pull out, with George and Gert sitting in the very back, their feet hanging over the tail gate. She gave the bread and wienies to Mr. Jones and waved to them. Somehow she was glad they weren't back in the hay. Maybe that was because Gert didn't want to get her fancy dress mussed.

"Grab this, will you, Mary?" She turned, and there was Dick, his hands full of parcels. "The one on top—take it off. Homemade chocolate cake. Best I ever tasted. That's for you and this is for Mother."

"For me? Why, Dick, aren't you sweet!"

"I guess I am, at that, but nobody tells me."

"What's in the other package?"

"This is chocolate coconut fudge, and boy, did I get gypped! I bought a dime's worth, and it was so good I got a pound. I asked who made it, and the woman said Dad donated it."

"The fudge Mr. Yaeger made from the old Easter eggs!"

"Exactly. And I paid seventy-five cents for a pound of it. It's really wonderful, though. I never thought of trying it in the store, or there wouldn't have been any to donate."

My, it couldn't have been a long hay ride. There was the truck again. George jumped off and helped Gert. They crossed over to the store through the heavy McClellan Street traffic, and she heard Gert say, "Thanks, George, it was fun. I'm on my way home, so I'll be seeing you."

When George saw Dick he said, "So you're back at last. Mind

the store for a while, will you? I want to take Mary for a hay ride."

"Maybe you'd rather take another ride with Gert. You asked her first." What in the world ever made her say that? She hadn't meant to at all.

"I couldn't very well ask you when there was nobody in the store."

"Come on, I was only fooling. George, let's get over as fast as we can, so we can get a place up inside, back of the driver."

Something was pushing against him, something warm and soft. George had the beginning of a pleasant dream that ended abruptly when he became fully awake and saw that it was that darn dog of Dickie's. He was about to give it a kick from under the covers, but it *was* cute the way it snuggled close, and besides, he knew that Dickie resented that it didn't sleep with him on his bed.

He began to pet Floyd's head, while talking to him loudly enough to wake Dickie, he hoped, and then noticed that the other bed was already empty. That was Dickie's way, doing everything quietly, almost underhandedly. But then, to be honest, George didn't want to get up when Dickie did, to take care of the early paper and breakfast business. It was no hardship to Dickie; he liked to get up early, or so he said, anyway.

What was today? Something special, he partially recalled. Sure, the fight last night, over the radio. Joe Louis had won over Braddock. All the people in the store, listening. A new world's champion! Not that it meant much to George, except for the business it had brought in. Then he remembered. Here he was, thinking about Floyd Gibbons and Joe Louis, when today was the decisive one in his life. By tonight he would be in charge of the new store, even though they wouldn't reopen for a week. He lay there for a while, luxuriating in thoughts of the stainless-steel back bar of the soda and lunch section, the matched Circassian walnut cases, the rubber-tiled floor and the soft indirect lighting, the wall cases with mirrors in back that doubled the apparent amount of stock in them.

For some reason his thoughts shifted to the day before yesterday and the block party. The hay ride with Mary. Somehow it had been more fun with her than with Gert Cameron. But what was he lying here for, when this was the day?

He pushed Floyd out of bed and, when he showed no inclination to go downstairs, put him out on the roof. Gosh, it was almost eight-thirty, and he'd have to eat in the store, which meant paying for his breakfast. He was darn certain that Kay and Dickie always ate there and never paid, but since he was the one who advocated it he'd have to, out of principle.

While he dressed he ticked off in his mind the things to be done. There had been no creditors in response to the legal notice; Popoff had been honest in that respect, and there was no reason to think he wouldn't be about the goods sold, since they had taken the inventory together, but he determined to check just the same.

Dad was taking care of the lease and the notes on the equipment. Oh yes, he had to remind the ice cream people to take out their cabinet, so Breyer's could put in theirs. And the sign man to call up. Jones & Son, they had decided on as a name. Dad had agreed, apparently without noticing that it wasn't plural, which left Dickie out, as he deserved, considering the way he had objected to everything.

Gosh, he was getting butterflies in his stomach just from thinking of all there was to do and from hoping that it would all turn out right, though he knew it would. One thing, though, was certain: He wasn't going to bother about breakfast, when there was so much work ahead of him.

## Chapter 15

It was George's idea to call the new store simply Jones's. They'd thought of Jones & Son, but if they did that, it would mean buying a whole new sign to replace the one that stretched across the front of the store above the windows or replacing Sam Pope's name with smaller letters. This way he only had to have the large raised gilt letters taken off. The sign man used the *s, o,* and *e,* so there were only four additional letters to buy, which was another economy. He'd wanted to have "Overbrook Branch" lettered on one of the windows, but Dad thought that none of the customers would be particularly impressed, so they'd made a saving there too.

The Breyer's people were putting up a new electric sign, which he didn't altogether approve of, but which Dad had talked him into. They were doing it free, to let folks know that the store was carrying the best now, instead of the cheaper kind Pope had sold.

He went outside and watched the Breyer's men adjusting the neon lights, but every now and then he'd look up at *his* sign, in gilt and dark blue—the colors Pope had chosen. Still they sure were beautiful.

There had been no customers yet, but it was still early and this was evidently a neighborhood where people ate breakfast at home. The newspaper delivery trucks had dropped off ten *Inquirers* and five *Records,* which didn't seem very many.

A florist's truck drove up. Pennock's, from downtown. The driver started toward the store door and hailed George.

"Mr. George Jones?"

"That's me."

The driver opened the back of the truck and brought out a flower arrangement that George thought must have cost at least twenty-five dollars, maybe even more. He opened the envelope perched on top. "Good Luck" was printed on the card, but there was no signature.

Now, who in heck could have sent that? If it was Dad and Mother, they should have saved their money; but it was sort of nice to get, just the same. He placed the flowers on a table close to the entrance, so they'd be seen.

A Buick roadster stopped out front behind the Breyer's truck, and a distinguished-looking man got out and came into the store. His first customer! He picked up a *Record* and an *Inquirer,* and then seemed to notice George for the first time. "Has this place changed hands?"

"Yes, sir. Beginning this morning. I'm George Jones."

Maybe he should give the man a cigar, explain that he was the first customer, but before he could the man said, "My name's Courtney. I've had an account with Pope ever since he opened. I suppose he told you." He reached into a good-looking wallet and took out a card: The Home Owners Loan Corporation.

"No he didn't. He never mentioned any accounts."

"I suppose mine was paid when you took over. I send out checks every month."

George tried to decide what he should do. They'd always done a cash business, except when Dad got softhearted once in a while, like he had with the Rivkins. But this man must live out here. He had an expensive car and he worked for the government; what risk could there be? Besides, he didn't want to offend a potentially good customer.

Mr. Courtney said, "I always pay for newspapers, of course. Too much trouble for you. But other things I'd rather pay monthly. I don't want very much. A box of cigars. Garcias. Pope kept them especially for me. If you're buying cigars, you might as well buy good ones, I say."

The whole bill amounted to over twenty dollars, and George felt a little uneasy. He entered the amount on a piece of paper and rang up the sale on the cash register.

Mr. Courtney said, "Good-by, Jones, and I wish you luck. Pope was hardly the man to make good in a location like this, but I think you will."

He'd barely gone when another car stopped. Who was it but Myra Lang's father. "George Jones. You haven't been around for some time. You and Myra have a spat? Get a job here for the summer?"

George tried to answer both questions at once, but Mr. Lang hardly gave him time. Gosh, but the men out here smoked good cigars. Mr. Lang took a half dozen Coronas, which you didn't even carry down on McClellan Street. "So long, son. Charge 'em. And drop around any time."

He hadn't even asked about credit and hadn't paid for his papers either. If Mr. Pope had only told him! Pretty near thirty dollars on credit already! It would take a fortune to carry trade like that for a month. He hoped Dad would come out soon, so he could talk to him about it.

He was relieved when an old Terraplane pulled up and Sam Pope got out of it. "I dropped by to wish you luck—and to see my store for the last time. All the nights I lay awake planning this place. Also there's something I forgot to tell you."

"Did you give credit to a Mr. Courtney?"

"Just what I was going to tell you. There's a good many government people—New Dealers—live out this way. It's bad dealers they are. Especially that Courtney. And that big bank fourflusher, Lang. I've written out a list of the good pay and the bad pay. Funny, it's only the no-gooders that ask for credit, anyway."

Before George could say anything Mr. Pope went on, "Say, don't tell me that Courtney has been in already, and you hardly opened?"

George nodded.

"What a buzzard! What a hyena! He hasn't been in here, not once, since the first month. He must of seen right away you were new." Mr. Pope shook his head from side to side. "And you fell for his line?"

"Uh-huh. Over twenty dollars' worth, including a box of those fifty-cent cigars."

This was no time to smile, but Mr. Pope did. "It ain't as bad as it sounds. Who would buy fifty-cent cigars these days that ain't out of his mind? Look at your inventory. Six boxes of Garcias, you'll see there, at two bucks a box, which is what I paid for them at an auction down on Second Street, just to help give class to this place. There's nothing gives class like fifty-cent cigars in a case, even though the customers all buy Cincos. Sam Popoff treated you right, kid, believe me. It's like them Coronas. I got 'em in the same lot. And you noticed all that cheap aspirin and milk of magnesia? All from the auction places. Bankrupt-store stock. You don't know about that? Except for a front, like on cigars, you buy only safe merchandise. Stuff that turns over good. You don't get stuck on standard brands. Most of the companies protect themselves by buying back up to the jobber's price."

After Mr. Pope left, George studied his list. Eleven customers with bad credit. Nine with good, who paid cash anyway. For the first time he felt misgivings. Like Dickie had said, when he'd been so angry with him, there was a margin of safety in hundreds of people living close by, instead of only dozens.

The family couldn't all come at once to see George's new store. It would have meant closing the old store. Mother and Helen came together, by elevated to Sixty-third Street, where they had taken a taxi. Later Mary came with Mrs. Waldman. Honest, you could hardly get Mary away from any part of the place. It was almost a good thing that there were so few customers. She had to be shown every last bit of equipment, and you'd have thought it was hers. When they were ready to go back to the city she said, "The flowers are pretty. Who sent them?"

"The card didn't say. I thought they were from Dad, maybe."

"Or that girl from your class? Or Gert Cameron?"

What had happened to Mary all of a sudden? So someone had sent flowers, and they had bucked him up a good deal while he was worrying about whether he should have given that Courtney fellow credit.

Before Mary and Mrs. Waldman left, Dad arrived by taxi. "Hello, son. How are things going?"

He had meant not to say anything about the credit he had given, but he did, and he also repeated what Sam Pope had said.

"You're bound to make a few mistakes at first, and I decided long ago how I felt about distress merchandise. There's something about it. A smell that goes with folks in trouble and losing their businesses. I'll be glad when we sell what you have here. Maybe it wouldn't be a bad idea to run sales on them, so folks around here get to know the place. Who sent the flowers?"

"I thought maybe you did. Maybe it was Mother."

A couple of newspaper sales. A few packs of cigarettes. The usual haggard-looking men for Bromo-Seltzers, but not much else. Dad hung around for a couple of hours, sitting on one of the comfortable, low-backed swivel chairs at the lunch and soda bar. A woman came in with a doctor's prescription, and George said, reading the name on the prescription, "I'll send it over as soon as it's ready, Mrs. Steinhaus."

He explained to Dad, "The pharmacist doesn't come on till one o'clock, as most of the drug business is in the afternoon and evening. It's pretty slow, isn't it?"

"We expected that. It takes time to build up a business."

The phone rang in one of the booths. "A woman wants me to send over two Cokes and three postage stamps. What do you think, Dad? We never had to deliver little things like that, ever."

"I suppose poorer people aren't used to having so much done for them. What did you say?"

"I said I would, right away. But we have only fountain Coke—Pope didn't stock the bottles. I hardly know how to carry it."

"There's some paper cups with lids; I remember seeing them when I took inventory. I bet that's what they're for. Make them up, and I'll tend store till you get back."

George made the delivery in the Lafayette, and when he returned he said, "Soon as we can afford it we ought to hire a boy with a bicycle. Maybe the oldest of the Green kids—William, isn't it?"

"William's the next oldest."

"In the meantime you don't mind my keeping the Lafayette out here?"

"Better for it than sitting in the garage. You know it's not much use downtown."

"That reminds me, Dad. When I left here yesterday, after getting things ready to open, I'd almost swear I saw Dickie driving a car. If he got caught it could cause a lot of trouble."

"Dickie has a license. I had to sign because he's under eighteen. He passed the test the first time, but whose car could he be driving? Oh, son, I think it's impossible."

"I only saw him for a second, but it sure looked like him, and there was a dog poking its head out of the window on the other side that looked like Floyd."

"You know he's never liked the store . . ."

"It's just that he's lazy. He's better at waiting on people than any of us except Mary. What he needs is a good talking-to, which you never give him."

"I do once in a while and always come out second best. He's a secretive kid, George, which you aren't. If anything was on your mind, you'd explode if you didn't get it off. Like telling me about giving credit to your first customer. I'd be willing to bet that you'd made up your mind not to tell me, but you did."

Dad knew more about human nature than you'd usually give him credit for. Imagine his realizing that! He went on, "I'd be inclined not to ask Dickie anything and I can't help feeling you're mistaken."

"It was a brand-new 1937 Ford coupé, and the funny thing was that there was some kind of washing machine tied on the back. Do you think he can be working at selling washing machines from house to house?"

At a few minutes past six Mr. Courtney came in again. George had sort of thought he would, and had decided upon the way to handle him. After all, he needed customers and also friends. Mr. Courtney sure made a good appearance, the way he drove up in his Buick. Who would think he didn't pay for the things he bought? There were folks like that down around McClellan Street, but for them there was the excuse that they had no money.

Mr. Courtney said, "Good evening, Jones. Think I'll take a couple of quarts of ice cream home to the family tonight. And a peacemaker of perfume. I've not been too good a boy lately. You know, between men, there's nothing to repair a breach between the sexes like a bottle of Lelong—or what do you have in stock?"

"After you came in this morning, Mr. Pope did too, to say good-by. He told me that what you said was perfectly true. You did have an account here and still do. It didn't figure in my buying Mr. Pope out, and I'd as soon forget it. Something you don't know was that you were my first customer here—the first customer I've ever had on my own. My father is helping me, but this store is strictly my job. I'd made up my mind to give whoever was first a box of cigars or a bottle of perfume, depending upon who it was, and it was you. I'd like you to pay for the other things you bought, and from now on it's cash. That's the way it'll be for everyone. But I'll give you every bit of service I possibly can, which is about all anybody can expect of a corner store, isn't it?

"What say, Mr. Courtney? I want you for a customer, and there are twenty-five good cigars say so. There's no other drugstore around here, and there'll be times you won't want to drive to someplace farther away. What do you say?"

"Say, you're quite a young fellow. So Pope told you I was bad pay, huh?"

"He said you had an account ever since he opened."

"And what do I owe you?"

"I make it $9.11. The cigars I want you to have as a gift. And you want ice cream and some perfume?"

"Two quarts of ice cream, but skip the peacemaker."

"Yes, Mr. Courtney. Any special flavor?"

"Peach in yet? Fresh, I mean."

"It sure is. Maybe you noticed I've switched to Breyer's, and they make just about the best fresh peach ice cream there is."

After Mr. Courtney had gone and George had rung up $9.11 on the front cash register and the dollar for the ice cream on the register by the soda bar, Mr. McCorkle, the pharmacist, came out from behind the partition that separated his little laboratory from the store. "Now, that was what I call diplomacy. I felt sort of sorry for you folks when you bought here, in spite of the fact that this is the best-equipped store I ever worked in. The location has been pretty dead, but maybe you'll bring it to life, at that."

The Fourth of July came on Sunday, which made a long week end, so that everybody who could get out of town had done so. Business was so slow that Chester sent Mrs. Waldman home, though Mary wasn't due to come in until seven. He sat on a stool in front of the soda fountain and smoked one of those fifty-cent Havana cigars he'd got out at the new store and listened to the radio account of the search for Amelia Earhart. It was two days now since she had radioed that she was over the Pacific with only a half-hour's supply of fuel remaining. What a terrible feeling that must have been for her and the man with her! Funny, they hardly mentioned him at all in the broadcasts. You'd think his life was less important than hers.

He got so interested in the account of all the naval vessels and airplanes that were searching for her (must be costing us taxpayers a pretty penny) that he realized only gradually that the telphone in the first booth was ringing insistently.

It was George. "Holy cow, Dad. I thought you'd never answer. I'm swamped. I put up that curb-service sign in the window, and every kid who has a car is out front. Mr. McCorkle is behind the fountain and I'm serving. Could you send out Mrs. Waldman or Mary by taxi?"

"I sent Mrs. Waldman home and Mary hasn't come yet. None of the Greens are around either. I'll close the store—it's like a morgue here anyway—and try to get one of them. If I can't, I'll come myself."

"Make it snappy. And send some chocolate sirup. We'll be fresh out in ten minutes."

Mary was home, Mrs. Plotko told him. Rather sullenly, he thought, she invited him into the parlor. She was stout and never took care of herself, but you could see that her hair must have been the color of Mary's and perhaps she had once been beautiful too. Some people took to drink and some to gambling. Chester didn't think she drank, but in the early days of the store she had practically lived on the telephone there, calling up bookies or waiting for returns. She hadn't been in since his last visit to the house, which was a good many years ago, when he'd threatened that he'd report her if she didn't behave better toward Mary.

She didn't look much changed. A little stouter maybe. She stood in the center of the parlor and, without moving to the hall, screamed so that undoubtedly it could be heard all over the house, "Mary, come down here. Old Man Jones wants you."

So far as he could remember, he'd never heard anyone call him that before, but maybe they did, behind his back. She didn't seem to mean to be rude, either.

"You'd think that girl didn't like her home, the way she stays in her room except when her old man's here."

Old man again! And Chester recalled that he always thought of him as Old Man Plotko, though he probably was about the same age as himself. He could hear footsteps running down the stairs, and then Mary brightened the dingy room. "Oh, Mr. Jones, has something happened?"

"Will you go out to George's place right away? He's started curb service and he's swamped."

"Do you really mean it? I'd love to."

"Hurry back to the store, then, and call a taxi. And take out a couple of gallons of chocolate sirup. I guess Mrs. Waldman's made up that much. I'll try to get her too."

"Please, let me go out alone. I'll work as fast as the both of us could. It means so much to me to see George make a go of it out there. I can't explain. Mrs. Waldman can take my place this evening."

Mary sure could look appealing when she wanted to. "O.K., but let's get a move on." Then, as they hurried toward the store, "Though why you're so anxious is beyond me."

She smiled, so that the dimples in her cheeks showed—the left dimple was deeper than the right. "It's that—that I've always wanted to try car-hopping; it looks like fun. George will have to buy me a uniform—with the tightest of black slacks."

187

Neither Mother nor Dad knew that Floyd slept on George's bed, now that George spent practically every night in the little room he'd rigged up in back of the Overbrook store. What they don't know won't hurt them, Dick thought. Thank goodness for one thing: he was practically fully grown and no larger than a fox terrier. Dick had taught him not to bark at night when he heard strange city noises or people passing, so there wasn't much that the family could gripe about the way they used to about Buddy, who had been killed by a car on McClellan Street.

Early this morning he had behaved sort of funny, pawing at Dick's hand until he'd become fully awake. Dick thought he wanted to go out on the back roof, but Floyd only whined to come in again and then growled until Dick gave him a slap that quieted him.

He seemed to be sleeping peacefully enough, but the moment Dick said, "Floyd Gibbons, it's time to broadcast," and opened the door, the dog was down the stairs like a shot. He began to growl low in his throat, and Dick was afraid he'd wake the folks, especially the baby.

A look at the store was enough to explain Floyd's behavior. Candy was scattered on the floor. The lending-library rack had been knocked over, and there were books every which way. The cash registers looked all right—they left them open at night ever since the last robbery, when the registers had been broken into. The cigar case had been emptied, and there wasn't a single pack of cigarettes in the rack behind it. The space under the candy case, where they kept full boxes, had also been emptied. Candy and tobacco seemed to be all they had wanted—stuff that would be easy to sell. How had they come to knock the library rack over? That's when Floyd must have heard them.

Dick went to the side door to let the dog out and saw by the forced lock how entrance had been gained. When he was satisfied that Floyd wouldn't wander onto McClellan, he considered what to do. Kay would be down in a few minutes. It would be better to wait for her to tell Dad.

The circumstances seemed to call for an extra double chocolate sundae. Then he let Floyd in and dashed out front to give Mr. Oberholtzer his morning paper in his six-day-a-week race with the streetcar. This morning it looked like a photo finish. As Mr. Oberholtzer flashed by, Dick handed him the rolled-up paper like a member of a relay team, passing the baton to his teammate. "No cigarettes, robbed last night," he called after him.

Mr. Oberholtzer nodded without slowing up and caught the streetcar just as the motorman began to close the doors. Just to watch so much exertion so early in the morning tired Dick so that he felt the need of another sundae, and by the time he had eaten it he heard Kay's steps on the stairs. He ran to the doorway and softly called to her, "Call Dad. We've been robbed," then went to the front door again to sell his papers.

When Dad came downstairs he didn't seem so much upset about the robbery as about the latest news of Amelia Earhart. He looked over the mess and said, "The last thing I heard last night was that sixty-two planes are searching for her. If she's not found now, she never will be. Now who could have done this? There doesn't seem to be much taken, outside of some candy and cigarettes."

Where had good old eager-beaver George come from? He was supposed to be out at the new place. Had somebody already telephoned him to come in? It could be, but it had been awful fast work. More than likely his nose had just smelled trouble. He had a little notebook in one hand and a pencil in the other, and he asked fool questions.

"How many Camels were in the rack the last you noticed?" he asked Dick.

"I'll have to go back to last Monday; I put in two cartons then. And how many did you sell Monday and replace?"

"If you'd stop clowning, maybe we could get somewhere."

"Ask me how many Melachrinos there are and I'll tell you. Also Fatimas. You know, within my lifetime they used to be pretty good sellers. What could have happened? Can't you be nonchalant with an Egyptian beauty?"

"You're deliberately trying to——"

There was no use letting this go on. "Why not settle with the insurance company, which I suppose is what's in the back of your mind, for Spewack's last delivery? That goes for candy and tobacco both. Up to closing time last night we hadn't used any of it, but we were pretty low."

"Now you're being constructive."

"Why don't you be?" Honest, but George could be a dope. "Meanwhile you'd do better helping Dad straighten out the books and behind the counters."

Somebody else came up to him with notebook and pencil in hand. "An alleged B & E take place here this A.M.?"

"Sorry, some of those initials whizzed past me pretty fast."

The man opened his coat secretively and quickly closed it. All Dick saw was an ordinary policeman's badge.

"You better talk to my dad. He's over there."

"I'll find out more just snooping around. I've figured out already how they got in—over that transom. That's the way with most of these store and taproom B & E jobs."

Dick said, "This fellow jimmied his way out, then—from the outside," and thought maybe he better shut up. "You look tired from thinking so hard. Let me fix you a cup of coffee."

"Why, thanks, sonny. I have been having quite a morning of it. Three jobs so far. Looks almost like a mastermind, don't it?"

"Sonny" tied it, but unfortunately Dick couldn't think of anything to do except to sweeten the coffee with arsenic, and they didn't have any of that around.

"Have any ideas on who may have done it?"

"Me? No."

"There's a bad street in back of your place."

"Fawn Street? We know all the families that live there. We never thought it was so bad."

"A lot of niggers on relief."

"So are most of the white people around here—or drawing money from sons in CCC camps."

"I'm against the whole business of handouts. Let people work, I say."

"Having a civil service job doesn't affect your thinking, does it? But I don't believe anybody on Fawn Street did it. I still think you should talk to Dad."

The plain-clothes policeman continued to sip coffee, so Dick said, "Myself, I think your mastermind idea is closer. For one thing, they must have had a car. We lost about forty boxes of penny and nickel candies that weigh two–three pounds each."

"Wait a minute! Candy in boxes?"

Kay left for work, and he waved to her. What had happened to George? Gone to the other place, probably, as it was almost nine. Honey and Mother coming in. Funny about Mother. Until the baby came she knew more about the store than anyone; now she was the last to hear anything. Except for the empty cases the store now looked as it always did, but Dad took her over to see the jimmied lock. What was the policeman saying now? Oh, yes, about the candy. "Sure. The nickel stuff, like Oh Henrys and Butterfingers, come in boxes of twenty-four and the penny candies twenty-one, with the two-fors and three-fors according."

"There's a lead there. Thanks, son."

Dick was watching him walk over to where Dad and Mother were still standing when Mrs. Koehler came in. "Hello, Dick. Hear you had a robbery."

"Yes. Not too bad—and we carry insurance since the last time, which was worse."

"Now, who would do a thing like that? Maybe starving people, that's what it could be. Honest, Dickie, when I think of all the starving creatures in the world my blood runs cold. Right now I'm feeding eighteen cats every morning, besides my own dear personalities. And cats *do* have personalities."

"So do dogs. I bet if my Floyd Gibbons could talk . . . Anyway his expression says more in a minute than his namesake can in ten, and he talks pretty fast."

"I know. I have some of the cutest mops of fur that I've taken in. I've given up taking in bigger dogs because the neighbors fuss so. I've no trouble on the Camac Street side, especially since it's gone colored. They seem to understand a dog's problems better. But around the corner I have trouble all the time."

Chester was talking to Mr. Meyer. Business had been off these last few days, and it was sort of nice to have him to talk to. Strange, now that he was on WPA, with at least the assurance of enough to live on, the old man seemed to be going downhill very fast. It was a hot mid-July afternoon, and the ceiling fans only seemed to stir up the overheated air, but he had on his old overcoat and there were more strings hanging from the buttons than Chester had ever seen before.

When Mr. Meyer asked for a package of Melachrinos, Chester told him about the robbery and the strange fact that the only cigarettes that hadn't been stolen were the few packages of those that were stocked for him and for Mr. Gerson.

"Gerson? Ah, yes, Saul's father. Tell me, does he hear anything from Saul?"

"He never talks much. For one thing, his English is very poor. Gertrude Cameron hears from him, I understand. She lives back on Fawn Street."

"I know the girl and her father. Strange people. Our window looks down upon their house. A good girl, though."

"Gert told my daughter Helen where Saul was fighting, but I don't remember what the place is called."

Chester was surprised to see that Mr. Meyer was crying. "Saul could have been a great violinist. Such a man should not be a soldier. It is a great tragedy, Mr.—ah—Jones. In instructing him, this old man had a reason to go on living. You know I fiddle now in a fifth-rate orchestra. Even for that I am not good enough. The hands—the arthritis in them. He was to have been my hands, Mr.—ah—Jones. The art of Paul Meyer would have gone on living in him. Instead he shoots Germans and Italians in Spain. The name of Freedom draws the soul of genius like a fata morgana—is that an expression understood in English?"

Chester nodded, not altogether sure that he did understand, and Mr. Meyer went on:

"Lord Byron, in Greece—but then, he was a poet. Musicians have no business in such things."

Eddie Bryant loomed in the front doorway. He'd been in for lunch only an hour before; what had happened to bring him back? Usually Eddie wore a broad smile that showed regular white teeth against his almost purplish skin, but right now he looked serious and upset. Chester felt particularly small when he stood next to the policeman, especially when he was in uniform. "Forget something, Eddie?"

Dickie used to say that Eddie Bryant's voice always sounded as if he were going to start singing "Swing Low, Sweet Chariot" the next minute, and it was so, even when he was as upset as he was now. "Is there anybody you could leave in the store, Mr. Jones, so that you could go down to the station house? They've caught two of the Green boys for that breaking and entering job in your place last night and they're treating them pretty rough. I'd mess in it if I could, but it would do no good. It ain't only the kids. I'm afraid that when Abe hears about it he'll go over and get in trouble."

Mr. Meyer offered a Melachrino to Eddie, who shook his head. "Can't on duty and don't smoke anyhow. Think you can get away, Mr. Jones?"

Chester pressed the buzzer. Helen had come in a while before, and he didn't remember her going out again. He hated to leave her in the store alone, but this was an emergency. She ran in, looking surprised to see only Eddie and Mr. Meyer there.

"Tend store for a little while, will you, Helen? I'm going down the street with Mr. Bryant. I won't be long. Excuse me, Mr. Meyer."

Chester walked along beside the huge policeman. Anybody seeing us likely thinks I've been arrested, he thought. When they reached the corner Eddie said, "I better leave you here. Go right up the stairs and then turn to the left. You'll likely hear them."

There seemed to be something always happening around the store, but he hated to think of the Green boys in trouble. In the station house nobody stopped him, and he followed Eddie's directions. To the left, he had said. He pushed open a door, and there were William and Horace Green on the floor; a man in civilian clothes stood over them, a broom in his hand.

"Come on, you. Where did you sell that stuff? Better tell quick, or I'll poke you in the face with this and put your eyes out."

Both boys were crying, and William kept repeating, "We ain't took nothin' and we ain't sold nothin'." Then he saw Chester. "Mr. Jones, please tell this man we ain't took nothin'."

The man threw down the broom. "What are you doing up here?"

"I'm Chester Jones. I've a store at Camac and McClellan."

"Yours the place was robbed last night?"

"That's right."

"We picked up these two in that nigger street in back of you. A mean little pair of bastards. I've beaten hell out of them, but they won't talk."

This wasn't a fellow like Yaeger or Eddie Bryant, whom you could talk to easily. He had the frozen-faced expression of the gangster who had tried to get them to put in gambling machines, and he spoke out of the side of his mouth. "What makes you think they did it?" Chester asked.

"This is what. Two full boxes of nickel candies and all these empty cigarette cartons. You know these two dinges?"

The kind of detective that made decent people into criminals. Horace had a goose egg on his forehead. What had he been hit with? And William kept rubbing blood from his mouth with the sleeve of his coat.

"Ever since they were born. They've run errands for me."

"It just goes to show. If I had my way, we'd get rid of all of them." William tried to say something, and the detective said, "Shut your trap or I'll kick your teeth in."

"Why don't you let him explain? I'll take the responsibility for these boys."

"Another softhearted guy. That's what makes our job what it is, guys like you butting in. Then the minute you get in trouble you call us for protection."

"Which doesn't include beating up an eight- and a thirteen-year-old boy. William, tell me where the cartons and the candy came from."

The two boys were still sprawled on the floor. William was shaking with fear, but Horace spoke up. "We *always* get the empty cigarette cartons, Mr. Jones. Billy, he makes 'em into trains for the young ones to play with." Sure, Chester remembered now how they always asked for them. "Dickie gave us the candy. He give it because the chocolate turned color. You give us candy like that too." Sure he had. Sure he had. Practically anything in the store that wasn't salable found its way to the Greens.

William said, "Mr. Jones, will you tell Ma where we are. She'll be worryin'."

"I won't have to. You're coming with me right now."

"Say, who the hell do you think you are?"

"At this moment I'd like to hit you over the head with that broom. We lost about twenty dollars' worth of candy and a little more of tobacco. I'd rather have lost twice as much than see what I've just seen. You try and stop me, and I'll make it hotter for you than you've ever known."

Funny thing. He'd no idea at all what he could have done, but it worked. When they got back to the store Chester said, "Run upstairs and get washed off. I don't want your mother to see you this way. And remember that all policemen aren't like that fellow. It was Officer Bryant who told me first what had happened."

"Since when have you started to beat up youngsters? Chester, I'm surprised at you." Ed Shaughnessy! Holy Moses, this was Thursday pinochle and his turn to give the party. He had clean forgotten.

"Hello, Ed. We were robbed last night, and the police picked up those two kids, who run errands for us. The cop on the beat tipped me off. When I got there they looked like you saw them."

"Merely being taught a little respect for law and order. From now on they'll respect your admonishment. 'Remember, my children, there are good cops.' Honest, Chester, sometimes you slay me. And don't you ever get anywhere on time, even to a game in your own dump? Max and Tony are upstairs looking over the new baby. I elected to stay down here and look over an older one. Has anybody told you that Helen isn't going to turn out like you thought she would, being so homely up to recently? I see glimmerings of real beauty."

Helen said, "Oh, Mr. Shaughnessy!"

"Mind staying on the job until Dick gets back?"

"No, Dad. There's no business anyway."

On the way upstairs Ed said, "You probably don't realize it, Chester, but you are the father of a looker."

"I realize it all right. Funny thing, we were having a lot of trouble with her. Not trouble exactly, but we were worried. Now all of a sudden she's become perfection itself. Kit and I hardly know what to make of it."

"Ask any bachelor. She played with fire and almost got burned. Right now she's scared, but she'll get over that. It's the nature of women to be good only so long as they're frightened—of someone or something."

They could hear Tony upstairs saying, "Now that you and Chester have started in again, you should keep it up. A nice-lookin' kid. What did you do, give Chester some of them hormones or something?"

"One of the things I like about Tony," Ed said, "his Italian humor. It's so basic."

"The best place to play pinochle in this house," said Chester, realizing that he had said it before, "is in the kitchen. The table in the dining room is too big. Do you mind, fellows? How about you, Kit?"

Her wonderful, comfortable laugh. "Honey is cleaning up the Green boys, so I already fixed up the table for you. And I bought new cards. Honest, Chester, your old ones were positively dog-eared."

Max said, "Pinochle is the one game supposed to be played with dog-eared cards," and Ed, making a face, "Now my luck is over."

Kit went out, and Chester drew Max for partner, while Ed won the deal. He was still shuffling when Tony asked, "Say, have you guys noticed how bad business has been the last week or two?"

# Part III

## Chapter 16

The kid looked peaked. Chester hadn't realized how hard George had been working—and how much he had been worrying. "The only thing we've built up is the curb service, and even that's spotty. If two or three cars stop, that brings others. But none of them are from around here, and they hardly ever buy anything else. That's the disadvantage of curb service, you never get the people in your store.

"Another thing that's different, Dad. People around our old neighborhood don't have cars. When they need something they run down to the corner and buy it. Out here they buy most everything they need in the city. All they come around here for is things they forgot. I do a heck of a big business in postage stamps."

"Maybe you should put in a vending machine. You'd make a little out of it, anyway."

"I've thought of it, but this isn't the time. Then, everybody around here has charge accounts at the stores in town. There's a Mrs. Betts comes in now and then. Last night she wanted a bar of castile soap. We've got a big stock that Pope must have bought up at auction. I said we were having a special on it and, if she used it right along, it might pay her to buy half a dozen. Know what she said? She buys a case at a time from Strawbridge and Clothier, when they have their annual soap sale, and just ran out. Imagine our people buying a whole case of anything."

"I'm glad you're beginning to think of them as your people. And business has slumped there too. One of the reasons I came out this morning was to have a talk when McCorkle wasn't around."

"He's all right, he's on our side. I hated to tell him we could only use him half time, but he understood. I think we're getting all the prescription business there is around, but it's not enough. There aren't the children around, always getting sick."

"You know how our neighborhood has been. It took a long time, but gradually living got geared to the depression. Prices went down, too, which helped. I can remember, after the World War, when beefsteak was sixty cents a pound. Things didn't get better, but they weren't getting worse. Now, the last two or three months . . ."

"The depression all over again," George said bitterly.

"That's where you're wrong, and it's not a recession either, like Roosevelt calls it. He implies that we got ahead a bit, for a while, and now are losing some of our gains. We didn't get ahead, we got adjusted. We've been at one bottom all along; now we're going to have to get used to a new bottom. You couldn't know this, and I couldn't, when we bought here. I'm sorry to have to tell you this, George, but I'm not going to be able to meet the payments on all the equipment notes this month and pay the rent out here too."

Chester saw a car park outside, and a man came in. "Morning, George."

"Good morning, Mr. Courtney."

"Big night last night and big head this morning. Fix me up a Bromo, will you?"

"You bet." George opened and closed the lever that measured out a dose of Bromo-Seltzer from the up-ended blue bottle in its metal stand; nodding toward Chester he said, "This is my father. Mr. Courtney is one of my good customers."

"Sure. Chip off the old block—I can see that now. You have a nice son. Did he tell you how we became friends?" Mr. Courtney drank down the fizzing potion. "A lifesaver, George, my boy. I couldn't face that damn office this morning without it. The dishonesty of it. The hopeful people I have to turn down—people who only want to save their homes. When you hear the name Home Owners Loan Corporation that's what you think of, isn't it? The most dishonest damn name there ever was. I was getting as bad. George will tell you, if he hasn't already. Dishonesty breeds dishonesty. A dishonest president means dishonesty all the way down to little Courtney, passing on loan applications that were never meant to be given, but people were told they were. Mr. Jones, this son of yours made me feel pretty small one day, and I've been glad that he did ever since."

A nice man, this Courtney, you could see that. "I'm glad you're glad," Chester said.

"You work for a government just so long and then you begin to feel exempt from the ordinary rules that other people have to follow. Do you know, Mr. Jones, that government employees are classed among the poorest of credit risks? Practically every one I know is a dead beat. Hell of a situation, isn't it?"

After Mr. Courtney had gone Chester said, "To return to this matter of the notes. I'm not too worried about it, and I don't want you to be, either. I'm going to the bank and arrange a loan to pay off the notes. I should have done that at the beginning. I don't think there'll be any difficulty. We've been dealing there for a long time, and they know me real well. Before I go, though, I think we ought to consider letting the companies take back some of these things. That's provided for in the contracts. This place is over-equipped. Take that refrigerator in the prescription department. We haven't sold much over a hundred dollars' worth of biologicals in the four months we've had this place, and we could keep all we need in the soda-fountain cooler."

"But Dad, it's over half paid for."

"Only at what Pope paid for it. We've paid four installments and owe seven more. Is it worth our while to pay the balance? Could we sell it for more than that? I'm inclined to answer no to both questions."

"Gosh, Dad, you could figure that way about everything in the store except the stock."

"I'm glad you thought of that and I didn't have to suggest it. We can use about seventy per cent of the stock down at our old place. The drugs we could probably realize something from. It might pay us to buy some of the equipment. The grill is a lot better than ours, and the deep-fat fryer is something we could make use of. Our whole loss wouldn't be much over two thousand dollars, which we could charge up to experience. There's the lease, too. It will cost us something to get out of that."

"You can't be serious! Four months isn't long enough. You said yourself it would take time."

"The question now is whether we can afford to take the time. Business here is about holding its own with what Pope did."

"That's only because of curb service. Mary does most of it, Sunday afternoons."

"Figure out how much extra that service costs you, son?"

"Mary won't take anything. She says it's fun and she makes enough on tips. Most everybody leaves a nickel or a dime on the tray."

Somebody was outside now, honking, and George hurried out. While he was gone the telephone rang and Chester answered. "Two packs of Luckies? Anything else? . . . What's the name? . . . No, I'm helping out; he's busy. . . . In a few minutes."

George rushed back to make a Coke in a paper cup, and Chester said, "Mrs. Woolman wants you to send around two packs of Luckies. She says you know the address."

"I sure do." The kid looked more exasperated than Chester had ever seen him. "Dad, I don't care. Do whatever you want. I'm serving a nickel Coke, and that Mrs. Woolman lives almost two miles from here. What really burns me up is that when I deliver the cigarettes I'll have to go around to the back door."

Another disadvantage of the new store—one he hadn't thought about much until they bought it—was how far away it was. While Chester changed from streetcar to elevated and then to streetcar again, he remained deep in thought. What would be the effect on George if they gave up the new store? Some good things had come out of having it—the boy had a better appreciation of his own neighborhood, for one thing. But would there be another hurt upon his spirit? Chester thought that perhaps he had been too sentimental when they had bought the place.

The alternative would have been to commit George to years of feeling that he had lost his best opportunity. The real mistake had been his, in not realizing that a country couldn't stand still so long. If it didn't go forward, it had to go backward, which was what it was doing now. All the expensive stopgaps had failed, and how much of the public wealth had been wasted? Why shouldn't he have realized? He had never believed in that golden voice over the radio, which said nothing so beautifully. George had been after him so often for remarks to customers who idealized, not really the man they had never seen, but the name that they associated with the voice. Give the man credit, he had seemed to have confidence at a time when that was a lost feeling, generally . . .

But he was trying to lift from himself the blame for a decision that was his. The more he thought about it, the more the feeling kept recurring that Dickie had been right. The place for a good store was where there were people. It was like Max, who always insisted that he made more money in his thickly inhabited Negro neighborhood than he ever could in a white one. Why, he doubted that there were as many human beings in all the area that George could serve as there were in one block of Camac Street.

I'll wait until I see what the bank will do, he kept thinking, and then began to consider all over again everything they had done. The fault in their calculations was the recession. What new word would be invented for the next step in the inevitable descent of an economy that from year to year produced less and less? But if he felt like that, what was the use of striving at all? No, he was tired most of the time, but he had to keep fighting for George's sake, and Dick was in his last year at high school; the store, the way things were, wouldn't be of much help to him. He never worried about Dickie making his way, though. Funny, sort of, wasn't it?

Mrs. Waldman was in the store. The cases were piled high with boxes of stationery and school supplies that had been sitting there since the fall school term had begun. This was the middle of October, and usually there would have been almost nothing left. They sold a few notebooks, pens, pencils, and rulers right along, but there wouldn't be any real sale again until February, and for the paper goods, especially, Chester liked clean stock.

Mrs. Waldman said, "I thought I'd try to find a place to put these while things are slow, but I'm having a job making room."

"I guess I overordered. I bought the same as I did last year, without thinking that folks weren't having children in 1931 if they could help it and those are the ones starting school this year. All those school bags are bought for beginners."

Mr. Oberholtzer came in. "Hello, Jones. The Postscript edition of the *Bulletin* in yet?"

"Be another hour. Say, isn't this a funny time of day for you to be in?"

"Layoff. Our place is closed down solid. Looks to me like it'll stay that way. Seventeen years I've been there. Thought I was fixed for life. They closed rather than unionize. I'm not a union man myself, but I think it was a pretty bullheaded thing to do. They might at least have talked it over."

"I'm real sorry to hear that."

"I'll be getting unemployment insurance, but it isn't much more than relief would be. The place I worked never paid enough so a man could save, but it was *steady*. Thought maybe if I got an early *Bulletin* there might be some want ads I could answer this afternoon."

"If you want me to, I'll send it down soon as it comes in. How's the missus?"

"Pretty blue right now. She's talking about going back to work. She used to be a waitress and she says she can always get some kind of job. I'd sure hate to see it come to that. A man would hardly feel right having his wife work while he takes care of the kids."

"There's lots that do, around here. They get used to it."

That night, at late supper, Chester remembered about Mr. Oberholtzer and told Dickie.

"So that's why he wasn't by this morning. Ever since I was nine, I guess, I've served the early-morning customers. That's six times fifty-two—three hundred and twelve—times eight: practically twenty-five hundred times I've opened the front door at four minutes of six and seen Mr. Oberholtzer coming down the street. Sometimes the streetcar would be late, but usually he'd be running for it. He only missed it two or three times and never lost a day that I can remember. Then today when I went out, there was the streetcar, way down at Eleventh Street, and no Mr. Oberholtzer in sight. I tell you, Dad, it was a real shock. I waited until after the streetcar went by and I thought, I guess this is one morning that Mr. Oberholtzer has overslept at last. I can't hardly believe yet that I may not ever see him again."

It was seldom that Dickie looked down-in-the-mouth, but he did now. Surprising he took something like that so much to heart. He looked down at his soup plate in deep reflection, then called out to the kitchen, "Honey, you'll have to bring me another plate to revive my spirits." When she came in he said, "Why don't we have pepper pot more often for supper?"

She laughed. "Dickie, you said the very same words last week about snapper stew."

Hard to realize that the baby was six months old. A beautiful child, Kit Jones thought. More beautiful than any of her other children at the same age and with more personality than any save Dick. She was the kind of baby that artists draw for advertisements. Right now Chester had a Mennen's Baby Talcum Powder ad sitting on the patent-medicine case, just because he thought the baby in the ad looked so much like Alice. She had pale blond hair that Honey loved to comb into a single curl on top of her head. Not that it was much of a curl yet, but you could see that it would be. She had gray-blue eyes, a perfect purse of a mouth, and full rosy cheeks. What was most interesting of all was how she noticed everything. After the first couple of months she was well behaved, too, which was a blessing, considering how hard it had been on Chester when she cried at night.

Right now the poor man looked worried. Was it because of going out yesterday to see George? Sometimes Chester was so much smarter at dealing with the children than herself. After he had showed her, she realized so much that she should have understood. All the days after George was stricken, his not knowing what was the matter, except that he was paralyzed; not understanding, except that he couldn't walk. The long, long, long way back. The very special courage that he'd had. After all that, she still had not realized that such a struggle must affect the spirit as well. Imagine

Chester understanding so much better than herself! But that was because he was smarter.

She was so stupid. She played with the baby, tickled the toes that were so nice and straight because they had never been malformed by shoes. Her baby! Wonder of it. But no wonder—Romeo and Juliet, Leslie Howard and Norma Shearer, had played their part. The way Chester insisted it was them. Wasn't he a scream sometimes?

She could sit like this for hours, just playing with the baby, forgetful that she had grown-up children—if being twenty-one made you a grownup—feeling that she and Chester were young again and that this was her first-born.

"Hello, Mother. How's the baby?"

"Kay, dear, I clean forgot the time, playing with the baby."

Kay slumped into a chair. "What a day! And I've news for you. Sig is being transferred to New York."

This was always Honey's time of the day to look after her own family, so Mrs. Jones put down the baby regretfully and prepared to heat up something for Kay.

"Don't bother, Mother. I'm not hungry."

"It's too long for you to go without food from lunch until we have supper."

"I'll have a cup of coffee, then. And a sandwich. Helen's in the store and can bring them up. I'd rather talk to you."

Sig being transferred, and Kay more than usually tired and tense. Maybe this was what she had been waiting to hear.

"Oh, Mother, don't put on that expression of 'Blessings, my children' even before I've said a word. Every time you think I'm not looking I've known you were watching me, waiting for me to say something, and ready to look maternal at the drop of a hat."

"I'm sorry, dear. There are things a girl has to settle for herself, and all I want is to be as much comfort as I can when you need it."

"I know. It's not you who needs to feel sorry, but me. I just haven't been able to make up my mind."

Funny, sitting here watching Kay, thinking that you had already had two children at her age but how much like you she looked. "When I saw your father I made up my mind right away."

"I *liked* Sig right away, but I've always thought I should be able to make a choice. I sound as bad as Helen does sometimes, I guess, but how can you know you really love one man unless you can compare him with somebody else who says he likes you too?"

"You've read too many novels—or seen too many movies. There they have to have two men falling in love with the same girl to make a plot. I don't think it's that way in real life—not among people like us, anyway."

"Then there are so many problems. I'd *never* get used to being called Mrs. Dobrzanski and I've so little in common with his folks. If we lived here, we'd be up at his house a lot of the time—they're all very close. And religion. He's willing to be whatever I want, but that's sort of selfish of me, when his folks care so much about him not changing and I know you wouldn't mind about me."

"We would mind, because your father and I were both raised Protestants and we wouldn't like for anyone to say a daughter of ours had to turn Catholic to marry. We're not asking Sig to become Protestant. If you had married Saul Gerson, which I thought maybe you would, once, we wouldn't have cared, because he wouldn't have wanted you any different from what you are. When Sig——"

"It's not Sig, Mother. It's his folks. And he's been awful patient with me, when I've said I'd marry him and then taken it back so many times. He doesn't get mad or excited or anything." She giggled. "Just to show the way I've behaved, I was angry with him for that, and he said he wasn't excited or anything because he knew that in the end I'd say yes. Sig wants me just as I am, religion and all—he's said so dozens of times. But I know it would make it easier for him if I turned."

"And harder for us, but do what you think best." She jumped up, remembering the coffee, went to the hall, and called downstairs. When Helen responded Kit said, "Bring up some coffee and a real nice sandwich for Kay. I think I'll have one too." Thank goodness, now that George was at the other store all the time, they'd stopped worrying about keeping count of things like coffee. She hadn't wanted to be so stiff with Kay about turning Catholic, either —it was only that if they did get married, she wanted it to start out right, which meant the two of them being honest with each other.

It wasn't a question of giving in on the part of either of them, but of accepting each other as they were.

She returned to her room, where Kay still slumped in the chair. One nice thing about her, she had never started smoking, like most of the other girls in the neighborhood. Otherwise she would probably have been puffing all afternoon, getting herself all worked up. "I suppose you think that because he's being transferred to New York you have to make some final decision. Take my advice and don't. If you don't see him for two or three months, you'll both know your own minds better."

"Not see him for months! Mother, I couldn't. I sit there in the office all day trying not to look at him . . ."

Kit began to laugh, softly as she could, so Kay would catch on to the real meaning of what she had just been saying, but Helen came with the sandwiches, with Chester right behind her. "Mary came in. She and Helen will hold the fort until Dick comes back. He said he'd be gone an hour, and it's nearer three. Meanwhile I'm sleepy. If you will clear out of here, I think I'll take a nap."

"Chester Jones, you never take a nap this time of day."

"I know I don't usually, but for some reason or other I couldn't sleep last night. Maybe it was the relief party at the Thomases'. Anyway I'm pretty tired."

"We'll hold the fort, but will we get the sauerkraut?" Helen asked.

"Don't try to tell me, Helen Jones, that you haven't been snooping in the Frigidaire," Kit said, and then, when Chester looked bewildered, "Dear, don't tell me you don't remember what we used to sing when the children were small and we were having sauerkraut for supper?" Heavens, she hadn't sung it in years, but she began, "Hold the forks . . ." and Chester caught on and joined in with Helen, "the knives are coming. Spoons are on the way. Put the dishes on the table, sauerkraut today."

# Chapter 17

Chester walked across to Tony's barbershop so deep in thought that he never noticed the oncoming truck until it was almost upon him, and he had to make a leap for the opposite sidewalk. Here he was doing the same thing he always warned Kit about, crossing at their corner instead of down at the traffic light.

Tony was sitting in his barber's chair, and Mrs. Tomolillo was on one of the row of chairs for customers, holding the baby. When he came in they were talking in Italian and a small radio that sat on the same shelf with the hair tonics and dandruff removers had on an Italian program. Tony turned off the program and began to speak English almost as though he were ashamed of speaking Italian. It was a funny thing, Chester thought, that the Jews and Poles and other foreigners in their neighborhood always spoke their own languages when they were together, regardless of who was around, but the Italians didn't.

Mrs. Tomolillo was extremely short and very slender—hardly the person you would think of to have such a large and fat baby. She gathered it up with all its clothes and said, "Tony will take care of you, Mr. Jones."

"If you're leaving on my account, don't," Chester said. "I won't be long—I just want a trim. Saw from our place that you weren't busy."

"Are you kidding? I haven't been busy in months. On top of

everything else, poor Mr. Roosevelt has a recession to contend with. You know what a recession is, Mr. Jones? It's one of those things. Mr. Roosevelt, he licked the depression fine, but how could he know this was coming up?"

Chester sighed and took the chair that Tony had vacated. He liked Tony, but like all barbers he talked too much. His idols were Roosevelt and Mussolini—today it looked as though Chester was in for a half-hour eulogy of Roosevelt. Tony looked up at his picture, framed, over the mirror. "What are people kicking about? He got us out of one jam, believe me, and he'll get us out of this." Tony always became angry at his imaginary detractors of the President. His scissors seemed to be charged with excitement; his electric clippers snarled with anger. "Do I like the recession? But why blame it on him? Customers who used to come in every week, like you, keep putting it off. You ain't been in for three weeks, Mr. Jones."

"And you haven't been buying over at our place like you used to."

"The Cokes-a-Cola, you mean? I say to the wife, I say, 'Why you drink all those things? My God, it's a recession,' I say. A Cokes-a-Cola she has to drink every hour. To pep her up, she says. 'Listen, baby,' I tell her, 'you got pep enough—too much sometimes, after I been in the shop all day on my feet.' "

Mrs. Tomolillo, sitting there holding the baby, protested. "You shouldn't say such things to Mr. Jones, Tony."

"The God's honest truth. 'Cut down,' I says. 'I ain't making enough in the shop to keep us in food, even. Why don't you drink wine, like I do?' I asks her."

Tony cut furiously and silently for a minute or two, then said, "What's bad for me and you is good for Joe, down the street. People ain't buying new shoes—they're getting their old ones mended. Joe says he's working twelve–fourteen hours a day mending shoes so old they should be put in museums. He's cleaning up, believe me. In his old age he should make money, when it don't do him no good."

They didn't get talking about Mussolini, anyhow, and it always appeared to break Tony's heart when Chester refused to have any tonic on his hair. "I guess not today. I'm going to the bank on business and I don't want to smell as though I just came out of a barbershop." He gave Tony a half dollar, said good-by to Mrs. Tomolillo, patted the baby, and slowly walked out. One thing he had never done was borrow money and he hated to have to try now.

In all the times he had been in the bank to make deposits he had never met the man who sat across from him now. He had always thought of the bank as a place where he was well known, and it was difficult to readjust himself to this stranger.

"I'm Chester Jones. I've had an account here for the last fifteen years." He went on to explain about the purchase of the new store and his wish to refinance the notes on the equipment; the man's face became increasingly expressionless. Folks were a lot more friendly when you made deposits in banks than when you tried to borrow from them. Even after he had finished telling what he wanted, the man sat there, his finger tips pressed together. Then he began to talk about a setback. Nothing serious, but a setback, when naturally the bank had to feel its way.

Why can't he just say no, Chester thought, and then realized that the man was like himself, when salesmen asked him to buy things that he didn't need. The man was trying to be kind, that was all. Chester felt better toward him, felt the need to help him say what he had to say. "I thought it would be more businesslike for my own bank to handle this, rather than half a dozen finance companies I don't know. If you don't want to get into this kind of loan business, I can understand easily enough."

The man beamed at him. "In ordinary times, naturally, we'd appreciate good, solid loans with long-time depositors, but right now, Mr.—ah . . ."

Chester had to smile, it reminded him so much of Old Man Meyer. "Jones, Chester Jones."

"Of course, Mr. Chester. In the future, when conditions change . . ."

When Mary entered the store, after Pop had gone to work, Dick was there alone. "Hello, Euchreanian, where you been? You're five minutes late."

"I've been playing euchre, you pinochlebian." That ought to hold Dick, but she knew it wouldn't.

"The word is pinochlesbian—one pinochle player loving another."

"O.K., so you win. I still don't like you calling me Ukrainian, even, and I know you only do it to needle me, but you shouldn't, Dick." She could see that he was really contrite.

"I'm sorry. Rough day, huh?"

"Sort of."

"Tell me. Do you folks have a washing machine?"

"Mom, washing? You make me laugh."

"I mean for clothes."

"Now you're being nasty. I *mean* for clothes."

"She sends the wash out?"

"To the damp wash. You know, where they bring it back ready to iron." Honest, but it was hard to understand Dick or what he was trying to get at, most of the time.

"She irons it?"

"I do, mostly."

"How long does it take, for you three?"

"Now, Dick, I know you're up to something, and you better not be. I'm sort of bushed."

"Pop?"

"I got him off to work. I don't know. Maybe it would have been better for him to lose a day, but he never has. You don't know how lucky you are, with folks like yours, and you shouldn't try to kid me the way you do."

"I say the same thing to myself. If I were as old as George, do you think I'd be as dumb as he is?"

"You're not as old and you're not as stupid." It was so hard to talk with Dick without having your mind undressed for you. Mary was glad when a car stopped out front. By this time she knew the Pierce-Arrow roadster of Gert Cameron's rich fellow, whom she would never take around to Fawn Street. They both watched Gert wave good-by, and then she came into the store.

"Dick! Mary! The most wonderful news! I'm engaged, and you're the first to hear about it. Lookie!" She held up her hand so they could see the flash of the diamond. Mary thought it was big and beautiful but that it wasn't the diamond that mattered, so much as the man who gave it. Sour grapes, she accused herself, and made twice as much fuss over the ring as she would have otherwise.

Dick said, "Tell me, Gert, what won you? It couldn't have been the Pierce-Arrow, could it?"

Mary liked the way Gert lifted her chin and answered back, "It helped undoubtedly. There are times, Dick Jones, that I would like to give you a sock in the jaw, though I realize that one in the belly would do more harm. Imagine a kid your age having a belly, even."

"You imagine. I can't."

"Let me tell you something. All my life I've been raised on helping the underprivileged. I'm so social-conscious I smell bad. I know the history of the AFL and the CIO from the time that Sam Gompers rolled his first cigar. I've got a dad who's stood on a soapbox ever since I can remember—maybe because it makes him look taller. We live on a colored street so he can study the psychology of the Negro. I'm going to marry a fellow whose father practically owns a bank. In addition he's a nice guy. Make what you want of it."

"You shouldn't be angry with Dick. He needles me all the time. Honest, Gert, I hope you'll be happy—awful happy."

"I am already."

Mary wondered if Gert wasn't a little too positive. She thought back to the day of the picnic in the store and the way she had noticed her looking at Saul Gerson—the way that she herself wanted to look at George and tried to keep from doing. She said, "Fathers have a lot to do with girls' lives—more than mothers, I think. Most mothers spoil fellows, and fathers make it hard for us."

"You ain't kidding. Not that mine isn't a grand guy . . ." She seemed about to say something else and thought better of it. Gert had never seemed beautiful until recently, but now she had a dark, slender, vibrant beauty that no doubt came from love. Mary wondered if sometimes she was also so affected, but no, it wasn't loving, but being loved, that did things to you.

When Abe Green came in to buy he wore his hat, but when he wanted a favor—from borrowing fifty cents to getting permission, which had never been refused, to sell Christmas trees out front—he took his hat off and held it in both hands, as he was doing now, and waited patiently until the store emptied to state the reason for his errand. It was a month early to ask about Christmas trees, so Chester decided that it must be a loan. After he'd sold the last newspaper and a box of Phillies cigars to Francis McGovern, the new Democratic committeeman, who was trying to get into his good graces, Chester asked, "What's the matter, Abe?"

"William's in trouble again, Mr. Jones, and I wondered if you could help me out."

"In trouble again? I always think of William as a real good boy."

"He is that, Mr. Jones, but ever since the police picked him up first for burglaring your place, they do it every time something goes wrong."

"Why, he had nothing to do with that."

"I know. But it gave him a police record. Every time something happens around here he gets picked up. Like the Lanzetti boys. Ever hear of them?"

"Pio and the others?"

"That's right. They never did anything either, but after one or two of them got picked up for doing nothing it was easy for cops to say, when anything went wrong, 'Let's pick up the Lanzettis,' because they had a record. That's what I'm afraid of with Billy."

"You should have said something while McGovern was in."

"I saw him, but I didn't want to say anything till I talked with you. Once the cops have a finger on you, you have to leave a place, that's all. This time maybe, or next, my boy will be softened up to put something on and a jury gets his record read. This is the fifth time."

"Why in hell didn't you tell me?" All the times he had talked about going into politics and hadn't. Dick kidding him about it. The need he would have for associating with cutthroats like McGovern, who used to run a little crap game back of a place down on Tenth Street before he became a Democratic machine worker. What was to be done?

"How did you vote last time?"

"Mr. Roosevelt. I know you were for Landon, Mr. Jones, but it was Mr. Roosevelt who got us relief, and where would me and my family be without it?"

"I can't leave the store right now, but you go down and see McGovern. I'll telephone him a little later."

"I'm not so much worried about Billy getting let go this time. It's that we're going to have to leave this neighborhood. I want to rent a drive-yourself truck to move with, but I got to have somebody sign for me. I was hoping maybe you——"

"Whoa there," Chester interrupted. "You mean you've rented a house somewhere else?" Where would they ever get other kids as dependable as the Greens?

"I found a place out near Twenty-second Street. Don't you worry none about the boys working for you. They'll come just the same. It's not much over a mile from here, but it's another police district. I hope I can sell Christmas trees just the same."

"Sure you can. And I'll sign for the truck. It makes me sore as hell just the same."

"Now, Mr. Jones, there are some things you got to be patient about and one is the police. We just have to accept that they've tied on to Billy. I'd rather not have to move just now, but we need a bigger house anyhow, the way the family has grown."

"Expecting an increase this year?"

"No, we're not. I said to Mrs. Green, 'Let's make it an even dozen,' but she put her foot down. She said that next year I'd want to make it a baker's dozen, and eleven is a lucky number anyway."

After Abe had gone his news seemed to be the last straw in Chester's burden of discouragement. He had heard of that kind of persecution by the law, but he had never actually known anyone who had experienced it. He felt helpless, as he did about his own affairs. In the next few days he had to make a decision of some kind. What was he to do? He was glad when Mrs. Waldman came in the side door, dressed in a freshly laundered white uniform and looking crisp and wholesome. That was one action to his credit anyway.

She said, "Oh, Mr. Jones, there's something I've been wanting to say."

What now? She never talked about her own trouble. He looked at her inquiringly.

"Well, it's the way business has been. If you want to cut my time or lay me off, I'll understand and I'll always be grateful anyway for all you've done."

"Now what gave you that idea?"

"I've been noticing how worried you look. I've thought maybe it was a mistake buying the new place, not knowing how things were going to go. One thing about being a waitress, you can always get work somewhere—and I can again, now that the business about Eddie has quieted down. You gave me help when I needed it."

That was pretty nice of Mrs. Waldman. "Business is bad. We're down almost a third from last November. What makes it worse is carrying over a lot of seasonal stock, like greeting cards and school supplies, that ordinarily we'd have sold. But so long as we're open we'll need help in the store. It's not like when we started and I could be on my feet from six in the morning until eleven."

A sailor came in and walked over to the cigar counter. Chester waited on him. "Camels and some matches. Remember me, Mr. Jones?"

He was tall and slender, and the way he wore his uniform suggested that he thought pretty well of himself. His hat was cocked over one eye, and a long dark lock of hair curled down his forehead. He only looked to be nineteen or twenty, but he had a self-assurance about him that Chester didn't like.

"No I don't place you. Did you used to live around here?"

"Well what do you know? I thought sure you'd never forget me. I'm Jimmy Gibson. Folks call me Hoot."

Chester gave him the cigarettes and made change for a quarter. Sure, Jimmy Gibson, who'd gone into the Navy three years ago, and good riddance to the neighborhood. A wonder he hadn't recognized him, after all the trouble he'd been, but he had grown and filled out. "The Hoot part is new, but I remember you now. Going to be around long?"

"Not too long." Whatever else he was going to say was interrupted by Helen coming down from upstairs. Jimmy Gibson whistled and walked back toward the soda fountain, where she had stopped when she saw him. He took off his hat, and two more curls dropped to join the one already there. "Hello, beautiful." Chester didn't like the way he said it or the way Helen reached back and felt if her hair was in place. Something told him that, in addition to all his other troubles, he was going to have her to worry about again.

The fellows still flocked into the store evenings when Mary was at the soda fountain. A lot of families had been moving out of the neighborhood, to double up with other members of their families, and a good many new folks had moved in, especially on Camac Street, where the Home Owners Loan Corporation had taken over practically the whole row and was renting for whatever it could get.

Chester tried to recall who the tall, carroty-headed youth was, standing up at the end of the fountain, and the stocky one next to him. They were arguing about the world series. Why the tall one thought the Giants had the better team, in spite of the Yanks winning four out of five, was part of that mysterious loyalty which seemed a part of being a fan.

Although every stool at the fountain was filled, and most of the seats at the tables, it was easy to see that none in the crowd had much spending money. They sat nursing five-cent drinks, talking about baseball and the Penn-Columbia football game on Saturday, while they waited for a chance to wisecrack with Mary. They kept the phone booths filled, too. Funny thing, you could almost always hear the women talking in the booths, but rarely the men. What were the four mysterious conversations now going on, with intent heads bent so closely against the receivers that even the movement of lips could not be detected?

Chester was busier than he'd been for a long time, chiefly because he had gone back to selling cigarettes at one for a penny, six for a nickel. Max had always done so, in his place, but in most stores the practice had died out.

Young Gibson came in. The trousers of his navy uniform looked skintight beneath his open pea jacket. He walked over to the fountain, where Mary was mixing a soda, and said, "Hello, beautiful," the way he had to Helen yesterday. What Chester didn't like especially was the way he pushed between the two fellows who were now arguing over whether Hubbell or Gomez was the better pitcher.

Mary had a nice manner about her—never forward, but not distant either. She said, "Hello. What can I do for you?"

"Plenty." He looked around, as though to accept applause for some special sense of humor. "But I'll settle for a double chocolate —a real Harold Teen, I mean."

Sometimes Chester wished that their evening soda business hadn't become so predominantly male; he would have preferred fellows coming in with their girls, like they used to. The fountain was at the far end of the store, which was a good thing, and the fellows were better off than they would have been hanging around a street corner or a poolroom.

Burke, from across the street, brought back his yesterday's harvest of mystery stories and began to browse through the rack. "Chester, you should put the screw on those library people. There isn't a book in the case that I haven't read, except some English ones that are too high-brow for me."

"I'll do that. Let's see now. You must read one or two a night."

"On good nights I read three. Especially those Crime Clubbers. I have a hard time going to sleep. Hell of a situation when a man's on his feet all day, cooking oysters, and then can't sleep at night. Of course, it would have been different if Sonny had lived or we could have had more. We tried and tried, but it was no use. The way it's been we've had nothing to work for, except to make a career of oysters. I think we put out the best stews and fries in Philadelphia, if I do say so myself."

"I've noticed our Dick seems to think so too. I see him at your counter almost every day. But to get back to books: two a day would be an average of sixty a month."

"Usually on Sundays I save the funnies to put me to sleep, but they're not interesting enough. Half the time I can't keep my eyes open to finish them."

"Well, say fifty a month. Do you think they publish that many?

I don't suppose they change more than seventy-five books altogether."

"The others are a waste of time and space, believe me. Last week I was desperate. You didn't even have any new mystery magazines in, and I tried to read that *Northwest Passage* the wife took out. What she saw in it I don't know. I was bored, plain bored. I couldn't stay awake long enough to read the first hundred pages."

Chester sort of lost track of what Burke was saying when he saw Helen come in from upstairs. She had her hair a new way and was made-up. She gave that Gibson fellow's sleeve a pull, but he was busy boasting about being in Shanghai when the Japanese attacked the Chinese and didn't turn around right away. Chester could hear him from here, describing how the Jap soldiers raped the Chinese women. Probably he'd have been more explicit except for Mary, but he was going pretty good just the same.

Helen gave his arm another tug, and Chester said, "Pardon me, Ed. There's something here I better attend to." Before he could reach Helen, Gibson turned around.

"Hello, beautiful!"

Helen didn't take it the way Mary had. "You really, really think so?"

"Sure I do. Come on, let's get away from the crowd."

She saw him coming, ran over, and caught one of the buttons on his coat. "Dad, you remember Hoot Gibson, don't you? He's invited me to see Clark Gable and Jean Harlow, at the Stanley. It's her last picture before she died, and I'm dying to see it."

"Your mother say you could?" Chester saw Gibson turn again to the fountain, with an air of indifference. "She knows you're going to the movies with this fellow who is practically a total stranger?"

Helen gave him the old, big-eyed, Vee Maguire approach. "Why, Dad! He's one of the boys from the neighborhood. He used to be in here all the time. Just because he's in the service! And you wouldn't want me to be embarrassed before all these fellows."

"You tell Hoot you've forgotten something and go back upstairs. He'll catch on in a little while, when you don't come back, and leave."

He watched the exaggerated way she told Gibson that she had

forgotten her lipstick, then dashed upstairs, probably to try a scene with Kit. He'd won this time, but it was a trouble that wasn't over. The only hope was that the sailor's leave was a short one.

When Dick came in with his customary "Sorry I'm late, Dad," and relieved him, Chester went upstairs. There was no sign of Helen, and Honey hadn't come back yet. He went into their room and saw Kit sitting there, within the light of the bridge lamp, knitting socks for the baby. He gave her a kiss, then tiptoed over to look down on the sleeping child. The feeling she gave him was worth all the drudgery of the long days. After kicking off his shoes and putting on slippers, he asked, "Where's Helen?"

"What happened? I was out in the kitchen when she came up crying, saying that you had mortified her before everyone in the store. I tried to talk to her, but she ran up to the girls' room."

"Remember Jimmy Gibson, who used to steal papers and snatch candy bars? He's in the Navy now and it hasn't improved him. He calls himself Hoot Gibson."

"Whatever for?"

"There's some cowboy star, used to be in the movies. He came in yesterday and Helen fell for his line. You know, with all the girls and fellows coming in here, I've seen it a thousand times, but it's hard to believe your own daughter can be so silly. She came down tonight. They'd made a date for the movies."

"She never said a word. And she's been so wonderful—so sensible —for months. I thought she'd outgrown that silly stage."

"I told her to tell him she'd forgotten something and go upstairs, so she couldn't have been too mortified. He caught on and left right after. I'm sorry to say, darling, that we have a problem daughter on our hands again."

"We've met problems before, haven't we, Chester?"

"This couldn't come at a worse time."

"Things aren't going well with the new store? I've been afraid of that, but you and George are so closemouthed . . ."

"We didn't expect it to catch on right away. Buying at the beginning of summer may have been a mistake, but what we counted on was this store carrying the other for a while."

218

"Dear! It couldn't mean losing this place? You and this store are what I put my trust in."

"I'm glad you included me with the store." Before he could say more there was a terrific thumping on the stairs and Kay's voice called.

"Mother, Dad, where are you?"

He slippered into the hall. "Don't forget you have a small sister."

"Get Mother. Bring her out to the kitchen."

What had got into Kay? He turned around, but Kit was right behind him.

"Sig and I got married. Tonight. We drove down to Elkton. I wanted you to know right away."

Kit was looking at him, but he shook his head slightly, so that only she should see and understand.

"Well, what happened to the groom?"

Kay giggled just like her mother always did. "He's waiting downstairs. Imagine, Dad, Sig is absolutely scared to death."

"Why, for Pete's sake? Call him up. I want to shake hands with a man who has the courage to take himself a wife these days."

Sig must have been listening at the bottom of the stairs, for here he came—not the usual serious and assured young businessman, but with his hair rumpled, possibly from driving, and in a state of stuttering confusion.

"He thought you might be angry about our going to a justice of the peace, but it seemed the only way out to us. We still have to tell his folks, and we don't know how they'll take it."

"Better than before a Protestant minister," Sig managed to get out.

Kit took on the determined expression that she rarely wore, and Chester knew that a twenty-four-year-old secret was about to be divulged. "For some reason your father doesn't want me to tell you this, but I'm going to anyway, because I think you should know. His people wanted us to be married by a Baptist minister, and you know from your grandfather how the Lutherans think they're better than anyone else. *We* ran away to Elkton."

"Mother! You didn't!"

"We did. And it's worked out real well, I think."

"Maybe it was the same man. A little white house on the left-hand side of the road, with a lighted sign out front?"

"It was daytime, but there was a sign—and the house *was* white and on the left side as you go in to town. The first place we came to."

"I bet it was the same. Do you remember his name?"

"It's on the certificate, which is put away out of sight of prying eyes. Now I've told you all I'm going to."

There was a sound of bare feet running overhead and then down the third-floor stairs. Helen, her face beaming with excitement—in nightgown and the kimono they'd bought for her when she was eleven, which now came less than halfway to her ankles—threw herself into Sig's arms, making him more flustered than ever. "I heard everything. Sig—Kay—isn't it wonderful, isn't it thrilling?"

When they had Helen quieted down Kit asked, "Where are you going to stay tonight? I better pack some things for you."

Kay didn't look directly at Sig when she said, "They're all packed and under my bed. Helen, run and get them. I sort of thought this might happen today."

Sig looked rueful. "I guess your daughter is far ahead of me, Mr. Jones. The fact is, I report at the office in New York tomorrow. We'll see my people and then take a sleeper. We have occupancy until seven-thirty in the morning, which will give me time to be on hand early—the first day, you know. Kay will come back here and be in the office by ten, which is late, but I felt that under the circumstances I could make an exception."

He seemed to be running out of breath, and Kay finished for him. "As soon as he can he'll get me transferred. I won't be able to work under him, of course, because there's a rule about relatives in the same department."

Chester tried to think of something appropriate to say, but all that came out was "Well, I'll be double damned."

## Chapter 18

What had happened to Mrs. Rivkin? Her eyes looked red from weeping and her mouth was set in a twisted, haggard line. She came over to where Chester was sitting at one of the ice-cream tables, sat down opposite, said, "Oh, Mr. Jones," and began to cry hysterically. Chester jumped up and patted her shoulder awkwardly, wondering if this was some new idea she had concocted for getting credit, and then blamed himself for thinking so. She was in real trouble—anybody should be able to see that. He ran to the fountain, made a Coke, and dropped an aspirin into it. How many times that had worked when one of the women around lost the whole of her husband's pay and just heard the news from her bookie over the phone.

"Here, Mrs. Rivkin, drink this. You'll feel better."

Her hands were shaking too much to lift the paper cup to her lips. He steadied the holder so that she could drink. "I'm afraid something has happened to the mister," he said, "but don't try to answer. Just relax."

She nodded and began to shake her head from side to side, which might have been her idea of relaxing, but it wasn't Chester's. "What has happened this day! To the both of us. Where can I go, I think, without going home, and I thought of here. You've always been very nice to us, Mr. Jones, and the few dollars we owe you you'll get back one day, believe me. And thanks for the drink."

"That's all right. Maybe now that you're feeling better——" He intended to say, "You should go home and lie down," but she interrupted.

"Thanks. You're a wonderful man, believe me. I'll wait here for him. Rivkin will stop here first, I'm sure, because when you need a friend, you are it."

I'm afraid of that, Chester thought, but there was something nice about her saying so, just the same. "But what happened?"

"You wouldn't believe. This morning began bankruptcy proceedings. Can you imagine? By debtors—people who we trusted, who we bought from, that we've been practically supporting for years. We were stunned. I tell you, we worked over that business. Before the help get there, we've got the work set up. Saturdays and Sundays I do the bookkeeping while Rivkin either goes to auctions to buy silk, or designs new items in the line. Our life's blood has gone into that business. Now, when our collections are slow, you'd think we'd get a break."

"Funny thing, Mrs. Rivkin, all the time you've come in here and talked about your business, I've never known what it is. I'm curious."

"You should ask that question. What I've always said to Rivkin. We don't advertise enough, I tell him. But all he thinks about is buying and production. Merchandising is what he has always been weak on and he won't listen. But still it seems impossible you don't know our line: Nikvir Nekvare. There couldn't be a better trademark. I thought it up myself. It rhymes, see?"

Chester realized that he must be looking pretty blank, for Mrs. Rivkin continued almost impatiently, in spite of the soothing effect of Coke and aspirin, "Men's ties. They've never been featured like they should, though God knows I've said often enough to Rivkin, 'If you'd pay less attention to saving a few cents a yard in buying and give more time to merchandising, you could get seven-fifty a dozen, instead of four,' I says."

"I still don't see . . ."

"Rivkin, spelled backward, and neckvare."

"Oh, neckwear."

"What I've been telling you."

The usual light afternoon trade for these times. The women in the phone booths, laying bets, and others buying *True Confessions,* which had just been delivered. A few of the persistent job seekers for the early edition of the *Bulletin.* Some transients for cigarettes or stamps, from the machine, until finally Mrs. Rivkin said, "I just had an awful idea. Rivkin will be taking this even worse than I am. Maybe he's committed suicide, though he's never done anything like that up to now, with plenty of excuses. Think I should go see?"

He had trouble enough of his own, Chester thought, and had done all he could to help Mrs. Rivkin with hers. "Maybe you better," he said, "but take a look home first."

But even then she didn't leave immediately. She sat up straighter, a new look of hopefulness in her expression. "Maybe we can make a settlement. Fifty cents on the dollar maybe. What do they gain if they put us out of business? At auction what would our plant and stock bring? Five thousand dollars maybe—a quarter of what we owe. That's what we'll do—call a creditors' meeting. Fifteen cents on the dollar I'll offer. But where can we get the money?" She thought a moment. "From Spiegel, that's who. A big jobber who owes us plenty. I'll go to him. I'll plead with tears in my eyes. I'll offer him an extra discount."

"Maybe he'll want to settle for fifteen cents on the dollar too," Chester said.

"After all the merchandise we've sold him? He couldn't do us a dirty trick like that. I'm going to him now, right away. The Rivkins ain't licked yet. Thanks, Mr. Jones, you did me a lot of good."

Poor Rivkins! Anyway, they had the courage to be independent. The people who lived on relief were actually better off, without working at all. *They* didn't have to divide a coffee cake for breakfast. He turned around, after watching her hurry down McClellan, and noticed George, sitting at the side of the fountain and looking as though he had been there for some time.

"Hello, son. Didn't expect to see you around this time of day."

"I couldn't stand it out there another minute. When McCorkle came on I just had to run in and see you. I hate to leave him out there alone. He's dependable, but the service that people around there expect!"

"You don't have to give Coke and aspirin to hysterical women, do you?"

"I've been watching. I didn't want to butt in, but I never can understand why you go on helping the Rivkins. She never paid for that Coke she drank, I'm willing to bet. And if she is able to pull off a creditors' meeting, do you think she'll include us? Besides, you know that business of theirs is no good for them. They've been starving ever since they moved down the street, keeping it going. Why don't they see that it would be better to get out of it and go on relief, even, than keep on with something that's hopeless? Nikvir Nekvare. Even the name stinks."

"They're on their own, George. But what's more important——"

"Us. Should we be other Rivkins? Dad, you don't have to say anything. We should have let the place go last month. Now that cold weather has set in we're not even doing curb service, unless I make it into a strictly hot-dog stand."

"All that has been holding me back is thinking how it would affect you."

"I'll take it hard, in a way, but as they say in the magazine articles, you're bound to make a mistake or two at first."

George was taking it better than he had expected. All the days that he had put off going out to see him. Before he could think up just the right, understanding answer, the kid said, "I've been reading about Woolworth. He failed two or three times before he made his first success, in Lancaster, in this very state."

God bless Woolworth and God bless Lancaster. "I've put off telling you how we stood. You've made it easy for me. The loss we'll take won't be too big, and we figured that it might happen, but we can't stand it as well now as we could have six months ago. Maybe the lesson we should both learn is to have a little more in reserve before we start trying to expand."

"All I want to do is to get back to people who aren't fourflushers. Here when customers are on relief they bring in their relief checks to be cashed and make no bones about it. Out there loads of folks have WPA jobs, but they still live in those swell houses and have big automobiles. They don't pay their rent and they owe on their cars—there's hardly a day but some finance-company investigator isn't in, but they act toward me as though I was dirt.

"The little things they cheat you out of. You sell a pack of cigarettes and the woman has forgotten her pocketbook. That's happened here, too, to Mrs. Rivkin and a few others, but at least they admit they owe the money. Out there they get indignant when you ask for the money the next time they come in, and they say they paid. Would you believe it, I have to ask for signatures, to show their husbands."

Mike Cameron's imposing white mane of hair appeared in the doorway and his sonorous voice drowned out whatever else George had been going to say. "Good afternoon, Jones. Still doing business at the old stand, I see. I almost wish you weren't, as apparently I forgot to return these two volumes that I was so injudicious as to rent some six weeks ago. Will it reduce the amount of unearned increment you will charge if I add that I was engaged in making free men of serfs, of automatons, of human machines who had lost the power of individual thinking through the dominance of the speed-up and the shutdown?"

It was hard to understand what Mr. Cameron was talking about, but his voice sure sounded nice. Anyway, he wanted to know how much he owed. Chester looked up his card. "Gosh, you *have* been away quite a time. September fifteenth, and this is—let's see—the twenty-eighth, at three cents a day. Suppose we call it a dollar each, and then I won't have to figure it out."

"Accepted." Mr. Cameron withdrew two crisp new bills from his wallet and put them on the counter. "Thank you for your aid to our cause. And now do you have a book called—let's see . . ." He consulted a slip of paper. *"If War Comes,* by George Fielding Eliot. The title intrigues me. War is already here. While we talk here, the people of Spain are succumbing to the fascist hordes. I predict that within six months of a Franco victory, he and his fellow criminals will plunge all of Europe into war. The Japanese have taken Shanghai. Thousands of innocent people are being killed by bombs dropped from the sky. Yet Mr. George Fielding Eliot says, 'If war comes.'"

That was the trouble with Cameron, whenever you waited on him you had to listen to a lecture on something. Chester looked through the books in a perfunctory manner. "I haven't seen it and it doesn't appear to be here. I'll put in a request for it."

"Do that. And now a tin of Prince Albert. My only association with royalty is to smoke the dear consort's dried-up old clothes."

Chester had heard this little joke a dozen times at least, but he smiled faintly as he handed over the tin of smoking tobacco. "Your *New Republic* is in. Want to take it with you?"

Mike Cameron paid for it and the tobacco, made a roll of the magazine and tucked it under his arm. He walked out, chin jutted forward, the great head thrown back, his short legs taking the most majestic steps of which they were capable.

George said, "There's an example for you. The lending-library company put in a case for me, but nobody rents anything but the latest best sellers, and if they forget and keep them out over ten cents' worth, they slip them back into the case when I'm not looking and claim they took them back and I must have neglected to mark them down. Mr. Cameron may be a labor organizer, but he's honest."

"Is, and no but."

Dickie's voice! Was the whole family practicing stealthy entrances so that he wouldn't hear them come in? Chester said, " 'Is, and no but'! What kind of language is that?"

"*Is* a labor organizer, *and* he's honest. What gives? Why are you here and not at Jones's store number two?"

"Dad and I have about decided to close up out there, on account of the way conditions are, and if you make any wisecracks about I told you so, I'll crack you—over the head with a Coke bottle."

"No cracks are necessary on any score, O wise and farseeing elder brother."

"There you go with that stuff again. I want you to cut it out, and I mean it." Chester thought, this is no time for Dick to be needling George, and the kid sure knows how to do it.

"May a mere child ask a few questions?" Without waiting for an answer Dick asked, "How much have you invested out there in original inventory?"

"Forty-six hundred almost," Chester answered, knowing that George resented the questioning.

"You should have reduced that some by this time."

"Not much. We had to buy a number of new items there were calls for."

"Except for the drugs, you can use most of that stock here. How much do they amount to? The things we couldn't use, I mean."

"Twelve hundred maybe."

George interrupted, "We've already been over all that he's leading up to. Why don't you tell Mastermind to find his way upstairs?"

Instead of being angry Dick grinned.

Chester said, "Because he has a right to know too. Go on, son."

"Thanks, O——"

"Cut it. We took over about nine thousand dollars of installment notes . . ."

"Call them leases, Dad. That's what they are, and it leaves you in a better position in your thinking."

"We got the down payment free, which in most of the leases was a quarter of the price, and one or two payments that Pope made, after."

"Has it occurred to you that good old diamond-in-the-rough Popoff might have sold you on an inflated deal? That he may be working the same thing somewhere else right now?"

"It did, but I don't think it's so. I investigated his old store, and in pricing his stock he marked loads of items below market—stuff that he'd bought cheap at auctions."

George was fit to be tied. "Dad, why do you let him? A high-school kid trying to show off how much he knows about business. Do you think we were complete stupes? I checked on every contract Sam Pope made, personally."

"You should have left it to your staff of lawyers."

"Make him stop. If he's going to keep this up, I'm going back to Overbrook."

"Good idea. Let us finish our discussion tomorrow, Dad, when we won't be interrupted by foolish questions. Has either of you discovered that when you're in a thoughtful mood there's nothing like panned oysters? Fries are for pure enjoyment, a stew is merely filling, but when Mr. Burke puts a nice, big hunk of butter in a pan, sets it over a slow fire, and slips a half dozen fat Maurice River Coves into it, you have the making of something that's really conducive to solid thought."

The continuing wonder of how Dickie came to be his. Why, the darn kid had even a better flow of language than Mike Cameron, and it made more sense. Chester could feel himself growing hungrier by the minute, and it was still early afternoon.

"Of course, the whole secret is that they shouldn't be cooked too much. Ever notice how Mr. Burke watches while the edges curl like a ballerina's skirt and then puts them, pan and all, right on your plate, where each oyster practically dances its way into your mouth?"

Chester watched Dickie's short, stocky figure walk across the street. He was much too stout, but then he was eating all the time. The damnedest youngster . . .

George was saying, "It seems to me that Dick is spending an awful lot of money. Every time I come down here he's over at Burke's. And I'm still convinced that was him I saw in the Ford that day. Do you think he can be stealing from the cash registers?"

Chester thought, if I could take those two kids and shake them together and pour them off again, like two sodas, there would be a big improvement in each. "This family has been living out of this store since long before you were born. If your mother wanted something at the butcher's, she took the money out of the register to buy it. We took quarts of ice cream every day, candy whenever anybody wanted it, sandwiches when we were hungry. We've used store tooth paste, talcum powder, and patent medicines, from Sloane's liniment to Carter's Little Liver Pills, which I think help me, though people say they're old-fashioned. You've all been raised to believe that anything in this store is yours, and when you say things like that I don't like it."

"There's still something funny about it. When I was seventeen you never gave me the freedom you do him."

"I understood you better. When I told you to do something I was fairly sure I was right. With Dick I'm usually doubtful."

"I like that! No wonder he's spoiled."

"Is he?"

"Well he makes me pretty mad. The way he behaves you'd think he was the oldest. But let's forget about Dickie. I got to get back. What shall I do, tell the finance companies to take their equipment when the next payment comes due?"

George was being as brave as he'd been over his sickness, and you had to admire him for it. "The big problem is the lease. The landlord can seize everything in the place that belongs to us unless we make some settlement. He can't touch the equipment, because he has notice that it doesn't belong to us until it's paid for."

Here came Dick, back from Burke's, wearing the expression of a cat that has just finished a bowl of cream. He came in and said, "Still here, George? I thought you were leaving in a huff—or did it go without you? I'm glad if it did, because I've solved your problem."

"Yeah? We can solve our own problems, midget marvel."

"Thanks, good and all-wise . . . Sorry, Dad. This is Thursday and tomorrow I'll be very busy, but Saturday morning I'd like to take you for a little tour of the city in my new 1937 Ford roadster, which lists for six hundred and ninety-five, or thereabouts, but cost me some six hundred dollars cash. Knowing elder brother, he probably thinks I stole it from the cash register."

"You dirty little . . ." Right there, in the middle of the store, George rushed in swinging, trying to take out on Dickie all his own disappointment. In spite of his build Dickie had always been surprisingly light on his feet. He backed away easily enough, but George tripped, fell, and began crying—the same kind of long, hysterical sobs that had racked Mrs. Rivkin earlier. Chester was angry enough to give Dick a sock himself. And suppose somebody came in and saw his sons fighting in the middle of the store?

Before Chester could say what he thought, or interfere, Dick was kneeling by George, holding his shoulders and whispering to him, "I'm sorry. I get carried away by words and ideas, but believe me, things aren't as bad as you think. Wait till Saturday and I'll show you. I'll bring Dad out and pick you up."

The fellow reading through the magazines on the rack had been there half an hour and Mary wanted to tell him that this was no free library, but right now she could see that he had the copy of *Esquire* open at the blond pin-up girl who looked so much like her that all the fellows were making cracks, and she didn't want to hear any from somebody she didn't even know, especially when she was alone in the store. Henry and Horace Green were sitting on the Camac Street curb and would come if she called, but they were only children. She didn't like the way the fellow furtively looked around the store over the magazine either, and occupied herself with filling the cigarette racks until he came over and bought two Camels from her.

Immediately she felt sorry for him. A strange fellow coming in and wanting to start a conversation would surely have bought a whole pack if he had the money. She smiled at him as she gave him three cents change out of the nickel, and he smiled back, a pleasant smile and not fresh, the way she'd expected he would be. "Sorry if I scared you, standing there so long. Think I was going to hold you up?"

"No, but I was afraid you might try to get fresh."

"Me? You're real nice, but I wouldn't have thought of doing that. I was going to hold you up, though."

"You're kidding!"

"No I'm not. I was trying to get up my nerve."

"I bet you don't even have a gun."

"I was going to point my finger in my coat pocket, like they do in gangster pictures."

Mary giggled. "I don't think I would have believed it was a gun unless I saw it."

"Then I tried to make up my mind about something else," the fellow went on. "I only had that nickel and I couldn't make up my mind whether to buy coffee or cigarettes."

Why, he must be hungry. "Come back to the fountain and have the coffee anyway. Mr. Jones, who owns this place, always gives coffee to anyone who asks for it."

"I hate to beg . . ."

"It isn't begging. Besides, it's better to beg than to steal." She turned up the heat under the only Silex that had coffee in it, and the fellow said:

"You can steal and still keep your self-respect. Thanks anyway."

She served the coffee and said, "Everything else has been taken upstairs, but there are two coffee cakes left over from lunch. They aren't awful fresh." She nodded to women coming in to telephone and waited on a few late newspaper customers. "You aren't from around here?"

"No, Detroit. Out there practically everything is closed down. If it's not a strike, it's a shutout. I thought maybe things would be better here in the East and I could get a job. Why I should think so, when there are over eleven million men out of work, I don't know. Anyway I took the chance."

"Couldn't you get on relief or something?"

"Who wants handouts? I'm sorry, this tastes wonderful and you're the first person I've met since I left home who's been friendly."

"Even though you were planning to shoot me with your finger."

"The crazy ideas you get when you're hungry."

"What's your name?"

"Aw, gee . . . don't pay any attention. This is the first I've eaten for a couple of days. No American girl, like you are, could pronounce my name. My mother's American—her name was O'Connor —but the old man's Ukrainian."

The Thomas kids came in for chocolate sundaes, at the table behind the phone booths, where the big colored policeman always sat when he was on day duty. Mary guessed they sat back there so their mother couldn't see them from across the street. She could hardly wait to get out and talk to the stranger again. "My folks are both Ukrainian."

"You wouldn't think so."

"What do you mean, you wouldn't think so? I like that."

The nice smile. "You should know what I mean. You want to be American, and all your life the kids have made fun of you and you want to be American worse than ever, but you're not going to be ashamed of your folks."

"It's my turn to apologize. Do you really want a job?"

"Like I want to live."

"My name is Plotko, Mary Plotko. My father's name is Anthony."

"I'm Pete Theodorevitch. Theodore's son, is all."

"You don't need to tell me. Pop has a job at an oil refinery. It's supposed to be dangerous, but he's been there since before I was born, so it can't be so terrible. He's foreman of a gang, and they're short one man—he was telling me before he left today. If you go there right now, I think maybe you could get on. They have a personnel department that it's supposed to go through, but in an emergency if he hires someone they usually approve."

Gee this was a nice fellow. Imagine him thinking of holding her up. He had a nice smile and nice eyes, and he had been through what she had. "You can't work all night on a couple of coffee cakes." What could she give him? Candy? "Like Oh Henrys?"

"Sure."

She put four in a bag, wrote out a note and folded it, writing the directions on the outside. "This is my father and this is where he works. Oh yes, carfare. You go out by the car that passes here, as far as you can, but ask for a transfer when you pay your fare. Then take a car south to the end of the line. And here's a half dollar."

"As one Ukrainian to another?"

"I can't——"

"O.K."

She watched him walk across Camac and along McClellan. Golly, what a nice guy! If she didn't like George so much, it could be possible that she might love Pete Theodorevitch, when she knew him better. George wasn't so good-looking and not so sweet, but he was so like his father that she couldn't help loving George more than anyone on earth.

Anyway I hope Pop gives him the job, and I'm sure he will, after my note, if it hasn't been filled, she thought.

Someone was coming across the street who walked an awful lot like Saul Gerson. It was Saul! She had thought she would never see him again, the way people were being killed in Spain. The way he walked, swinging his arms, she could see that he wasn't wounded, either. Thank God for that.

"Hello, Mary!"

"Saul! I saw you first, crossing the street. This is wonderful!" He

232

was thinner than she remembered him. There were deep lines to either side of his nose. And he was sunburned almost black.

"When did you get home?"

"Today."

"And you weren't wounded?"

"Only in spirit. We were sent home. I guess I knew it was a lost cause when I went. You know the government has moved to Barcelona. When that falls there will be a few months of consolidation and then all Europe will be taken over by the fascists—or have to fight."

"You sound like Mr. Cameron."

There was a change in his expression. Should she tell him that Gert was engaged? She decided not to—he'd find out soon enough for himself. He said, "There should be more Camerons." He made a gesture of futility with his hand. "It's hard to realize that there won't be an air raid in a few minutes. And I'm not used to the silence, with no guns booming in the distance. Tell me—does Gert come in often? How is she?"

"She should be in in a few minutes. She usually waits here for——" She caught herself and finished lamely, "She's usually in about this time." To cover up she asked, "How long have you been gone?"

"Six months, that's all, but I feel ten years older."

He looked it too, and it gave him a quality he'd never had before. He'd always been nice-looking, but he'd just been one of the fellows in the neighborhood. Now he was handsome—distinguished-looking was more what she was trying to think.

Mary said, "Here comes Mr. Meyer. He'll be glad to see you. He asks if anybody has heard from you every time he comes in, which is almost every night." She hadn't realized how thin and bent over the old man was. She smiled at a recollection. "You remember the first Coke he ever drank, at our picnic here in the store a year ago last Labor Day? Now he comes in for one almost every evening. And he's stopped smoking Melachrinos. If anything ever happened to your dad, Mr. Jones would be stuck, because nobody else smokes them."

Mr. Meyer was so feeble he had trouble opening the door, and

Saul ran to help him. At first the old man didn't seem to recognize him. "Don't tell me that you've forgotten your star pupil."

"Saul! I can't believe it. Mary, take my other arm and help me to a chair. I can't stand." When he was seated he asked, "Your hands —they are all right?"

"Fine."

"A cause for celebration. Mary, two Coca-Colas and one for yourself. This is the happiest occasion since I made my American debut. You will allow me to instruct you again? But of course you must."

"Sure. But I have a living to make, too."

"Have you any plans?" Mary asked.

"I'm to speak around at a lot of anti-fascist rallies. Tell what I saw in Spain."

"Up where Pop takes me to church once in a while, everybody says the side you were fighting on is communist."

"While I was in Spain the government took in the first communist. There are republicans, socialists, anarchists—all kinds supporting the government."

"Politics! A musician has no business bothering with politics." Mr. Meyer threw his hands into the air. "Almost the world lost a man who can be a great violinist. For why?" He shrugged his shoulders.

"Here I guess I'll be working with communists mostly. They seem to be the only ones who see the danger—except for a few people here and there, like Gert's father."

"She's coming now."

Gert stopped short when she saw Saul, and her hand went to her throat. "When did you get back? I didn't know . . ." Her speech drifted away. "You look different. Older, but it's more than that . . . Saul, you left. I thought you would never come back." Mary could see that Gert was trying to pull herself together. "You didn't get hurt? Whatever you think of me, I've thought of you over there, fighting for all of us—alone maybe. Or hurt. You weren't wounded?"

Gert was wearing another new dress and when she came in she

had looked carefree and attractive, but now she seemed haggard and nervous.

Saul said, "I was lucky that way," and Gert said nervously:

"Come around tomorrow. Please. I have to run now. Good night, Mary."

She almost ran out of the store and up Camac Street. Mr. Meyer just sat there, and Saul looked surprised, but Mary knew that Gert wanted to reach the next corner, to head off her rich fiancé before he reached the store.

# Chapter 19

As he reached the top of the stairs Kit called, "Have a nice time, dear?"

"Guess I'm a little late. We started later than usual, talking about that sales tax the city council is trying to get passed. Fortunately Mayor Wilson is against it."

"Sales tax? What is it? My goodness, I thought we were taxed enough already."

"This would be terrible for storekeepers. We'd have to collect two cents on every dollar's worth of sales. First off, everybody would be angry with us for charging it, and then we'd have to turn it in on some kind of complicated form. We storekeepers have troubles enough without making tax collectors out of us." Chester sat down at the kitchen table. "Then, business is pretty bad, and we talked a bit about that. Ed Shaughnessy was really in form today, but do you know, I can't remember a damn thing he said."

"Chester, I wish you wouldn't use such language."

"Why, for Pete's sake?"

"Its effect on the baby, for one thing."

"At six months? Where is she? I want to play with her a bit."

"Sleeping. The way you act, you'd think she was only some kind of toy."

What was ailing Kit? "A pretty nice toy, I'd say."

"I think it's about time you told me how things are out at the new place and here."

That was it! And Kit was right, as usual. He had meant to tell her, but the boys' quarrel had come in between. "The long and short of it is that business is terrible here and we can't afford to keep the other place going. I'm afraid I made a mistake there anyway. I let myself be taken in by the store equipment. The kind of place a man dreams about having. That, and trying to get George on his own feet."

"It won't affect us here?"

"Only that we'll lose two or three thousand dollars, which we might need to see us through a bad time. And this *is* a bad time, as sure as God made little apples."

"Apples?" Kit looked puzzled.

"Never mind. Something funny. Has Dick told you he owns an automobile?"

"Dick? Heavens, no! Where would he get the money?"

"That's what I'd like to know. He and George practically had a fist fight in the store about that before I went to Ed's place for our game."

"It's hard to think of our Dickie fighting. Usually he's the best-natured boy."

"He didn't really, but he got George riled. It's been hard on the kid, out at that store practically day and night. He's nervous and edgy—and naturally disappointed."

"Isn't there some way——"

"I wish I knew one. The bank turned me down on a loan. Dick seems to have some crazy idea. He wants to take me out Saturday in that car of his. Brand-new and he paid over six hundred dollars for it, he says."

"I don't believe it."

"Funny thing. George told me some time ago he thought he saw Dick driving a car, with Floyd sitting beside him."

"The two are out together the minute he's home from school. I don't know what to make of him."

"I'm to learn the great secret Saturday, anyway. One thing, whatever he's done, it's been on his own, and if you ever saw a cocky kid, he was one this afternoon. What in hell do you think he's been up to?"

"There you go again."

"She's sleeping. I tell you, Kit, there are times I just have to cuss, and when I think about Dickie is one of them."

Kit looked at the electric clock over the gas range. "Kay's late." She giggled. "I called her this morning and asked to speak to Kay Jones. You should have heard the way the girl at the other end said, 'You mean Mrs. Dobrzanski?' Honest, Chester, I'm sorry for her. Schweitzer was bad enough, and with a z in it, too. How I loved it when I became Katie Jones!"

"While Kay has to go from Jones to ——"

"Don't say it, Chester. And Sig is a nice fellow. She's really lucky to get such a sensible man."

"Too sensible, almost. But then, Kay is too. Imagine a honeymoon of one night in a Pullman!"

"They took a compartment, anyway. To listen to Kay, you'd think they had been extravagant doing that much. What I was going to say is that her transfer has come through. She was all excited, over the phone. Sig has found an apartment for them—of all things, it's over a store."

"Which should help to make her feel at home," Chester commented. There was a faint cry from the direction of their bedroom. "Now I'm going to play with the baby. Just to watch her gurgle is a treat."

Dick heard the hammering and looked at his alarm clock. A whole hour before he needed to get up. He settled back in bed, and then there was another barrage of blows that sounded as though someone was trying to kick in a door. From George's bed came the low growl of Floyd Gibbons. Dick ran to the window, opened it wider, and looked out. Darned cold in nothing but these pajamas, he thought. Most of the leaves were off the trees, and through the branches he could see the unmistakable outlines of a red police car. Why, it was in front of Mary's house. The hammering began again. Had Mrs. Plotko really cut loose this time? Or the old man? But no, he would be working. Maybe that was it. Maybe something had happened to him out at the refinery. Mary was always talking about how worried she was about the danger in his job. He pulled on trousers and shirt, slipped into unlaced shoes, and sneaked downstairs with Floyd behind him.

He left the store door open—nobody would try to get in, with the cops just a few doors away. By the time he got to Mary's house, she was there in the doorway and her mother was standing behind her.

Mary said, "Dick! Am I glad to see you! Something has happened to Pop."

The police sergeant, who evidently had made the sounds that first roused Dick, kept saying, "I'm sorry, Miss Plotko, coming around at this time of the morning," as though accidents didn't have to happen when they did, but could be planned for somehow.

Mrs. Plotko was being pretty bad. Mary was standing in the doorway so that her mother couldn't come out, but Dick could hear her, and Mary's whispered but commanding "Mom, go inside."

She shut the door behind her. "Dick, do you think your dad would mind if you called him? You're a sweet kid and I appreciate your coming, but something tells me I'll need him."

Dick wondered why George didn't have more sense—for Mary sure looked beautiful, even in that old wrapper, with her hair every which way.

She asked the cops, "Will you give me five minutes to get dressed?" and the sergeant said:

"Sure, lady, but we don't have room for anyone else."

"I've got my car a block away. I'll follow you."

The sergeant said, "Room for her, too? It won't look so good, us driving with a looker like her."

Dick called back, "Sure," as he ran toward the store. No use waking Mother and the baby. He tiptoed upstairs, intending to shut Floyd in his room, but the dog whined so much that it seemed easier to take him along. He didn't remember ever trying to wake Dad during the night before, even when only he and Mother were in there. It didn't seem altogether right to open the door and sneak in, but he did, prepared to back out if it seemed the right thing to do. He shook Dad into wakefulness without waking either Mother or little Alice. "Something has happened to Mary's father. I think he's dead, but the cops who came for her won't say. Dad, she's asked for you to go out with her. You will, won't you?"

239

What a guy Dad was! He was up and putting on clothes automatically, while he kept repeating something to the effect that Mary was one of the family.

Dick whispered, "Wait at the side door. I'll pick you up there," and tiptoed out and downstairs.

The police car was still there. He ran down McClellan to Twelfth and turned south to the row of stall garages where he kept the Ford. He had to circle the block in the car, because of the one-way streets, but he arrived at Mary's house just as she was coming out. He heard her say, "Now Mom, behave yourself," before she closed the door.

Dick said, "Floyd, up in back," and called, "Right in here, Mary."

She was grave and in complete control of herself. What a girl she was!

The sergeant said, "Know how to get there, kid, in case we lose you?" Dick nodded and the sergeant went on, "Well be waiting for you at the refinery gates."

"O.K." Dick waved and drove down the street to the store, where Dad was waiting; this wasn't the way he had intended to show off his closely kept secret, but that couldn't be helped.

Dad said, "Hello, Mary," and took the seat next to her. "This the car you were going to surprise me with tomorrow?"

As the police car pulled around them, Dick said, "You'll get more surprises tomorrow, but this is no time to talk about them." He swung west on McClellan, trying to keep the taillight of the police car in sight; but at Broad he had to stop for traffic, while the police car, claiming the right of way, went on through.

Out of the corner of his eye he watched Mary's expression. In the dim light of early dawn she looked impassive. Whatever her feelings must have been, they were hidden beneath the bleak, flat contours of her face. Now Mary looked like a Slav, Dick thought. Who else could have such complete control in such tragic circumstances?

There was the police car, waiting for them, and Dick followed into the refinery grounds. In a moment they were in a scene of crying, hysterical women, come to identify their dead. Mary said, "Mr. Jones, you'll come with me?" and Dad went along, holding her arm, while Dick stayed in the Ford with Floyd. Accidents must be a commonplace, working around something as volatile as gasoline. All that he could learn, from overheard conversation, was that six men had been burned to death.

Dick began to think of the store. Now that Mr. Oberholtzer was out of work, it wouldn't matter if he didn't get back until six-thirty, though he still opened up earlier, out of habit. Here came Dad and Mary. She was still dry-eyed, but she was really leaning on Dad's arm now. It must be pretty rough to have to identify someone you loved after he'd been burned to death.

He drove halfway back to the store before Mary said a word. She just stared through the windshield until he almost hoped that she would cry to ease her feelings. When she did speak it was in her usual soft, unemotional voice. "Thanks, Mr. Jones. I had to have someone, and you know how Mom is."

Dad said, "Yes."

"The other fellow—the one they didn't know about—I knew, but I couldn't tell them then. All I wanted to do was get away. It would have meant questioning. I couldn't have explained. How could I explain?"

Instead of asking questions Dad said, "Sure, sure." Dick thought, he might have said, "Yes, yes," but the other is better for Mary, the way she is now.

Mary was talking again, which was good for her. "He came into the store yesterday afternoon and hung around. He bought two cigarettes finally and gave me a nickel. I gave him three cents change. One of them was an Indian head. I remember, because I used to save them. I don't any more, but I still notice them."

It was fully light now, and looking at her, the times when he had to stop at crossings, Dick tried to understand why she seemed more upset over the stranger's death than over that of her own father.

"He had come in to hold up the store," she went on. "Imagine, he didn't have a gun. He was going to stick his finger at me through the pocket of his coat. He was nice, Mr. Jones. You know, nice. I gave him a cup of coffee. I knew you wouldn't mind. He was nice, and he said he was Ukrainian, and I said I was too. 'When there are eleven million folks out of work, why should I think I can get a job?' he said, or something like that. Then I remembered Pop telling me they were one short in his gang. Pop always said it was dangerous work that he did, but when he'd been saying that all his life and nothing ever happened . . . Do you understand?"

Dad said, "Sure, sure," again.

"Pete, his name was, and he was nice. One of the nicest fellows I've ever met, even if he did come in to the store to hold us up. There were two coffee cakes left over, and I gave him those too and four Oh Henrys, which I paid for, because he had to have something. Pop has often been shorthanded and had to take on somebody for his gang at the last moment, so there was nothing wrong in that, was there?"

"Sure, sure."

"I wrote him a note to give to Pop and gave him a half dollar of my own."

"Sure, sure."

Dad meant well, but what had been the right answer minutes ago was wrong now. What was coming up was something that Mary might worry herself over for years, if it wasn't killed now.

"What you're trying to say is that you gave him the half buck, sent him down here, and then arranged that the right spark would strike the right fumes. Even you couldn't figure all that out."

"Thanks. You've sort of put it right. It's more than that, though. There's another side. Pop must have taken him on on account of me. Whatever happened, could he have been the cause, out of not knowing better? Maybe he lit a cigarette out of force of habit."

Dick had circled around by Twelfth Street, so that they reached the store first, and Camac was one-way in the other direction—but who would bother at this time of the morning?

Mary said, "Please, can I stay with you? I can't go home right now."

Again Dad said, "Sure," and this time it made sense, for it was practically time to serve the morning newspapers, and George was still sleeping out at the Overbrook store, so there was no reason why Mary couldn't get a little rest in George's bed, which hadn't been slept on, except for Floyd.

Mrs. Waldman found the story in the late edition of the *Inquirer,* and there was a photograph of dimly visible figures carrying stretchers. It wasn't much of a story, three short paragraphs to mark the end of six human beings, and in the list of victims Old Man Plotko's name was misspelled. After Mrs. Waldman had refolded the paper and put it on top of the pile on the floor, she said, "Seeing something printed in the paper makes it seem realer than it would otherwise. When my Eddie first got in trouble I couldn't believe it. I just *couldn't* believe it until I saw it in the papers. They got all the facts wrong and made out a lot of things that weren't true, but there it was, all printed out, and I knew it was so. That's how it will be with Mary."

Chester shook his head. "No. She knows it was so. We both do. There's no fact stronger than what we saw."

"Poor Mary."

"Her problems have been reduced by fifty per cent. She's up with her mother now, and what I'm afraid of is that she'll transfer her loyalties to her. Mary is someone who has to be loyal to somebody."

"I know what you mean. It's a good feeling, too. I go up to see Eddie every visiting day. It's a long trip, but I know he's counting on me being there. And he knows I'm not running around, that I'm waiting for him. I've told him all about how nice you've been and I talk about all the folks coming in the store and all the things they're up against—things almost as bad as what we have to face. When I tell him about Mary next week he'll feel just as sorry as anybody—because, believe me, Eddie is sensitive—but at the same time it'll make him feel better about what he got into, not meaning to. Funny, ain't it?"

"You know, Mrs. Waldman, the first time—or one of the first times—that you came into this store you said that. I remember, because I say the same thing all the time, about things that aren't funny at all."

Why had he said that? He remembered the time, well enough, but he had never thought of it since, until now. He had to make Mrs. Waldman understand. "Maybe they *are* funny. Like the other week, when Old Man Plotko went back to the house with a couple of quarts of beer in a bag. When he passed, all I thought was that maybe he'd started in again and Mary would be having trouble. Then his foot caught on the bad paving over there, or maybe the sweating of the bottles got the bag wet, I don't know. One bottle fell and broke against the bricks, then the other followed. The expression on his face made me laugh fit to kill myself, but it wasn't funny to him. You know, now I come to think of it, that's about the last remembrance of Mary's father I have—his expression then."

By this time everyone who came in seemed to know about what had happened, the way it is in neighborhoods, and Chester tried to tell them all that he knew, because of the way everybody liked Mary, but he was glad when she came back to the store and told them her plans, so he didn't need to say over and over that he didn't know where the funeral would be held.

She was wearing a plain black dress, against which her smoothly combed hair looked more blond than ever. Did women always keep on hand the clothes for such emergencies? Chester wondered if he even owned a black tie, but he wouldn't have been surprised if Kit had one all ready if something happened to her Pop.

"Anything I can do to help?"

Mary put her hands in front of her, palms up, in a way she had. "Honest, maybe people are like this all the time. First I'm going to make myself a Coke."

Chester said, "Let me," but Mrs. Waldman was already pumping sirup.

"All Pop's gang were laborers. And the work was dangerous— he always said it was. But all but Pete—the fellow I sent down, whose last name I can't remember no matter how I try—worked with him for years. I thought it would be nice, and Pop would like it, if there was a funeral service for all of them together. The families thought so too, when I suggested it, but are the priests putting up a kick! I thought they were all Eastern Orthodox, but Mike Morusca, who was closest to Pop, belonged to Holy Ghost, near Fairmount Avenue, which is Rumanian, and a couple of the other poor fellows were Russian Orthodox, but not the same kind. The payoff is Nick, the guy Pop was always talking about because he was so dumb. He went to a Holy Ghost too, but a church way down near the refinery that's Greek Catholic that comes under the Roman Catholic and so isn't really Greek Catholic at all, it seems. Soon's I get my breath back I want to do some phoning to those families and tell them the trouble I'm having. I'll bet they'll be as mad as I am. When you live in America you shouldn't have a European religion."

"Now, Mary, you're all excited," Chester said. "That's what the Ku-Kluxers are saying, with their burning crosses and all."

He'd never seen Mary look so beautiful as she did when she answered angrily, "It's not the same. The Kluxers are after Jews. Do the Jews take orders from somebody in Jerusalem? Do the Presbyterians or the Lutherans or the Baptists? Take all these people, my people. I don't like to learn that they take orders from someone in Turkey or Russia or Rome. There were other places, but I can't remember. Metropolitans of this and that. The Holy See. What is the Holy See?"

Chester said, "I don't think you should bother about it now, Mary. Your father didn't and you shouldn't." He stopped, never having seen her look like that and not knowing what to say.

"You haven't been kidded all your life. All of us people, born here, like I was, or not born here, but not wanting to be called foreigners anyway. Dick, your Dick—he's nice, but he never stops kidding me about it. I suppose it's like in street fighting—you take what advantage you can. We never stop being told what we are, so we return to our religion. Isn't it wrong? It seems so to me."

As it turned out, the service for five of the men was to be held in the Russian church on Fifth Street, because that seemed like a sensible compromise. Nick's family wouldn't consent, Mary told Chester over the phone, and he was to be buried as a Ukrainian Greek Catholic, which was Roman and not Eastern Orthodox.

"It's too complicated for me," he said, "but it seems everybody in the neighborhood wants to go. Your mother all right?"

"Better than I expected. A lot better."

"Kay would come except she doesn't want to disappoint Sig, who'll be waiting for her in New York. She knows you'll understand."

245

"Oh, I do."

Chester couldn't remember talking to Mary on the phone before. Her voice sounded even more gentle than when you were talking to her face to face, but you'd know it was Mary any time.

"An awful lot of the neighbors want to go—even people you'd never think of, like Mike Cameron. He's taking Mrs. Koehler, who has all the animals, and Mr. Meyer, if he doesn't forget by to-morrow. There will be a good many cars, I'm afraid."

"I don't mind. It's nice to think there are so many people who care."

"You and your mother will go in our car, I hope, with Mrs. Jones and Helen. Dick will bring George and Mrs. Waldman."

"Mrs. Waldman? What about the store?"

"We're closing it, after the morning newspaper trade. Dick just made a sign, 'Closed until twelve o'clock, on account of death in family.'"

There were sputtering noises over the phone. Why, it sounded as if Mary was crying, and he hadn't heard her cry once since the accident. He said, "Mary, Mary—what's the matter?" but she kept on crying. He could tell that she was still not herself when she said, so low that he could hardly hear, "I can't talk any more now. Until tomorrow," and hung up.

Kit often said that he was inclined to be stupid where women were concerned, and apt to say the wrong thing, but what in blazes could he have said to Mary to make her behave like that?

# Chapter 20

Floyd Gibbons jumped into the Ford and then looked around at Dick inquiringly, as though he knew that today was a special occasion. And it was. After keeping his secret more than a year Dick found the three-day postponement caused by the funeral of Anthony Plotko an endless period of excitement. Dad didn't matter so much; what he wanted was to see George's face when he'd finished showing them. He picked up Dad and drove out Overbrook Avenue.

Dad said, "Haven't really had time to tell you what I thought of this little roadster. I'm still curious to know what you used for money."

"Really, Dad, I hate to keep you waiting, but it will be easier to show you than to explain now. When I first had the idea I was afraid you mightn't approve and I wasn't too sure I was right. Then, when it went over so much better than I expected, I could hardly believe it and I decided to play for the limit, instead of being satisfied with something small. I've felt pretty mean, not telling you, just the same."

Why hadn't he driven out through the park, instead of this way, with the worn streetcar tracks ready to cut a tire if you crossed them at too small an angle, and the hard-to-see potholes caused by missing Belgian blocks in the street paving? He made such good time, though, that finally Dad said, "You better take it slower, son, or neither of us will get to see what you want to show me."

He turned on Sixty-third, and in a few minutes drove up in front of George's place. Dick pressed the horn button, and when George came running he explained, "We have a lot of stops to make, so I didn't want to lose any time. Jump in." He drove halfway to Market Street and pulled up before a large and rather shabby-looking red brick apartment house. "I'm beginning at the beginning. Come on, Dad. Floyd, mind the car."

He led the way down the alley marked "Service Entrance," turning several times to enjoy the look of mystification on their faces. He passed the first fire-tower stairway, which led to the kitchen entrances of the apartments overhead, pressed a bell button marked "Janitor," and opened the door beside it. "Go right in."

This was really something to watch. George and Dad both looked around the low basement room, with lines of asbestos-covered steam pipes overhead and a cement floor underfoot. At the end of the room two women were operating washing machines. A colored man came toward them and Dick said, "Afternoon, Ellis. How's business?"

"Real steady, Mr. Dick. I sold those two other machines for you."

"Good. This is my father and brother. I'm showing them around."

Dad said, "Glad to meet you. I don't quite know yet what my son is supposed to be showing me."

"Oh, the washing machines," Dick said. "This is where I put in the first one, over a year ago. It's attached to a coin meter. Here it's twenty-five cents for half an hour, but most places it's twenty minutes. They fill the tub first and begin putting in clothes before they put in their quarter. Most of them wash and wring out two tubfuls. There are over a hundred families in this place, a lot of them doubled up, and one machine wasn't enough. They were still washing at ten at night. I give Ellis, here, a quarter of what I take in and ten dollars when he sells a machine. He does pretty good, don't you?"

"Sure do. Almost doubles my pay, and I need it, with a houseful like I got. Mr. Dick is a nice boy and sure treats me fair."

"You treat me fair, so we both do pretty good."

A woman came in with a basketful of dirty clothes, sat down in a rocking chair, and picked up a magazine from a table strewn with them.

"Those two rocking chairs and the table I just put in a month or two ago. Gives the women a place to sit while they're waiting."

"You ain't checking now?" Ellis asked.

"No, but you can give me the hundred from those machines." He really had George goggle-eyed, watching the janitor count out the money. "I'll be seeing you, regular time."

When they got out to the car again, Dad said, "Renting washing machines! Now what in blazes gave you that idea?"

"Being lazy, I guess. I just never could see working hard, the way you and George do, so for a long time I'd been thinking of some way of getting folks to work for you and pay for it, at the same time. Then one night, a little over a year ago, I got hungry and raided the icebox. Going back to bed I barked my shin on Mother's washing machine, and I got to thinking that she only uses it one day a week and the rest of the time it sits around for people to bang against. I figured that if I could rent a washing machine for so much an hour, it might pay."

Again Dick stopped the car before an apartment house, a smaller one. "I've only got one machine in here, and it does fair, partially because the janitor isn't as good as Ellis, but there's no use going in, as it's about the same setup. We'll go on to a place that I do want you to see."

He stepped on the gas and went on, "To get back to what I was saying—then came that slot-machine business, and I got to thinking some more. If you could rig up a slot machine with a timer that would deliver current for a fixed period, and mount it on a washing machine, that would be ideal. The women would do your work and you'd collect. I began saving money like mad, beginning with that jackpot I won during the raid. I hunted up coin-vending-machine companies—there aren't many. None of them had just what I wanted, but I got one to make up something like what I had in mind. That took my first hundred bucks." He slowed down, pulled into a driveway, and parked in the rear of another apartment house. "This is my best place. It's all one- and two-room efficiency apartments and mainly women or young married couples. I want you to see this."

Chester watched the self-assurance with which Dick walked ahead of them. How many of these places did he have? Again they went in through a back door, but this time they continued down a narrow hallway to a cheerful little room in which they saw a row of four machines, a pair of laundry tubs behind each, curtains at two high windows that showed that the room came below ground level, and a suite of painted wicker furniture.

"I'm proud of this place. I put one machine in here and it was busy all the time, but the owner started to kick—said it was using too much hot water and was a nuisance. The janitor tipped me off that most of the women did their washing in the bathtubs and there was a lot of trouble with them running over, and one thing or another. Also, they all ironed in their apartments and scorched tables and so on. I sold the owner on this regular laundry. He paid for the plumbing, and I bought the furniture and had the wiring done. In the next room are ironing boards and outlets to plug irons into. Right now the place is empty, because most of the women work, but early in the morning and from five to midnight it's crowded. Here I only pay the janitor fifteen per cent, because of my bigger investment, but he makes as much from this as from taking care of the whole place."

You had to give credit to Dickie, but Chester still had his doubts. "It's a little hard for me to see any substantial business in all this. How many of these places do you have?"

George said, "Washing machines!" and made a face, but Dickie only smiled.

"I'm getting hungry, Dad, and there's a place around here that sells the best Hoagies."

"Hoagies?"

"You know, submarine sandwiches. They call them that because they're made out of small loaves of Italian bread, which look something like submarines. They're filled with all kinds of stuff: salami and peppers and onions and tomatoes and—oh, a lot of other things.

An Italian has this place and his Hoagies are really good, believe me. Let's pile in."

They only went about a square and stopped before what was nothing more than a hole in the wall, with a sign saying "Hoagies Today" over the door. Dickie, cocky as could be, ushered them into a room that was furnished with two tables and chairs, a wooden-topped counter with stools in front, and a white-enameled electric refrigerator. A man that to Chester looked like a human sparrow, his eyes were so bright and his movements so quick, ushered them to the rear table.

Dickie said, "Three super-dupers, Joe," and then, to them, "If you've never eaten Hoagies before, you might as well try the best there are."

The man practically flew behind the counter, put a cutting board on it, and cut three rolls with single strokes of his knife. Then he opened the refrigerator and really went to work. Leaves of lettuce, slices of radish, tomato, and onion, fillets of anchovy, slivers of meat. He cut, spooned, and forked—his mop of black curly hair shaking like the orchestra conductor's at the Fox Theater.

Joe still seemed to be overcome with his efforts when he served them on squares of waxed paper. There was a sign on the wall, "Pay when served," to which Dickie apparently paid heed, for he dug into his pocket, brought out a dollar and two dimes, and said, "Keep the change."

The darn things looked good and were good, though Chester had trouble in opening his mouth wide enough to take bites and decided to eat on the right side and not trust the bridge that he had on the upper left. He hadn't half eaten his sandwich when Dick, who had finished, began to talk.

"That first meter and machine cost me almost two hundred dollars, with connection costs and buying the machine on time. It earned net, after paying Ellis, about eighteen dollars a week, so it paid for itself in a little over two months, except that I only had five dollars a week to pay and in six weeks had the down payment on another machine in the same place. That brought the income per machine down a little, but by the third month I had four machines and had paid for the first machine. The fourth month I had eight machines and had paid off two more. The next month I didn't buy any machines, because I found I could get a half dozen from a jobber at forty per cent off, and besides, I had one location that wasn't so hot and brought the average down. The sixth month I owned my eight machines, which were earning over a hundred dollars a week, and before the month was over I'd bought six more for cash."

Chester said, "You're as bad talking as you are driving, son. You go too fast for me."

"Take a pencil and paper, George, and put down these figures so Dad can keep up with you and me."

"I'm not keeping up either." George prepared to take notes, just the same.

"Put down at the end of six months, fourteen machines with meters, all paid for and earning around fourteen dollars a week each after all expenses, except depreciation, which I'll explain later. Over eight hundred dollars, which I put back into six more machines. The seventh month somebody broke open a meter and stole ten or fifteen dollars, but I earned over fifteen hundred dollars that month. Six hundred I took to buy the Ford, which I needed by this time as I didn't want the jobber, who was delivering the machines, to know too much about what I was doing. I bought six more machines, which made twenty-six."

"I make it twenty-four," George interrupted.

"You make it wrong," Dick answered snappily for the first time today. "I practically know the serial numbers of every machine I have. That was May and the best month per machine I've had. I bought a dozen machines and got thin finding locations for them."

"That was a time I missed——" Chester began, but Dick cut him off.

"Wait till I finish, Dad, so George won't have any occasion to straighten out my figures. Well, June and all those machines brought down my net per machine to a little over twelve dollars a week, which amounts, if you care to count it up, to over seventeen hundred dollars a month. Meanwhile I found a newer and cheaper meter, so I was able to buy twelve more machines, most of which I put in locations where I already had one or two, like at this place

252

we just saw. That makes fifty machines and meters, even. With more machines, the net per week goes down; it runs around eleven dollars now."

George was pretty good at figures too, even if he had made a mistake before. "Over twenty-two hundred dollars a month! It's impossible."

By golly, with Dickie nothing was impossible. He reached his hand into his inside coat pocket and brought out a bank statement showing a balance of $9,012.27. "That's four months. Up to the first of November."

Wouldn't George ever be satisfied? "I still don't think you're so smart. If all you have to do is buy more machines to make more money, why didn't you buy more, instead of socking all this away?"

That confounded, funny grin of Dick's. "Two reasons, dear brother. In the first place, after the first couple of months I thought I had a foolproof business, where the women who washed did all the work, and the worse times got, the more they would want to save by using my machines. The last part is true. Net weekly earnings per machines are going up, but also, I'm working almost as hard as I do in the store, counting money and moving machines and getting new locations. In the second place, when you and Dad bought that Overbrook place I figured I better begin saving money to bail you out."

When Dick was the way he was now, Chester could understand why he rubbed George the wrong way, even when he was being generous. The kid had a devil in him of some kind, which knew the little chinks in someone's self-respect and put his knife—of look or word—into them.

"Will anybody have another Hoagy?"

Chester and George both shook their heads, and Dick said, "I'm weak from talking so much. Think I'll have a standard twenty-center, just to keep the steam up."

The little Italian went into his act again, and Dickie said, "Where was I? Oh, yes. From present experience, I can count on about twenty-two hundred a month—in quarters. There's almost no upkeep and no depreciation. Know why? Another angle I figured out. When the machines get to be six or seven months old, Ellis sells them for me. I keep a permanent ad in the paper, 'Washing machine, less than a year old, for sale at half price.' That's sixty dollars, and now I'm buying new machines for that, so all I lose is the ten bucks' commission I pay Ellis."

"Well, son, you certainly have worked hard," Chester said, as Dick bit into the new Hoagy.

The kid winced. "Dad, don't remind me. I've worked like a dog and I don't like it. That's why I want to take you and George in with me, as equal shareholders. Jones Enterprises is my idea for a name. I'll put in my washing-machine business and enough cash to bring my investment up to fifteen thousand."

The damn assuredness with which he talked! And not yet eighteen. What was he doing, Chester wondered, looking at a business tycoon in the making? He watched the way George sat forward, prepared to object, without knowing what to object to.

"The investment of Dad and yourself is your stock and equity in that Overbrook store, and J.E.—almost like G.E., which will inspire confidence—will take over the lease."

George said, "But you talked about equal shares. You'll have twice the investment of the two of us put together."

"You confuse terms. We'll invest according to ability, but share equally. I owe it to Dad, and to you too, for your fine example during my formative years. But I have two conditions."

"I thought there would be." Why couldn't George let Dickie finish?

Dick grinned. "The first is choice of officers. I want Dad to be president, you to be V.P.—that's the fellow who does the work— and I'll be secretary and treasurer—which maybe I can't be legally until I'm twenty-one. I'll have to consult my attorney about that."

"You mean you have a lawyer?" George almost screamed.

"Why the surprise? You don't think I'd run a business the size of mine without legal advice? Oh yes, the other condition—and this is only a quasi condition, if there is such a term." In two seconds Dick's manner and expression had changed completely. He was being direct, sincere, and simple. "I believe I can make a go of the Overbrook location by completely changing its character. I'd like to have a free hand—with your advice and assistance, of course. Think it over, both of you. The Joneses have ample capital that's already paying ten per cent a month, and the world is our oyster.

"Which reminds me. Let me drop you off at your place, George, and Dad and I will buzz into town. I have an order in with Mr. Burke for five o'clock, and we just have time to make it. Your next note installments are practically due, so we need to work fast. If you're agreeable, we'll meet at my lawyer's the day after tomorrow and sign incorporation papers."

Chester headed off whatever George was about to say. "But son, no lawyer will be able to do things that quick, from what I know of them." The constant wonder—what forebear of Kit or himself was responsible for this fat and chunky yet strong and athletic kid whose mind was always so far ahead of you? He was being taunting again, as he picked up a remnant of his second Hoagy.

"A tidbit for Floyd, for guarding the car. As for the papers, they've been ready for a month or more, waiting for the time when you two would reconcile yourselves to having made a bad deal and make a sacrifice to get out of it."

By the time they arrived at the store Chester's head was reeling with facts and figures. Dick had told him all about the many brands of washing machines he'd tried, the advantages of enameled over aluminum tubs, of soft-rolled wringers over the whirl-dry ones, about jobbers' discounts and wholesalers' and why there was a difference. About the types of meters he'd tried and ways of hooking them up to the machines so customers couldn't tamper with them, of ideas he had for installing metered radios that would play a half hour for a dime. The disadvantages of renting electric ironers the same way, the rules for cleaning out the tub properly after use. "I've wanted to tell you all my problems right along, Dad," he had said, "but at first I didn't believe in the idea too much myself. What I mean is, I didn't believe in renting washing machines the way George believes in storekeeping. Fact is, I don't believe in it that way now. The minute there'd be a lot of competition, or landlords would begin to wake up to the fact that they could buy a few machines and get the income for themselves, I'd sell out. In fact I've already figured that when that happens—and it's almost inevitable, eventually—it's the landlords I'll sell to."

There was a place to park on Camac Street, and Dick backed in with a single cut of the wheels. "I know you want to relieve Mrs. Waldman, and Floyd likes fried oysters as much as I do. Don't you, Floyd?"

Funny, the way the dog put his head to one side, the black patch over one eye giving him an especially ludicrous expression, and then gave two short barks. When Chester got out on his side the dog jumped over the door on the other, then ran over to the pavement, his stump of tail wagging eagerly. Chester watched the boy and dog walk toward Burke's together. Why, Floyd was actually getting as fat as Dick—and no wonder.

When Chester entered the store he said, "Sorry to be so late, Mrs. Waldman. Dick has been giving me a lesson on how to make money."

"That's all right, Mr. Jones. It's been slow, and I had nothing to do anyway. I'm glad you came, though. That Cameron girl was just in. She asked for you and was disappointed you weren't here. She seemed real upset. I'll stay awhile longer if you want to go around and talk to her."

Now, what could be bothering Gertie Cameron? "You sure she went home?"

"I imagine so; she went out the side door."

"Maybe I better."

He left the store and turned down Camac, thinking that he hadn't been on Fawn Street since the days of the committee to clean it up, after the polio epidemic when George had been stricken. As he turned into it he thought that it could be a pretty little street, with its tiny, steep-roofed colonial houses of old-fashioned red brick. The street was too narrow for automobiles, so children could play in safety. It was real warm, in spite of the fact that it was November, and there seemed to be dozens of them—little girls playing jacks or carrying brown-skinned dolls, boys playing marbles and pitching milk-bottle tops. From an open door came the bang of an out-of-tune piano, and a sweet little voice sang, "I like coffee, I like tea, I like the fellows and they like me. I wish my mother would hold her tongue; she had a fellow when she was young." That reminded him—what had happened to Shirley Stratford since her family moved from the neighborhood? What a wonderful voice the child had! And the Green children. It seemed funny not to see the whole tribe back here.

The door to the Cameron house was painted bright red and had a polished brass knocker and doorknob. He knocked and waited. In a moment the door opened and Gert stood there, in the kind of blue jeans and shirt she used to wear. "Mr. Jones! I saw you in the 'busybody' upstairs. I was just around to the store. Did Mrs. Waldman tell you?"

"That's why I came over. She said you were upset about something."

"I didn't know I showed it, but I'm awful glad to see you. Come in."

Inside, partitions had been knocked out to make one good-sized room out of two small ones and a hallway. A funny-looking room it made, Chester thought. One wall was painted a red as bright as the door, and another a deep blue. The other two were covered with cloth that looked like the kind that potato bags are made from. On each hung a picture you couldn't make any sense out of, except the lines in it were about the same red and blue as the colors of the other walls. Running around three sides of the room were low shelves with so many books in them that Chester wondered why Mike Cameron ever wanted to rent any out of his library. On the top shelf, all around, were pieces of wood or stone or metal that looked slightly like women's heads or bodies or animals of some kind or other, but none of them enough so that you could really recognize them.

"The old man has an amusing collection of sculpture," Gert said, noticing where he was looking. "Are you interested?"

"They don't make much sense to me," Chester said, feeling that perhaps he was being rude.

"I'm sort of pleased that you don't care for them." On the side of the wall where there was no bookcase stood a large radio and phonograph combination, with cases of records by it. "Like classical music? Or jazz? We pride ourselves on our understanding of both."

Gert was in an odd mood. He didn't know whether she meant what she was saying, because of the peculiar way she said it. Instead of answering he waited.

"I came over to the store because I felt that I needed some advice and I didn't know who else to turn to. You're always so sensible . . ."

Chester had to chuckle, thinking of this afternoon. "If you want advice, you should ask Dickie. He's a lot smarter than I am."

"This time I need somebody more like a father, and I can't go to my old man, because I know just what he'd say and I'm not sure he'd be right. Oh, I don't know. I thought, Mr. Jones is just the one to help me, but now I don't know how to say what I want to. But we're still standing. Do sit down."

The chairs were as strange-looking as everything else. They looked like horses' saddles with oddly slanting legs and a funny back, which pressed right under your shoulder blades, but they were more comfortable than they looked. Well, if Gert wouldn't take the plunge, or couldn't, he'd have to.

"You know, being in the store all day, a lot goes on that I can't help seeing. Most of our customers are neighbors too, folks we've known for a long time. With you, we were all glad to hear about your engagement. Your fellow never came into the store, but that didn't matter. I saw him through the window a few times. He looked nice and clean-cut, though I don't know how much that means."

"He is nice."

"Then Saul Gerson came back."

"Yes. You realized he meant something to me?"

"You used to stop in quite a bit together."

"Mr. Jones, I don't know what to do. I don't. What do you think I should do?"

"Me? I can't tell you what you should do. I wouldn't try, even, because I might be wrong. Naturally I've thought something about it, like I do about all the girls and fellows coming in, as well as my own children. With them, I try to stay out of the way unless something begins to get completely out of hand the way I see it, and even then I'm not always sure I'm right."

258

"Please tell me what you think I should do."

"I can't tell you what I think you should do, but I *can* tell you more or less what I've thought about you three people that I know —you and your father and Saul—if you really want to know and especially if it will help you make up your mind the right way."

Hell, Chester thought, I hadn't meant to get so technical, but Gert said, "That's just what I *do* want."

"Have you noticed that ever since Saul has been grown up he and your father seem to get excited about the same thing? They're not much alike otherwise, but in their way of thinking they are. I'd call them idealists. Now, Gertie, maybe you can help me out. I don't mean that that's wrong, but sometimes there's no judgment behind their idealism. They're too—too . . ."

"Sentimental?"

"Exactly. They're sentimental idealists. A pretty good phrase for me!"

"Maybe you have something. I never thought of the old man and Saul in the same breath."

"It might be a good idea for you to think about having lived with and listened to your dad this far in your life and listening to somebody else like him for the rest of it."

"God forbid!"

"It was an idea I had before Saul ever went to Spain."

Suddenly Gert jumped up, walked over to the shelves farthest from her, and picked up a square block of wood with what seemed to be a face carved on it.

Chester cried, "Hey, what's got into you?"

"The old man bought it, and Saul said he admired it, the last time he was here, but I have to look at it every day. I want to throw it through the window."

Chester got up slowly from the funny chair and said, "I'll be getting back to the store."

# Chapter 21

Chester wondered whether he would ever have an opportunity to tell Kit about Dickie's amazing business venture. First of all, when he came around after talking to Gert Cameron, he had to run into her father, who seemed completely unaware of the crisis in his family. *Maybe he's right, letting things take their course,* Chester thought. But Gert had come to him for help and not to Mike.

He was all steamed up about the President's appointment of Senator Black to the Supreme Court. "To appoint to the highest court of the land a man who was ever a member of the Ku Klux Klan is a direct affront to every Negro, every Jew, every Catholic," Mike orated.

"He doesn't belong any more," Chester objected mildly.

"But he *did.* Any man so injudicious as to join an organization dedicated to intolerance and hate isn't fit to sit on the Supreme Court bench."

He kept on talking until Chester said, "As you know, I haven't much use for a lot of this New Deal business because it's not honest. It pretends to be doing things it's not doing at all and not even trying to. This HOLC is an example. When you see its sign in the window of an empty house it doesn't mean that Home Owners Loan tried to keep the home of some poor old couple and failed, but that it bailed out the investment of some insurance company or bank, and now that it has done its job it doesn't care whether the property is kept up or not. Take a look at the HOLC houses around here, the way they're falling to pieces. Now about Black. Seems to me he's been a real good senator and at the same time he seems to believe in the things you do, including all this alphabet stuff, but you don't like him because once, a long time ago, he had some ideas that you don't believe in—and I don't, for that matter. In your kind of thinking can't a man ever change his mind?"

Honest, there were few times that Chester felt so steamed up about something. Here was a man honest enough to admit that at one time in his life he had believed in an organization strongly enough to join it. Then, because he later came to believe it was wrong, he had renounced it. What was so awful about that?

"You call yourself liberal in your thinking," he went on. "By damn, in some ways I think you're narrower than I am. I admire the new Justice because he has the courage and the honesty to acknowledge that sometime in growing up he made a mistake." Just the same, he was sorry he had got into an argument with a customer. That was one thing George was always warning him against.

After Cameron had gone Dick came in to relieve him, but meanwhile Mrs. Malone had started to explain her new system. Malone was probably at home right then, stewing because the twins weren't being taken care of properly, and the thought made Chester uneasy.

"From now on I'm only playing winners. You make less, but it's sure."

How sure is sure, playing horses? Chester chuckled inside while Mrs. Malone went on talking. "Take War Admiral, for instance. He's won his eighth straight. But does he pay to win? He doesn't you might say, but by my system . . ."

Mrs. Malone's beautiful, dark Irish features, all excited, the way they were now, and Malone waiting at home for her. The first few months after the twins were born she'd had her hands full, but now she spent most of every afternoon in the phone booths again. Gambling did something else to women, if they kept it up long enough. What was it? Something hard to put into words. A loss of a sense of values, maybe. Mrs. Malone wasn't the sweet girl any more that Malone had first brought to their neighborhood. But then, Malone had changed too.

When Mrs. Malone left he got upstairs at last, but just as he took his shoes off, preparatory to telling Kit about the afternoon, Honey came in. He could hear her whistling *"Bei Mir Bist Du Schoen"* all the way up the stairway and she sounded happy enough, but the minute she saw him she began crying.

"Now what in hell's got into you?" he asked.

That wasn't altogether the right attitude to take toward somebody who had worked for them as long as Honey had, and was bound to them by every tie of love there was. "I'm sorry, Honey. Right now I'm mad over two people, Mr. Cameron and Mrs. Malone, but that doesn't give me any right to take it out on you."

Who in the whole world had a smile like Honey's? Or more courage? Or more understanding? Maybe understanding was the most important of all. Chester began to think of all the situations he might have worked out among his customers if he had only possessed more understanding of them and their problems at the times that they needed him.

Around here the colored people called Honey bright-skinned, but it didn't begin to describe the peculiar beauty of her complexion. Of course the perfect, youthful appearance of her teeth helped. Even Helen didn't have teeth so beautiful. Honey worked twice as hard as any white woman he knew. She put in a full day with them and took good care of her own family besides. She never complained, and he was shocked to think that so far as he could remember he had never seen her look unhappy before.

She must have been, and had put on some happier face to conceal how she felt. It must be pretty bad, whatever had happened, if she couldn't do that any longer. She could forget her own troubles enough to say, "Mrs. Malone is just rotten spoiled, that's all. If he'd beat the living daylights out of her, instead of sucking the bottle, they'd all be better off. Why you're mad with Mr. Cameron, I don't see. At least he tries."

"You've put it just about right."

Honey said, "I sure made a fool of myself, but it ain't easy to keep a family together and I have to manage mine. Not that

Shelley is a worthless man. He ain't. But he figures that as long as he don't run after other women and brings in all he makes a week, he's done his part. Mr. Chester, we got to look ahead, with children growing up."

"Now, Honey, what happened?"

"Shelley lost his job."

"At that spaghetti joint?"

"Uh-huh. Not that he can't cook it good as any wop, but the way things is . . ."

"Don't worry. For one thing . . ." Chester searched for words. What were all those phrases when you had to seek public help? Honey didn't give him time. "We've always forded our own creeks when we came to them, and I aim to do so right along."

"You know that as long as the Jones family keeps afloat you'll be riding with us."

"And when it starts to sink I'll be the first to go."

"You wouldn't say that without having thought a lot about it."

"I have. These are days that you have to."

"Not now. Dick has found a way. You might have been right. Honey, the way people like us make up their minds isn't always fair."

"I know, Mr. Chester."

"You would. You ought to know me better than I know myself."

"Sometimes I've thought that. Like that new store. Often I wanted to come down and nudge your elbow and tell you not to mess up with something like that right now. Because why? We feel the pressure long before you do."

What had happened to Kit? He was about to call when she came in—from their room, he guessed—and then Helen burst in on them. Recently she had acquired a new way of expressing herself with her hands, throwing them out together to the right or left, with the fingers bent and thumbs somehow more noticeable than usual. She sure began to put on an act now.

"Well, kid, what's bothering you?"

"I'm a grown woman, Dad. Why should you treat me like a child?"

He tried to laugh easily and not snort, but whatever came out didn't help.

"Aren't you satisfied with ruining my life"—there was more of the play of hands—"without being amused over what you've done?"

All he could think of to do was to ask, "Say, Kit, what the hell is going on?"

"Now don't get excited. Helen is a little upset."

"Mother! I'm furious. My whole life ruined. Believe me, I've nothing left to live for."

"Say, are you two in cahoots at going crazy? What am I supposed to have done?"

"It's about that Gibson boy—the sailor. His leave was canceled and Helen didn't get to see him before he left."

Chester was going to say, "Good," but realized in time that it would only complicate matters, so he lied like a gentleman and a father. "Well now, I'm sorry to hear that. A nice, clean-cut boy. But why blame me? I'm not the U. S. Navy."

"You humiliated me before him. He never even came around to say good-by."

"No doubt he'll write. I'm sorry, Helen, but a father has some responsibilities."

"And I missed seeing a perfectly marvelous movie that I'd set my heart on."

"That actress that died and the fellow with the big ears?"

"Dad! Clark Gable is wonderful—and Jean Harlow was the great love of his life. This was her last movie."

Kit said, as though she meant it, "I've wanted to see that picture too. It's still playing. Chester, darling, let's go, and take Helen."

Chester had to laugh at a certain remembrance. "I don't think we should go to the movies together. It's not safe. You and Helen go to the matinee Saturday."

Honey went downstairs to clean up around the fountain, and Helen, partially mollified, went to her room.

"Well, that's that. I've been waiting to tell you about Dickie."

"What I've been wanting to know is where he ever got the money to buy that car."

"The Ford? My dear, that's the least of it. Do you realize that right now Dickie has more money in the bank than we've ever had in all our lives? He's a washing-machine magnate, that's what he is, and he's offered to take us in with him on equal shares, with him putting up fifteen thousand dollars and George and I putting up the equity in the other store, which we were going to lose."

"Fifteen thousand dollars! Where would our little Dickie get that much money?"

"Renting washing machines. Kit, it's fantastic. Let me tell you . . ."

"Quite a remarkable son you have, Mr. Jones."

Chester roused himself from his daydream. "What? Oh, yes."

Dickie grinned at him. "You don't sound very enthusiastic, Dad."

The lawyer sat there, that kind of half-smile on his face that lawyers appear to use when they don't altogether know how to deal with a situation. If doctors have a bedside manner, lawyers might be said to have a deskside one, handy for reading wills to bereft families, compromising litigation, or having a younger son take his brother and father into business with him.

"Tell you the truth, Mr. Baxter, when I think of what he's done this last year, with his family knowing nothing about it, I'm a little—well . . ."

"Nonplused is a good word, Dad. I don't know exactly what it means, but at this point it would sound good."

Why doesn't George help me out? Chester asked himself, then thought, he's even more in a daze than I am.

"I'm afraid that when Richard first came in to see me I wasn't inclined to take him seriously—his obvious youth and his—do you mind if I say so?—assuredness. He'd evidently just picked my name at random, and——"

"Ho-o-ld up right there, Mr. Baxter. It's not fair for you to say that. Soon as I saw I had hit on a way of making a good bit of money, a lot for the Jones family anyway, I decided that sometime I might need a lawyer. I was thinking of some woman getting caught in a wringer or something like that. I figured it would be better to pick one out before, than wait until something happened. I could have gone to the lawyer Dad's used a few times, but he's an old fogy. Finally I decided that the people who would know the most about lawyers would be the men who had to listen to them. By being real persistent I got in to see quite a few of the judges across the street in City Hall. I told each of them that I was the oldest son of a widowed mother who needed good, honest legal advice that wouldn't be too expensive, and could they give me a list of four or five lawyers from which I could pick. Some didn't want to, at first, but they all did eventually. Mr. Baxter, your name was on the lists more often than anybody else's."

Suddenly George came to life. "I think that was an awful thing to say about your family, especially when it's not true."

"I told you I was anticipating, didn't I?"

Mr. Baxter was obviously pleased. "Why, Richard, you never told me that. I never realized I was held in such high esteem by our judiciary."

Chester thought, if I know Dickie—and the longer I'm around him, the less I'm sure that I do—he's built up this story in the last two minutes.

By damn, he was right. Even after sitting there for an hour, listening to all the whereases and heretofores that Dickie had cooked up and Mr. Baxter had put into legal form for them to sign, Chester felt that he was doing pretty good to recognize that funny anticipatory look that Dickie always had when he was leading somebody into a verbal trap.

Mr. Baxter may be good and honest, but he still doesn't know Dickie the way I do, Chester thought, when the lawyer went on to ask, "Just as a matter of curiosity, how many lists was I on?"

Why did the kid get such enjoyment out of something like this? He put his pudgy hands in his side pockets and smiled that devilish way he had. "Two, Mr. Baxter."

Now, as he looked around the place, it was hard to realize that he had ever thought it was the most beautiful store in the world and that he had dreamed about it for nights running. How much more experience he had now—gained the hard way maybe. George thought of the long days that he had been out here, the wakeful nights while he faced facts. The fact that stainless-steel equipment showed every touch of a finger, even when it wasn't in use. The fact

266

that alternating black and white rubber tiles showed tracks the way a more mixed pattern or battleship linoleum wouldn't have. The fact that a backlog of old prescription files was more important to a drugstore than an attractive counter. The fact of all facts, that it was customers that made a store. Every now and then Dick came out with a really bright remark. What had he said the other day? Oh, yes. The British Empire had supported itself on four hundred million starving Indians. The kind of thing you might expect from Dick, but there was truth in it at that.

And he had been pretty darn decent about putting up the largest investment in Jones Enterprises and insisting that each of them was to own an equal share of the stock. Just the same it wasn't fair that after all his years of work and planning, Dick, who never worked when he could get out of it, should make all that money on something as silly as renting washing machines. Also, he hadn't been too smart, or he would have insisted upon being president of the new company, or vice-president at least.

Dad nudged him. "You better listen to this, son."

When Dick got going you had to admit he could talk. Mr. McCorkle was sitting back there listening, and that wasn't such a good idea; a man who was working for you shouldn't sit in on a purely family matter. Dad couldn't resist Dick, and George felt that for the good of the family he would have to take as objective a view as he could.

"We are hooked with a lease," Dick was saying, "also with a lot of furniture and fixtures and stock. We must agree that the location is no good for the kind of store you had, because you were ready to take a loss, but did you ever analyze what kind of business might be successful here? By accident George came close. This is not a good neighborhood location, but a wonderful one for automobile traffic. What kept this place going all summer was curb service, from Cokes through sandwiches. As a side line to running a drugstore, remember?"

When Dick started to talk George still felt resentful, but gradually he began to see what Dick was driving at.

"You go to a drugstore to eat only if you think you're not going to find any place better. Then, let's look at it another way. Cases, counters, refrigerators we can move with no expense, but all that 220-volt wiring and the plumbing around the lunch counter we couldn't. Curb service is too much work. Here we have an ideal setup, I think, for what is going to be the light-lunch stand of the future. There's plenty of parking space in front. The fact that the store is back of the building line was bad the way we've been running it so far, but now we can take advantage of it."

Dick hadn't once said that he'd done wrong, George thought, and what he said amounted to good merchandising, the way the magazines talked about it.

"My idea is to specialize in sandwiches and put on an act, making them like Joe does in that Hoagy place I took you to. I thought maybe we'd get Shelley and dress him in a chef's outfit, with a high white hat. Two hundred varieties of sandwiches, we'd advertise on our signs."

"Wouldn't that mean keeping an awful lot of fillers in stock?" George asked.

"Let's take four basic fillers: ham, cheese, tomato, and egg. We'd serve lettuce with everything, for looks. There's ham sandwich, and cheese, and ham and cheese. There's ham and tomato, and cheese and tomato, and ham and cheese and tomato, and plain tomato. Then we'd serve tomato and egg——"

Dad interrupted. "O.K. I guess we get your point."

"We'd have a terrific menu, with each sandwich numbered. I can think of five kinds of hamburger right off. The name I thought of is the Earl of Sandwich, and the slogan 'Each Sandwich an Aristocrat.' They would be, too. We'd hire Mary to run the place on salary and a share of the profits."

Dad interrupted again. "I'm afraid you'll have to count on somebody else for that job. Just this morning Mary and her mother left for Buffalo, to live with Mary's aunt."

Mary going to Buffalo? Why, she couldn't do that! George was surprised by his feeling of—of—what did he feel, exactly? Well, Mary shouldn't have gone without saying something to him. "She's gone, without saying anything to me?"

"She told me the other day. There's been so much happening, I forgot to tell you."

"But she works for me. She had no right——" Dick was looking at him, that funny way he had, and George stopped in the middle of the sentence.

"She works for me too. Every day. There's nothing to be excited about, son. Naturally she thought I'd tell you, and I fully meant to."

"I'm not excited. Only . . ." Only what? Well, she should have told him anyway, told him personally and not through Dad. It was hard to get his mind back to what Dick was saying.

"We'll get a girl to run it, anyhow. Maybe Mrs. Waldman, and put somebody else in her place."

Mary had gone to Buffalo. How far away was Buffalo?

"So much for the front of the store. My idea is to run through a partition halfway back and then divide that part . . ."

And not saying anything to him! What was the matter, was he poison or something? Here they'd known each other all their lives practically. Was that any way to treat him? When he saw her again he'd tell her just what he thought of the way she'd behaved.

Dick was saying something about storing his old washing machines in one room in the back and making the other part into a laundry. George tried to put his mind on what Dick was talking about. After all, he was vice-president of Jones Enterprises and this would be their first undertaking. It was his duty to disagree, or to suggest other ideas, but the trouble was that you never knew what Dick was coming up with next, and besides, he kept getting back to thoughts about Mary.

Why should I think of her any more? he asked himself. If that's all she thought about me, the sooner I forget about her, the better.

"Practically nobody around here has a washing machine—I've made a survey. They send out to laundries—mostly damp-wash— and they've run up bills with most of them, which they couldn't with me, as it's pay first."

Honestly, the way Dick talked you'd think that all that mattered in the world was business. He didn't seem to care about what happened to Mary, alone in a strange city with a mother who wasn't really fit to take care of herself. Mary wasn't anyone to strike out on her own, after living on Camac Street all her life. Why, she had always come to him or to Dad for advice when she'd had trouble.

What would she do now? Couldn't Dad, even, see how serious this was, instead of going on interminably when he should be giving a little thought to what was really important? He became increasingly impatient while Dick was explaining his reasons for not wanting the laundry business to share part of the store front.

"When people catch on to the possibilities the competition will be killing, the way it is in the damp-wash laundries now. This won't depend on location, but going from house to house and getting a few people started, the way I did in the apartment houses. Once a few try it they'll tell others."

George tried to forget Mary long enough to ask, "Why you should think people would come to a laundry when they wouldn't to a store . . ."

"The automobile," Dick said. "The automobile encourages people to buy out of their own neighborhoods, where they can get things cheaper, but I'm hoping that women who wouldn't be caught dead carrying a bundle of wash won't mind taking it in their car. I found out something else, too. Even women who you wouldn't think cared don't like to think that their clothes have been washed in the same water with some other woman's." He shrugged his shoulders. "So if it doesn't pay, we can recover our investment by putting the machines in some of the locations I already have."

Ideas about what to do with the prescription department and the purely drug stock. Ideas about another store, farther south in South Phillie. "I know George won't be happy unless he's running a store, and there's a place that's a giveaway—the place where I won the jackpot the time of Mayor Wilson's raids. We could doll it up with some of this equipment, because what's there is old stuff bought up piecemeal."

At last Dad opened his mouth. "How do you know it's so good, son?"

"There's more people there to the block than down at our place, even—with only a few hundred bucks' investment. We'll only take it if the landlord makes the right kind of lease, which he will, the way locations are going begging."

The way Mary's hair fell in a soft, blond sheen down to her shoulders. The grave way she had of looking at you with those eyes that were so difficult to define in color because of the way they changed from gray to green. The way she moved when she was serving people at the fountain or at the curb out here on Sundays. Why, just to watch her was wonderful. Funny that he had never dated her, but it must have been because she was always around.

Besides, she had never cared much about him, that he had noticed, and this was proof, going away without even saying good-by.

Dad was talking again. "Now, don't ask me what I think about all this. The truth is, Dickie, that I haven't been able to think since you showed me your first washing machine. It looks like you're going to be the idea man of this corporation and George and I will furnish the work."

Honest, when Dick looks like that I hate him, George thought. Here he was thinking he was so smart and not even giving a thought to what might be happening to Mary right at this minute.

"All I'm trying to escape is work."

"I guess you're going to be like George and not even want to finish high school, much less go to college."

"Whatever made you think I was ever like George in anything? Sure I'm going to college."

They still hadn't said anything about Mary. He had to find out something. "Did she leave her address?"

Dad's face looked blank.

"Mary, I mean. Did she say where she was going to live in Buffalo?"

"Why no, George. I don't believe she did."

"It seems to me that the least you could have done was to have got her address."

"Whatever for? She's gone to live with her mother's people. I wouldn't be surprised but what she wanted to cut away completely from around our neighborhood."

"Why, for Pete's sake?"

"Well, for one thing, everybody knew about her family, about the way Old Man Plotko drank."

For a man who could be so wonderful sometimes, Dad sure

wasn't showing much sense now. "What does her father have to do with it now?"

"Her mother is no prize package either. I just don't see why you're getting so excited about Mary. You never seemed to before, and she's lived a half block from us all her life."

How can my own father be so stupid, thought George.

"Forget about Mary," Dick said. "We're transacting business. I had started to say that I thought Saul Gerson would be a good fellow to handle the laundry. He's dependable, and a regular job would get him away from the half-baked radical group that's making him into a hero while they keep him in spending money."

George simply stopped listening. He was glad when Dad suggested that it was time to get back to Camac and McClellan. Dick said he'd stay and take measurements of where he wanted to put partitions.

Funny, George thought, he'd never realized until the last few weeks how commercially minded Dick was, but today had certainly shown him up, though he'd been generous enough about little things that didn't count.

Chester said, "If you don't mind, I think I'll drive. Between you and Dickie, I hardly get a chance any more." Most of his time was spent in trying to understand what was going on in the minds of his youngsters, and generally, when he tried to guess, he was wrong.

This time, though, it was pretty apparent that George was carrying a grudge toward Dickie, in spite of the generous way the kid had treated them and the deference with which he had asked their advice, though he was so far ahead of them in his thinking that it was like a one-man race.

"Now George, you shouldn't hold it against Dickie that he's smarter than we are. He bailed us out of a big loss, for one thing."

"Dad, believe me, I'm not even thinking about Dickie. I don't care what he does or what happens about anything."

"You mean because we didn't make a go of the store the way it was? You can't always figure about those things. You yourself said that Mr. Woolworth failed several times before he hit a winning combination."

Chester was so engrossed in trying to get George out of his unhappy mood that he almost plowed into the rear of a Lancaster Avenue trolley car, which would have done no damage to the streetcar, but plenty to the Lafayette.

"Maybe I better drive, Dad."

"Just because that damn streetcar stopped so sudden? Now, George, believe me. You're taking an attitude I didn't expect from you. Dickie has ideas neither of us would think of. Take Lord Sandwich, for instance. Who else could have thought of a name like that?"

"The *Earl* of Sandwich, who used to spend so much time gambling that he stuck meat between two hunks of bread so he could eat without losing time. Any schoolkid knows about *him*."

"It's a good name just the same." There was that five-way traffic light on the west side of the Schuylkill River bridge, and Chester waited a bit impatiently for it to turn green.

George said, with more passion than he'd ever known the kid to show, "You two give me a pain. All you think about is washing machines and how we're going to make money, when Mary is in trouble."

"Mary? Mary Plotko? Why, her trouble is over. She's taken her mother to relatives. I don't see why that worries you so much."

"Just as though she didn't have enough trouble here, and never showing it. She's never said what a hard time she was having, but you could tell. And all that trouble with those foreign priests when her father died."

"All the time I've known you, George, I never thought you cared for Mary."

George didn't seem to hear what he was saying until just before they pulled to the right to turn south on Seventeenth Street, when he said, "I don't care what you say, if there's a train to Buffalo tonight, I'm going to take it. I *have* to talk to Mary myself."

"To Buffalo? We don't know her address."

"I'll find her somehow. I just can't stand the thought of her being up there helpless."

"It always seemed to me that Mary was a pretty self-reliant girl."

"Dad, I simply can't understand how you let her go that way. Let me out, before the light changes, and I'll go over to the station and find out about trains."

"There's no need to." Chester turned the corner and stepped on the gas. "I know there's a night train from Reading Terminal, over the Lehigh Valley, because Mary was thinking of taking it." Sometimes it was pretty hard to understand George, the way he was behaving. "I think you should take a couple of days to think this over and——" he started to say, but he was cut off.

"There's nothing to think over. Please, Dad, hurry. I'm going to have a lot to do."

"Just what do you intend saying to Mary?"

"I don't know. I haven't got that far. That I can't live without her, I guess."

Chester suddenly realized that he was driving much too fast, because of his own reaction to George's excitement, and slowed down, even though the kid became increasingly impatient. There was just room to park next to the "No Parking from Here to Corner" sign that was almost in front of the store. George was in the store and up the stairs as though the devil were after him. Helen, who was behind the fountain serving coffee to some passer-by, said, "Dad, whatever has got into George?"

"I told him about Mary going to Buffalo."

"He didn't know? She told me days ago." Then, with one of those new expressions that Chester didn't like, "Don't tell me he's found out he's in love with her. Honest, Dad, can you imagine George being in love with anybody?"

"A little difficult, I guess. Excuse me a few minutes, will you? I need to wash up. I'll be down to relieve you soon as I can."

One thing he wished he had done when they remodeled, and that was leave the kitchen downstairs, as well as a bathroom. He didn't go up to the second floor so often, but still it had become a chore. Halfway up he heard Kit saying, "Of course Mary gave me her address, but why the excitement? You always seemed to treat her like part of the soda fountain."

"I don't know." George was almost screaming.

By the time Chester reached the kitchen George was already

on the way to his room—anybody with ears could hear him pounding the third-floor stairs.

Kit should have been all upset, but instead she faced him with a placid smile. "You know, dear, I think George loves Mary."

Honest to God! "What's so wonderful about that? I love her too, and have ever since she was little."

"Chester darling, remember when she was so little that she could hardly walk, in those dirty clothes, coming in to buy cigarettes for her mother? Wasn't she adorable?"

"Of course she was. I don't object to George loving her, if he does. You don't have to sell me on her." Honest to Jesus, to listen to Kit, you'd think he'd been obstructing true love all these years.

When he returned downstairs to relieve Helen the Green family was waiting for him—all thirteen of them. It was unusual to see Mrs. Green on the street, but of course she wasn't expecting this year. "Mr. Jones, we're in trouble. It's over this turkey raffle I been running."

"Turkey raffle? I never heard about that."

"Honey bought a ticket. I only sell to colored folks. You can see how the talk might go around if you were to win on my raffle."

"But Honey's buying makes it legitimate. How's William doing since you moved?"

"Fine. William, say 'Fine' to Mr. Jones."

That would be George, coming down the stairs two at a time. He dodged around the Greens, almost knocking Horace over with Chester's old Gladstone that he was carrying. Chester said, "Good luck, son," but all he received in return was a reproving look, because, apparently, he had done everything wrong. "Take the car to the garage, it's on your way," he called, and watched, amused, while the kid changed directions and dashed toward where the Lafayette was parked.

"George's going out of town on business," he explained. "Now, Abe, what's this raffle about?"

"Well, I've been selling tickets for twenty-five cents. First prize a fifteen-pound turkey, second prize a twelve-pound goose, and third prize a fat hen. Trouble is we've been using the money to live on, as I haven't had any relief checks for two months. I'm just about at the end of my tether."

"You mean you haven't bought the prizes?"

"That's the long and the short of it. We had the drawing this morning, and I just got to deliver those fowl."

"Seems to me you should buy the prizes first."

"Nobody ever does that. Usually we win one or two of the prizes, but this year we haven't had any luck." Chester thought Abe looked at his wife reproachfully, as though she were responsible somehow.

"Doesn't that look bad, when you win prizes in your own raffle?"

"That would look very bad, Mr. Jones, but I buy tickets in other raffles, hoping to win prizes for my raffle. That's how raffles are run. Take Honey's Shelley, now. He runs a raffle. He won my twelve-pound goose, which I got to deliver so he can give it to the man who won it in his raffle. He runs a raffle too and needs it for *his* second prize, so you see there are a lot of people depending on that goose."

"You mean this goes on every year and I never heard about it before?"

"I guess you wouldn't be hearing now except I'm in this fix. And it isn't only the goose. The man who won the turkey, he runs a raffle . . ."

"That's enough. I'm getting dizzy." Chester pressed the "No Sale" key on the cash register. "How much are you going to need?"

Abe's face took on a very serious look. "I'm going to have to buy all three prizes, Mr. Jones. The first time *that* ever happened. I ascribe it to us not doing the Lord's will."

Mrs. Green snapped, "The Lord's will nothing," in a way that Abe didn't seem prepared to contest. He began to figure aloud:

"A fourteen-pound turkey at thirty-five runs to four-ninety, and an eleven-pound goose I may be able to buy at a quarter, but better figure on thirty, which is——"

Chester interrupted, "Anyway, ten dollars will cover it. But I thought you promised a fifteen-pound bird."

"I know just what you're going to say. I'll fill their crops with dried corn to make up the weight. That's considered legitimate."

Chester thought, as he watched the Greens troop out, well, anybody who thinks he can learn to know this neighborhood in a lifetime has another think coming.

He sat on one of the stools and thought of Thanksgiving coming and Christmas just around the corner, of Dickie's projects and of George going to Buffalo, of Kit upstairs and the baby. He wanted Dickie and George to make money, but particularly to learn to understand each other. For himself this place was all he wanted, just so he could go on making ends meet.

## Chapter 22

When the store had emptied Chester said, "Helen, I wish you'd either sing that song or hum it. You've repeated 'castles on the Rhine' about twenty times, and then the line you're singing now."

"Oh well, it was swell while it lasted," Helen was singing. She stopped for a moment and reached her hand behind her neck to feel whether her hair was in place. " 'Thanks for the Memory'—you should like it, Dad, it's right in the groove."

"Besides, I don't think you should hum, or sing either, while you're waiting on customers, whether it's in the groove or not."

"Dad dear, business is slowing up and Dick will be in in a little bit. Can I go to the first show at the Avon with Shirley? It's Ronald Colman, and I just adore him, he's so smooth."

"Shirley? Shirley who?"

"You mean you don't know my very best girl friend? Shirley Cotton, of course."

"Oh, her. Come to think of it, I have seen you two together quite a bit. Somehow you always seem to pick out friends I don't care for. But it's all right with me if your mother approves."

She threw her arms around him. "You're just a killer-diller of a Daddy!"

Helen was always like this when she wanted something or had to get permission to do something, but it gave him a nice feeling

278

anyway, especially when she kissed him on the cheek before running upstairs.

Mr. Meyer came in for his Coke, and Bill Thomas to look at the *Bulletin* help-wanted ads. It must have been eight years since he lost his job, but he kept on looking. Mr. Oberholtzer rushed in. "Say, Jones, do you have anything that's good for a sick kid? The wife won't be home until ten."

"Which boy is it? What seems to be wrong with him?"

"Jimmy. I cooked supper for them both, and he wouldn't eat his. After I washed the dishes I noticed his face looked flushed. I came in to call the wife, but she doesn't like me to phone where she's working."

"Last time he was sick you bought some mineral oil. You haven't used it all?" When Mr. Oberholtzer shook his head Chester added, "I'd try that. It's mild and won't do any harm, anyway."

Years of chasing streetcars must have got Mr. Oberholtzer in a habit of perpetual hurry. He almost ran past the window, and Chester mused, funny times we're living in, when the men stay home to take care of the kids so the women can go out and make a living.

He sat on one of the stools and thought, just for a change, of Dickie's projects and of George going to Buffalo. Four days without a line from him. Maybe Mary would help to make George a little more tolerant, if he succeeded in persuading her to come back. Chester told himself that he might as well admit that Mary's going to Buffalo, so soon after Kay's leaving, had made a pretty big hole. It wasn't only missing her around the store, but you couldn't sort of keep an eye on her for more than sixteen years without . . .

His thoughts were broken when a brass-buttoned blue policeman's overcoat loomed in the front doorway. The head of the wearer was cut off by the shadows, but Chester knew it was Patrolman Yaeger, who would be on the four-to-twelve shift this week.

There was another patrolman behind him, young and with a reddish complexion. Before Yaeger could say anything the younger man said, "The name is Regan. I'll be on this beat regular. Dutch, here, thought I ought to drop in with him and get acquainted."

"That's right. This is my last week," Yaeger said. "Go on retirement Sunday. I used to enjoy the police business, but the last few years it's been getting pretty crumby and I've looked forward to getting my time in. This is still going to be a hard week for me, though. Funny, ain't it?"

"I'll be sorry, for one, not to see you coming in," Chester said, and then held out his hand to Regan. "Glad to meet you. If there's anything I can do . . ."

"You never can tell. Dutch says you're a square guy."

"I try to run a nice place. We don't write numbers or have punchboards, anyway." To Yaeger he said, "What are you planning on doing?"

"Well, I have a little place down in Wildwood—near the Burkes, across the street. We've two married daughters live down there."

How long and how well you could know people without knowing *about* them. Hard to imagine Yaeger with a family. Chester had never seen him when he wasn't in uniform. "Never knew you had a family."

"Seven, and all living and married except the youngest. He's ten. Kind of an afterthought, like the one you had, if you don't mind my saying so. I'd like to get him started where living is clean . . ."

It was easy to see that Regan wasn't interested, and Chester understood when Yaeger let his voice sort of die away. "How about a cigar?" He got out the box of White Owls, which Yaeger liked, and after he'd selected one, Regan said, "My smoke is Phillies."

Before Yaeger could tell his story about the Italian and the cop and the apples, Regan took a half dozen from the fresh box that Chester offered him and put them away in the top of his cap, while Yaeger watched with an expression of disapproval.

The telephone booths filled with youngsters calling their dates, and a couple of others ordered Cokes at the fountain. Chester wished he hadn't let Helen off early. It was easy to see that the new cop on the beat wasn't going to be as dependable as Eddie or Yaeger—one of the new breed, Regan was. Chester got back to the cigar case, where they were still standing, in time to hear the veteran say, "The way I always figured it, the more trouble I could prevent before it got started, the better cop I was."

"That's all right for a fellow like you, who never cared about getting ahead. But for me, I don't see it like that," Regan answered. "How can you make a record that way? I want to be in at the pinch, that's what I want. Why should I go down and give two kids a sob story, like you were telling about, not to get into the trouble you seen coming? Perhaps they don't do it then, but the next time. And will you be copping the pinch?"

Language that Chester hardly understood, except that he knew Yaeger was always running around taking care of kids and older folk that seemed headed for trouble.

There were her light footsteps on the stairs, and Helen came into the store, her face made up more or less within the limitations that Kit had set, but in a way that Chester still didn't like.

Yaeger said, "You sure are getting to look grown-up. Hard to realize I was on this beat when you were born."

Instead of answering Mr. Yaeger, Helen exclaimed, "Oh!" and dashed for the side door. At first Chester felt angry at what seemed a lack of courtesy, but then he saw that a Yellow cab had stopped on Camac Street and there was George climbing out of it. By damn, he could see the smooth sheen of Mary's fair hair in the shadow of the cab's interior. Mary really a member of their family! The thought sure made him feel good—different from anything he had felt about Sig when he married Kay.

By this time he was out on the pavement, greeting the pair and trying to help with their luggage while the cab driver stood there looking bored. No doubt he had witnessed hundreds of such scenes.

Dick appeared from somewhere—well, it was time; he should have been in ten minutes ago, but he couldn't complain any more about Dick's being late, now that he knew all the kid had to do. Dick said, "Let me take those, Dad. It looks like elder brother has got some sense at last, but you're the one to tell him so."

Helen began to hug Mary, which only added to the confusion. George said, "Dad, you'll have to pay the taxi driver. I'm clean out of money."

This was an occasion for being generous, even if the fellow did look pretty sour. How much was the meter—$1.10? Chester handed over two dollar bills and said, "Keep the change."

Patrolman Yaeger was shaking hands with George and Mary and saying to his companion, "Knew them both since they was born—the kind of kids that can be raised down here if you go about it right, instead of just looking for pinches."

Helen was practically screaming, and to lessen the confusion Chester said, "Your mother is going to be awful mad at missing all this. You better run upstairs and tell her that George's back with Mary."

It was easy to see that Helen didn't want to go, but she did, while Chester got everyone into the store. Mrs. Waldman came running in, breathless, to say, "Horace Green just rang my doorbell to say that George and Mary are married. My dear, I'm so glad for you."

"But we're not married." The wail in Mary's voice made Chester realize that he had thought they were too, and must have behaved accordingly. What was George thinking about?

Honey's voice saying, "Mrs. Jones, take it easy on them stairs. Marriage lasts a long time, but legs break awful quick."

Kit rushed in on them. "Mary! My dear, dear daughter."

Chester said, "Keep your shirt on, Kit. They're not married."

It was time George began explaining, instead of standing there like someone in a fog. "I wanted to go to a justice of the peace, like Kay and Sig did, and you and Dad, but . . ."

Gert Cameron added her voice to all the talking that was going on. "Mary! Henry Green just told me!"

Talk about Paul Revere's ride! The Greens were alerting the neighborhood. Suddenly Mary wasn't flustered at all, but her usual quiet, poised self. "Hello, Gert. The Greens are anticipating a little. It's my fault. I want a church wedding."

"With me and Frederick! Mary, George, would you?"

"It's all Mary's idea. I don't care where, just so we get married."

"St. James the Less. It's so fashionable I'm sort of scared to go alone. If you would too . . ."

St. James the Less! Now, who could he have been? Chester asked, "Is that the name of a church? Who was St. James the More Important, I'd like to know?"

Mary was shaking her head. "No, Gert. You're sort of like me, wanting to be sure of things. No, that's not it either. I want to belong. I want to begin belonging, and I couldn't there, Gert, really I couldn't. I told George that I want to be married at the Eighth Presbyterian, the one that has the block party on Camac Street every year. It's where we live. It's where I want to go, after. People from here. When I go to church I want to hear the service in English. Oh, Gert, it's hard to explain. You had things too different."

"Problems of my own, kid. Problems of my own."

Gert was a damn nice girl, even if she was putting on like she used to. Maybe that was to help Mary out. And it was funny, the way Dick wasn't taking part in what was being said. There was a youngster nobody would ever know. Look at him, sitting there on the soda-fountain stool but figuring out everything from that new Irish cop to what Gert was going to say next.

Kit said, "I think we should all go upstairs and let Honey get us something to eat," and for the first time since he had carried in the luggage Dick opened his mouth:

"I think that you are a woman after my own heart. Honey, it sure looks like work for you."

Everybody in the neighborhood seemed to be coming in, to buy one thing or another, and Mrs. Waldman was taking care of them, rushing around almost as fast as Mary could, though she wasn't supposed to be on duty. Chester was going to ask if she thought she could manage alone, but she anticipated him. "You go right ahead —I'll make out."

Mrs. Koehler came in, without her dogs, as the two policemen left. "Billy Green told me about George and Mary," she began, and then, seeing the look on everyone's face, "Don't tell me it's not so."

The others were already on the way upstairs, so Chester answered, "They're not married yet, whatever Billy told you, but they will be soon, it appears. Come on upstairs and have a snack with us."

What a little wisp of a woman she was, but how many animal lives depended upon her, Chester thought, as she answered, "No, really I can't. Twinkletoes isn't feeling well and Goldyeyes is expecting. I should be getting back this second, but Mary was always such a dear child and I think George will develop."

In spite of himself, Chester began to laugh. "He has, within the last month. You'd be surprised how much. Come on up for a minute."

She wouldn't, and he watched her pull her coat close around her neck when she stepped outside.

Upstairs, everybody was sitting at the table. Evidently Helen had forgotten her interest in the movie at the Avon, and Honey, instead of working desperately over the range, as he had expected, was watching the scene with what was almost a maternal look. Kit must have noticed his surprise, for she said, "I've sent over to Burke's for oysters and French fries, and told them to come too, if they can."

"I doubt that they'll be able to. You know how full their place is, most times."

George was telling all about going to Buffalo. A long trip for a youngster away from home for the first time, Chester thought. Mary was explaining how she had always thought he didn't care for her at all and how surprised she had been when he turned up at her aunt's place, just as they were sitting down to breakfast.

After the first oysters and French fries came over—Mr. Burke hadn't bothered to put them into his usual cardboard boxes, but had arranged them on platters, with the oysters piled up like walls that enclosed the potatoes—things quieted down for a bit. Two full bottles of Burke's homemade ketchup kept going from hand to hand, and there was a continuous flashing of forks as everybody speared from the rapidly diminishing piles.

When he had eaten his fourth oyster Chester said, "This is too early in the evening for me to eat—I haven't any appetite," which acted as a signal for the talk to start up again.

Dick said, "Haven't reported yet on what I was doing today. Honey, your Shelley has a regular job again, for one thing."

"That so, Dickie? He was to see that Democratic committeeman down our way about getting on WPA . . ."

"This will pay better, and he can vote Republican if he wants to." Dick turned toward Chester. "Then I got to thinking about McCorkle and all that drug inventory. He's a good man, but too old to go out and get another job easily. I've found just the spot for him—a small store, well established, that one man can handle. It's nothing for Jones Enterprises, not worth the time and trouble——"

"How do you hear about these places?" Chester interrupted.

The kid's funny look. "Remember the storekeepers' committee to call on Mayor Wilson? I made a point of keeping in touch with all of them. But about McCorkle—setting him up in business provides a market for all the drugstore stuff out at Overbrook, including the fixtures, without losing any money. He's enthusiastic."

Chester looked over to where Mary was sitting. "I guess you heard about Dickie's adventure in washing machines."

Kit said, "Our Dickie a business typhoon! Hard to imagine, isn't it?"

Dick, spearing the last oyster and two French fries, said, "You mean the big wind of 1937? Don't believe all you hear, O beautiful and glamorous betrothed of elder brother."

Dickie starting that stuff again. It wasn't what he said that made it sound so bad, but his manner. Fortunately everybody began to laugh at Kit's mistake, and then Gert Cameron came to Mary's rescue. "Don't let him tease you, Mary. He teases me all the time, but I overlook it. I admit he's done remarkably well for a mere child . . ."

"For that, dirty Gertie Cameron, I challenge you to a duel. Oysters, at six paces." There you were. One moment Dickie was a little stinker, if there ever was one, and the next, so likable you couldn't resist him, though you knew he was acting all the time.

Gert Cameron had sure turned into a pretty girl. Right now, with her head thrown back, laughing, showing the evenest white teeth, she was as pretty as Mary or Helen, in her own way. They were like the three favorite varieties of ice cream—chocolate, vanilla, and strawberry.

Gert said, "If I ever have a daughter, I won't name her Gertrude. All the misery I went through, growing up! Often I went home and cried after the kids called me that. You were one of the worst, Dick."

Dick looked surprised. Did anything ever really surprise him? He seemed surprised, anyway, and very serious. "Is that really so, Gert? You're not making it up?"

"It's so, all right. Of course I don't mind any more, but living in Fawn Street and being called that . . ." She shrugged her shoulders. "It doesn't matter now, does it? Mary, I'm so happy for you and George. I'll come in often and see you."

"I won't be here. George is opening a store down on Snyder Avenue, and I want to help him with it. Of course I'd like you to visit, but you'll soon forget about us when you live out on the Main Line. Running a store isn't so much, but it's the only life George really likes, and I do too."

Honey brought up another platter of oysters, and everybody seemed to find room for more. Gert turned serious. In some ways she took after her father, especially in getting steamed up over ideas. "I think running a store is very important if it sets an example for a neighborhood, like the Joneses have done. You know, George, that everybody around here looks up to your dad. A store isn't just a place with windows, and things inside for sale. It's a lot more. It's the people who run it, for one thing. You know, my mother died so long ago I don't remember her at all. When I think of a mother, it's Mrs. Jones, being nice to me."

"Why, Gert Cameron, I never treated you any differently from the other children," Kit said, looking astonished.

"Maybe that's part of what I'm trying to say. Anyway Mary, I won't forget you and I'll come down and visit, and I hope you'll come out to see me. But there's still something I want to get off my chest. Getting like my old man, I guess. All right, so his washing machines and Lord Sandwiches——"

"*Earl* of Sandwich. But maybe historical accuracy should be sacrificed for commercial expediency. If you and Dad both insist on Lord, maybe that's what it should be."

"Don't interrupt. Maybe you will always make money——"

"I know what you're going to say. There are other things in life that are more important."

"People who see both sides of an argument are among my pet hates."

Chester began to be worried about Mrs. Waldman, all alone downstairs, but there was a clumping on the stairs and Ed Shaughnessy came in. "Hello, Chester."

"My God, don't tell me the Green kids went all the way to your place!"

"The Green kids? Oh, the little colored kids that run errands for you. No. Max has sold his store and there won't be any game this Thursday. The guy who bought from him only plays bridge. Can you imagine a bridge player making good in Max's neighborhood? But that's how it is." The exaggerated Shaughnessy double take. "But what's this that's going on?"

"Mary, there, from up the street——"

"Sure. Used to work at your fountain sometimes. You're a looker, kid."

"——is marrying George."

"Don't do it. The boy's a dope. Takes after his old man."

That was Ed for you, always kidding. Dick was whispering something to George about hiring Mr. Oberholtzer to take care of the washing machines. Maybe he should be listening to that, but, after all, the store was the most important thing of all, and Mrs. Waldman was alone.

Chester said, "Now Ed, you just stay awhile and have some of the best oysters you ever tasted. I have to go downstairs. You understand, don't you?"

Ed looked at him with an expression that reminded him of Dickie. "Sure I do," he said.